For Nicola

Because it was crazy enough to work.

SHE CARRIED
THE DEAD

BLOOD IN THE GUTTER

"ALL RIGHT, BOYS," WILLIS said as he polished off the last of his watered-down beer and smacked the mug onto the bar. He was a muscular man who'd worked at the docks since he was a boy. His once jet-black hair had turned shades of grey, and his beard was already stark white. "That's it for me."

The Port of Call was a dank, grimy dive, its air thick with the scent of cut-rate drunks and bad decisions. The lights, kept low, masked cracks and cockroaches hiding in corners. Longshoremen clustered along the scarred, beer-stained counter, attentive to the radio's murmur: half of them absorbed in the day's ball game, the other half catching sporadic updates on the war in Europe—Germany had its claws dug deep into Poland and was advancing on France.

The place reeked of smoke, booze, and diesel fuel. Sepia photographs haunted the walls—a silent tribute to the harbor and the men who had lived and died there. When a train from the dockyard rattled past, bottles of rag water clinked on uneven shelves, the lights sputtered, and the radio faded momentarily into hush until the rumbling ceased.

Willis shrugged into his denim workman's jacket and, with his broad, rough hands, slapped the backs of Cramer and Toby, both nursing their beers. Cramer, potbellied and liver-spotted, was the oldest on the docks—even older than Willis—while Toby, a lean and sinewy Cajun, was the youngest. Both had drawn up seats beside Willis at the bar.

"Already?" Cramer said. "It's only just past nine."

"I've got the early ship in the morning."

Cramer chuckled. "You best be careful walking home. Dangerous place, these docks."

"Yeah," Toby added, grinning. "Heard there's monsters out."

Willis narrowed his eyes. "What are you boys getting at?"

Cramer leaned back, a satisfied look on his face. "You ain't heard the stories?"

"What stories?"

Toby leaned in over Cramer. "Stories 'bout evil things around these parts."

Willis looked skeptically at the two of them "You pulling my leg?"

"You really ain't heard?" Cramer said. "Must not have been around Bull much these past few days."

"Yeah," Toby agreed. "He's been going on and on about what he seen in one of them boats." The Cajun shifted his eyes back and forth. "One of Lazaretto's."

"He's getting everyone worked up about it," Cramer said. "They're saying Lazaretto's bringing something unholy into our town."

Willis chuckled. "You two don't go out for that sort of thing, do you?"

"No," said Cramer. "But we sure do get a laugh out of it."

Toby grinned stupidly. "You gotta hear the crazy Bull's been spoutin' about."

"Hold on, we'll get him." Cramer—his cheeks and nose flushed red against his scraggly gray whiskers—looked across the bar and called out. "Hey, Bull," he shouted, too drunk to suppress his broad grin. "Willis ain't heard your story. Y'know, about what you seen in that boat."

Bull was a bald, broad man, with a strong back and arms like tree roots. He looked up sharply from his beer, his low brow furrowed. "Keep it down, Cramer," he shouted back, his voice sputtering and tight.

Toby joined in, ignoring the look of terror that had twisted Bull's face. "No, no, really. Willis here wants to hear 'bout it."

"He's leaving. He'd best know what's out there," the old man said. "You know, to watch out for it." Cramer and Toby both broke out into boisterous laughter. Cramer slapped the counter; his laughing turned to a wheeze.

Even Willis was smiling a bit. "What'd you see, Bull?"

"I'm telling you, this ain't something to joke about." Bull stood from his stool and shouldered his way over to the three of them through the crowded bar. A few of the other patrons had paused their own chatter, watching the men shout back and forth at each other. "If you'd seen what I seen, you wouldn't be laughing, none of you."

"No, course not," said Cramer. "We'd be piss-pants scared, just like you."

"But we wouldn't go telling folks," Toby said, still laughing.

Bull scowled. "Shoulda never told you nothin'."

"You did, son. Now go on, tell him," said Cramer, calming down.

Bull looked the men over. Cramer and Toby, drunk and acting the fool, paid little mind, but Willis appeared serious—he always did. One of the oldest on the docks, Willis possessed a wisdom and patience rarely seen in the city's rough places. When he spoke or asked a question, he did it with purpose.

"All right," Bull finally said. He leaned on the bar, bringing his head down, hunching his shoulders like he was bracing against a cold wind. He spoke softly, eyes locked with Willis', avoiding the stupid grins slapped across Cramer and Toby's faces. "For you, Willis, but don't go spreading it around. We ain't supposed to be saying none of this."

"Course," Willis said.

"The docks ain't felt right lately," Bull began, casting a nervous scan over the crowd. "Things have gotten strange."

"Strange how?"

"For starters," Bull said. "They been making us carry these."

Bull reached into his back pocket and removed his billfold. Inside was a tattered tarot card, creased and torn, dirty and worn around the edges. On the front of the card was the image of a man, a laborer, his back turned and hunched as he carried a load of ten heavy sticks across a field toward a distant village. On the other side, the back of the card was beautifully ornate. Two bats at the center mirrored each other, touching at the feet, their wings outstretched, reaching the top and bottom of the card. They were bordered by an intricate, golden filigree that swooped and curled around the edges, leaving pockets in each of the corners, which were marked by different phases of the moon.

Willis took the card, running his rough fingers along the edges.

"Why?" Willis asked as he passed the card back to Bull.

"Because they don't want nobody snooping around who shouldn't be," Bull said, taking the card back.

"It's Lazaretto," Willis said. "It's only a fool goes snooping around his boats."

"It ain't Lazaretto, though," Bull said. "They're just using him."

"Who?"

"I wish I knew."

"Well, what are they bringing in, then?"

Bull leaned in close to whisper. "Coffins."

"They're smuggling coffins?"

"Not quite," Bull said. "They say they're steamer trunks. Got these young girls from Europe, bringing them in. They look like coffins, though, and they're smuggling what's inside 'em."

"And what's that?" Willis asked.

Bull shifted in his seat, uneasy. He swept the room with his eyes, lingering longer this time. He swallowed hard, Adam's apple bobbing, and then lowered his head toward Willis, voice barely a whisper.

"Vampires."

The breath went out of Willis. The room around him was still boisterous, but there was silence between him and Bull as he searched the other man's face for a hint of flippancy. Willis didn't find any.

Cramer's hand came down, slapping Willis across the back.

"See what we were saying?" Cramer said, the noise of the room flooding back in. "Nonsense."

"It ain't nonsense, old man," Bull said. "I seen 'em with my own eyes."

"Where?" Willis said.

"I took a peek in one of them trunks—one of them coffins."

"This's what we wanted you to hear," Cramer said, clapping Willis' shoulder. Smiles returned to both Cramer and Toby.

"Quiet," Willis said, motioning for Bull to continue.

"There was a man inside—or what looked like a man—lying stiff, hands folded on his chest. His skin was pale, clothes were old and dark, hair black as pitch."

"It was a vampire?"

"Sure as hell," Bull said.

"How you know?"

"Because it woke up," Bull said. "Like it sensed me, smelled me. Its eyes came open, red as embers, and its lips split in a grin so I could see them pointy teeth, like two needles—both of 'em stained pink with blood."

Willis slowly straightened up in his stool. He could see the fear in Bull's eyes.

Another train passed, and the lights flickered. Cramer slapped Bull's arm.

Cramer slapped Bull's arm. "Quit those Lazaretto ships; they're making you paranoid."

"Even if the money's good," Toby said knowingly.

"The hell with you," Bull said. "I know what I seen."

"I know, I know," Cramer said. "One time I was working upriver, I would-a sworn I'd seen a wolfman. Big, burly fella smelled like hell and did nothing but growl. Course, turns out, it was just some bum who'd got drunk and fallen in the swamp. The sheriff told us as much, but damned if I wasn't certain I'd seen some creature that night, too."

"Wasn't no bum in that boat. They ain't got red eyes and fangs!"

"Hell, sounds like most of the ladies working the whore-houses these days. The red light gets in their eyes, I'd swear most of 'em were vampires too."

Toby snorted. "Those are his favorites."

Cramer swelled into laughter again. "You remember that one he was falling for—what was her name?"

"Margaret? Marcy?"

"Mona!" Cramer shouted.

"Big-boned Mona!" Toby howled with laughter.

Rage bubbled over Bull. "The hell with you all," Bull said again, shouting it this time. "I'm leaving too." He stormed back to his stool and grabbed his jacket from off the bar. As he left, he could hear the laughter start again at his expense. He could hear Cramer and Toby telling everybody what he'd been saying. A few of the other longshoremen had joined in, and they called out after him.

"Be careful out there, Bull!"

"Take some garlic. Or a cross!"

"Let's get some holy water blessed for you!"

"Don't let them near your neck!"

Only Willis stayed silent, watching Bull as he left the bar and walked out into the moonlit street until he faded into the shadows and the fog.

The lonely wail of a trumpet was carried from a few streets over, where the bars were still serving, and the jazz men were still playing. Where Bull walked, away from the clubs and the cathouses, the New Orleans streets were ominously still. He was alone, stewing about the laughs the others had had. There wasn't anything funny about it.

He muttered to himself about what a fool he'd been for telling them in the first place—and for doing it again. Jamming his hands into his pockets, he walked stiff-legged through Jackson Square, passing under the high steeples of the St. Louis Cathedral. He tried not to think about them. Then he tried not to think about what he'd seen—that coffin, those eyes, those blood-stained teeth.

The empty streets suddenly seemed too quiet.

Unlike downtown, where everything had gone electric, the old gas lamps still burned in this part of the city, radiating their oily, orange light. The flames made his shadow dance across the walls of the darkened storefronts.

Bull passed an alley just outside the square and startled out of his thoughts. Sitting alone at a small table tucked away from the street was a raven-haired woman. Dressed all in black, she was poised, casually shuffling a deck of tarot cards. Her flowing hair framed her pale face, which seemed bright under the moonlight. His eyes fell to the sandwich board that sat beside her, illuminated in the flickering glow of a streetlight, adorned with fanciful Victorian script.

MADAME LOVEBITE

FORTUNE TELLER

KNOWS ALL AND SEES ALL

Bull's foot scuffed the ground as he took a faltering step, entranced by the woman. She didn't look up, only continued shuffling her cards. Her dress was elegant, and her hands were covered with long, silk gloves up to her elbows, bangles jangling around her wrists. Bull shook his head and continued walking.

"Would you like to know your future?" The woman asked, just as he was past the alley.

Bull stopped and turned back to her. She was looking at him now. Her face was beautiful. Her full lips were a dark crimson, bold against her ivory skin, and just above the corner of her mouth—which curved mischievously—was a dark beauty mark. Her emerald eyes glittered in the dancing light, set against charcoal shadow.

Her stare made Bull's heartbeat quicken. Her voice and her movements seemed sensual; there was a danger about her, which only added to her allure.

"Sorry, lady," he said. "I don't have time for that."

"Please, Bull," she said, leaning forward. "Come learn what the Fates have planned for you."

Bull stiffened. "You know my name?"

She laughed gravely as the corner of her mouth curled slyly. "I know everything."

He looked around, searching for anyone, any sign that he hadn't stumbled into a dream. But the streets were empty, and only the woman—the Madame Lovebite—was there, looking at him, beckoning him to sit and see the future.

He nodded.

She smiled again when he sat down across from her. It was an enchanting smile, but there was a cruelty in it. Her eyes, as deep and captivating as they were, had the same shadow of cruelty lurking behind them.

The Madame placed a tarot deck neatly on the table, face down in front of him. Bull recognized the symbol on the back immediately, the bats clutching one another's feet and stretching their wings out above them.

"I have a card just like that," he said.

"Has it brought you fortune?" she asked.

"I suppose."

"Let's see what else awaits," she said, pushing the deck towards him. "Touch it."

Gingerly, he reached out, putting a finger to the top card, letting it linger just a moment, and then recoiling his hand as though the cards had been hot to the touch.

"Three cards," she said. "Three cards to tell you all you need to know."

With delicate, entrancing, rhythmic movements, she began to shuffle the cards once more. Cutting the deck, fanning them together again and again. Bull stared at the precise, fluid movements of her hands. When she stopped, he looked up and met her eyes as she gracefully removed her silk gloves.

Her hands and arms, Bull was shocked to see, were covered in tattoos. Across each knuckle was a phase of the moon, spanning across both hands. On the back of each was a bird—on the right was the outline of a dove, and on the left was a jet-black raven, their wings raised in flight. Her left wrist was wrapped in a thorny vine, twisting itself around an hourglass, each bulb marked with MORTE and VIVANTE. On the other wrist, down along her veins, was a dagger dripping blood towards her palm.

The Madame placed her hands flat on the table, the deck of cards between them. With an easy, flowing motion, she peeled three cards from the top and placed them face down.

"Are you ready to know your fate, Bull?" she asked. He could only nod.

Deftly, she took the first card and flipped it over.

"The Moon," she said, leaving the card on the table. A full-faced moon beamed down across a desert nightscape. Animals—wolves, Bull thought—looked up at it, almost worshipping it, calling to it. Owls and bats fluttered through its light.

"Your troubled mind keeps you awake at night, Bull," she said. "You're afraid of something—something you saw, something you felt, something that quickened your beating heart." Her voice was calm and inviting, speaking slowly, taking time with each word as she said it.

Before Bull could say anything, her hand moved to the second card and turned it over. This one depicted a beautiful woman, dressed in fine robes and seated on a throne between two pillars, with a crescent moon at her feet.

"But don't worry," the Madame said, "your problems will all soon be over." She pointed to the woman on the throne. "The High Priestess brings relief. A woman shrouded in mystery holds the remedy for your troubled mind."

This time, Bull was able to grunt out a laugh. "I could use some of that," he said, but the Madame paid no attention to him. She reached for the final card, flipping it over.

This one showed a man, face down on the ground, ten swords stabbed into his back, blood pooling around his body.

"What does that mean?" Bull asked.

"It means you talk too much."

Quick as a viper, Madame Lovebite pulled a pistol from beneath the table and leveled it at Bull's forehead. Just as he looked up, she pulled the trigger.

The shot rang out in the alley, and Bull's broad-shouldered body slumped over to the ground.

Madame Lovebite stood; she hiked up her dress and tucked the pistol away into the holster around her thigh. She snatched her gloves and the tarot cards from the table and picked up the sign. She turned down the alley to the darkness beyond the flickering gaslight, where she had parked her long, black Mercury coupe. The trunk was open, and she tossed the sign in. As she walked to the driver's side door, she stopped and looked back at the shadowy lump of Bull crumpled on the ground, the gun smoke swirling up over his body like mist off a lake.

She reached into her purse and pulled out a gold cigarette case, clicking it open. She brought a long, slender, black cigarette to her lips, the filter wrapped in shimmering gold foil. Lighting it, she took a drag and blew out the smoke before she stepped into her car.

The engine growled to life as she sped away and disappeared into the night.

PART I
They Kill By Night

CHAPTER 1

CHARLIE BAPTISTE TOSSED THE dice across the table, looking to roll ten. The dice bounced against the green, felted rail and settled—both fives.

"Hard winner," the stickman called out. The crowd around the table cheered.

Everybody got paid.

Charlie smiled, shooting his cuffs and adjusting his cufflinks. He was hot; the dice were behaving tonight. He was up nearly five hundred, almost enough to buy a new car. The last three months had been hard. He'd had to leave one apartment behind already. He'd heard of at least one debt collector who was asking around about him. He'd been down to only one suit, the rest worn to rags. To get into a place like this—a place to win big—you needed to look sharp. He bought a tuxedo: crisp, white, tailored, complete with a bow tie and a black pocket square. It cleaned out his stash and started his problems, sending him on the lam again. But without the tuxedo, he wouldn't be here tonight, and he wouldn't be up five hundred whole dollars.

A redhead across the table gave him the eye. Charlie Baptiste smiled, warmth rising inside him as his confidence swelled with each glance.

He ran a hand through his slick, blonde hair. He was clean-shaven and handsome. In one smooth motion, he grabbed the cocktail glass off the rail, swirled it, then knocked the drink back. The glass landed empty. He touched his finger to his lips. On his left pinky, a gold signet ring with an onyx inset gleamed—the ornate "B" etched into the stone caught the light. He kissed it, tossed another stack of chips to the pass line, and scooped up the dice before sending them across the table.

"Natural winner," the stickman said when the roll came up seven. The crowd cheered again.

Natural winner, Charlie thought. He liked the sound of that.

He looked around the table. People were happy as the dealer paid out their winnings. Charlie felt a lightness in his chest, a warmth rising from the buzz of alcohol. Was it happiness, or just the booze? He couldn't tell, and maybe it didn't matter.

As the excitement swirled around the table, Charlie noticed a man approach, looming over the redhead's shoulder. The man's face was grim; his eyes looked dark and hollow. A neatly trimmed Van Dyke brought his chin to a point. It reminded Charlie of the Devil and made him shiver with a rush of fear and discomfort. The man met Charlie's gaze and nodded. Charlie, heart pounding, nodded back, striving to appear calm. The man's look made him uneasy; it was killing his buzz. Swaying a little, head just fuzzy enough to feel comfortable, Charlie looked up and away from the man with the Van Dyke, scanning the revelry for an anchor to steady his nerves.

The Rag & Bone Club was an old Creole building, done up in a gaudy Rococo motif. Wall sconces flickered low along the walls, and large chandeliers hung from the high ceiling. Once, it had been a music hall—or perhaps an opera house; Charlie couldn't remember. For most of his life, it was nothing more than a shut-up husk, a ghost of a better time. Then, less than a year ago, someone purchased, renovated, and reopened it. Now it was a place to see and be seen, to woo, drink, dance, and gamble. It was a place where you could feel alive.

The gaming tables were on the ground level, along with the dance floor and cocktail lounge, which faced the grand stage where a soulful diva was fronting a thirteen-piece swing band. A long bar wrapped around the joint, corralling all the patrons in the middle of the room. Pretty women in tiny outfits walked the floor, delivering drinks and selling cigarettes.

An open gallery on the second floor overlooked the action. It was packed with more people smoking and drinking. Some leaned on the handrail to watch everything below. But above them was where the real action happened. The third floor was a mystery to Charlie. He had never been up there, nor did he know anyone who had. He heard whispers about the wealthy patrons who were "top-floor only"—crime bosses and oil magnates. These were men and women who had enough money to buy themselves into or out of anything.

Someday, Charlie always told himself, he'd make it up there. He'd be counted among the wealthy, the elegant, the mysterious who spent their nights at exclusive parties held just for their crowd. But for now, this would have to be enough.

Everywhere he looked, there were people; they were talking, laughing, dancing, high on one thing or another. They were spending money at the bars or making it at the tables. Whatever they were doing, everybody was trying to get lucky. He looked back over at the redhead who'd been giving him the eye. She bit her lip coyly.

He smiled again, bigger this time. He tossed the dice. Another winner. Everybody hooted and hollered. The redhead clapped her hands joyfully. Even the grim man beside her with the Van Dyke couldn't bring him down. This could be his best night in a long time. Maybe the best night of his life.

Then his eyes flicked over the redhead's shoulder, and the smile melted away. The frantic, worried face of Petey Beech was coming up behind her.

Beech was a gambler who knew the Queen of Diamonds better than his own mother. He was short and doughy, with a garish taste and a tendency to worry. He was wearing a tuxedo too, cut for his stumpy frame. Gold rings lined each hand. A flop sweat beaded across his forehead. Looking at him, Charlie felt embarrassed to know him. He wondered why they continued to let him in places like this—places where folk were decent. Charlie kept thinking someone would complain, have Petey kicked out for looking the way he did. But it never happened. Petey kept coming back, hitting the town, looking for action night after night. He came up fast around the table and spoke rapidly into Charlie's ear. Charlie could smell mothballs under the little man's cologne.

"Slits is here," Petey said breathlessly.

"What?" Charlie asked. "Where?"

Beech pointed.

Back in the crowd, Charlie saw "Slits" Nicotero—a wiry bagman with slicked-back hair and a pair of scars on his left cheek below his eye. He was as skinny as a knife and just as deadly. Two heavy-set thugs with big arms and sour faces flanked him as they strolled through the gaming hall.

Charlie shook his head in disbelief. A sense of dread grew in his chest—this was all terribly wrong.

"Want to borrow my rod?" Petey asked, opening his coat just enough to show Charlie the handle of the heavy revolver he had tucked into the waistband of his trousers.

"What?" Charlie said, distracted. He looked back at Petey and saw the gun under his coat, realizing what the little man had asked. "No, put that away, Petey, you'll get someone hurt with that thing."

Petey shrugged. "Long as I'm the one doing the hurting."

That gave Charlie the idea.

"Go distract them for me," he said.

"Distract them?"

"Make a scene or something."

"I can't do that; they'll kick me out."

"They'll kick you out someday anyway."

Petey looked hurt.

"Look, just do it for me, would you?" Charlie said.

"I'll see what I can do, but I'm not gonna raise any ruckus."

"I'll owe you one, pal."

"Yeah, I'll count on it," Petey said.

Charlie wasn't listening. He backed away from the table, taking his hands off the rail. Slits hadn't seen him, but urgency took hold; Charlie couldn't wait around. He pushed Beech aside and grabbed his chips, tossing one to the stickman, who thanked him flatly. He took one last look at the redhead, who watched him, confused.

"Sorry, sugar," he said, and fled.

Charlie shoved his way through the crowd of swaying drunks, past the poker tables and roulette wheels. He looked back over his shoulder, searching the waves of faces for Slits and his two goons. He saw them, by the dance floor, casually walking the room. Petey approached them, the short man's head barely visible through the crowd. He greeted Slits, slapping him on the arm, acting like buddies. Slits looked annoyed. The two goons started to push Petey away, and he played it for laughs.

Bringing a hand up to scratch his eyebrow, Charlie tried to hide his face. He made his way to the cages and pushed his pile of chips to the cashier, who smiled.

"Well done, sir," she said.

"It's my lucky night." Charlie looked over his shoulder again. There was no sign of Petey or Slits. He began to tap his finger nervously on the mahogany countertop.

"One, two, three, four, five hundred," the cashier said, counting out the bills, stacking them neatly on the counter. "And ten, twenty, thirty, forty, fifty-five."

Charlie looked back, trying to grin through his nervousness. He slid two tens back to the cashier. "Thanks," he said, hurriedly. "Have a good night."

He headed into the crowd, stuffing the wad of bills into his coat, making his way towards the entrance. The doors were tall, padded in red velvet. Beyond them was the vestibule, with the coat check. After that was freedom—outside, where a long patio stretched to the street. Folks sat at bistro tables, sharing drinks and smoking cigarillos while listening to a jazz trio that started playing at dusk.

Charlie still couldn't spot Slits, and sweat beaded on his flushed face. The air grew suffocating and stale, the press of bodies stifling. The music blared. He couldn't focus—it was as if the drunken crowd engulfed him. The door vanished from sight. Panic simmered, threatening to erupt.

Just as the nerves were taking hold, the crowd parted, like the Red Sea, and Charlie caught sight of the door; he almost ran for it. He heard snippets of the jazz trio's set outside as he neared the exit; he could just about taste the fresh air wafting in.

And then he stopped—somebody grabbed his arm; cold, steely fingers wrapped around his bicep.

Charlie turned; his jaw clenched. He expected to see Slits' face when he looked back, but Slits wasn't there—it was the man with the Van Dyke.

He was taller than Charlie, who had to look up to meet the man's face, which was comely and aristocratic with a broad, angular chin and an aquiline nose; he was one of those ageless types who could have been in his thirties or his sixties, but damned if Charlie knew. His dark, wavy hair was combed back neatly, and his eyes, set deep, were pale, faded out, but the irises caught some of the low light and refracted it like a cat's. They glowed like dying embers.

The man was dressed well, but boldly; a red ascot tucked into the open collar of his shirt, matching the handkerchief tucked into the breast pocket of his pinstripe tailcoat. His pants were black, his shoes were shined, his cufflinks the color of polished redwood. In one hand, he held a homburg hat, and in the other, he grasped a black cane, the gold handle in the shape of a crow's skull. An imposing figure with broad shoulders, the man had an air of old aristocracy that made Charlie feel inadequate.

The man took his hand away. "I wanted to thank you for your roll at the table," the stranger said. His voice was resonant and calm, laced with a French accent. "I was smart to bet on you."

"Sure, sure," Charlie said, stepping back. "I made out pretty well myself."

"You left the table so quickly. I wondered if I could buy you a drink." The man motioned toward the bar with his hat.

"Sorry," Charlie said. "Next time." He turned, leaving the man standing on the edge of the crowd, and pushed his way through the nearest door. Charlie stormed through the vestibule and through the exit to the patio. Charlie took a deep breath of outside air as the doors slammed shut behind him.

The jazz trio was playing feverishly, and affluent good-timers mingled together, tipsy and oblivious. Charlie exhaled, relieved.

Another hand clamped down on Charlie's shoulder. He thought maybe it was the man from the table—he even dared to hope that it was—but the vice-like grip told him it wasn't.

"Charlie the Cheat," Slits said, stepping into view while one of his strong-armed thugs kept hold of Charlie's arm. "We need to talk."

If nothing else could be said of Charlie "the Cheat" Baptiste, he could at least take a punch.

He'd already taken eight of them, sandwiched between Slits' two big palookas — "Fat Phil" LaRasso and "Knuckles" Mc-Queen—who held his arms back while Slits went to work on him.

Slits bounced on his toes like a boxer, balling his hand into a fist and throwing another right hook across Charlie's face, bringing the total up to nine. His sleeves were rolled up to his elbows; his suit coat was folded and gently laid across a stack of crates. They were in the alley behind the casino, where the two gorillas had dragged Charlie after they'd laid hands on him.

Blood dribbled from his mouth; his lip was split, his nose was bleeding, his left eye was black and swollen. When his head drooped, Fat Phil pulled it back up by the hair.

Dropping his hands, Slits stopped his boxer's bounce and crouched down to look up at Charlie's face. "I thought I made it clear that your ticket was due, Charlie," he said. "In fact, I remember telling you distinctly that unless you ponied up the dough you owed, I'd kill you the next time I saw you."

Before Charlie could answer, Slits reached into the pocket of Charlie's tuxedo and pulled out the wad of bills. He counted them, peeling them off the roll as he went. He whistled. "Not a bad night for you," Slits said. He looked over at Fat Phil. "What was it he owes?"

"About two large."

"Two large," Slits said, almost sounding impressed. "That's more than some guys make in a year—honest guys with storefronts and mortgages. No wonder we're working so hard to find you."

"I'm gonna pay you back."

"Pay us back? With this? Turn him around, boys." Slits twirled his hand overhead. The two thugs shuffled Charlie around to face the back of the casino.

"You know who owns this place?" Slits asked.

"Lazaretto."

"And do you know who I work for, Charlie?"

Charlie answered hesitantly. "Lazaretto."

"Ding-ding-ding. Right-o, Charlie. But here's the big-money question: If you owe Mr. Lazaretto money, and you go to his joint to win money, then whose money are you going to pay Mr. Lazaretto back with?"

"It's not like that, Slits," Charlie said, desperately.

"I'm sure."

"I swear!"

"Even if I believed you, Charlie, how am I not supposed to kill you now?"

Charlie spoke frantically. "I can't pay if I'm dead."

Slits pointed to the casino. "You really think Lazaretto needs the money?"

"Isn't that what you want?"

Slits shook his head. "You just don't get it, do you, Charlie?" He smacked Charlie across the face with the cash. "I got five hundred from you right here, and the truth is, I don't think you're ever going to be worth much more than that."

"Give me a chance—"

Slits held up his finger. "Quiet, Charlie," he said. "I have." Slits looked at the two thugs. "You know what? Take this guy down to the river and wash him out. When I say I never want to see him again, I mean it."

"Slits, wait, I'll get you your money. I'm good for it, I swear, I'll have it for you tomorrow."

"It's not about the money, Charlie."

Slits turned away, hand in his pocket; he grabbed his suit coat and walked back to the casino. Charlie kept shouting as the two big men forced him toward the back of a car and stuffed him in the trunk.

They drove for almost an hour, Charlie bouncing around in darkness, crammed beside the spare tire. When they finally stopped and popped open the back, Charlie heard the sound of crickets. Fat Phil and Knuckles hoisted him out, tossing him to the ground.

They were on the banks of the Mississippi, out in the bayous, where the land turned soft and the bald cypress trees clustered like gossips.

Charlie stumbled trying to stand and run, but Knuckles punched him in the back of the head, sending him sprawling back to the dirt. The big man put a foot on his back, leaning his weight on Charlie, and pointed a sausage finger at him.

"Stay down, you little weasel," he said.

Fat Phil busied himself, loading his snub-nosed .38 revolver that looked small in his pudgy hand.

"What else you think this rat got on him?" Knuckles said.

"Dunno," Fat Phil said. "Shake him down."

Knuckles leaned down, taking his foot off Charlie's back and feeling through Charlie's pockets. He took out Charlie's wallet, which was empty, and tossed it to the ground.

"If you guys want money, I can get you some," Charlie said. "Maybe Lazaretto doesn't need it, but what about you?"

"Shut up," Knuckles said harshly as he continued to search Charlie's pockets, finding them all empty.

"Slits has me all wrong," Charlie said. "Just give me till tomorrow, and I can get it for you."

"You think we're idiots or something?" Knuckles said. "You know how many guys beg us for one more day? We know you ain't got it. You ain't gonna get it." He pawed at Charlie's left hand. "Nice ring though," he said, sliding the gold signet off. He held it up, examining it in the moonlight. "This might be worth something."

"It's a lucky charm," Charlie said.

"Must be broken, then," Knuckles said.

Fat Phil snapped the chamber closed on his snub-nose. "Slits was right, this guy really is hung out," he said.

"Wasn't his family rich or something?"

"A long time ago," Fat Phil said. "They lost it all. Ring's probably all that's left. Toss it in the car, we'll see what we can get."

Knuckles put his foot on Charlie's back again. "Stay down," he said as he stepped over him, Knuckles' weight pushing Charlie deeper into the mud and forcing the air out of his lungs.

The big man opened the passenger door and dropped the ring onto the seat. When he closed the door and started back towards his partner, he stopped. "You open this?" he asked, looking at the back door, which was resting just slightly ajar.

"What are you talking about?" Fat Phil asked. He was standing over Charlie, eyeing him through the iron sights on the revolver.

"Nothing," Knuckles said, leaning against the door to shut it.

"Then get back over here and let's do this damned thing. I want to get out of here."

As Knuckles returned, Charlie gave one last plea. "Really, I can get you money, whatever you want."

Fat Phil scoffed. "If you could get money, you wouldn't be here." He looked at Knuckles. "This guy," he said, shaking his head.

Charlie closed his eyes and let his head drop to the ground. His body began to shake.

"What's going on with him?" Knuckles asked, his foot still on Charlie's back. "Is he choking?"

"I think he's crying." Fat Phil sighed and shook his head. "Let's get this over with."

Charlie sobbed. He heard Fat Phil approaching, heard him pull back the hammer of the .38. He closed his eyes and braced himself for the cold, black embrace of whatever followed.

But there was no gunshot. Instead, he heard a gurgling scream and felt the warm spray of blood over his back. Fat Phil's body collapsed on him, making him gasp.

Knuckles jumped back, taking his foot off Charlie. He scrambled to the ground, picking up the little revolver. He leapt to his feet, turning around nervously again and again, his arm raised, pointing the gun straight out like he was using it to ward off evil.

Charlie didn't move. He lay still, face down in the mud with Fat Phil's corpse smothering him, blood leaking over him from the gaping gash in the fat man's neck. He shut his eyes tightly.

"What the hell?" Knuckles said, his voice filled with confused terror as he searched the empty black around him. He fired the little snub-nose three times into the trees. The gun sounded feeble in the vastness of the murky swamp, like a kid and his cap gun.

Knuckles paused. There was silence. And then he screamed—a final, gut-wrenching wail that was suddenly and permanently cut short.

From beneath Fat Phil, Charlie heard a crunching, tearing gush. It was wet and gristly, and it spilled out onto the ground.

And then, once again, there was silence.

Charlie didn't dare move. The swamp had turned deathly still, the crickets and frogs all quiet. Even the breeze had stopped, like the bayou was holding its breath. There was something else there with him; he could feel it, feel its eyes on him. It was prowling, circling him and the bodies like a predator.

Coaxed by fear of whatever it might be, he moved his hand; he could feel the warm blood seeping into the mud, pooling around him—and then he felt the handle of the gun. He grabbed it tightly and jumped up, pushing Fat Phil's body off him. He spun around, waving the revolver.

There was nothing there.

Mist shifted through the swamp. A humid breeze rustled the leaves of the cypress, fireflies flickered through the bluish blackness, but Charlie was alone.

Wiping the mud from his eyes, he looked at the bodies. Laid out before him was a horror show.

Fat Phil's eyes bulged out of his head, looking absently towards the sky. Where his throat should have been, there was a ragged hole of bloody flesh. His jaw was broken, set at an odd angle, which left his mouth agape as though frozen in a silent scream.

Knuckles was worse off. He was still sitting up on his knees, his broad torso folded in over itself. His midsection had been left a scramble of bloody scraps, ripped through to his guts. Blood spilled out of him, soaking everything beneath him in red. Dropped in a position of penitence, his thick arms hung at his sides, his knuckles lay on the ground with his palms facing up, and his insides pooled up around his knees. His throat was a mangle of tattered skin, and his head hung unnaturally to his chest.

Charlie's confusion was quickly overpowered by dread that swelled up from his gut. He needed to leave. He had to get away. This place was not right.

Propelled again by fear, Charlie started rifling through the dead men's pockets, looking for an escape. He found a wad of cash in Knuckles' jacket that he wasn't too proud to take, but it was Fat Phil who'd had the car keys. He grabbed them, and he stumbled to their ride, scratching the lock as he tried frantically to open the door—too panicked to realize it was already unlocked.

When he finally got the key in, he yanked the door open and jumped into the driver's seat, slamming the door behind him. He exhaled for the first time in what felt like hours. Relief washed over him. He began to laugh. His laughter turned to sobs.

After he laughed and cried all the tension out of his body, Charlie took three deep breaths. He tossed the gun and the cash on the passenger's seat. His hands were still shaking, covered in blood and dirt. His tuxedo was ruined. Grabbing the steering wheel, he looked out through the window. Everything felt like a dream.

Charlie knew it wasn't. This was real, and he had lived through it. He started to laugh again, running his hands over the steering wheel's leather cover.

The longer he sat there, the more he came back to himself. He needed a plan.

He had a wad of cash, a gun, a car, and a decent head start. It'd be morning, at least, before they found the bodies. Maybe they'd think he was dead too. Maybe they'd never come looking for him at all. Maybe he could start fresh somewhere.

His mind began to clear.

He could go west, or maybe north—not New York, but Baltimore or Boston. Maybe Atlantic City was the kind of place for him. Wherever he went, though, he knew he was done with New Orleans.

For maybe the first time in his life, Charlie felt free. There had always been someone to keep him down—but now it was just him, alone, and he was giving himself a chance. There was no one left to ruin him, he thought.

"Good evening," came a voice from behind him.

It was familiar, deep, it could have even been called serene if it hadn't terrified Charlie so much. Charlie checked the rearview mirror—he seized up in fear when he saw who had spoken.

The man with the Van Dyke sat coolly behind him, cloaked in shadow. His posture was straight, and his manners were proper, just as he'd been before. But, this time, his beard and the lower half of his face were covered with blood, which he was politely cleaning away with a handkerchief. He pulled the handkerchief away from his mouth and smiled.

Charlie's eyes widened with fear, his mouth went dry, his stomach tightened, and the color drained away from his face. He tried to scream, but his throat clenched so tightly he could only rasp out a single word.

"Vampire."

The stranger opened his mouth in a grotesque smile, bearing two needle-like teeth.

Charlie reached for the gun, but the stranger lunged out from the back seat, grabbing his hand, holding it down.

"No, no, no," he said. "No need for that."

"What do you want with me?" Charlie asked, his voice pinched with desperation.

The vampire grinned.

"I want you to drive."

CHAPTER 2

THE ATTIC OF THE Old Ursuline Convent had been converted into a dormitory for the orphan girls who lived there. It was a long, narrow room with dozens of mismatched beds lining the walls. Most of them were filled. The girls were all young—the oldest was eleven. When she turned twelve in a few months, she'd be sent to Sacred Heart Academy, a boarding school supported largely by the church. There, young women could learn a few skills before being turned out into the world.

Sister Magdalene walked down the aisle of beds, watching over the girls as they readied themselves for the night. Beneath her black habit, she was young and slender. She clasped a rosary across her stomach as she listened to the girls kneeling at their bedsides, murmuring the words of their nightly prayers quietly to themselves.

As she passed, one of the younger girls—a small little thing named Martha—called out to her.

"Sister Magdalene," she said, "would you tuck me in?"

The sister stopped and smiled, kneeling to be at Martha's level.

"Of course, dear," the sister said softly, gently gathering the comforter and tucking it beneath the little girl. Magdalene smoothed down Martha's wild, auburn hair and saw the girl's eyes shining with unshed tears, her lower lip trembling as she tried to keep her composure.

She cupped Martha's cheek with a warm, tender hand, thumb brushing away a tear. "What's wrong, little one?" she asked, her voice a gentle caress, fingers lingering to offer reassurance in each stroke through Martha's tangled hair.

Martha's chin quivered. "Nothing."

"It doesn't seem like 'nothing.'"

"I was just—" the girl paused. "Sister, do you believe in monsters?"

The sister's lips turned up in a tender, understanding smile. "No, sweetheart," she said, gently brushing Martha's hair back. "Is that what all these tears are about?"

The little girl gulped. "What about devils? They're in the Bible."

"They are, yes, but you don't need to worry about them." The sister stopped stroking the girl's hair and held her head. "You're safe here in the convent. The other sisters and I wouldn't let anything happen to you."

"You promise?"

"Of course, Martha. What's all this about?"

"Some of the girls were telling stories."

"Oh?"

"Scary stories."

"Were they trying to frighten you?"

"No, Sister. They told me to leave, so I wouldn't get scared. I told them I wouldn't, I told them I was old enough—" Martha faltered, shame clouding her expression and her voice wavering. "But they scared me," she admitted, barely above a whisper.

"There's nothing wrong with that," Magdalene said, her tone warm and understanding. "I get scared too, sometimes." She offered a gentle, knowing smile. "Do you want to tell me what the stories were about?"

Martha's eyes lowered, and she looked about the room like she was preparing to whisper a secret. She leaned in towards the sister. "Vampires."

"I see," Magdalene said. "And who was telling these stories?"

"Jane and Hyacinthe." Martha looked past the sister. "Juliette was telling them, too."

Magdalene raised her eyes in surprise. "Juliette? Really?"

"Hers were the scariest."

"How is Juliette doing?"

"I think she may be sick—she's been coughing and shivering."

Magdalene frowned with concern. "We can have a doctor in tomorrow to look at her," she said.

"She's quiet, too," Martha said. "Except for her stories."

"Give her time. She's only been here a few days. Sometimes it takes a little while for people to speak up." Magdalene touched the tip of the little girl's nose. "It might help if she had someone to talk to."

"I can do that," Martha said. Her eyes wandered towards Juliette's bed. "Where is she?"

Magdalene turned and looked. The bed was empty; the sheets still pulled tight from when it had been made in the morning. "I think I might know," Magdalene said, looking back at Martha. "But don't you worry, just rest, and dream of nicer things."

Martha smiled again, then closed her eyes and settled in under her covers. Magdalene doused the lamp beside the little girl, smoothing her hair one last time before leaving.

Without drawing attention to herself, Magdalene quietly slipped out the door of the dormitory. She moved silently down the wide stairs to the ground floor, while the other nuns stayed upstairs, tending to the girls. During Juliette's short time in the convent, Magdalene had already found her in the same place three times before, so she walked with purposeful steps, knowing where she would be.

From the bottom of the stairs, Sister Magdalene started towards the chapel. The convent was quiet and still. The only sisters who hadn't already retired to their chambers were upstairs with the girls. The halls were empty and dark. They were lined with faded oil paintings and worn wooden statues of saints; Magdalene still struggled to remember their names. All of them—the statues and the figures in the paintings—seemed to watch her as she walked briskly down the hall, their eyes following from their dark niches.

She passed by the tall, arched windows, pausing to close and lock one of them. She lingered for a moment, appreciating the cool air outside and breathing in the scent of rain. Standing there, she looked out at the rolling fog rising off the river in swirls. As the moonlight dimmed beneath the roiling storm above, she knew there would be rain tonight. She loved its sound—the pattering against her window and the moan of the wind making the convent creak. She found the sounds oddly comforting.

At the end of the hall, Magdalene approached the wide wooden door to the chapel and quietly pushed it open, entering near the transept.

The chapel was a single, long room that stretched out on both sides away from her. To her left, the space was filled with pews, and to her right stood the apse and altar, where a huge crucifix hung. The door creaked shut behind her, and her footsteps echoed hollowly in the rafters of the high, vaulted ceiling.

The only light was from streetlamps outside, which glowed through the stained-glass windows; it was so dim that both ends of the nave—the apse and the entrance beyond the pews—were barely visible. A primordial fear twisted in her belly, and fine hairs on the back of her neck stood on end. She realized she was holding her breath; she had been ever since she'd entered.

Magdalene exhaled quickly and shook her head, feeling foolish that she'd been so afraid of the dark. This was the chapel, she reminded herself, a place of God, with nothing inside to fear. Still, she paused briefly near the altar and made the sign of the cross.

She took a candlestick from inside a niche and lit it with a match from the rack of prayer candles. The soft glow was comforting in the oppressive dark, and she would need it as she passed into even greater darkness.

Beside the altar, tucked away and mostly out of view, was an unassuming set of stone steps that led down to the crypt below. It was the oldest part of the building, and although they'd tried desperately to control it, the crypt often felt soggy and damp due to the saturated earth. Water would trickle from invisible fissures in the stone walls and pool in muddy puddles on the floor. More than once, the crypt had flooded, and the musty smell of decay had never left.

With one hand, Sister Magdalene lifted the hem of her dress so it wouldn't drag on the steps. Holding the candle out before her to light the way, she carefully made her way down into the darkness below.

The iron gate at the base of the stairs groaned as she opened it. Beyond the gate was an overwhelming maze of columns and subterranean chambers, filled with caskets and the bones of the faithful departed. The stagnating air was cool, almost cold, and a shiver ran down the sister's spine. Beyond the meager glow of her candle, she could see nothing but black.

"Juliette?" she called out, pausing for a response. "Juliette, it's Sister Magdalene. Are you here? It's time for bed."

She waited again for a response, but none came; there was only the empty sound of wind beginning to blow overhead. She strained to hear, and she thought, maybe, there was a faint scratching somewhere in the distant dark. Magdalene stepped forward, toward the sound, passing by old tombs and alcoves where the dead had been laid to rest.

"Juliette?" she called out again, and this time, in the returning silence, she was certain she heard something—a tiny cough. Beyond the light of her own candle, she thought she could see the soft glow of another.

As she continued through the crypt, she worried about finding her way back. She had never spent more than a few fleeting moments there before Juliette had arrived. For whatever reason, the young girl favored the dark seclusion the crypt offered, and whenever she could, she escaped down here, hiding away to be alone.

Magdalene reached the far wall, a stone coffin lying on the ground in front of her, the name of the occupant illegible, its etching worn away by the relentlessly damp air. On the other side of it, a small, flickering light tossed soft shadows along the ground. She heard another cough.

The sister stepped around the coffin, and there sat Juliette, dressed and ready for bed in a light blue nightgown. Her waist-length blonde hair was fine, brushed to a golden sheen that shimmered in the candlelight. She was huddled against the wall, as if taking shelter. A blanket had been laid out on the ground where she sat, a small tea light lit beside her. The girl was turned away, working on something in the low light.

"What are you doing down here, Juliette?" Magdalene asked.

The little girl spun around, hiding her work away. Her eyes were wide and innocent with shock.

"It's time for bed, you can't be down here, you'll freeze in a nightgown like that." She touched the girl's forehead. "You're already freezing," she said.

The girl's forehead glistened with beads of sweat, and she shivered, hugging her knees to her chest. Martha had been right. Juliette looked sick, dark bags forming under her eyes. The little girl coughed again.

Magdalene bent down and gently helped Juliette stand. As she did, Juliette quickly snatched the paper she had been working on and slipped it into her nightgown. Glancing at the ground, Magdalene noticed a stack of blank pages and colored pencils neatly lined up along the wall, evidence of what Juliette had been doing.

"Have you been drawing down here?" the sister asked.

Juliette nodded sheepishly.

"You're not in trouble—not with me," Magdalene said. "But we need to get you upstairs where it's warm."

The girl seemed resistant, silently looking at her makeshift bed and her collection of art supplies. Magdalene leaned down, gathering the blanket, pencils, and paper, and blew out the girl's tea light.

"Come with me," she said, taking the girl's hand. "We'll get you some medicine and into bed."

Together, they walked back to the stairs and up into the chapel. It was fully dark when they reached the top, the moon completely hidden by the storm clouds. Magdalene could hear the first patter of raindrops against the windows. The girl was still shivering, but except for her coughing, she stayed silent.

As they left the chapel, Magdalene tried to coax the girl into talking.

"Do you like to draw?" she asked.

When the girl didn't answer, the sister tried to recall the French she'd learned as a child. "How do you say it? *Tu dessines?*"

"Draw?" the little girl said, finally breaking her silence. "Sometimes."

Magdalene smiled with relief. "I used to paint," she said, but the girl didn't respond. "Have you ever painted?"

The girl nodded.

"Which do you prefer? Painting or drawing?"

At first, the girl didn't answer, and Magdalene thought she wouldn't. She was about to change the subject and ask another question when the girl finally spoke.

"Painting," she said. "But I could only find pencils."

Magdalene smiled. "I think," she said, "that I might have some of my old paints and brushes." She looked down at the girl's face as they walked. "If I find them, would you like to borrow them?"

Juliette bit her lip, thinking about it, but she couldn't hide her enthusiasm and nodded.

"I'll look for them tonight," Magdalene said as she cleaned a smudge of dirt from the young girl's face. "If I find them, I'll give them to you tomorrow."

Juliette smiled; the first Sister Magdalene had seen from the young girl. It was sweet and warm, her lips tightly pressed together.

"I'd like that," Juliette said.

"As would I."

They passed the stairs to the dormitory, stopping at a supply closet where the nuns kept basic medicine. Magdalene shook out two tablets of aspirin into a small paper cup and handed it to Juliette. Then she led the little girl to the convent's kitchen, where she filled a glass of water.

"Let's hurry," she said, handing the glass to the girl. "The quicker you're in bed, the quicker I can find my paints."

She held out her candlestick, the girl's blanket, and pencils tucked under her arm. With her free hand, she took Juliette's and headed back towards the stairs. At the base of them, though, someone was waiting.

Still as a statue, stood a dark figure, her black habit and veil cascading down her body and the stairs like melted wax, her coronet obscuring her face with inky shadow. She clasped her hands at her waist, holding a ring of keys.

As Magdalene and Juliette drew near, the light from their candle illuminated the woman's face. She was a bland, unpleasant woman whose sharp features came to a point at the end of her nose. Her bloodless lips were pursed disapprovingly as her vulture eyes glowered down at them.

"What is going on here?" she asked, her words as sharp as her face.

"We're just going to bed, Mother Superior," Magdalene said.

"The girl should be in bed already."

"She's sick, I was just getting her some medicine."

The Mother Superior put a hand to the girl's head and quickly brought it away. "She's faking it," the old woman said. "She has no fever. And you're indulging her lies. Now get to bed, both of you."

Magdalene nodded, holding her tongue, and curtsying slightly. She took Juliette's hand and pulled her away to the stairs. The Mother Superior remained at the base, watching them closely as they skirted her and climbed to the attic, only leaving when she heard the dormitory door shut behind them.

Inside the girls' room, Sister Agnès was waiting for them. She was a round, old sister with a kind face and smiling eyes behind horn-rimmed glasses.

"Did the Mother Superior find you?"

"Unfortunately," said Magdalene.

"I'm sorry," Agnès said. "I tried to steer her away, but she was livid when she saw that you and the girl were both missing."

"It will be fine," Magdalene said.

"It is never easy with a woman like her in charge," Agnès said.

"It's not all bad."

Agnès smiled slightly. "Keep your attention on the girls here. They love you for your compassion."

"Thank you," Magdalene said, touching the older nun lightly on the arm. "I'll try to remember that."

"Do," Agnès said. "Now get the little one to sleep, and yourself as well."

The older woman smiled and left as Magdalene guided Juliette to her bed. The little girl put her aspirin and water on the bedside table as Magdalene quickly stuffed her blanket and pencils into the chest at the foot of her bed. When she was finished, Magdalene walked to Juliette's bedside.

"Isn't this better?"

The girl shook her head. "I don't like my bed," she said.

"What's the trouble with it?"

"It feels—" the girl paused. "How do you say it? *Exposée?*"

"Exposed?"

"Yes," Juliette said. The girl coughed again and shivered. Magdalene put her arm around the girl, holding her close to warm her.

"You'll get used to it," Magdalene said. "It will just take time."

The little girl shivered, and Magdalene ushered her under the covers. As she tucked the blanket tightly around Juliette, the girl turned to look at her.

"I'm sorry you got in trouble," Juliette said.

Magdalene feigned a smile. "There's nothing to be sorry about. The Mother Superior just has her way." When she finished with the blanket, Magdalene knelt down. "Have you said your prayers?"

Juliette shook her head.

"Would you like me to pray with you?"

"No," Juliette said.

"Very well," Magdalene said. "I'll leave you to it. And don't forget to take your medicine. It will help with the fever."

"I don't want to pray," Juliette said.

"Why not?"

"It's foolish."

The answer surprised Magdalene. Not the idea itself, but the way she'd said it. The little girl had been so certain and so calloused, she sounded like a woman hardened beyond her years.

"What makes it foolish?"

The girl looked blankly at the sister. There were no tears in her eyes, but there was pain.

"No one listens."

"What do you mean?"

"Men prayed as our village burned, but it didn't save them."

The war. Magdalene's heart sank. Of course. Realization dawned on her. That's why the girl stayed in the crypt, why she felt afraid up here. Magdalene had listened to the news, heard the stories about Germany and their Hitler, about his bombing sprees across Europe. Families had been told to take shelter in their cellars for safety. For Juliette's family, Magdalene thought, it must not have been enough.

Sister Magdalene put her caring hands on Juliette's shoulders. "Believe it or not, I didn't use to pray either," she said. "I was scared, and I was angry, and I didn't think God, if He even existed, cared about me."

"What happened?" Juliette asked

"I lost my family," Magdalene said. "Or rather, they lost me. I ran away, and when I tried to go back, they wouldn't take me."

"Why?" The girl sounded genuinely confused; the hard edge in her voice had dulled.

"They didn't want the trouble," Magdalene said. She paused for a moment. "That's when I stopped painting, too."

"Why did you start to pray?" the little girl asked.

"Because I needed to," Magdalene said. "I needed someone to hear me. I needed someone to help. I didn't want to be scared or angry or alone anymore."

"And it helped?"

Magdalene met the young girl's gaze. Beyond the pain and the anger, she thought she saw a small glimmer of hope in the young eyes.

"That's why I'm here," Magdalene said. "You don't have to be frightened anymore, Juliette. You're safe now."

Juliette sniffled. "How do you know that?"

"The war is behind you. All you have is what's ahead."

"But what if—" the girl paused. She coughed. "What if something came with me?"

"I'll protect you, Juliette."

The little girl pushed away and looked into Magdalene's eyes; her face was grave, and this time the tears were there. When she spoke, her words choked up in her throat.

"But—" she paused. "What if you can't?"

"Nothing," Magdalene said, "will stop me."

CHAPTER 3

SEBASTIAN NIGHTINGALE SMACKED A crumpled pack of cigarettes against his palm. He'd smoked all but three of them already, and he was just getting started for the night. He leaned against a lamppost, watching the street, surrounded by saloons; the red lights above the door bathed him in crimson light.

The place was as lively as a graveyard. Everyone was inside, had been since sundown. Word had spread: the neighborhood was closed for business. A few johns still came out, just the kind looking to share a drink with some company. They sat in the cathouse bars, nursing thinned-out bourbons, making small talk to pass the time. The women mostly obliged. They flirted, joked, faked smiles—always with a watchful eye and a hand on the knives they kept tucked into their garters.

Nightingale considered lighting another smoke when he heard delicate footfalls behind him. He turned to see a woman in the glow of the streetlight. She was a foot shorter than he, built with firm muscle. He'd heard she had been a gymnast with the circus before becoming a burlesque dancer. Her face was soft, her red hair cut to a bob.

"Quiet night." She had dropped the baby-soft coo she used when talking to the clientele; even now, it sounded sultry, but with a hard edge and a pint-of-gin rasp.

He nodded at her. "Ruby," he said, in greeting.

She extended two fingers, silently asking for a cigarette. He shook one from his battered pack without hesitation. She took it, holding it cool between her lips as he lit it. She leaned beside him against the lamppost.

Ruby exhaled smoke. "Waiting for trouble, detective?"

"Trouble's late."

"You sure have a way of finding it, though."

"It tends to find me first," he said.

Ruby straightened up, glancing down the dark street with one arm over her stomach. "You really think it's a vampire?"

Nightingale looked at the last two cigarettes in the pack, still debating whether to light one with her or save both for later. "I saw the bodies. I'm sure."

She took another drag. "They said they didn't have a drop of blood left in them. You ever seen anything like that before?"

Nightingale looked back at the pack of cigarettes. "Yeah," he said, "I have."

She blew smoke through her nostrils. "Of course you have, detective. Silly me."

"You probably shouldn't be out here," he said.

She smiled again. "I thought you could use some bait."

"Ask a worm how that goes," he said.

Ruby tossed the butt and snuffed it out with her shoe. "Plenty of those around here."

From a block away, a shrieking scream cut through the night.

All around them, lights inside darkened rooms flicked on. The door that Ruby had come out of opened, and a gaggle of call girls came spilling out, holding their long robes and lace kimonos closed, frantic questions spilling from their lips as they wondered what the scream had been and who had made it.

Without hesitation, Nightingale took off towards the sound, dropping his pack of cigarettes in the gutter.

"Get them inside!" Nightingale called to Ruby before he bolted out of sight. "And stay safe."

The woman's cry was cut abruptly short, and in the sudden silence, Nightingale heard the back doors of a delivery truck slam shut. He rounded the corner just as the truck was grinding into first gear and disappeared around the block.

Nightingale turned hard, dashed through back-alley courtyards, his soles slapping tile and pavement, the sound echoing off high row house walls. He dodged a low fire escape ladder and leapt over a toppled trash can, sending rats scurrying into the sewer.

His long, wool overcoat billowed out behind him, flapping like batwings. His fedora was pulled down low, the brim casting deep shadows across his face. And the heavy revolver holstered under his arm thumped against his chest with every pounding step.

Out on the street, he could hear the truck's creaking chassis, and in the narrow gaps between buildings, he caught glimpses of its taillights.

Nightingale was puffing for breath. Block after block, the chase continued. He sprinted through backyards and hopped fences. The truck rattled along, loud. His legs ached. His lungs burned. Any moment, the truck could peel away and leave him behind. Still, he kept running. The truck stayed in sight.

Rampart Street crossed in front of him. He heard the truck's brakes squeal and its heavy frame groan as it slowed to make a turn.

Just as Nightingale hit the sidewalk, the truck rushed by him, and he came face to face with the broad side, locking eyes with a smiling pig chomping down on a sausage link, and in big letters that arched across the top was the company name.

BELLE CHASSE MEATPACKING CO.

He was headed to the slaughterhouse.

Nightingale made a sharp turn on his heels and bolted after the truck. He reached out with his hand, feet still pounding the pavement, chest heaving with breath; his fingers danced along one of the handles on the back—but the truck was just out of reach. It bumped along the road one beat faster than Nightingale could run as he splashed through puddles behind it.

He was losing steam; he could feel the truck beating him. With a grunt, he lunged forward, throwing himself towards the truck. He caught the handle with his off hand and wrapped his hard fingers around it. Growling in exertion, he pulled himself up, hoisting his body. A gust of wind caught his hat, pulling it from his head and sending it flying to the street behind him, where it landed in a puddle of dirty water.

Nightingale jumped onto the bumper, but his wet shoe slipped. As he fell, his free hand swung across to grab the opposite handle. Hanging across the doors, he managed to pull himself up and plant his feet, steadying himself.

The truck rumbled on through the empty streets, and Nightingale stood spread-eagled against the back of it, his hair mussed in the wind and his coat whipping out against his shins.

Rampart turned to McShane, then St. Claude, as the delivery truck bounced through the Lower Ninth Ward and Holy Cross, dropping off the paved roads and onto the dirty gravel ones that crisscrossed through the industrial district.

Brick and steel buildings lined the road, unadorned and uninviting. The warehouses were dark, the factories silent, except for a few running night shifts. Their smokestacks belched ash, steam, and poison, as if about to blow. The air grew hotter, more fetid, and foul as they neared. Nightingale knew they were close.

The brake lights flashed, and the truck made a wide turn towards a gravel courtyard. Nightingale jumped from the back and dashed across the street, clinging to the shadows. He ducked behind a pile of crates and peered around them as the truck came to a squeaking halt—they had arrived at the slaughterhouse.

The Belle Chasse Meatpacking Company was a towering structure, a monolith of death silhouetted against the dim glow of the crescent moon. The industrial windows—framed in steel and made of small, square panes—ran the full height of the building; grimy, they were covered with the sheen of fat and oil that had been cooked onto them by the hot, Southern sun. The coppery miasma of blood and rot was pungent. The air was alive with the buzz of flies, turned gluttons by the piles of offal that were left heaping after the day's slaughter.

The grounds stretched out over a full city block, a labyrinth of connected buildings, a temple to the industrial art of killing.

High above them, two tall smokestacks reached up like the hands of a penitent sinner praising God.

Stopping between the biggest structures, the truck parked in front of a low-roofed delivery bay. The driver's door swung open. Out slid a skinny man. He was long-limbed and slender, with lean, sinewy muscles. His face was pale with sallow, sunken cheeks and dark, deep-set eyes, obscured by the shadow of his Cro-Magnon brow. He dressed in dingy workman's clothes—ratty denim and heavy boots—that hung off his slim frame like drying laundry. He turned his head and coughed. A deep, hacking cough bubbled up from the bottom of his lungs. Then he spat into the dirt.

His name was Walter Grange, and Nightingale had been looking for him.

A delivery man for the slaughterhouse, who'd worked there for years. But lately, he'd been going missing.

Grange walked to the back of the truck, darting his head side to side like a lizard, double-checking that no one was around. As Grange reached up to open the back door of the truck, he stopped. His lanky frame leaned over as he looked down, running a hand across the bumper. Nightingale watched him—and as Grange studied the bumper, Nightingale remembered slipping from it and thought of the muddy shoe prints he must have left behind.

Nightingale crept to the edge of the crates and reached a hand into his coat, resting it on the butt of his hefty revolver—a blue-steeled revolver loaded with six shots of silver-tipped .45.

He was just about to pull it, but Grange moved first. He whipped out a handkerchief from his back pocket and ran it along the bumper, wiping the muddy prints away. Grange then grabbed the doors and pulled them open. With a single, high step, he climbed in, disappearing into the dark.

Exhaling slowly and quietly, Nightingale took his hand away from the gun. Across the road, the truck jostled, and the suspension creaked. He could hear the clanking of chains inside, a faint grunt of effort, and a dull thud as something fell to the floor.

When Grange emerged into the moonlight, he carried a canvas sack slung limply over his shoulder—the type of sack the meat packers used to cover the larger slabs of meat. It was just big enough to hold a person.

Grange stepped to the ground and walked quickly to the door of the slaughterhouse. He unlocked it, pulling it open, and with a final paranoid glance over his shoulder, he entered.

As soon as the door clicked shut, Nightingale sprang from his hiding place and sprinted across the street, gravel crunching beneath his feet. He ran to the front of the building, put his back to the wall, and slunk around the corner as quietly as possible. He moved to the door Grange had used, checked it, and found it locked.

"Damn," Nightingale said under his breath.

He searched for another way in.

High above, he could see a metal balcony. On the ground, three stories below it, was a scattering of cigarette butts. Some-one, Nightingale thought, took his smoke breaks up there, and frequently—maybe even enough that he'd leave the door unlocked.

Nightingale moved to the cab of Grange's truck and climbed onto the hood. From there, he could reach the low-pitch roof above the delivery doors. He jumped, pulled himself up, and kept low as he crept over to the wall of the slaughterhouse.

A plumbing pipe ran down the side of the building. Grabbing it with both hands, he put his feet against the brick and began to climb, walking himself up towards the balcony.

When he was high enough, Nightingale reached out, grabbed the railing, and leapt to it. He checked the handle and the door clicked open—unlocked, just as he'd hoped.

Inside, Nightingale paused in the darkened office of M. Garvey, General Manager, according to the name painted across the glass panel of the door; a panel dirty with the same grime that covered the other windows. Even in the high office, the smell of the slaughterhouse crept in, assaulting the senses. No wonder, Nightingale thought, the man smoked outside.

Before he left, Nightingale bummed a cigarette from M. Garvey's pack sitting on the desk. Making his way silently from the hall, he took the stairs down three flights to the ground level, and then he doubled back to the front of the building. He moved as quickly as he could, staying quiet and low as he navigated the narrow hallways, passing rooms that looked like hellish operating theaters, the white tiles stained pink with blood, and the drains clogged with slimy, unwanted bits of animals that no one had cared to clean up.

He found the door that Grange had used, and from there he followed the faint sounds of struggle until he arrived at the double doors of the killing floor. The smell was even worse here, and the buzz of flies more aggressive. Inside, he could hear Grange's shuffling.

Nightingale pushed through the doors slowly. The room was long and open all the way to the high beams overhead.

A shaft of moonlight shone through the dingy windows. The place was a labyrinth of buzz saws and butchery tools; bloody skins, stripped from the meat, hung from frames. Conveyor belts snaked around pillars, pipes, and rails crisscrossed overhead, and heavy chains with twisted hooks hung from them like vines in a blood-soaked jungle of steel and glass. A staircase along the far wall led to a walkway above, and in the moonlight, he could read the stenciled name of the station on the dirty wall.

SLAUGHTER HALL

A ramp from outside connected to the walkway, where the pigs were brought in from the pen behind the slaughterhouse. It led to the drain rack, where the pigs were killed, hung on hooks, and left to bleed out through the grated floor.

From there, the pigs were pushed along the walkway on rails to the scalder, a long, narrow oven the size of a hallway that spewed flames and steam to heat the skin, making it easier for the meatpackers to scrape the hair off the bodies. Dead and hairless, the pigs moved to the killing floor or one of the other anonymous rooms of the slaughterhouse, where the bodies were cut up, packaged, processed, and shipped away.

It was at the drain rack where Nightingale spotted Grange. The slender man was bent over, hard at work. The canvas bag he'd brought in was now empty, and it hung over the railing. He had lowered one of the chains and was wrapping something around the hook. Nightingale crept to the stairs and up to the slaughter hall, where he could see what Grange was working on.

A young woman lay on the floor, her eyes closed, her chest moving slowly with breath—alive, but unconscious. Her hands and feet were bound, her mouth gagged. Grange had attached the hook to the bindings at her wrists. His back was to Nightingale as he pulled on the length of chain, hoisting the girl up until she dangled with her feet just above the grating. Grange steadied her, his hand caressing down her body.

Nightingale could hear the wet sound of a smile split Grange's lips. He pulled his revolver just as Grange gave another hacking cough. That's when Nightingale moved.

He rushed up behind Grange, the sudden sound of the clanking metal making Grange turn just in time to see the dark shadow of Nightingale swoop in, revolver raised high before it came crashing down against his head.

Grange collapsed to the floor, a stream of blood trickling down his face. His eyes rolled back, and his eyelids closed. The man was out cold.

With the corner of Grange's jacket, Nightingale wiped off the butt of his gun. He rolled the man onto his back and opened Grange's mouth, pushing up his lips.

His teeth were yellow, crooked, even a little rotten, but they were the teeth of a man, not the elongated incisors of a vampire, just the decaying teeth of a chronic dipper.

For the last three days, Nightingale had been looking into Grange. He liked him for the murders. The truck had been the first clue; some of the women—Ruby included—had seen it around on the nights the victims had gone missing, others had seen it where their bodies had been dumped. None of them had seen the driver, and most hadn't seen the truck in detail, but when Nightingale had talked to enough of them, it gave him something to go on.

It brought him to the slaughterhouse, where he'd started asking questions, learning about the drivers and anything out of sorts. That's when he learned about Grange.

The man worked early mornings, staying up through the night and sleeping most of the day. The people at the factory were the only ones who knew him, and they said he'd changed. Some said he'd gotten sick, that his health had slipped. He'd been taking a lot of days off, sometimes just going missing. This week, no one had seen him at all.

When he'd seen Grange tonight, he thought he'd had it all figured out. But Grange wasn't the killer—not the vampire Nightingale thought he was.

"If it's not you," Nightingale said to the unconscious man, "then who?"

Just as Nightingale asked the question, he heard the shrill, scraping noise down below of a sewer grate being pushed up and slid to the side.

Nightingale turned, raising his revolver again. Slowly, quietly, tensely, he walked to the railing, careful not to make a noise, and peered over the side.

There was nothing below but shadows.

He scanned the room, looking for movement, listening intently. He stopped when he saw the sewer grate. It had been lifted off the manhole and set beside it. Stringy bits of blood and refuse gathered at the edge of the hole, which descended into the black underground.

Quietly, he thumbed back the hammer of his gun. His breath caught in his throat as it clicked. His heart was pounding; the blood rushed in his ears.

The vampire was here.

With the clarity that sudden fear often brings, Nightingale understood. He'd made a mistake. Grange was a thrall—a crony, a servant, what some in the Old Country called a *raklo*—the living attendant of the thirsting dead, an emissary of the daylight who carried out the bidding of his nocturnal lord. Grange brought the victims here, but it was his master who did the killing.

A chain rattled behind him. Nightingale spun around, but the vampire was already there. In the moonlight, its skin was pale, nearly translucent. Its bulbous head was bald, except for a few long, white, wispy strands of hair. The vampire's eyes were a deep red, and its long limbs ended in gnarled fingers with sharpened nails.

It hissed, bearing its blood-stained fangs and raising a claw-like hand.

Nightingale brought his revolver up and fired, but the vampire was faster. It swiped at his arm, tearing his coat, spilling fresh blood from his veins. The shot boomed, echoing in the empty rafters of the slaughterhouse, as the bullet ricocheted between the machinery. Nightingale yelled in pain; the revolver fell from the detective's hand and went clattering to the floor below as he collapsed to the grating.

The vampire hissed again, its tall figure looming over Nightingale, craning its neck to stare down at its prey. He clutched at his bleeding wrist, but seeing its hungry eyes, Nightingale forgot the fiery pain and scrambled backwards. With loping steps, the vampire followed him, advancing on his retreat, a predator playing with its prey.

Nightingale pulled himself along the slaughter hall, passing under the heavy chains of the drain rack and onto the scalder.

The brick walls, scorched by the heat and flame, were claustrophobic, pressing in around Nightingale. The moonlight disappeared in the narrow passage, and the darkness gathered.

A grotesque grin slithered across the vampire's face, crinkling its papery skin.

Still crawling backwards, Nightingale made it through the scalder where, in the dim light, he could see a gas valve and a large dial next to a red button marked IGNITE.

The vampire was only feet away; Nightingale had to act.

He kicked the valve open and leapt up, jamming the dial as far to the right as it would go and slapping the red button.

Somewhere below them, machinery rumbled to life. The pipes hissed and clanked. Then, the nozzles erupted into flames, spitting out tongues of orange, yellow, and blue that licked at the walls and ceiling, sending the vampire tumbling backward, howling. An infernal heat exploded through the hallway.

Nightingale ran. He could still hear the pained wails of the vampire as the fire raged, illuminating the hallway ahead. The cuts on his wrist flared with stinging pain. He pulled a handkerchief from his pocket and tied it around his wrist, then turned down a flight of stairs into the darkness beyond the flames.

Directionless and practically blind in the deep dark, Nightingale charged through the depths of the slaughterhouse, down hallways splashed with grime, lined with chains, filled with gore and the putrid stench of death. The building was a maze of nightmare rooms, and he felt himself getting lost. He slowed just a bit, catching his breath. Somewhere behind him, there was a woman, tied up by her hands, hanging near a raging fire. Below her, lying uselessly on the killing floor, was his gun. And, somewhere between here and there, was a vampire, furious and bloodthirsty.

Stopping to turn, Nightingale headed back in the direction he'd come. Groping in the darkness, he passed more carnage-filled rooms until he found the stairs that led to M. Garvey's office. He breathed a sigh of relief. From there, he returned to the long, dark hall, back to the swinging doors of the killing room. The bright flicker of flame outlined the entrance: light streaked through the gaps and across the ground. He hustled ahead, wary, still holding his throbbing wrist. As he neared the doors, they swung violently open.

In the doorway, silhouetted against the dancing fire behind it, stood the vampire.

The flames had burned the side of its face, the pale skin charred black; the monster held its badly scorched arm close to its chest. In the firelight, Nightingale could see its full figure. Its shoulders were hunched, a slight hump on its back. Its ears were large and pointed, its nose knobby and hooked. With its good hand, the vampire held the door open as its sharpened fingernails scraped mindlessly at the metal. The creature's red eyes, once so sure and predatory, were wild with bloodlust. It wanted Nightingale, and it was coming for him—not to feed, necessarily, but to kill.

Nightingale stopped sharply and flattened himself against the wall, retreating around a corner. The vampire hadn't seen him, but he could hear it sniffing the air. The light from the fire vanished as the doors swung closed. In the darkness, he heard the shuffling footsteps of the limping vampire coming towards him down the hall.

He backed away from the sound, moving slowly, fighting the temptation to run. When he could, he turned, heading down another hall, leading further into the slaughterhouse. He paused and peered around the corner just as the vampire came into view at the far end. It dropped to the floor, moving on its long limbs like a spider. In the dim light, it examined a dark spot on the ground. The vampire sniffed at it and then, parting its thin, purple lips, revealed a long, viperous tongue. It licked at the ground, tentatively at first and then greedily, lapping at the stain.

As the vampire slurped away, Nightingale looked at his wrist, slashed and bleeding. The handkerchief was soaked through with blood, which dripped to the floor. A foot away was another drop, and another before that—all the way down the hall, where the vampire skittered along the ground on its long limbs, licking it up, drop by drop.

It raised its head, turning it slowly side to side.

"I can taste you," the vampire said in a high, unsettling tone that was almost playful. "I smell your blood. And your sweat. And your fear."

Nightingale left the corner, fleeing the vampire. He untied the handkerchief from his wrist, and when he reached another hallway, he tossed it away from him and continued in the other direction.

He hurried down a flight of stairs, into the basement where pipes ran along the ceiling and the walls dripped with rust and bile. Under the steps, he ditched his long, gray coat, then further up, in a room filled with hanging slabs of pig, he tossed away his suit jacket—both had been soaked in his blood. He took his tie and tied it tightly around his wrist, trying again to stop the bleeding. All the while, the vampire followed, taunting him, its voice echoing through the empty rooms and hallways. Each time it found a piece of bloody clothing, it would laugh slowly, resonantly. Each time, the laughter was closer.

Down in the bowels of the slaughterhouse, the drone of flies returned. Ahead of Nightingale, the hall dead-ended with a set of double doors, a single word stenciled across both.

SANGUINARIUM

When he pushed his way through the doors, flies swarmed in the darkness. The room was lined with tall, rusted tanks and boilers. The ceiling was covered in a weave of pipes, which dripped with dark, viscous fluid. In the middle of the room, between the tankers and set against the back wall, was a huge vat, at least four feet deep, filled almost to the rim with whatever dripped from the pipes.

Nightingale approached, dipping his fingers into the vat, and brought them close to his face. The liquid was rich and red—it was blood, gallons and gallons of blood. What was drained from the pigs ended up here, festering in the dark.

Somewhere in the hallways behind him, the vampire continued its taunting call. "I wonder if I'm the first of my kind that you've met," it said. "Because you are not the first of your kind that I've killed." The vampire cackled.

Its voice was close, and Nightingale was out of options.

He kicked off his shoes and tore off his socks, stashing them behind a boiler under a bundle of dirty rags. He lifted his legs over the side of the font, sending a cloud of flies buzzing away angrily, and stepped into the pool of blood, slowly lowering himself down.

In the darkness, above the cacophony of flies, he could hear the scuttling sound of the vampire crawling closer—it was just outside the doors.

They creaked open. Nightingale, who had been waiting with his nose just above the surface, took one last breath and submerged himself entirely. Just before he went under, he saw the pale hand of the creature clutching the door.

Immersed in blood, Nightingale waited. He could hear the muffled noises of the vampire around the vat. In his mind, he counted, "*one-Mississippi, two-Mississippi, three-Mississippi*" while he waited, hoping the vampire would leave.

He could sense the flies shifting away, buzzing angrily as they were disturbed again. The vampire stood at the edge of the font; Nightingale could almost feel those hungry, red eyes searching for him, driven mad by the scent of blood. He could hear the monster sniffing the air, crouching close to the surface.

"*Seventeen-Mississippi, eighteen-Mississippi, nineteen-Mississippi…*"

The blood rippled as the vampire plunged its taloned hand into the font, thrashing through the gore, searching for Nightingale. He flattened himself to the bottom, near the back, the blood sloshing as the vampire cut through it again and again, just inches above his face.

Nightingale held himself to the bottom of the font, continuing to count, holding his breath, biding his time. As quickly as it had started, the vampire whipped its hand out of the vat. The blood sloshed wildly for a moment until it finally settled and stilled. Nightingale didn't move, just listened, waiting. He heard the door swing open and closed, and the buzz of flies resumed unmolested above him. The vampire had left. His lungs were beginning to throb, but he continued counting. *"Thirty-five, thirty-six, thirty-seven…"*

When he reached forty-five, Nightingale guardedly rose from the font, blood streaming down his face. He ached to breathe, but he fought the urge to gasp for air, exhaling slowly before taking a long, steady breath in.

He was alone.

Nightingale stepped from the font, grabbed one of the dirty rags nearby, and cleaned the blood from him as quickly as he could. After putting his shoes back on, he stepped to the door and checked the hallway. Silence.

Blood-smeared and cautious, Nightingale started back the way he had come, following the tongue-smeared stains of blood on the floor, grabbing his long, gray coat on the way.

When Nightingale reached the killing floor, the fire was burning wildly out of control. The flames licked up, consuming the second and third floors; the light danced along the walls, bright as day, casting long shadows onto the street through the grimy windows.

On the walkway, over Grange's limp body, the vampire stood, its shadow gigantic against the far wall. It was petting the face of the young woman with one of its long, crooked fingers. The vampire sniffed her, touched her hair, twirling a lock in its hand. Thankfully, she was still unconscious.

Nightingale crept up the stairs to the drain rack, behind the vampire. His revolver still lay on the ground below, but he had forgotten it; there was no time or need. In this place of death, Nightingale had his pick of instruments.

As he approached from behind, the vampire pulled the woman's head back; it bared its fangs, preparing to bite into the tender, sweet flesh of her neck.

Grabbing a meat hook that dangled from a chain, Nightingale raised it high over his head, his shadow emblazoned on the wall behind him. Before the vampire could bite, Nightingale swung the hook down, bringing it over the vampire's shoulder and plunging it into its chest. He wrenched the hook upward, twisting it so that the sharp point pierced the creature's heart and stabbed out through its back.

The monster howled in pain, arching its spine, its hands reaching out, flailing. It turned towards Nightingale, its red eyes alive with fury and anguish. Nightingale met its fierce gaze and smirked. He grabbed the length of chain and pulled, throwing all his weight into it, hoisting the vampire into the air. It cried out in pain again, slashing futilely at Nightingale, who stood just beyond its reach.

As the flames danced, claiming the slaughterhouse, Nightingale watched the life finally drain from the vampire's eyes. Its head slowly lowered until it fell to its chest with a final and sudden drop, its hands collapsing limply at its sides.

The vampire was dead.

Nightingale took a long, deep breath, puffing out his chest. From a tray of tools, he grabbed a rusted pair of pliers. He opened the vampire's mouth, finding its long, narrow-edged teeth. Gripping them with the tarnished pliers, he pulled the fangs from the monster's maw.

Old blood dripped from the vampire's gaping mouth as Nightingale rifled through its pockets. He found bones and keys, a few coins with Cyrillic script that he couldn't read, and faces of old men he didn't recognize. All of it was worthless and uninteresting until he found, in the inside pocket of the vampire's tattered dress coat, a tarot card. The back was black, with golden embellishment along the edge and two bats clutched in the middle.

He turned it over to see the card's face. It showed a skeleton, draped in a black cloak, sitting astride a pale, sallow horse. A scythe rested against the skeleton's shoulder, and its hand clutched an hourglass. Across the bottom of the card, in jagged letters, was the name of the figure.

DEATH

Nightingale pushed the hanging vampire along the rail, sending it into the flames, where the body quickly charred. The delicate skin began to crackle and flake. The limbs withered; the eyes popped and sizzled. When Nightingale turned away, it had already started to turn to ash.

He tucked the tarot card into his pocket and lowered the girl down from where she hung—she was still breathing. Hopefully, Nightingale thought, she'd never remember any of this. He carried her out of the burning building, stopping to collect his revolver.

Grange awoke in darkness, his cheek stinging with a fresh pain, the back of his head aching with a sharp but distant throbbing. He was on the dirty floor of a warehouse, dark, except for a blazing flame outside. Through the greasy windows, he could see his truck, parked where he'd left it; behind it was a wall of fire.

Nightingale loomed over him, backlit by the flickering light. He was tall and rough, his shirt stained red, his hair bedraggled, his face streaked with blood, his wrist crudely wrapped in a tie. His figure was cruel and powerful, with his broad shoulders and barrel chest. The holster around his shoulder was empty, the revolver clutched in Nightingale's hand.

He stared down at the man on the floor.

Grange tried to lunge forward, but his hands were shackled, and Nightingale easily kicked the man over.

"Stay down," Nightingale said, his voice a growl.

"Are you going to kill me?" Grange asked as he erupted into a violent cough.

"Sounds like that's already taken care of."

"It's my lungs," Grange said, coughing again. "The doctor said I only got a year at best."

"That's why you were working for the vampire," Nightingale said.

Grange hung his head. "He said he would cure me."

"What did you promise in return?"

Grange didn't answer.

"I know your type," Nightingale said. He pointed behind him. In the cool darkness, the woman he'd pulled from the slaughterhouse lay on the floor, still unconscious. "Trading her life for yours."

"What was I supposed to do?"

"Die, just like everybody else." Nightingale holstered his revolver and crouched down on his haunches. His coat was lying over a railing beside him, and he searched through the pockets. He pulled out the tarot card and showed it to Grange. "You know what this is?"

"Never seen it."

"You sure? Seems like it must have been important."

"I told you, I never seen it before."

Nightingale sighed and returned the card to his coat. He pulled out the cigarette he'd bummed from M. Garvey along with a lighter.

As he lit the cigarette, the glow of the flame gave Grange his first good look at the detective. He was somewhere around forty; the hair at his temples glittered with streaks of silver that were starting to spread, and crows' feet reached out from the corners of his storm-blue eyes. His jaw was strong, rough with the day's stubble; his brow was low and heavy, his nose was pronounced with a tell-tale scar across the bridge that said it had been broken more than once. On the left side of his neck, Nightingale had another scar, this one thick and ragged; it started under his jaw and disappeared below his collar. Even with it dirtied by blood, Grange could see two rough fang marks in the marbled flesh.

"You've been bit?" Grange sounded astonished. "By a vampire?"

"Close," Nightingale said. "But I got to it first." He snapped the lighter shut, leaving only the glow of the cigarette. He took a long drag. "I was in France the first time I saw a vampire. In the war. They sent me to the north, to Villefère, where the trees outnumber the people a thousand to one.

"There was something out there, something old and evil. The locals told stories about it, but the soldiers didn't believe, not until it started killing them too. And in the end, it killed all of them—all except me," he said. He pointed at his neck. "Not for lack of trying.

"A priest found me, nearly dead. He patched me up and told me how blessed I was to have survived. And then he gave me this—"

Leaving the cigarette in his mouth, Nightingale opened his fist and struck the lighter. In his palm was what looked like brass knuckles, but across the front of it was a crude iron cross that reminded Grange of the brands used on cattle.

Nightingale slipped the piece on so that when he closed his fist, the cross protruded above his fingers. He held it up to the lighter, moving the cross through the flame.

"He told me this was from the Inquisition. To brand heretics. He'd branded his own neck to keep the vampires from getting him. He told me, once I healed, I should do the same—I didn't, though," Nightingale said. "One scar from that night was enough."

The brand was beginning to glow as Nightingale moved it slowly back and forth above the flame. "I kept this, though," he said. "I thought it might be useful. In case I met someone—like you—who wanted to be like them."

Snapping the lighter shut, Nightingale grabbed Grange's hair, pulling his head back and exposing the man's neck. He brought the glowing brand up to Grange's throat, who began to shout, but as the hot metal seared into his flesh, his scream turned into a gurgling cry of pain.

The room filled with the smell of cooked meat. Grange tried to struggle away from Nightingale, but the detective was strong; he placed a knee on the wriggling man until he pulled the brand away, and the sizzling stopped.

Grange whimpered on the ground. His neck was raw, marked with a dark symbol of the cross. Nightingale dipped the brand into a pail of water, and the metal fizzled.

Nightingale grabbed his coat, replacing the lighter and the brand in the pockets. He walked away from Grange, who gurgled on the floor, clutching his neck and thrashing his legs in pain.

Taking the handle of a heavy wooden door, Nightingale pulled it open. Light flooded into the dark room; the slaughterhouse was a towering inferno. A wail of nearing sirens pierced the air.

Beside Nightingale, the woman stirred on the ground. He crouched beside her. As her eyes opened, her face flashed with fear and confusion. Nightingale reached out, holding her shoulder lightly. "It's okay," he said. "You're safe."

The woman looked around, blinking away the bewilderment.

"You're the detective," she said. "You're Nightingale."

Nightingale nodded. "They'll be here soon," he said, pointing towards the sound of the sirens. "They'll have lots of questions—I shouldn't be an answer to any of them."

The woman understood.

He took the cigarette from his mouth and offered her a drag. She took it. When she gave it back, he flicked the butt out into the gravel. They could see the lights from the fire trucks and police cruisers flashing on the side of the building.

Pulling his collar up around his neck, Nightingale stepped out into the night, disappearing into the darkness.

CHAPTER 4

CHARLIE DROVE WHITE-KNUCKLED, LEAVING the swamps and bayous behind. Rain fell as they entered the city. The wipers squeaked across the windshield. Streetlights reflected off wet asphalt. Steam curled from the sewers, swirling in the headlights.

The wad of cash and Fat Phil's revolver sat on the passenger seat. Charlie glanced at them, then checked the rearview mirror—the vampire behind him gave terse directions. He had cleaned the blood from his mouth; the handkerchief lay crumpled on the floorboard.

Charlie didn't dare speak, just focused on the road ahead, driving, until the vampire told him to stop.

Charlie pulled to the curb, the front wheel bouncing up. He left the engine idling as rain pattered on the roof. The vampire pointed ahead. Charlie looked through the windshield—he strained to see.

Ahead of them stood a plastered stone wall, thick cracks veining its surface. A wrought-iron gate closed the entrance, flanked by two heavy pillars, topped by a sign.

CEMETERY SAINTES-MARIES

"We're going in," the vampire said, stepping out of the car.

Charlie grabbed the gun and the cash, stuffing them into his pockets just before the vampire reached over, opened Charlie's door, placed a cold, firm hand on his neck, and pulled him out of the car.

They walked to the gates, the vampire guiding Charlie with a hand on his neck. They waited as a man in a knee-length coat and a wide-brimmed bolero hat appeared. His face was long and gaunt, mouth drooping in a frown.

"I'm a guest," the vampire said. "I'm here for my belongings."

"Who's this?" the man asked, pointing to Charlie.

"A friend," the vampire said.

The man nodded grimly. "The Groundskeeper's in the chapel," he said. He grabbed the gate, opening it; metal creaked against metal. Stepping aside, he waved Charlie and the vampire in.

They trudged down the muddy path, passing collapsing mausoleums and crooked memorials sinking deeper into the sodden earth. Rain-washed stones appeared sallow. Wild vines choked old graves, hacked back in places to reveal names carved in the rock, or to clear passage into the tombs.

Ahead, the road ended, forking sharply left and right. At the top of the junction stood a small, Gothic chapel—narrow, tall, and leaning to one side. Its spire vanished into the darkness above. Mottled grey stone, nearly black in places, lined the building. The open doors revealed flickering candles, their light pouring onto the wet ground through cracked, stained-glass windows. The vampire pushed Charlie up the steps and into the chapel, fingernails digging into his neck.

Inside, the ceiling was high enough that the candlelight didn't reach it. Overhead, Charlie could hear the squeaking and fluttering of bats. Looking up, he could just make out the shifting, shadowy mass of them inside the steeple.

No crosses hung inside. Empty niches stood cleared of statuary. The altar was gone, replaced by a large oak desk. Behind it, a skeletal man with wrinkled skin and a hairless, liver-spotted scalp, ringed by straight gray hair, hunched in his chair. He closed a leatherbound tome and smiled, showing crooked, crowded yellow teeth.

"Marquis," the man said. "What a pleasure to see you again."

"I'm closing my account."

"So soon?" The man clicked his tongue as he shook his head.

"I have business that needs tending," he said.

The groundskeeper smiled. "We'll need to settle your bill." He opened a desk drawer and pulled out a thick ledger, thumbing to the last page. He ran a finger down a column of names, then tapped.

"Here we are," he said. "The Marquis de Sang." He uncapped a fountain pen and held it out towards the vampire, pushing the ledger across the desk.

The Marquis pulled out a tarot card and tossed it onto the open book. Charlie saw it was marked DEATH.

"This should be sufficient."

"Of course," the groundskeeper said. Raising his eyebrows, he examined the card, turning it over to show the intricate back—two bats at its center. "I didn't realize you were one of the Monsieur's guests." He returned the card and crossed out the box by the Marquis' name.

"I hope you've had a pleasant stay," he said, with a final, unsettling smile.

"I have," the vampire said. He bowed his head and turned Charlie around towards the door. The Groundskeeper returned to his work, and the bats rustled overhead.

They returned to the muddy road. The vampire led them to the left. Charlie walked stiff-legged, the gun in his pocket thumping against his leg with each step. His heart pounded. He tried to swallow but couldn't.

The vampire halted before the rusted gates of a derelict mausoleum. The crumbling stone bore decades of grime and neglect. A shattered cross once crowned the flat roof; only the base and a solitary arm survived. Above the door, REQUI-ESCAT IN PACE was etched deep in the stone, and a tarnished plaque proclaimed: DOCTOR ALMERO ASHTON, PILLAR OF THE COMMUNITY - BELOVED FATHER AND HUSBAND. The Marquis shoved the groaning gate open, and they stepped inside.

Inside, the tomb was musty and humid. Water dripped from the leaky roof. Wind whistled through the broken windows. An empty coffin sat on a stone pedestal in the middle of the room; its lid was on the floor beside it.

The vampire finally released Charlie's neck, walked to the coffin's head, bent down, and picked up a black leather physician's bag. Its gold clasp matched the bird skull on his cane.

"I'm sure you have questions," the vampire said, turning to face Charlie—but the tomb was empty, Charlie was gone.

He ran, arms and legs pumping, sharply turning down a narrow alley lined with mausoleums. He had no direction—just getting away from that vampire was enough for now.

Vampire. He felt like a fool even thinking it. He wondered if it was chasing him, but he didn't dare look back. He didn't hear anything behind him, no footsteps, no breathing, no flapping of wings—which he wasn't sure if vampires had.

Charlie turned down a sunken stone path. Ahead, beyond the garden of graves, streetlights glowed. He ran faster, then paused.

Outside a tomb stood a shadowy figure. As Charlie neared, he saw a woman in black with a billowing dress, her face hidden by a lacy veil.

She turned as he approached, and Charlie stopped. Even behind the veil, he felt her icy gaze. Instinct screamed that something was wrong.

"What are you doing here?" she asked.

Charlie shook his head, breathing heavily after his dash through the cemetery.

The woman lifted her veil. In the darkness, her eyes glinted red. She sniffed the air and grinned hungrily. Charlie could see the long, sharp teeth.

He cried out, turning around to run, but another figure was behind him. A woman, too, this one had silky, white hair that cascaded around her shoulders, her skin glistening from the rain. She bore her fangs and hissed.

As he stumbled backwards, Charlie fell against a third vampire—a plump, ashen man with a monocle over his eye and a beauty mark drawn on above his lip. He smiled, his pointed predator's teeth protruding over his fat lips.

Charlie turned again, tripping against the gate of a mausoleum. He grabbed at it, yanked it open, and scrambled inside. The uneven stones sent him sprawling. The vampires crowded in the doorway, blocking his escape as Charlie crawled backward. Their eyes glowed red; their teeth dripped with saliva.

It was the woman with the veil who entered first, pushing her way past the other two. She looked gleeful as she lunged at Charlie.

Then a voice came from outside, shouting, and the vampires froze.

"Halt!"

The two women and the fat man turned, allowing Charlie to see through the doorway. In the middle of the path stood the Marquis de Sang, as the groundkeeper had called him. He was a looming monolith of shadow. Cast in black, it was only the metallic handle of his cane and the long, white teeth in his sinister grin that Charlie could see.

"Leave," the vampire said. "He's mine."

Without protest, the other three vampires skulked away out into the night, their heads hung low, not daring to look at the Marquis.

The vampire stepped into the tomb.

Charlie cowered on the ground and tried to crawl away, but his gaze stayed fixed on the monster approaching him. Remembering the gun in his pocket in a rush of panic, he pulled it out with shaking hands and raised it.

"Stay back," Charlie said, his voice trembling.

The vampire paused, his lips curling up even higher over the fanged teeth in a grotesque smile. "Have you ever killed a man?" he asked.

Charlie didn't lower the gun, nor did he answer. The vampire took another step towards him.

"You haven't," the vampire said. "Could you, though?" He took another step. "What if it doesn't work, Charles? What if you do pull the trigger, but I'm still standing? Then what will you do?" He took another step. If Charlie wanted to, he could have reached out and touched the fringe of the black coat that was draped over the vampire, but Charlie didn't dare move.

"Does Charles Baptiste have what it takes?" With a swipe of his cane, the vampire knocked the gun from Charlie's hand. It went skittering into the dark, and Charlie pulled his hand in close, holding it to his chest like an animal with an injured paw.

"What do you want from me?" Charlie asked, the words dripping with fear.

The vampire towered over him, cruel and magnificent. A gust of wind outside brought a sheet of rain across the doorway behind the vampire.

"Your help," the vampire said.

"My help? Why my help?"

The vampire crouched down, bringing his face down to Charlie, and looked him straight in the eyes. "We're family."

Charles looked horrified. "I haven't got any family."

"None living," the vampire said.

"Who are you?"

"I have had many names." The vampire held out his hand, showing Charlie the golden signet ring he wore on his little finger. It was set with an onyx, a B etched into the stone, identical to the one Charlie had worn. "But I was born Vermilion Donatien du Baptiste."

"If you're hoping for money," Charlie said. "It's gone. Long gone. I never even got a cent of it."

"I'm not here for money," Vermilion said. He put out his hand. "I want something more."

Charlie looked up from the ground, first at the vampire's outstretched hand and then at his face. It was emotionless, expressionless, yet it looked strong and determined. He looked for a family resemblance, but saw none, probably because he'd never seen a Baptiste who didn't look defeated.

"I can't think of a single reason why anyone who wasn't a Baptiste would ever claim to be one." Charlie took Vermilion's hand, and the vampire hoisted him off the ground.

"That," Vermilion said, his predator's eyes darkening as another sinister grin crawled up the sides of his mouth, "is exactly what I want to change."

"What do you need me to do?"

Without saying anything, Vermilion held out Fat Phil's snub-nosed revolver. "Whatever I ask," the vampire said.

Charlie looked at Vermilion and then at the revolver.

He reached out and took it.

"What's the plan?" Charlie asked.

The vampire stood in front of him, his hands both clasping the bird skull that topped his cane. He nodded to Charlie.

"Take me to the convent."

"The convent? Why?"

"For the rest of my belongings."

CHAPTER 5

SISTER MAGDALENE AWOKE WITH a shake. Sister Agnès was over her, holding a candle, the flickering light illuminating her worried face.

"Sister," Agnès said, "come quickly."

"What is it?" Magdalene asked, her voice tight with tension. "What's happened?" She turned on her bedside lamp and glanced at her clock; it was just past three. No good news came at this hour.

"Juliette," Agnès said. "She's missing."

Jumping from her bed, Magdalene pulled on her dressing gown and followed Agnès down the long, empty corridors of the old convent. They quickly climbed the stairs to the attic. The room was awake and alive as a dozen other nuns settled the young girls down, kneeling by their bedsides—some attempting comfort, others threatening punishment. In the midst of it was the Mother Superior, her thin lips pursed. When she saw Magdalene, her eyes narrowed.

"Everything's under control here, Sister Magdalene," she said. "There's no need for your coddling."

"They're my girls," Magdalene said, pushing past the Mother.

The old nun grabbed her arm. "They're orphans, Sister Magdalene." Her voice was sharp, her words stern and staccato. "They don't belong to anyone."

Magdalene glared and wrenched her arm out of the Mother's grip. She turned, walking brusquely to the end of the long room with Agnès to the empty mattress and the open window above where Juliette had slept. The glass of water had fallen from her nightstand, shattered on the floor in a puddle; the two aspirin lay beside it.

A draft from the window swept past Magdalene, making her shiver. The wooden shutters had been torn apart, hanging loosely on their hinges and creaking in the wind. The curtains blew half in and half out of the splintered frame; they were soaked through with the pouring rain.

Magdalene ran to the window, standing on the unmade bed to look out.

"What happened?" she asked.

"She was taken," Agnès said. "Someone was in here."

"Who?"

"We don't know."

"Who saw him?"

"Martha."

"Where is she?"

"I'm here, sister." The little girl, dressed in her nightgown, sat on her bed, holding her knees, her face streaked with tears.

Magdalene jumped down from the bed and opened her arms. Martha ran to her and buried herself in Magdalene's embrace.

"You said we were safe here," Martha said through tears.

"I know," Magdalene said. "I believed it." Magdalene clutched the little girl as she wept. Martha's tiny hands gripped the folds of Magdalene's robe so tightly they began to shake.

"What are we going to do?" Magdalene said, looking at Agnès.

"Nothing." It was the shrill voice of the Mother Superior that answered.

"Nothing? The girl was taken."

"The girl ran away, that's all there is to it."

"They saw someone in here—"

"Their imagination," said the Mother Superior. "They're frightened little girls. They'll come to their senses."

"We need to tell the police!"

"We will do no such thing. Wasting their time and ours."

"But—"

"But *nothing*, Sister Magdalene." The Mother Superior looked around the room. "She's not the first girl to leave; she will not be the last. Now help get these girls back in bed."

As the Mother Superior walked away, Magdalene sat on the bed, Martha still clinging to her. When she sat, she heard crinkling beneath the pillow. She reached in and pulled out a crumpled piece of paper. Magdalene recognized it from earlier that night; it was the paper with Juliette's drawing.

As she unfolded it, Agnès watched over Magdalene's shoulder, bringing the candle close. She gasped when she saw the drawing. Martha's eyes went wide with fear, and she buried her face in the young nun's chest.

"That's the man," Martha said, sobbing. "That's who took her."

Crudely drawn in a child's hand was a macabre image. Bodies lay on the ground, blood spilling from their necks, hands clutching at the mess like they were choking. Standing above them was a man dressed all in black. He was tall and thin with a pointed goatee and eyes that glowed red like embers, resting his weight on a cane. His face dripped with blood, and protruding from his sinister grin were two elongated fangs.

"It's the vampire," Martha said, sobbing.

Magdalene's eyes went to Agnès, searching for help.

The older nun sat down on the bed beside Magdalene and took the drawing.

"I think I know someone who can help."

CHAPTER 6

NIGHTINGALE HAD SHOWERED, SHAVED, and managed to sleep for at least a few lousy hours. His wrist still throbbed with dull pain, but he'd cleaned and dressed it, and a white bandage was taped neatly across the slashes underneath his cuff. He'd tossed away his clothes from the night before—the ones covered in blood—burning them in the basement furnace. Now he was dressed in a fresh suit and a crisp banker's shirt. He'd cleaned his shoes. The grime was gone, and he'd polished out the scuffs. He bought a new hat first thing as he went out. Only his overcoat showed the signs of the night before. He'd been able to wash out the blood, but the right sleeve was still shredded from where it had been slashed by the vampire.

He carried the tarot card with him—the one marked with Death. He'd thought about it all night, even dreamt about it. He had questions, and he knew a man who might have the answers.

The rain had subsided to a drizzle, but the storm clouds still gathered overhead. He caught the St. Charles trolley to the 11th Ward and walked down Washington Avenue, passing the Queen Anne mansions and Center-Hall cottages. He moved along the crumbling, white-washed wall of the Lafayette Cemetery—overgrown by moss and creeping vines.

The mausoleum roofs and gnarled treetops peeked out over it. He crossed the street and turned the corner, stopping outside a clapboard storefront. The shop's name was painted in gold across its big window.

DR. BONE'S EMPORIUM HISTORIA
RARE BOOKS, COLLECTIBLES, AND CURIOSITIES

The bell above the door chimed as Nightingale stepped in. The store had the musty smell of age, like an attic or a cathedral, and there was a stillness about it, as if the things inside had not been disturbed for centuries.

The shop was a jumble of objects from distant lands and ages past that a museum curator would envy. The shelves held singing bowls from the high mountains of Tibet, saw-toothed war clubs from Polynesia, and scrimshaw from the Bering Strait among hundreds—thousands—of other items just as interesting and exotic, each one labelled and priced. Fanous lanterns from Egypt hung from the ceiling; Turkish rugs were rolled and stuffed above them in the rafters. A suit of armor from an English court stood in the corner, and the hide of a Niger giraffe was pinned to the wall opposite. The back of the shop was covered in floor-to-ceiling shelves crammed with books and scrolls, all of which the proprietor, Dr. Bone, claimed to have read.

Against the far wall, behind a varnished counter, beside a heavy, brass cash register and a little sign that read "THE DOCTOR IS IN," was the man himself.

Franklin Bonaparte was handsome, his face a tapestry of wrinkles that somehow seemed to glow with energy, even as he neared his sixties. His black, coiled hair was trimmed to the same length as his beard, which turned stark gray at the chin. He dressed with flair—a black silk shirt, pinstripe pants, and a rust-colored vest; a gold chain glinted at his collar. He leaned forward on the counter, eyes bright, hands animated, as he spoke to two enraptured young women, each about 20 years old. The girls listened intently, their eyes wide as they hung on his words.

"Oh yes," Nightingale could hear him say, pretending to browse as he eavesdropped. "Those old graves open up from time to time." Bone was waving his hand towards the cemetery across the way. "We see plenty of the dead."

"Ghosts?" one of the girls asked. She was brunette, her hair curled and swept to the side.

"At best," Bone said, nodding. "At worst—they're vampires." He smiled when both the women gasped.

"I told you, Ginny," the other girl said, slapping her friend's arm. This one was blonde and tall with bright red lipstick.

"It's just so hard to believe, Alice," Ginny said. "You really think it was Old Lady Mable?"

"Dr. Bone says so," Alice said. "Right?"

"I've seen plenty of strange things in this city."

"But," Ginny said, "do vampires ever look *younger*?"

"Younger than when they died? It happens."

"Because the woman I thought I saw sure looked like Old Lady Mable, just not as old and frail."

"With rosy cheeks and fuller face?"

"Exactly."

"Ah," Bone said. "She's not younger, then, just full."

"Full?" Ginny asked.

"Yes," Bone said. "Of blood"

Both girls gasped again, instinctively reaching for each other's arms. Their eyes flicked nervously toward the door, as if expecting something frightful to appear at any moment.

"How wretched," Ginny said, wrinkling her nose.

"That they are," Bone agreed.

"Oh, what can she do, Dr. Bone?" Alice asked, almost whining. "Is Ginny in danger?"

"That's hard to say." Bone leaned forward, lowering his voice. "Would Old Lady Mable have any reason to come after you, Ginny?"

"No, no, of course not."

"You sure?" he asked. "You never said anything *impolite* about her?"

"Never," Ginny said. "Not to her face."

Bone leaned back, stroking his beard again and raising his eyes as he hummed contemplatively.

"Dr. Bone, please tell me, am I done for?" Ginny asked, pleadingly.

"Well," Bone began, "I think it's best you keep your windows locked and stay inside at night. If she doesn't see you, she might not bother you. But all the same, you may want one of these."

Bone opened a wooden chest on the counter beside him. Inside was a collection of linen sacks, each about the size of a purse. A sign hung at the top of the box that read "VAMPIRE WARDS."

He picked up one of the bags and handed it to Ginny. "Everything you need to stay safe is in there," he said. "I usually sell those for four, but a pretty, young girl such as yourself, I'll do you for three."

Ginny reached into her purse. "You can never be too safe with things like this," she said, pushing the bills into Bone's hand.

"You sure can't," he said.

"I'll take one too," Alice said, slipping Bone another set of bills and grabbing one of the small sacks from the case.

"If you ladies ever need anything else, anything at all, you just come ask it. "Especially," he said, gravely, "if Old Lady Mable starts giving you trouble."

"We will, Dr. Bone, we will," Alice said.

Ginny clutched the little bag to her chest, her voice catching as she said, "I can never thank you enough." Relief and anxiety mingled in her trembling smile.

Bone waved at the girls as they ran off out of the store, bells above the door clanging as they did. As soon as the girls were out of sight, Nightingale stepped out from behind the shelves and walked to the counter.

Bone smiled. "Detective Nightingale," he said. "I never know if it's good or bad to see you this early in the morning."

"You trying to put me out of business, Bone?" Nightingale reached into the case and pulled out one of the sacks for himself. The top was synched closed with twine and clasped with a silver cross the size of a half-dollar. He untied it and looked inside. The bag contained a crucifix, a wooden stake, two cloves of garlic, two glass vials—one filled with holy water and the other with colloidal silver—and a small, leather-bound book with a selection of scripture. He pulled out the book and opened it.

"And fear not them which kill the body, but are not able to kill the soul," he read.

"But fear him which is able to destroy both the body and the soul in Hell," Bone recited from memory.

"Quaint," Nightingale said, closing the book and tossing it back into the bag.

Bone pointed a finger at the bag like he was scolding it. "I sell at least two of those a week." He put out his hand. Nightingale clasped it, and Bone's face broadened in a smile. "But it still can't beat a professional's touch."

Nightingale chuckled. "Need me to look into Old Lady Mable?"

"If you have time." Bone waved his hand. "But not even a starving vampire would have stuck his fangs into Margery Mable's leathery old hide," he said. "It's probably just a couple young girls getting themselves excited."

"You gave them plenty of help."

Bone laughed. "I can't help it sometimes." He put out his hands in mock penitence. "They want excitement, I give it to them."

"Always the salesman."

"Extermination isn't the only business in the vampire trade," Bone said. "How's work? You take care of those working girls?"

"Closed the case last night."

"I thought as much," Bone said. "I heard about a fire at an abattoir."

"Yeah?"

"They found a man there yelling about vampires and a girl he was trying to kill. They say she got the better of him. I thought she looked familiar."

"Nothing gets past you, Bone, does it?" Nightingale reached into his pocket and pulled out the vampire's teeth. He tossed them to Bone, who smiled gleefully as he studied them, running his fingers over the yellowy fangs. "I've got your cut, too," Nightingale said, setting an envelope down on the counter.

Bone waved his hand away. "You know I don't need that."

"It's your finder's fee," Nightingale said. "You send me the best clients."

"I'm just trying to help."

"You did."

"The bastard go down easy?"

"Not as easy as I'd like," Nightingale said. "Got this for my trouble." He held up his arm to show Bone the tattered sleeve of his coat.

"Nasty fella," Bone said, shaking his head. "Go see Sadie over on Union, she's the best seamstress in the city, she'll fix you right up."

"Is there anybody in this city you don't know?"

"Only if they aren't worth knowing."

"You know any fortune tellers?"

"A few. Why?"

"I've got another question for you."

"Let's hear it," Bone said.

"The vampire had this on him last night." Nightingale reached into his pocket and pulled out the tarot card. "Ever seen a card like this?" he asked, passing it to Bone, who dropped the teeth to the counter and took the card, raising his eyebrows as he studied it.

"Seen plenty of tarot around here," he said. "What you have here is the thirteenth card of the major arcana, featuring our familiar friend Death." Bone held it up and tapped the figure with his finger. "He's been part of the tarot deck from the very beginning. Centuries, we're talking about; although, back then, they just called it 'the card with no name' so as not to frighten people." Bone ran his thumb along the edge, feeling the weight of the paper stock. "This one's not so old, though. I wouldn't say it's been around for more than a year or two. Maybe even less."

"What about the pattern on the back? You ever seen that? Maybe know where it comes from?"

Reaching into his pocket, Bone pulled out a pair of bifocals that he rested on the tip of his nose as he further scrutinized the card, studying the designs. He brought the card closer to his face and pulled it away again before bringing it close once more.

"You said the vampire had this?"

"That's right," Nightingale said. "And he's not the first. That's the third one I've seen in the last few months." Nightingale leaned against the counter as Bone continued to study the card. "I didn't pay much attention to the first one, but the second one made me wonder, and now this—it can't be a coincidence."

"No, it cannot," Bone said, stroking his beard. He sighed. "I haven't seen a card like this, not exactly, but I might be able to tell you something about it."

"Like what?"

"Hold on a minute," Bone said as he opened the flap in the counter and walked to the back of the shop. He faced the bookshelves, scanning the old spines, holding his thumb to his chin, muttering the titles of the books as he read them.

"Ah-ha," he exclaimed, putting his finger on one of them. "There it is." He pulled a narrow hardcover from the shelf and carried it back to the counter, where he laid it down in front of Nightingale. The book's title, FOLK ART OF THE ROMANI PEOPLE, was embossed on the plain canvas cover. Bone flipped it open and thumbed through the pages until he found what he was looking for. He opened the book to a full spread and ran his hand down the middle, so that the pages lay flat. Taking the card, he placed it on the book, where the pages were filled with illustrations.

"These ones here," he said, running his finger over the thatched design along the border beside the golden flourishes. "These look like the *laimas slotiņa*." Bone looked up at Nightingale. "Laima is the patroness of fate and luck."

"Makes sense for a tarot card," Nightingale said. "What about these?" he asked, pointing to the moons in each corner of the card.

"Those are moon phases, but—" he squinted down at the card, "if you look close, you can see something else there." He turned the page and pointed to another symbol that matched. "The *meness krusts*," Bone said. "The cross of the moon. It's a symbol of creation and destruction, life and death, the ongoing cycle, and what have you."

"They're Romani symbols, then?"

"Baltic, originally, but Romani who travelled through there adopted them, and the way they're displayed here, on the card, they definitely look Romani to me."

"What about this design in the middle of the card?" Nightingale asked.

"The bats?"

"Any symbolism there?"

"Darkness, night, take your pick. But in Romani art, it might just depict something they've seen."

"What do you mean?"

"The Romani are nomadic—generally speaking—and their art reflects the things they pass. You're familiar with the carts they move around in?" Bone turned the pages of the book, finding one with photographs of Romani wagons. "They're called vardo. They're elegant, ornate, carved with images of places they've been and animals they've seen." Bone tapped the bats at the center of the card. "This could be something like that. Each family or caravan—or whatever you want to call it—has distinct patterns and images associated with them because of the experiences they've had and how they choose to express them."

"Then a pattern like this," Nightingale said, "could belong to someone specific. A family. Like a crest."

"Could be, yes," Bone said. "The other cards you found; they had the same pattern?"

"Identical. Same image too." Nightingale turned the card over to show the grinning reaper on the other side. "Any ideas why that might be?"

"Maybe," Bone said, "I've heard stories. The Romani leave messages for each other, but they leave them in code. Some of them use tarot cards. They'll leave them hidden in a place so that if another group comes by, they know what's going on. Each card means something different. Maybe the Wheel of Fortune card means there's money to be made in a town, or the Judgment card means to watch out for the law, or the Death card—"

"Means someone's a vampire," Nightingale said.

Bone nodded. "Exactly," he said. "Just a guess, of course. I'm no expert—but let me ask around."

"I owe you, Bone," Nightingale said. He grabbed the book off the counter. "Mind if I borrow this for a bit?"

"I'll trade you for these." Bone held the vampire's teeth in the palm of his hand.

"Deal," Nightingale said. "Make a necklace or something."

Bone laughed. "I'll add them to the collection."

CHAPTER 7

THE GIRL LAY ACROSS the backseat as Charlie drove. Vermilion sat up front. The girl slept fitfully—her breathing shallow and fast. Charlie glanced nervously at her in the rearview mirror. He could see she was unwell. Her eyes were sunken. She murmured to herself. Sweat beaded on her face.

"I don't get it, Vermilion," Charlie said. "Why do we need the girl?"

"She's important," Vermilion said.

"Important how?"

"Important to me."

Charlie shook his head. He didn't like any of it. He hadn't liked climbing up to the convent roof or prying the window open. He hadn't liked racing down to the car after Vermilion burst out with the girl. And he didn't like having the girl with them, coughing and shaking.

"What are we doing?" Charlie asked. "Where do we go now?"

"Where do you live?"

"We can't go there," Charlie said. "Lazaretto is going to be looking for me. And with the girl, somebody's gonna notice her."

"Then we need to leave the city."

"No kidding," Charlie said. "I don't know any place outside the city. I never left." Then he remembered. "Except for the family homestead."

"Take us there," Vermilion said.

"It's a wreck. No one's lived there in decades."

"Perfect."

Charlie headed to the highway, then turned off outside the city. As he took the country backroads through farmland and countryside, his chest tightened with a mix of nostalgia and apprehension. He was bound for his ancestral home—a testament to the rise and fall of the Baptiste family.

Manoir Vert had been built during the Antebellum years in a misty grove of Southern live oak. A long, wide drive led from the road to the house itself, where it circled a marble fountain.

The house was tall and wide, with huge columns in front. A large, open balcony wrapped around the second story. It was called the Green Manor due to the lush forest surrounding it. The trees had been cleared to make room for planting crops behind the house. It was once a beautiful homestead for the Baptiste family. They spent long Louisiana afternoons playing croquet in the yard or riding horses in the pastures.

That was before Bernardin Baptiste died and the house passed through generations. They squandered the family's name and wealth. Soon, the Green Manor stood boarded and forgotten. The once-glorious house was now all decay, a ghostly ruin left desolate in the marshy backwoods.

The woods they'd cleared a century and a half ago had grown wild again. Now, they reclaimed the land. They closed in on the road and the house, blocking out light from above. Even during daylight, the grounds appeared gray and dusky.

Vines crept up the columns, through some of the windows, into the rafters. They pulled away clapboards and shutters, crawling along the hallways into the rooms and the attic. The fields had gone to weed, overrun by snakes and rats that made their way into the old manor through broken windows and collapsing walls.

The fountain was filled with rainwater and debris, thick with spongy moss. The rich marble, where visible, was yellowed. Frogs splashed through the slimy basin, croaking and feasting on fireflies. Snakes slithered through the water, feasting on the frogs.

There were those who still knew where to find Manoir Vert, those who still remembered stories of the extravagant parties and luxurious lifestyles of the Baptiste clan—stories passed down through generations, cautionary tales about greed and excess. Those who remembered had given a new name to Manoir Vert, one more fitting of its desolation. They called it Manoir du Ver—The Mansion of Worms.

It had been hours since they left the city when Charlie turned from the dirt road they were on and drove slowly up the drive, through the looming trees, careful of the potholed road. Glowing eyes reflected from the bushes as they passed. Mist clung to the ground in ghostly vapors.

Years had passed since Charlie last visited the family home. As a child, his father—sober enough to be sad—sometimes brought him to look at the house. He'd remind them what the family once was, before Charlie's father, uncles, grandfather, and great-uncles drove them all to ruin.

Charlie never liked visiting the Manor. He would cry, which earned him a slap on the face. He knew what people called the place, and he hated that he agreed. He hated missing out on the good times when the Baptiste name had meant something. Now, as he drove up, he hated it again.

When it seemed as though the road would go on endlessly, the headlights finally revealed the vacant manor, and Charlie pulled the car around the old fountain, stopping in front of the entrance. Climbing out of the car, Vermilion stretched and smiled as he looked at the crumbling homestead.

"Are you enjoying this?" Charlie asked.

"I have often wondered after this house," Vermilion said. "Bernardin thought it would be a new beginning in a new world." The vampire paused as he looked over the ruined house. It sighed with the breeze, as if it were tired. "He was wrong."

"Bernardin?" Charlie asked, and then, in this place of reminiscence, a memory of the name Vermilion Baptiste puzzled itself out in his mind. He had only heard it once, maybe a few times at most, but he'd heard it. Someone from the family had said it when he was young and there was still family around, invoking his name when one Baptiste or another had gone on a bender or cheated on his wife, saying he had a bit of Vermilion in him.

Charlie remembered now. Vermilion Baptiste had been the playboy, the rascal—at least that was the story he was told, with a hint that there were other stories much too dark for young ears. Vermilion's life had been rich and decadent until, Charlie had been told, it was suddenly cut short.

"Bernadin was your brother," Charlie said.

"*Younger* brother," Vermilion responded scornfully.

"They said you were a libertine."

Vermilion nodded deviously. "Only when they were being polite."

Charlie was stunned. "How old are you?"

"Old enough to have enjoyed every pleasure this life has to offer." He smiled. "But not long enough to tire of them."

Vermilion took the creaky steps up to the house. He placed his hands on both doors and pushed them open. Wind gusted through the entryway, blowing away leaves and dirt that had lain there for decades. The entrance hall had high, vaulted ceilings, empty and expansive, thick with cobwebs. A tarnished chandelier hung overhead. A grand staircase led up to a broad balcony on the dark second floor.

Deep within the house came a low, leathery, flapping noise. The sound grew louder and louder, getting closer and closer. Charlie heard high-pitched screeches tangled up in the clamor. The sound was almost on top of them, rushing down from the attic and over the stairs towards the open doors. Charlie realized what the sound was and ducked just as hundreds—thousands—of bats flew over his head, shrieking, and disappearing through the overgrown trees.

As the sound of fluttering faded, Charlie stood up cautiously. He looked at Vermilion, who seemed unaffected, taking a step across the threshold of the old manor, removing his hat like a gentleman as he did.

The air inside was stale and heavy—abandonment weighed on every room. As they walked in, the floor groaned like an old ship. Most furnishings had been sold, hocked for a few extra dollars to keep the family afloat. What few pieces remained were covered with heavy canvas, trying—but failing—to keep off dust and dirt.

An owl perched outside on a tall chimney hooted. Its call echoed down the fireplace and through the house. Frogs croaked and crickets chirped, filling the air to the lofty ceilings. Another gust of wind blew into the house, moving dried leaves and rippling the canvas coverings.

Vermilion wandered the house, opening glass doors and windows, their panes caked in dirt. Moldy curtains billowed in the breeze, moving like ghosts. Charlie followed dazedly behind him, coming to terms with the shame he'd felt his whole life for being born a Baptiste too late to enjoy it. But maybe, with Vermilion here, that would change.

They walked all through the house, Vermilion leading the way, winding through the many rooms, and ending at the French doors in back, where he pulled away the boards and stepped into the backyard.

Thorns and briars curled through the long grass like writhing serpents. Decomposing trees had fallen into the lawn, and new ones sprang up, wearing Spanish moss like a veil. The stables were rotten and collapsed, the horses long gone, sold for glue because they'd been too old and diseased for the family to sell them off to stud.

Tucked away to one side of the yard, in a shadowy grove overgrown with vines, was the family gravesite, covered by a gossamer blanket of low mist. Bernardin Baptiste had fathered eleven children between two wives—all of them, and all their descendants, had been buried here, in this family plot. Even Charlie's father had been laid to rest in this solemn ground, though Charlie hadn't attended the funeral.

There were crumbling mausoleums surrounded by tomb-stones eroded by the elements. The vines had crept past the iron fence and crooked gate, laying claim to the burial mounds. Vermilion walked through the thorny deadfall, around the jumble of errant headstones. He stopped, standing above a once-elegant tomb, reading the name etched into the briar-bound marker above the door.

BERNARDIN ALPHONSE DU BAPTISTE

"Found you, brother," Vermilion said with a grin.

Charlie trampled up beside the vampire, looking at the stone chamber and the name etched into it. "Why didn't you come with them?"

"They came here *because* of me," Vermilion said. "They ran." He looked grimly back at the tomb. "They told their friends I was dead—if they acknowledged me at all. They wanted to forget." The grin returned to his face. "Now look at them."

The vampire spat on the ground.

"You hate them, don't you?"

"More than anything."

"Then why did you find me?" Charlie said. "If you hate family so much, why would you want my help?"

"Do you not hate them too?" the vampire asked.

Charlie was silent.

"When I arrived, I asked after Bernardin's descendants to see what came of them. I thought, perhaps I might exact some revenge, take what was rightfully mine. But you're all that's left."

"They blew it all."

"They robbed you of your birthright," Vermilion said. "Just as they did me."

"That's why you want my help, then? To get it back?"

"No," Vermilion said. "To start anew. I want more than Bernardin ever had."

Charlie licked his lips. "When do we start?"

"I need rest," Vermilion said. "And I'll need a coffin." He raised a crooked finger and pointed towards the dark interior of the old mausoleum where Bernardin's old bones were interred. "Give me his."

CHAPTER 8

THE ORLEANS PARISH CORONER'S Office was a dilapidated, low-ceilinged building at the bottom end of Uptown. It smelled like antiseptic and death. Fly paper hung in coils near the windows. A long hall ran the length of the building, lined with refrigerated rooms where they kept the dead. The farther down the hall one walked, the lower the temperature dropped.

In the farthest room, beneath the dim light of a single bulb, three men stood at the side of a white ceramic examination table. Frenchy De Angelis, handsome and well-groomed, squared his shoulders, fussed with his starched white shirt, and set his horn-rimmed glasses into place. In the opposite corner, Geno Gentil cracked his knuckles and shifted his weight. A known sadist and killer, it wasn't often he was seen without blood on his knuckles and a twisted smile on his face.

Between the two of them was a tall, broad, brute of a man, built like a brick house and dressed in pinstripes. His overcoat was draped across his broad shoulders like a royal mantle. His fedora sat crooked on his bald head. Jet-black hair ringed his scalp. A hefty gold watch was wrapped around one of his thick wrists, and his fat fingers were adorned with chunky rings. He had a bulbous nose and a small mouth that looked cruel and dispassionate. His invisible lips wrapped around the fat stump of a cigar. His name was Anton Lazaretto.

The naked body of William "Bull" Buford was laid out on the table, covered from the waist down by a white sheet. The toe tag said he was deceased, and the cause of death was a gunshot to the head, the hole squarely between the dead man's eyes.

Lazaretto puffed on his cigar before plucking it from his lips. "What a waste," he said in a low growl. The words sounded mushy in his mouth, like his tongue was too big to fit between his teeth. Taking another puff of the cigar, he balled his hands into veiny fists and rested his knuckles on the table like a gorilla.

"You sure it was them, boss?" Frenchy asked.

"They found that tarot card in his pocket, didn't they?"

There was a knock at the door. A lanky, humorless man dressed in a white medical smock poked his head inside. His dark, combed-back hair was noticeably thin. "Mr. Lazaretto," he said nervously. "She's here."

"It's about damn time," Lazaretto said. "Send her in."

The coroner disappeared back into the hallway, and Lazaretto fidgeted with the rings on his fingers, straightening them while he waited.

"Never liked that witch woman," Gino said from his corner. "Something ain't right with her."

"Don't worry about it," Lazaretto said, cracking his knuckles. "I'm gonna take care of it."

The door opened again, and this time the woman entered. She flowed in, dressed all in black, her movements poised and economical. Rain shimmered on her black coat trimmed with fur. With a gloved hand, she drew her scarf, which covered her head like a hood, lifting her chin as she locked green, discerning eyes with each man, a crooked smile teasing at her lips with each encounter.

"Madame Lovebite," Lazaretto said.

"Anton," she said, standing across from him on the other side of the table—Bull's body between them. "Is this where you bring all the ladies?"

Lazaretto gave a hollow chuckle. "Only you," he said.

The Madame slipped her hand into her purse and drew out her gold cigarette case, snapping it open on the examination table beside Bull's body. She plucked a long, black cigarette, tapped it once against the metal, then brought the gold tip to her crimson lips. She flicked her lighter, the flame jumping up, and held it steady until the end glowed. She inhaled, letting the smoke linger in her chest before exhaling in a narrow stream. "You wanted to talk?" she said.

"I do," Lazaretto said. He pointed his cigar at Bull's body. "One of my men at the docks got himself killed last night."

"My condolences."

Lazaretto gave another joyless chuckle. He took a puff of his cigar. "I've been thinking about it all morning," he said. "The lazy bastards at the police station are happy to call it a mugging, but seeing as he still had a wallet full of cash, that don't quite sit right with me." Lazaretto adjusted his shoulders. His spine cracked. "That got me wondering," he said. "It couldn't be a mugging. And if it couldn't be a mugging, then what could it be?"

Gino folded his arms and smiled as he watched Lazaretto work.

"My first thought was maybe an enemy of mine did him in—Lord knows I got plenty of those. But that didn't make much sense either. If somebody wanted to get at me, there are a lot of people they could kill, and this guy? He ain't one of them." Lazaretto took another puff of his cigar, then ground it out on the table. Gino chuckled to himself in the corner. Frenchy looked on; his arms folded across his chest.

"Then I started thinking about my friends," Lazaretto said. He rested his knuckles on the edge of the table again and leaned forward, looking grim as the light overhead cast stark shadows down his face. "Because if it wasn't a random act of violence and it wasn't an enemy, who else is left?"

There was silence in the cold room.

The Madame smiled at him. She put one hand flat on the table and leaned forward, almost flirtatiously. She took another drag, then held her cigarette near her face, pointing it up towards the ceiling.

"Do you want an apology, Anton?" she said.

Lazaretto leaned back slightly. He gave another chuckle, still joyless, but this time it sounded incredulous. "I want to know why my man got killed."

The Madame brought the cigarette to her crimson lips, twisted in a wry smile. "He had a big mouth," she said.

Lazaretto's nostrils flared, and he gritted his teeth. "I don't like it when my people get gunned down in the street."

Putting both hands down on the table, the Madame leaned over Bull's body like a wildcat on the prowl. Shadows ran down her face.

Gino jumped up from his corner and pointed a thick finger at the Madame. "Don't tell Mr. Lazaretto his business."

"Shut up, Gino," Lazaretto said, his voice raised. He didn't turn away from the Madame, his eyes locked on hers. "You know, I work with a lot of people, and none of them have enough nerve to kill one of my guys, then tell me it's my fault."

"Because they don't pay you what we do."

"You want a discount or something?"

"I want you to do your job," she said.

Lazaretto snorted. "Let's get one thing straight," he said. "I don't work for you. You pay me that money, and I *allow* you to bring in whatever you want through those docks. I don't ask no questions and I make sure nobody else does either."

"Then keep your men in line," the Madame said, jabbing a finger into the dead man's side. She looked at Gino. "And keep your dogs on a leash—or we'll have to take our business elsewhere."

"Is that a threat?"

"It's business," she said. "If you can't provide Apophrades, Inc., with the services we need, then we'll find somebody who can."

"I run this town," Lazaretto said with a snarl. "Nobody can do what I do."

"Then we shouldn't have any more problems," the Madame said. She took a final pull from her cigarette before grinding the butt on the table like Lazaretto had done. She snatched her case and dropped it back into her purse.

"We have a shipment tonight," she said. She glanced down at the body. "You'll need a new man."

"That's going to be expensive," Lazaretto said.

The Madame withdrew a wad of bills from her purse. With a sharp flick, she tossed it onto Bull's stomach, the money thudding against the cold flesh.

"Don't worry," she said. "We'll cover it."

Lazaretto picked up the wad of cash. He felt something hidden between the bills and pulled it out. It was a tarot card with a picture of a high, ivory castle that reached up into a stormy night sky. A powerful bolt of lightning crackled down from the dark clouds, striking the building and setting the roof alight. Flaming bricks rained down to the fathom below. A man, helpless, his fine clothes on fire, fell too, screaming toward the stony ground and his inevitable death. At the bottom was the card's name.

THE TOWER

"What's this supposed to be?" Lazaretto asked.

"A reminder," the Madame said, the corner of her mouth curling up again into a smirk, "of who you're dealing with."

CHAPTER 9

NIGHTINGALE TOOK THE TROLLEY downtown. He brought his coat to the tailor and stopped at a diner—Cushing's, his favorite—for a cup of joe. He slogged it down and retrieved his coat before heading toward his office.

The rain was picking up again. He kept the book Bone had given him tucked inside his coat. Despite the weather, he strolled unhurried, savoring the walk. Water streamed from the brim of his hat. At his building, he stepped through the marble lobby, shook off the rain, and climbed three flights to his office overlooking the street. The sign on the door was hand-painted on pebbled glass.

NIGHTINGALE INVESTIGATIONS
WE WORK IN THE DARK

The lights were off inside as he unlocked the door and entered. There was an empty vestibule where his secretary would sit if he ever thought to hire one. He continued through the next door, which was marked PRIVATE.

In the sunless, rain-soaked morning, gray light filtered through the blinds, casting inky bars of shadow across the room. Water streaming down the window made the light shift as if alive, writhing, though it never quite reached the murky corners.

The furnishings were spartan. There was a desk, two chairs in front of it for clients, and a couch along the wall across from a row of filing cabinets stacked high with papers. A credenza sat below the window, a hot plate and coffee pot on top of it; a bar cart was parked in the corner. The ceiling was high with stamped tin panels. The raw brick walls were naked, except for a few travel posters advertising Paris, Cairo, and Rio de Janeiro that had been left behind by the previous occupant—a travel agent. An award with Nightingale's name, presented to him by the city of New Orleans for distinguished service in the line of duty, hung crooked on a bent nail.

Another door led to a narrow room adjacent to his office that Nightingale had blacked out into a usable dark room.

He tossed Bone's book on the desk, shrugged off his coat, and hung it with his hat. He clicked on the banker's lamp, green light illuminating coffee-ringed papers. Sitting in his slat-back chair, he opened the book, studied the Romani folk art, and skimmed notes on their meaning. He compared styles to the tarot card, searching for clues.

In the hush of the slow, dripping morning, he heard footsteps in the lobby—the crisp click of heels on marble. The footsteps mounted the stairs, ascending—one, two, three floors. When the footfalls angled toward his office, he set his book aside and eased open the top drawer of his desk, where his gun rested atop a pile of files.

The woman stopped in front of the door. He could see her through the vestibule, her shadow behind the pebbled glass, shading his name. His hand rested on the revolver.

When the knock came, he shouted that the door was open.

When the nun walked in, he closed the drawer and stood politely.

"You lost, sister?" he asked. He flattened his suit with his hands and straightened his tie.

"Aren't we all, detective?" she said, a faint, sad smile flickering at the corners of her mouth.

He smiled back. "It's what keeps me in business."

Nightingale put out his hand and motioned to the chairs in front of the desk. "Take a seat," he said. He quickly closed the book with the tarot card inside and walked to the wall where he flipped the light switch. The bulbs flickered for a moment before the current became steady and the light filled the room, banishing the shadows. "Can I get you a drink?" he asked. "Coffee?" He picked up two glasses from the bar cart. "Bourbon? Gin?"

"I'm fine, detective," she said, sidling into one of the chairs, hands clasped over her purse in her lap.

Nightingale sat, lit a cigarette, and studied her: blonde hair beneath a white veil, confident light eyes, fair skin. She sat straight, hands on her purse. Younger and prettier than the nuns he knew, yet visibly troubled. Her arriving smile was nervous, not cheerful. He exhaled smoke.

"I hope you don't mind if I smoke, Sister—?"

"Magdalene," she said. "Sister Magdalene. And no, I don't mind at all."

He smiled his uneven smile again and took another drag. "We don't get many members of the cloth around here."

"Thankfully," she said, "it's not often we need to be."

"What brings you to my door?"

"A missing girl," she said.

"Oh?" He took the cigarette from his mouth. "The police weren't any help?"

"I can't go to the police."

"You got trouble with them or something?"

"No, it's just—" she hesitated. "It's complicated."

"Tell me about it."

The sister shifted, her gaze dropping to the floor. "Some-one—some*thing*—took a little girl."

"Something?"

The sister looked more sheepish than she already had, like she'd walked onto a stage and discovered her fright. She fiddled with her hands.

"I—" She paused, embarrassed. "I think it was a vampire that took her."

Nightingale sat back. He rapped his fist on the desk. "What makes you think that?"

"Because I found this." Magdalene pulled Juliette's drawing from her purse, gently unfolded it, and placed it on the desk in front of Nightingale. "The girl drew that—Juliette. One of the girls says that's the man who took her."

Nightingale picked up the drawing and narrowed his eyes as he studied it.

Magdalene tapped her fingers nervously. "Do you think I'm a fool, detective?"

"No," he said. "But I'm not sure it's a vampire."

"Why not?"

"If you came here talking about a vampire, it's because you know the kind of work that I do. It sounds crazy until you've seen one. And I've seen more than my share."

"Then, what is it?"

Gently setting the picture down on the desk, Nightingale shrugged. "It's just to imagine a vampire breaking into a convent."

"Could one?"

"It's possible," he said. "Not likely, though. Imagine trudging through the sewer or digging through a dump. It's not something they'd like to do."

"Not even to take a little girl?"

"She'd have to be important," Nightingale said. "Vampires are animals. They sleep and they eat, and they're not going to head into a convent for a meal when there are easier meals outside of them."

"What if the girl was somehow special to him?"

"She'd have to be—vampires aren't the sentimental type." Nightingale tapped the girl's picture. "And I don't know if a drawing is enough to convince me."

The sister took a deep breath. "I know I sound like a fool," she said, her voice raw as she choked back tears. "But Sister Agnès told me to see you."

"Sister Agnès," he said. "I didn't know she was still around."

"She is," Magdalene said. "She said you would help."

He knocked on his desk again. "And she thought it was a vampire?"

"She did."

Nightingale sat silent, the rain tapping against the window behind him. "I'll take a look, sister. See what I think."

Magdalene looked relieved. She smiled. This time, the tension was gone. "Thank you, detective," she said. "Thank you."

"Don't thank me yet," Nightingale said as he put on his coat. "You'd better hope it isn't a vampire, because if it is, then you're going to have to pay me."

CHAPTER 10

"SHE THINKS SHE CAN talk to me like that?" Lazaretto was shouting. "Disrespect me, in my town?" He brought a rocks glass to his mouth and gulped down the bourbon inside.

He was in his office on the second floor of the Rag & Bone Club. The walls were paneled in dark-stained oak; the blinds were drawn, but there was a lamp in each corner and one on the desk—all of them were on, their lampshades all red. He stood near a wall of floor-to-ceiling windows that looked down over the casino and dance floor. Below, the club was dark, most of the lights were off, and the windows were blacked out. Only the stage was well-lit, where the crew worked to reset the chairs and stands for the musicians. One man sat at the grand piano, playing lightly, stopping whenever he hit a note just a touch out of key, then he'd reach inside to adjust it before setting back in at the ivories.

In the rest of the club, busboys wiped down tables, custodians swept, dealers replaced old decks of cards with new ones, cashiers in their cages counted their chips while the pit boss watched, and bartenders washed glasses, tapped fresh kegs, and emptied the heaping ashtrays.

Gino sat in an overstuffed chair in the corner of the office, drumming his fingers and watching Lazaretto as he paced angrily. "I keep saying, we can't trust that Gypsy witch," Gino said. "She's dangerous."

"They all are," Lazaretto said, stalking back to the bar cart behind his desk to refill his glass. "Her boss, too, Monsieur Du Vide." He said the name with a mocking French accent. "Coming into my city, flashing cash, thinking that buys influence."

"We gotta get rid of them, boss."

"You think I don't know that?"

"Of course," Gino said. "Then why don't we go hit 'em, right now?"

"We can't go in half-cocked like that," Lazaretto said. "We can't just shoot our way out of this."

"Then what are we gonna do?"

"We're gonna wait," Lazaretto said. "See what Frenchy learns at the docks."

"You think that's gonna work?"

"Who's the boss here, Gino? You or me? Of course, it'll work. Once we know what they're bringing in, we cut off the supply. Then we'll see how demanding little Miss Witch and her big bad boss are."

"We're still going to bump them off, though, right?"

"Of course, we are—but after we get our hands on their business."

Gino chuckled. "Can't wait to see the look on her face," he said. Then, as if a switch had been turned on, concern furrowed his brow. "But boss, what if she knows what we're planning?"

"You ain't going to rat to her, are you?"

"No, course not—but—"

"But what?"

"She knows things—things she ain't supposed to."

Lazaretto's gaze fixed on the tarot card that sat on his desk, the one the Madame had given him. He snapped open his humidor, took a cigar, and sheared off the tip with a swift flick, sending the piece flying to the floor.

"We'll see about that," Lazaretto said, bringing the cigar to his mouth and lighting it.

A knock came at the door.

"Who is it?" Lazaretto said.

"Slits."

Gino opened the door, letting Slits Nicotero saunter in. As usual, he looked lanky and dangerous, but his face today was crestfallen.

"What's wrong now?" Lazaretto asked.

"Bad news," Slits said. "I found Fat Phil and Knuckles."

"Where are they?"

"The swamps—what's left of them, anyway."

Gino clenched his fist, like he was looking for something to hit. Lazaretto raised an eyebrow.

"What happened?" Lazaretto asked.

"Last night I shook down Charlie Baptiste for what he owes. He only had about five hundred on him, so I sent him up the river with Fat Phil and Knuckles." Slits tossed the wad of money onto Lazaretto's desk. "Guess he had more fight than I thought."

"Charlie the Cheat?" Gino asked. "He killed them both?"

"Tore their throats out," Slits said, pouring himself a drink. "No open caskets for them two."

Lazaretto put a finger on the wad of bills, pushing it back towards Slits. "Take this. Put it on Charlie's head. No one disrespects me like that."

Slits shrugged. "He's probably long gone by now."

"Then find him," Lazaretto said. "Five hundred to whoever puts him in the ground. Cash on delivery." He turned to Gino. "That includes you, too."

Gino nodded, cracking his knuckles.

"You got it, boss," Slits said, collecting the bills from the desk. He paused when he saw the tarot card. "Been seeking guidance or something?"

"No." Lazaretto shook his head as he picked up the card. He raised his cigar and burned a hole through the center of it. "Just a parting gift from an old friend."

CHAPTER 11

FRENCHY SHOOK THE RAIN from his coat as he entered the Port of Call. The caustic smell of sweat and cigarettes hung in the air. The bartender wiped the counters. A few working men ate steak and eggs, conversing in low, gruff voices. Others slept off hangovers, heads resting on tabletops. One man wheezed loudly as he slept on a ratty couch in the corner.

Frenchy approached the bartender, set his hands on the counter, then quickly pulled them away, finding it sticky. He wiped his hand with a handkerchief. The bartender paused his own wiping and leaned against the bar, arms stretched wide.

"What'll it be, captain?" he asked with a yellow-toothed grin.

"I need to know about a man who drank here," Frenchy said.

"Lot of faces in my bar," the bartender said. "I can't remember all of them. Memory ain't what it used to be. Not so early in the morning."

Frenchy glanced at the clock; it was nearly eleven. "We'll see if we can jog it." He gave up cleaning his hands, pulled out his checkbook, and dropped a twenty in the tip jar.

"I'm starting to wake up," the bartender said.

"Good." Frenchy pushed his glasses back up onto his nose. "The man worked the docks. People called him Bull."

"I know him. Always pays his tab."

"That's good news for you."

"Why's that?"

"Because he's dead."

The two men eating at the counter stopped talking and turned to look at Frenchy.

"You a cop?" the bartender asked.

"Do I look like a cop?"

"Who are you, then?"

"Just an interested party."

"How interested?" the bartender asked, pulling the twenty from the jar and snapping it tight between his fingers.

Frenchy gave a weary smile. "I'm sure you know my employer," he said. "He owns property around the city—including this bar."

The bartender stood at attention. "I didn't know you worked for Lazaretto," he said. "I was just—"

Frenchy held up his hand. "Protecting it. I understand."

The bartender handed the money back, but Frenchy refused to take it. "It's a gift," he said. "Just tell me about Bull."

"I know him—knew him," the bartender said. "Not well, though. He drank here, like the rest of them. Drank here last night, even."

"With whom?"

"That sorry sack over there was one of them." The bartender pointed to the wheezing man on the couch. "That's Cramer. They was talking last night."

"Very good," Frenchy said, standing up from the bar.

"How'd Bull die?" the bartender asked.

"Shot," Frenchy said, bringing a finger to his forehead. "Right between the eyes."

The bartender looked relieved. "You sure it wasn't nothing unholy, right?"

Frenchy looked confused, staring at the bartender, trying to figure out just what the hell he could be talking about. He slowly shook his head. "No," he said. "Just a murder."

Frenchy walked to the couch. Cramer slept, his belly exposed. The old man stirred as stray whiskers from his unkempt mustache tickled his nose. Frenchy sat across from him and kicked the sofa. Cramer's eyes shot open. He looked at Frenchy with glazed-over eyes, lowered his head, and slurred, "Whattayoowant?"

"I need to know about Bull," Frenchy said. "I heard you talked to him last night."

"Why you want to know?"

"Because he's dead, Mr. Cramer."

Suddenly alert, Cramer propped himself up, his joints popping and his bones aching. His breath was acrid. He licked his lips with a dry tongue and scratched at his wiry beard. "They got him."

"I'm sorry, Mr. Cramer, but who got him?"

Cramer licked his lips again, hunched over, his head dropping below his shoulders like a vulture as he lowered his voice to speak. "It must have been them vampires."

"Vampires?" Frenchy asked. He turned around to look incredulously at the bartender, who nodded emphatically. When he looked back at Cramer, he reached into his coat, pulling out his checkbook again. "Tell me more."

CHAPTER 12

SISTER MAGDALENE DROVE A powder-blue Studebaker that handled like a boat. Nightingale sat beside her, watching the rain-soaked city glide past the window.

"You're not from New Orleans?" the sister asked. She'd been questioning him since they left his office.

He shook his head. "Baltimore, originally. But my family ended up in Philly for my father's work." He glanced at her. "You're not from here either."

She laughed politely. "Am I that obvious?"

"I'm a detective."

She laughed, more genuine this time. "New York. Not the city, the state."

"And how'd you end up here?"

"One mistake after another." She quickly glanced away from the road and met Nightingale's gaze for a moment—her eyes were big and knowing. The look she gave told him she wouldn't elaborate. She turned back to the road. "I found my way, eventually."

"To the church?"

"Not what I planned, but it's where I ended up," she said. "What about you? Why did you become a detective?"

"It was either the cops or a factory."

"But you're a private investigator, not a police officer."

"I used to be on the force. Philadelphia and here."

"Why'd you stop?"

"It didn't work out." He looked over at her, giving her the same look she'd given him that meant he wasn't going to say anything more.

"Do you like it?"

"I'm good at it," he said.

Sister Magdalene smiled. She started to say something, but had to crank the wheel as the big car took the corner. "Here we are," she said instead.

The Old Ursuline Convent came into view. Thick, grey fog that blew in off the Gulf with the storm clung to the place like cobwebs. It was an austere, lime-washed building on the edge of the French Quarter. Shaped like an "L," it stood three stories high, with gabled windows jutting out from the roof. The grounds were surrounded by a tall stone wall, topped with wrought-iron spires. The sister maneuvered the car around the back of the building and stopped in front of a wide metal gate.

"Would you mind, detective?" She asked, handing him a key for the lock.

He took it and stepped out of the car into the rain. He opened the chunky padlock and swung the heavy doors wide for her to pass through, closing them again once the big car was inside.

She parked beneath an overhang, and Nightingale met her at the door, opening it for her. She thanked him, and together they approached the convent, following a narrow path around the building. The courtyard garden was bounded by clipped hedges, with a walkway lined by marble statues of saints, some of which Nightingale recognized; the white stone streaked gray.

Magdalene stepped close to him and grabbed his arm. "Her window's up there," she said, pointing. Near the joint of the building, Nightingale saw a set of broken shudders in one of the gables, hanging loosely and blowing in the storm. Curtains billowed from the shattered window, the wooden slats flapping in the wind.

"We'll see more inside," she said, moving on. She stopped outside two ornately carved, wooden doors. "I'll ask you to wait in the chapel for a moment," she added. Nightingale nodded as she grabbed one of the thick metal rings that hung off the door and pulled it open.

Behind the doorway, the chapel stretched out ahead of them. Nightingale dipped his fingers and made the sign of the cross over his chest.

"You're Catholic?" Magdalene asked.

"Occasionally."

"When they built this," she said, "they were still very much interested in the European style." She was staring up at the high ceiling. "They wanted us to feel insignificant, to remember God's power."

"It works," he said. "It's impressive."

"It's no cathedral, but it's something," she said, tempering a smile. "I'll just let the other sisters know you're here so we can go up to the dormitory."

"Are they expecting me?"

"Some of them are."

"Will it be an issue?"

Magdalene shook her head. "Not for you," she said and left him at the entrance. She slipped through the door at the far end of the chapel.

He stood behind the pews, hand resting on the back. Tapping his finger, he scanned the chapel. The air was heavy with smoke and incense. Candlelight flickered, shadows dancing on the walls. The rain's drumming echoed inside.

Reaching into his coat, Nightingale pulled out his pack of cigarettes and lipped one of them. He flicked his lighter, which sparked, but didn't ignite. He slipped it back into his pocket and, with a glance around the church, he walked to the stand of candles, bent down, and lit his smoke on one of them.

He took a drag as he looked at the Virgin statue in the niche above the rack. Her hands were outstretched, welcoming, a glowing halo arched over her head.

"Thanks," he said through the cigarette.

At the sound of soft footsteps entering the chapel, he looked at the door and saw Sister Agnès standing inside.

"I hear you've been giving my name out," he said.

"Only when needed," she said, stepping closer.

Nightingale chuckled, then took a quick pull and blew the smoke out the side of his mouth. "You really think this was a vampire?"

"I don't know, detective," Sister Agnès said. "But things aren't right here."

"What things?"

"I'm not entirely sure," Agnès said. "But there is something wrong with the girls coming from France."

"Juliette. You mean?"

"Not just her—all of them. All around the city."

There was muffled commotion outside the door to the convent, which made them both turn to look.

"Go with God," the nun said, patting his hand. "And keep Magdalene out of trouble. She's a good one." Agnès turned and slipped out through the wooden doors into the rain.

At the other end of the chapel, the commotion continued. He heard raised voices coming closer.

"And who told you to do that?" one of them said; it was a woman, and not Magdalene. This one sounded older, harsher—like the nuns he remembered. "Bringing a detective here. It's almost blasphemous."

"He's already hired." That time, it was Magdalene's voice.

The door opened, and Magdalene walked in; Nightingale could see she was angry. Behind her trailed a stone-faced crone who looked like she had a bad taste in her mouth. A third person followed, his long, black robes sweeping the floor. He was a priest, judging from the collar, and he walked with his hands clasped behind his back.

"Is there a problem?" Nightingale asked.

"No," Magdalene said. "This is Detective Nightingale. He's here to investigate."

"There's nothing *to* investigate," the other nun said. She turned to Nightingale. "Now please, leave us be."

"Nothing?" Nightingale said. "A missing girl isn't nothing."

"She's a runaway," the woman said. "Nothing more."

"Care for a professional opinion?"

"We already have one," the woman said. "I've been raising these girls for decades. We've never had a kidnapping."

The priest finally stepped forward. He was a bit older than Nightingale, in his late 40s at most, with sandy blonde hair highlighted with gray and the kind of easy confidence that played well with congregations. "Mother," he said, speaking to the older woman. "There's no harm in letting the detective look around."

The nun looked horrified, but before she could speak, Nightingale stepped forward. "I'm sorry," he said, "but who are you people?"

Bowing his head courteously, the priest answered first. "I'm Father Renault, from the diocese."

"And I am Mother Constance," the sour-faced woman said. "The Mother Superior here." She straightened her posture as she spoke.

Nightingale nodded. "Then who's in charge?"

"This is my convent," the Mother Superior said.

"Which is part of the diocese," Father Renault said with gentle authority.

Nightingale looked at Magdalene, who was trying to hide her smile as she watched the Mother Superior flounder. The detective turned to the priest. "I'm going to get to work, then, if you don't mind."

The Mother Superior pursed her lips tightly and breathed heavily. She glared at Nightingale. "We don't allow smoking here, detective. Not in the chapel, nor the convent."

"Then take care of this for me," he said, handing her the lit cigarette.

Magdalene brought her hand to her mouth to stop from chuckling.

"I'll walk with you," the priest said. He looked at Magdalene. "Might I have a word alone with the detective?"

Magdalene curtsied. "I'll meet you upstairs."

They left the chapel. Magdalene hurried ahead while the Mother Superior stormed toward her office. The priest and the detective walked side by side down the wide hallway. Father Renault kept his hands clasped behind his back and his head slightly bowed, moving slowly.

"Detective, I wonder if you know what's happening in Europe."

"Sure," Nightingale said. "There's war—again."

"I was there the first time," Renault said.

"So was I."

The priest turned to Nightingale, surprised. "You seem too young for that."

"I lied," Nightingale said. "I looked older than I was back then."

"I was fresh from the seminary," the priest said. "It was the worst of humankind that I've ever seen—I don't need to explain that to you."

"No," Nightingale said, scratching at his neck. "You don't."

"These girls—Juliette, in particular—are escaping those horrors."

"I can't blame them."

"Neither can I," the priest said. "Which is why I'd like you to tread lightly. They didn't deserve to see the things they've seen. I'd hate to cause them any more trauma now that they've arrived."

"I'm here to help," Nightingale said. "That's all."

"I appreciate that," the father said, nodding. "And I'd also appreciate you keeping me up to date with what you learn."

"When I can," Nightingale said.

The two men reached the bottom of the stairs. The detective put out his hand, and the priest took it.

"Follow these to the top," Renault said. "Let me know what you find."

Nightingale found Magdalene at the foot of Juliette's bed. The sister was shaking her head. The bed had been made—the corners of the sheets and top blanket were pulled tight and neatly folded under. The pillow had been fluffed and replaced at the head.

"I told them to leave the bed as it was," Magdalene said angrily.

"I don't think they want to listen."

Over the bed, the broken shutters flapped back and forth in the wind, the wood shattered into splinters. The hinges had been almost completely torn from the frame. Outside, the rain was picking up, and the curtains, soaked through, fluttered half in and half out of the room.

"Mother Superior," Magdalene said. "I don't understand how she can pretend nothing happened. A little girl is missing for heaven's sake."

Nightingale opened the footlocker, found it completely empty, then closed it again. "It's easier this way," he said. He walked to the head of the bed, opened the drawer and the cupboard of the nightstand. Inside were a few pencils and sheets of paper, a Bible pushed far to the back and turned upside down. "Or somebody wants to get rid of the evidence."

"You really think that's possible?"

"Can't rule anything out yet," Nightingale said. He knelt on the floor, looking under the bed as he spoke. "But this place has been cleaned out."

"There's truly nothing?"

"Not yet," he said as he put a foot on the headboard and hoisted himself up to the broken window. Nightingale looked at the frame and the shutters. He paused, furrowing his brow. He ran his hand along the edge, then he looked back at the sister. "You nail these shut?" he asked.

"Perhaps for the storms?" The sister climbed up onto the headboard beside the detective. She smelled of floral greens, with just a touch of citrus.

"Using silver nails?" He pried one of them from the splintered wood and turned it over so he could look at the head. A symbol was stamped into it. "Marked with a Papal seal?"

"What does that mean?" she said, taking the nail from him.

"They've been blessed." Nightingale climbed back down from the window, drying his hands from the rainwater on his coat.

"What would they be blessed for?"

"Good for keeping vampires out."

"That works?"

"It can. Some places used to nail coffins shut with silver to keep the dead from rising."

Sister Magdalene turned to climb down from the bed. Nightingale offered his hand to her, which she took, to help her descend.

"It didn't seem to do much here."

"Maybe it wasn't a vampire," Nightingale said. "Or maybe the vampire had help."

"This all sounds like superstition."

"A lot of it is," Nightingale said. "But it all comes from somewhere."

"What can you tell me about them?"

"Vampires?" Nightingale said. "They're nasty, I can tell you that."

"But how do they work? Is it magic?"

Nightingale shook his head. "Honestly, I couldn't tell you." Nightingale began searching the girl's bed. He lifted the pillow, pulling the case off and dropping it unceremoniously when he found nothing. "They were dead and now they're not. Because of that, things get turned around."

"Turned around how?"

"For example, most people sleep at night and are awake during the day. Vampires are flipped. They become nocturnal. They can be up during the day, just like we can stay up during the night, but instinctually, they sleep when the sun is up."

Nightingale pulled back the blankets from the bed, one by one, searching the folds of fabric. "Or take the drinking of blood. We eat food to sustain us, to keep our hearts pumping. It doesn't work that way for a vampire. Instead of food sustaining life, they need life directly."

"Do they always kill their victims?"

"No," Nightingale said. "They can feed off a victim for weeks, months, years."

"Wouldn't they turn into a vampire?"

"That's not how it works." Nightingale tossed the sheets and blankets to the floor and scratched his jaw as he looked over the stripped bed. "There's a ritual. They call it different names in different places. In France, it was *Le Sacrement Rouge*, the Red

Sacrament. For three nights, a vampire drinks the blood of the living, and then the person drinks the blood of the vampire. On the third night, after drinking the blood, the person dies—but not for long."

"Why three nights?" Magdalene asked, taking a seat on the footlocker at the end of the bed.

Nightingale shrugged. "Why did Jesus spend three days in a tomb? I guess it takes that long to be reborn." He sat down beside the sister. "And that's the thing about vampires. Whatever mysticism there is about them, it's evil. They like to sleep in places underground, because the living walk above it. They're repelled by holy symbols because religion is supposed to attract and comfort. They kill people to increase their numbers because, while we can create life, vampires have to destroy it."

Sister Magdalene looked troubled. "Can somebody be turned into a vampire against her will?"

"Sure," Nightingale said. "I've seen that happen." Moving from the footlocker, he began to search along the side of the bed. "If you're wondering about Juliette, yes, if she were taken by a vampire, she could become one. That means we have a hard deadline." He flipped up the mattress, but finding nothing beneath it, he lowered it back down onto the bed frame. "And there's nothing here to help us."

"There must be something more we can do."

"Tell me about the girl."

"She loved to paint," the sister said, almost smiling. "She was precocious, smart, her English was practically perfect. But I could tell she was frightened, the way she carried herself—it was like she'd been aged beyond her years. I suppose surviving a war will do that to a child."

"Where else did the girl spend time? The classrooms? The chapel? The garden?"

Magdalene smiled excitedly. "There is a place," she said. "And no one knows about it but me."

Water dripped from the ceiling of the catacombs as the rain fell outside, saturating the earth. Sister Magdalene led the way, holding a candle as they navigated the dark underground beneath the chapel.

"I think Juliette's village was bombed," Magdalene said. "She would come down here to feel safe."

"Quaint," Nightingale said as he followed behind the sister. "How much time did she spend down here?"

"As much as she could."

They walked further into the dirty underground, Magdalene retracing her steps from the night before, trying to remember which tombs she had passed. She studied the names as they passed, and she turned to talk to Nightingale as they walked.

"It's a frightening business you're in, detective."

"It pays the bills," he said.

"There are that many cases?"

"Around here? There are enough. But I don't only deal with vampires."

"Why do you deal with them?"

"Because I can," Nightingale said. "I know what they are, I know how to find them. I know how to kill them."

"Is that what you did for Sister Agnès? You killed a vampire?"

"What makes you ask?"

"It was only after I told you she sent me that you agreed to take the case," Magdalene said.

"She's helped me out—more than once."

"Then take a look," Magdalene said. "We're here."

The sister held out her hand and showed him the tomb where Juliette had hidden. She offered her candle to him, but he reached into his pocket and pulled out a penlight instead. He crouched down.

"Not where I'd expect a little girl to set up shop."

"She was frightened," Magdalene said.

"She must have been." Nightingale reached around the back of the coffin, into a tiny gap between it and the wall. He could feel something back there. Grabbing it, he pulled it out, and a pile of crumpled papers spilled out onto the ground. As Nightingale sorted through them, Magdalene joined him.

"Are those drawings?" she asked.

"They look like it." Nightingale held one up. It was a countryside, however crude it may have appeared. There were trees, streams, and cottages. Another was a drawing of a street in a small village, lined with shops. Others showed an exotic marketplace and a harbor full of boats.

"I was supposed to give her my art supplies today," Magdalene said, holding her arms as she shivered in the cold, musty air. She choked back a sudden rush of tears. "She was excited for it."

Nightingale held up the stub of a ticket hidden among the pages.

"That must have been hers," Magdalene said, leaning close.

"She had a room in steerage on the S.S. Myrkranna," Nightingale said, reading the details from the ticket. "The boat left from Morocco and arrived here on Monday."

"She came to the convent Tuesday morning," Magdalene said. She reached out and took the ticket from the detective. She pointed to a line at the bottom of the ticket.

"It says her fare was purchased by Apophrades Incorporated. Have you ever heard of them?"

"Never," Nightingale said.

As he returned to the pile in front of them, he paused, seeing a familiar design. He pushed the other papers aside and picked up the item.

"What is that?" Magdalene asked, bringing the light close.

"It's a tarot card," he said, holding it up for the sister to see.

The back had the same Romani designs as the death card he'd found the night before. On the front, there was a woman and a child huddled together under blankets on a small boat. Beside them were six swords, standing on point. A ferryman guided them along a dark river, steering towards land.

"What does it mean?" she asked.

"It means I'm on the case."

CHAPTER 13

LIGHTNING SPLIT THE SKY, and thunder crashed as Madame Lovebite drove home. Rain fell harder, and fog spilled into the streets. The Italianate lamps along the sidewalk glowed like moons in the mist.

She parked her long black sedan at the curb across from a storefront. It was nestled between a cigar shop and a tailor. The neon lights in the windows glowed brightly in the dark day: a hand, the palm facing the street; the other, a crystal ball. Between them, above the door and below the first balcony of the apartment above, hung a blade sign with the shop's name.

THE HOUSE OF THE RISING SUN

TAROT – PALMISTRY – TEA LEAVES

Madame Lovebite took her keys and purse, left her car, and walked to the door. She stepped inside. The building was overwhelmingly fragrant, filled with the scent of sandalwood, jasmine, and patchouli, with hints of nutmeg, pine, and to-bacco. Sheer drapes hung over the windows. Curtains of fine, colorful silk hung from the ceiling. Potted ferns and palms rested in the corners, tall candlesticks beside them. The melted wax was so old and heavy, the candles looked as if they'd grown from the holders. Shelves overflowed with charms and curios: incense, bags of herbs, bottles of oil, and jars of mysterious roots. Books of arcana and the occult were stacked haphazardly among the items. Even a human skull sat there, its empty eyes staring into the room, pennies stacked inside. At the center, surrounded by plants and candles, stood a round table draped in purple velvet and fringed in golden tassels. A glass orb perched atop a gilded pedestal.

There was a counter behind the table that held more charms and potions, all marked with prices. Standing at it, casually flipping through a magazine, was Lady Sabine—the Madame's aunt.

"Where have you been?" she asked without looking up.

Sabine was twenty-five years Lenora's senior, but the difference between the two women looked no more than ten. She was beautiful, full of life and vigor. Her lips were full, her cheekbones were high; her silky, black hair was swept to one side. The resemblance between the two was clear, and those who didn't think they were mother and daughter thought for certain they were sisters.

"I was out on business," the Madame said.

"You were out on business last night, too."

"The Monsieur has lots of business."

The Madame's aunt finally looked at her niece over the top of her magazine. She slowly pursed her lips.

"You're not sleeping well."

"I'm sleeping fine."

"You can't lie to me, Lenora," Sabine said.

"I'm not lying to you."

"To yourself, then."

The Madame sighed. "Loose ends."

"Are they tied up?"

"For now."

Sabine shook her head. "You're taking on too much, Lenora. Relax. Go upstairs, take a bath."

"I can't. I need to speak with Du Vide."

"He can wait. Go. Have a moment. I'll mind the shop."

"Are you sure?"

"Of course," Sabine said. "I've been doing it longer than you."

"If Du Vide calls—" the Madame began to say, before her aunt cut her off.

"If he calls, I'll tell him to call back." Sabine went back to her magazine, waving her hand at the Madame. "Now, go."

The Madame opened the back door, which led to a vestibule and a flight of stairs to the first of two floors above the shop—both of which the Madame owned. She walked up towards the door to her residence.

The apartment was empty and, except for the steady rain pattering against the windows, it was silent. She hung up her coat on the rack and walked into the parlor just off the entrance, where she set her bag down on a chair beside the door.

With the heavy curtains drawn, the room was dark; not even the flashes of lightning nor the murky streetlight made it inside. It was furnished with overstuffed chairs and cherrywood end tables. The walls were covered in striped wallpaper and adorned with collections of butterflies and beetles framed and mounted behind glass. There were two doorways—one from the entry, which the Madame had just used, and another to her left that led to the dining room and the kitchen beyond that. In front of her was a fireplace and mantle, and in the corner, near the window and balcony doors, was a tall birdcage covered with a dark drape.

She walked to it, drawing the cover aside. Two birds were perched inside, their heads tucked beneath their wings. One was a raven, the other a dove, and their placement mimicked that of her tattooed hands—the dove on the right and the raven on the left.

They cooed softly as the Madame petted each of them. She closed the door to the cage and left the drape open.

Leaving the birds, she went upstairs to the third floor, where she had her bedroom. Sauntering towards the bed, she unbuckled the holster from around her thigh and hung it on one of the posts, the gun dangling from the strap. Then she slinked off the silken gloves, laying them gently over her vanity.

She looked at her hands, placing them palms down and splaying her fingers—the moons across her digits and the birds flying towards one another. The thorny vine around one wrist wrapped itself up around the rest of her arm, blooming into roses along her bicep and across her shoulder. The roses extended along her other arm, with astrological constellations and their symbols hidden throughout the thorns and flowers.

The Madame continued undressing in front of her mirror, stepping out of her black dress, stockings, and undergarments. Tattoos covered the rest of her body, stark against her olive skin. Beneath her breasts was an ornate Romani design. Skulls, candles, and tarot characters marked her back and abdomen, extending down her legs. More Romani designs cascaded down the backs of her thighs, with the thorns and roses continuing, wrapping around her legs. A snake coiled around her left calf. The tops of her feet were marked with the sun and the moon. Alchemical spells and magical words were inked among the larger works. Finally, below her navel was a bat with wings spread across her waist, its fangs bared—a match to her tarot cards.

She ran a warm bath, sprinkling lavender and eucalyptus oils into the water, which filled the room with fragrant steam. Putting up her hair, she reclined in the clawfoot tub, the water rising to her neck. She stayed there for more than an hour before stepping out, drying off, and slipping into a black, silk dressing gown.

The rain was still pouring as she stepped onto the balcony, her skin prickling at the kiss of the cool, damp air. She had gone downstairs to the kitchen and prepared a cup of hot tea; now she drank it as she looked over the empty streets below.

Lightning flashed and thunder cracked like a whip, and the Madame watched it unflinchingly from her balcony. The sky was a dark, tumultuous gray, and the bloated clouds were dumping rain in sheets. Once she finished her tea, she looked at the leaves clumped together at the bottom of her cup and around the edges. She thought at first to read them; instead, she held the cup out into the pouring rain for a moment, long enough to wash the tea leaves loose, and then dumped them out over the railing.

A wet chill crept over her, and she left the balcony, returning to the darkened house. She carried the teacup back downstairs to the kitchen, but as she went to turn on the light, nothing happened; the room remained dark. There was another flash of lightning. She thought, at first, the storm had knocked the power out, but that didn't feel right. There was something in the air, something that made her nervous. The house felt still, but not as it had before. It was too still now, even with the muffled tempest raging outside. She knew she wasn't alone.

"Aunt Sabine?" she said.

No one answered.

She opened a drawer and grabbed a knife—not a kitchen knife, this one had a long stiletto blade, one of many she had hidden around the house. She held the knife at her side, the long blade against her wrist, ready to strike.

Opening the door to the dining room, she side-stepped in and then moved to the parlor, where she pulled the pocket door open. With the lights out and the curtains still drawn, the room was black as pitch, but she could feel the eyes on her from across the room.

"Who's there?" she asked.

The raven cawed in response. Then, lightning flashed, and a beam of light poured through the doorway across the floor. In the brief light, she saw a man sitting in the chair by the window, legs crossed. He wore a black three-piece suit, and his neck was covered in a silken cravat. The flash of lightning had only revealed part of the man's face: a jawline rough with gray stubble and a full, black-haired mustache. His eyes remained in darkness, but the Madame didn't need to see them.

"Monsieur Du Vide," she said.

"My dear, Lenora," the Monsieur replied, his voice deep and smooth and rich. Beside him, the birdcage was open. The dove had remained inside, but the raven was perched on Du Vide's hand. Its eyes were closed as he stroked its feathered head.

"I wasn't expecting you," she said, setting the knife down on a bookshelf. Taking a match from a wooden box, she struck it and lit a candle on the table beside her, offering some light but still not enough to reveal the man's face.

"I wanted to see how our little bit of business went last night."

"It's been taken care of."

"Good."

The Madame took one of her long, black cigarettes from a wooden box on the shelf and lit it with the candle.

"I spoke with Lazaretto," the Madame said. "He wasn't very pleased."

"I wouldn't expect him to be," Du Vide said. "Any trouble?"

"Not yet," she said, taking a drag. "But we shouldn't trust him."

Du Vide nodded. "Keep a watchful eye on him."

"That won't be a problem," she said.

"Not for you," Du Vide said. "As problems go, though, we have another."

"What now?"

"There was trouble last night at the convent."

"What sort?"

"A vampire broke in."

"What did he do?" The Madame said, leaning back and flicking the ash from her cigarette into a tray on the end table beside her. "Feel up a nun?"

"He took a girl—one of ours."

The Madame grew serious. "Is she dead?"

"I don't know, but the nuns have hired a detective. A man named Nightingale."

"Do you want me to take care of him?"

"That might raise more questions," Du Vide said. "I think it would be best if we discreetly removed any connections."

"What do you mean?"

"The girl didn't arrive alone," he said. "If the detective finds the others, they might lead him to us."

"You want me to kill the other girls?"

"Precisely."

The Madame shook her head. "No," she said. She took a drag and stared into the darkness towards the man.

"It's the cost of doing business," he said.

"That's not our business." The Madame took another drag.

"Then what do you suggest?"

The Madame straightened her posture. "Give me a day," she said. "I'll find him—make sure he doesn't find us."

Du Vide stopped petting the raven as he brought a rough hand to his face and scratched at his scruffy chin. She could feel his eyes on her, looking her over from the darkness, considering her offer.

"Fine," Du Vide finally said. "One day."

"Thank you."

Du Vide set the raven on the cage door. "I'll leave you to it."

Turning, he grabbed his coat and hat, which he had laid over the back of his chair. "See me tonight, tell me how it goes," he said as he shrugged on his coat and walked towards the open door, where the Madame had come in. As he passed, he placed a hand gently on her shoulder. "What would I do without you, Lenora?"

"Much worse," she said, stamping out her cigarette.

PART II

The Traffic of the Dead

CHAPTER 14

WILLIS HAD WORKED THE boats since before dawn. Now nearly noon, he trudged along the docks in the rain, finally taking his break. The wind was cool coming up off the river, mottled gray clouds churned overhead, and fog billowed over the harbor like a witch's cauldron. The big ships docked there groaned as they bobbed in the current.

Other longshoremen, some just starting, unloaded burlap sacks of Colombian coffee, Ecuadorian bananas, and Caribbean cane sugar. They strained and heaved; some paused to wave at Willis as he passed, wiping sweat and rain from their brows.

He nodded at them and mumbled a few "how's-it-goings," and continued down the waterfront to the dock house with his hands in his pockets.

When he arrived, he saw a group of men huddled inside, talking in low, excited tones. Willis pushed his way into the crowd, where Cramer and Toby stood at the center. As Willis stepped into the circle, everyone turned their attention to him.

"What's the hubbub here?" Willis asked.

"Bull's dead," said Toby.

"Bullshit," Willis said.

"It's true," Cramer said. "I heard it from Lazaretto's man myself this morning. He's not one to joke."

"You talked to the mob?"

"Bull was executed," Cramer said. "Because of what he told us—because of the vampires."

An uneasy silence fell over the men, all of whom had been at the Port of Call the night before, until a voice from the doorway broke it.

"The hell is going on here?"

The voice belonged to Eugene Tatopoulos, the foreman, who'd been a good, strong worker once, but spent most of his days now behind a desk in his stuffy little office above the docks, letting his waistline expand and his hairline recede.

"Bull's dead," Toby said again.

"I heard," Tatopoulos said, "which means you all need to pick up the slack."

"We're just taking a minute to mourn," Cramer said.

"I don't have a minute. What I got is a shift tonight that's a man short, so which one of you lazy louses is going to fill it?"

"A shift tonight?" Toby asked.

"That's right?"

"Lazaretto's boats?"

Tatopoulos' face went sour. "I don't know what you're talking about. Anton Lazaretto is not, nor will he ever be, associated with the New Orleans Harbor nor the workers' union here."

"Right, right," said Toby. "But, you know, tonight's shift, it's one of our, uh, special deliveries, isn't it?"

"There's a cash bonus, yes."

The stevedores glanced at one another, uncertain, but none replied. With eyes cast downward, they looked away, like schoolchildren avoiding a teacher's gaze.

"That's how it is, then? No one wants extra pay," Tatopoulos said, turning to leave. "Then get back to work."

The huddle broke. As the men dispersed and Tatopoulos climbed the rickety stairs to his office, Toby and Cramer remained behind with Willis.

"What fool would take that offer after what happened to Bull?" Cramer said.

Toby shook his head slowly.

"Have to be someone who's been here a while," Willis said, mostly to himself.

"What you thinking, Willis?" Cramer asked.

"I'm thinking I'll pick up an extra shift," Willis said as he followed after Tatopoulos.

Eugene Tatopoulos's office was a cramped closet of a room. A battered desk was wedged against one wall, and the foreman had to suck in his gut to squeeze behind it. When opened, the door nearly scraped the desk's edge. An ancient filing cabinet and a bent coat rack squeezed the space even tighter. The room roasted in summer and froze in winter; only on soggy days like this was it comfortable, aside from the leaks dripping into Tatopoulos's array of mugs and trash bins.

Tatopoulos had just taken a seat behind his desk when Willis stepped in, closing the door behind him and squeezing himself in front of the desk.

"What do you need, Willis?" Tatopoulos tried making himself look busy.

"An extra shift."

"What you got in mind?"

"I'm taking your offer."

Tatopoulos stopped his charade and looked up at Willis. "You know I was just saying what I had to down there," he said. "These are Lazaretto's clients."

"I ain't a fool," Willis said, "I've been on these docks longer than you have."

"You ain't ever wanted a hand in Lazaretto's business before," Tatopoulos said. "Why now?"

"Worked out for you, didn't it?" Willis said, looking at the narrow office. "Maybe I just want to get my due."

"Wouldn't think you cared, Willis."

Willis sighed. "Truth is, I got me some debts."

"I never knew you was a gambler," Tatopoulos said, leaning back in his chair, resting his hands across his stomach.

"I like to keep my problems to myself," Willis said. He leaned closer. "And ain't that what you need on that ship tonight? Someone who knows how to keep his mouth shut?"

Tatopoulos thought it over for a moment, breathing out through his nostrils. Then he nodded. "Never thought I'd see the day. But I'd never turn a good worker down, either." He sat forward and rummaged through his top drawer. "The ship comes in late. I still need you here today, so you'll be working double. Go take a long break, but be back in a couple hours to finish this morning's work before the shift tonight. We'll get you set up for the right rotation next time."

"I owe you, Gene," Willis said.

"Just don't let me down," Tatopoulos said. "But first—" he closed his drawer and tossed a matchbook to Willis, who caught it. On the front flap, it read THE HOUSE OF THE RISING SUN. Tatopoulos pointed to it as Willis read the name. "Go get your fortune told."

Waiting across the street from the House of the Rising Sun, Willis put the matchbook back in his pocket. When a car passed, he crossed over and entered the shop.

The fragrance of the place was overwhelming, and he could smell it even before he walked inside. The lights were low, and the heavy drapes that hung from the ceiling made the gray day even darker. A woman behind the counter greeted Willis. She was beautiful, with dark hair and pale skin.

"How can I help you?" she asked.

Willis walked to the counter and set the matchbook down. "I was told I needed to see you," he said. "Eugene Tatopoulos sent me."

The woman smiled. She picked up the matchbook, struck a match, and lit a candle beside her. "You're a man of fortune?" she asked.

Willis nodded. "And I've come to seek my fortune," he said, repeating the line that Tatopoulos had told him to use when the woman asked him a question.

"Very good," the woman said, taking the candle and walking over to the table in the middle of the room. "Then let us see what awaits you."

He followed her to the table and sat across from her, the crystal ball between them. She took out a deck of tarot cards and placed them face down on the tablecloth. As she did, Willis noticed the familiar design from the card Bull had shown him the night before.

"What is your name?" the woman asked.

"Willis," he said. "John Willis."

"I'm Lady Sabine," she said. "And I will tell you your future." Taking his hand in hers, she studied his palm, caressing the deep lines with her finger. "You're a strong man. A hard worker. You've worked all your life."

"Anybody could tell that from looking at my hands."

"You have a good heart, though," she said. "And a brave soul. So, I wonder what it is that brings you to me."

"I'm worried about a friend."

Nodding slowly, Sabine watched him, taking in his presence. "Very well," she said. She took the card from the top of the deck and slid it across the table to Willis, still facing down.

"What's that?" he asked.

"It's yours," she said.

He reached out and flipped the card over. It was the Ten of Wands, the same as the card Bull had shown him the night before. On the other side of the table, Sabine smiled.

"May it bring you good fortune," she said.

CHAPTER 15

CHARLIE STARTLED AWAKE. MOST of his morning had been spent cleaning out the old mausoleum for Vermilion, tossing out Bernardin's bones and sweeping out the years of debris. He had found a moldy mattress in a room upstairs to sleep on and had collapsed on top of it from exhaustion. Now, at midday, rays of gray light came through the gaps of the boarded-up windows. In that haze, he saw the little girl, Juliette, staring at him from the open doorway. Pushing himself up on the rotting bed he'd slept in, Charlie wiped the sleep from his eyes, running a hand over his face.

She watched him silently for a moment, standing still in her blue nightgown, but her illness seemed to have passed. The darkness around her eyes had faded, and the fever didn't seem to bother her.

"What's your name?" she asked. He told her. "Are you a vampire?"

"No," he said.

"Do you want to be?"

Charlie stared at her, uncertain what to think of the little girl standing in the doorway. He dodged her question, asking his own instead. "What do you know about vampires?"

"Almost everything," she said.

"And what about Vermilion?" Charlie asked. "How do you know him?"

"He watches over her." Vermilion's voice carried in from the hall as his shadowy figure stepped into the doorway and placed a hand on the little girl's shoulder.

"Have you met my nephew?"

Juliette nodded. "Yes."

"And what do you make of him?"

"He smells."

"Very true," Vermilion said.

Charlie straightened up. "When are we going to get started, Vermilion?"

"Started?"

"You know, the money and the power."

"Ah," the vampire said. He wrinkled his nose. "After you've cleaned yourself up."

"There's no clothes or water here," Charlie said.

"Find some, then."

"Where?" Charlie said. "Lazaretto's people will be looking all over for me."

"I'm sure you can figure it out," the vampire said, turning the girl and guiding her out of the room. His voice floated back. "We'll await your return."

Charlie looked at himself in a cracked mirror. It was true; he was a mess, covered in mud, moss, and blood. He ran a hand through his matted hair. After putting his shoes back on, he grabbed his coat—the cash and the gun still in the pocket—and Charlie walked to the car. Still tired, he started the engine and pulled away through the long, tree-lined lane, headed for the city.

It rained the whole way to New Orleans, the car chugging along the bumpy, muddy road. He'd have to clean it out, too, he realized. When he was close enough to his apartment, he found a garage, pulled in, and gave the grease monkey a dollar to wipe it down and another five to not ask any questions. The man accepted the money happily, and Charlie told him he'd be back in an hour or two before slipping away into the alley.

At the edge of downtown, Charlie entered the Unser Arms, a seedy high-rise sandwiched between the Business and Warehouse Districts. Avoiding the main entrance, he climbed through a broken basement window and made his way to his apartment on the third floor.

As he crept down the hall, he fished the keys from his pocket and stopped outside his door, 11C, hesitating to put the keys in the lock. Charlie was holding his breath. His hand was shaking, his fingers wrapped tightly around the keys so that they wouldn't jingle. After the last twelve hours, he knew something had to be waiting for him behind that door.

Instead of entering, Charlie slipped back down the stairs and out the basement window, heading straight into a nearby diner. He found a payphone booth just inside and ducked in before anyone noticed the smell. Fishing coins from his pocket, he plinked them into the slot, and when the operator clicked on at the other end, he gave her Petey Beech's number.

The phone buzzed and popped, and when the lines connected, the voice on the other end was groggy.

"Petey?" Charlie asked.

"Who wants to know?"

"It's Charlie."

The voice came awake, and Charlie could hear Petey shoot up in bed. "I thought you was dead."

"Me too," Charlie said.

"How the hell did you get away from Slits?"

"It's a long story, pal," Charlie said. "Come to my place and I'll tell you all about it."

"Your place? It's safe there?"

Charlie brought his hand up to the mouthpiece. "We're gonna find out."

Petey was sweating as he walked towards Charlie's door, the keys in one hand, the other one resting on the big gun tucked into the waist of his pants. He waited for a moment as he took a deep breath, then slid the key into the lock and turned it, stepping into the dark apartment.

At first, there was stillness as Petey walked past the threshold. The blinds were closed over the windows, and he could hear the patter of rain outside. It was a one-room hovel with a narrow bed and a kitchenette, but not much else. As he stepped inside, the door slammed shut, and large, muscled arms like steel cables wrapped around him.

Petey kicked and thrashed, feeling for his revolver, but before he could grab it, the attacker yanked the gun away and tossed it across the room. The assailant forced Petey to the ground with a thud, grabbed the back of his head by the hair, and slammed it against the floorboards, knocking him into a daze. As Petey struggled, a knee dug into his back. He reached out, trying fruitlessly for the gun—it was just too far. A heavy shoe pressed down on his hand, grinding it into the floor. The strong man on top twisted Petey's other arm painfully behind his back, holding it there. Petey yelped.

"Where's Charlie?" the attacker asked, growling the words.

Petey hesitated, asking himself the same question. Where *was* Charlie? He was supposed to be here too, coming up the fire escape, but Petey didn't see a sign of him.

"Where is he?" the attacker asked again.

A jolt of pain seared through Petey as he felt his arm wrenched further behind his back. He was about to cry out that Charlie was outside in the alley as his arm was pulled further behind him.

One more time, the attacker asked angrily. "Where is he?"

"Right here."

Petey heard Charlie's voice. As the attacker eased his grip and the knee lifted from Petey's back, there was a sudden whack—something hard striking something harder. Instantly, the hold on Petey's arms released, and the attacker tumbled backward across the floor, knocked out cold.

Charlie didn't help Petey up. Instead, he stood there, stunned as he stared at the body of Gino Gentil lying across the floor of his apartment.

Scrambling off the ground, Petey looked at the body sprawled across the floor, then back at Charlie. "Holy mackerel. Is he dead?"

"No," said Charlie. "He's breathing."

"What are we gonna do with him?" Petey asked as he walked to the other side of the room to get his gun, tucking it back into place.

"I don't know yet," Charlie said.

"He's a big fish," Petey said, sounding satisfied. "They don't get much bigger than Gino."

Charlie finally blinked away his shock. "We'd better tie him up."

Petey went down to the basement for some rope, while Charlie emptied Gino's pockets. He found a few crumpled bills but not much else, which disappointed him—until he saw the gun holstered under the big man's arm. Charlie drew the heavy automatic, admired the pearl-handled grip, then slipped his old .38 into his pocket. He closed one eye and looked at Gino through the gun's sights.

The door opened as Petey returned, a coil of rope slung over his shoulder. He looked at Charlie's new piece. "That's some pea-shooter," he said. "That Gino's?"

"Mine now," Charlie said.

"To the winner go the spoils," Petey said, chuckling. He handed the rope to Charlie, and both men knelt, tying it around Gino. "What are we gonna do with him?"

"We're taking him," Charlie said. "I got someone I want him to meet."

CHAPTER 16

MAGDALENE AND NIGHTINGALE WERE in the back room of the New Orleans Office of Immigration and Naturalization. It was windowless and poorly lit, full of filing cabinets and shelves. The detective had slipped ten dollars to the man at the front desk, who had quietly hidden it under the mat on his desk and kindly opened the door for them. He hadn't been much help otherwise and left the two of them to sort through the files, most of which hadn't been organized at all—just tossed in a box.

Nightingale had planned to go alone, but Sister Magdalene had insisted on joining. She drove them in her powder blue Studebaker, making small talk as they approached the waterfront. Once inside the back room, Magdalene positioned herself under the lamp and began sifting through a stack of unorganized files, while Nightingale searched with his penlight. Their conversation continued as they worked, trading comments as they pulled records off shelves and inspected paperwork.

"How often do you hunt vampires?" she asked.

"Some weeks there are more than others, like this one."

"It's a whole new world to me," she said. "And you just go about it, like a normal case?"

"There isn't really such a thing as a normal case," Nightingale said. "You're always getting into the life of somebody else. If you do it long enough, you learn to take it in stride."

"Then this is just another case for you?"

Juliette's ticket sat on a shelf, right at eye level. With it sat the tarot card—face-up to show the women in the boat. He looked at it as he spoke. "No," he said. "This one feels different."

"Different how?" she asked, taking her eyes off the files for just a moment to glance at the card too.

"I'm still not sure why a vampire would go to so much trouble," he said. "In this city, they've got plenty of victims to choose from—it seems like a lot of work to steal a girl from a convent."

"Maybe he wasn't just looking to feed."

"That's the other thing," Nightingale said. "I don't know why else he'd want her. Vampires don't really keep pets."

"What do they do?"

He looked at the nun, pausing for a moment. "They're debaucherous, we'll say."

"You don't have to hold back because I'm clergy, detective. We do live in the world, too."

"We don't need the details anyway," he said, half-smiling back.

"What else can you tell me about them?" she said. "That tarot card you found, do vampires use those often?"

"More and more each day," Nightingale said, returning to the box of files he was searching through. "But that's what makes this case strange, too—vampires don't organize."

"What do you mean?"

"I mean, there's no conglomerate, no secret council. Secret codes and stuff like this—" he tapped the card on the shelf. "That's not what vampires do."

"Then I suppose somebody must be helping them," Magdalene said.

Nightingale nodded. "I'm hoping that's what we find out."

There was a roll of thunder outside, and they could hear the muffled bellow of fog horns from the ships going in and out of the harbor. Magdalene sat up. "I think this is it," she said.

Nightingale straightened up and crossed to where Magdalene sat, lifting his penlight to better illuminate the stack of papers in her hands. Magdalene set the file on the shelf in front of her, flipped it open, and together they leaned toward the pages as Nightingale held the light steady.

"You have the ticket?" she asked.

Nightingale reached back to where he'd been standing and picked the ticket up, handing it to the sister, who set it down beside the ledger. He pointed to the name of the ship. "Look for the Myrkranna," he said.

Magdalene nodded, and Nightingale watched over her shoulder as she flipped through the pages of manifests, looking at the names of the ships and the dates they docked. There were dozens of ships, each of them holding passengers.

"Here it is," she said, putting her finger on the page. "The steamship Myrkranna. It left from Tangiers, arrived in New Orleans on Monday, September 22."

Nightingale looked at the ticket. "That looks right," he said.

"It says the ship was chartered by a company, Apophrades Incorporated."

"Same as the ticket," Nightingale said. "Is her name on the list?"

The sister flipped the page over, looking at the loose papers that had been clipped to the back, angling them under Nightingale's light. She ran her finger down a column of names, all written with an elaborate hand, the cursive letters full of swoops and flourishes. She stopped when she saw the girl's name.

"Juliette Cantrell," she said. "Twelve years of age, and she has the convent's address listed as her destination."

Nightingale looked at the names below Juliette's. There were three other young girls—fifteen, sixteen, and seventeen. "You think they traveled with her?"

"Anne-Marie Decuir, Louisa Lavoie, and Antonia Havron," Magdalene said, reading the names. "They're certainly French, too."

The sister began flipping through the rest of the papers that had been attached to the manifest.

"What do you have there?" Nightingale asked.

"Exit visas, I think," Magdalene said. She pulled four of the papers out of the stack and set them on the desk. "One for each of those girls, granting them permission to leave Europe and travel to the U.S." Concern furrowed her brow as she studied the documents.

"What's wrong, sister?"

She pointed to the signature at the bottom of the page on Juliette's visa. "This was sponsored by the church," she said. "That's a Catholic seal beside the signature here." She pointed to the bottom of each visa, noting that the signature and seal matched on all of them.

"The Church was bringing these girls over?"

"I knew we were taking some of them in," she said, "but I didn't realize we were responsible for bringing them over." She looked up at Nightingale, troubled. "Is someone in the Church involved?"

Nightingale scratched at his chin. "Maybe that's what Sister Agnès was getting at," he said. He looked back at the manifest in his hand. "We need to talk to these other girls."

Magdalene took the page and reviewed it. "Where are they staying?"

"They've got a different address than Juliette listed."

"I know it," she said. "The Sacred Heart Academy—it's a boarding school. We send the girls from the orphanage there when they're old enough. The church helps pay for it."

Grabbing a pen and a loose scrap of paper, Nightingale began writing down the names of the other girls and their ages. "The church seems to pay for a lot of this," he said.

"I know," said Magdalene. "That's what worries me."

CHAPTER 17

THE POLICE STATION WAS a two-story building of grey stone, with bars on the windows and a wrought-iron gate around the front. Heavy columns beneath the eaves made the place look imposing and brutish, and the rain made it look like it was bleeding.

Madame Lovebite walked through the open gate and entered the tall front doors into the vestibule, where a policeman sat reading the sports section at the desk. Behind him, in the station, she could hear the clatter of typewriters and the laughter of men.

She breezed past the officer, who opened his mouth to stop her until he realized who she was, then quickly put his head down, hoping she hadn't seen his mistake. Gaggles of cops, huddled around desks, turned to watch her as she strutted through the office, head held high and confident on her slender neck, never once meeting their gaze.

Pearson's office was on the second floor, towards the corner along a row of other, identical offices, all with pebbled glass and barred windows that opened just enough to let a draft in. The Madame entered without knocking.

Pearson leaned back in his chair behind his desk. His window was open, so he could hear the rain and feel the breeze.

The fan mounted on the high ceiling rattled overhead, keeping the air moving. Another officer, half sitting on Pearson's desk, watched the Madame as she entered.

As she walked in, unannounced, Pearson snapped up into a straight back. "Beat it," he said to the other cop, who did as he was told.

Detective Pearson was a clean-shaven man in his mid-thirties who looked ten years younger than he was, with round cheeks, brown hair, and no signs of weariness. He was handsome, if not boyish, and he wore a dark suit that almost fit him perfectly.

The Madame sat down, crossing her legs. Pearson straightened his tie, chuckled nervously, and smiled. "My lucky day," he said. "I thought I might be seeing you."

"Oh?"

He nodded, opening his desk drawer and pulling out a tarot card. He slid it across the table to her, and she took it in her gloved fingers.

"Found that on a dead man today," he said. "You should be more careful."

"Nobody knows what it means."

"My partner thought it was interesting."

"I'm sure you took care of that."

"Of course," Pearson said. "But still, we find too many of those, and people might ask questions."

"There shouldn't be a reason to find any more."

Leaning back in his chair, Pearson took a cigarette from the pack on his desk and lit it. "My superior skills of detection tell me that wasn't what you came here to talk about," he said.

"You never cease to impress, Pearson," the Madame said. "I'm wondering if you know a man."

"You got a name for him?"

"Nightingale," she said.

"Oh boy," Pearson said, shaking his head and blowing smoke. "Been hearing that name a lot today."

"You know him?"

"Not personally, but he was on the force here some years back. A lot of the guys around here know him. He worked with my partner, in fact. I know he had some sort of scandal, but it didn't seem to tarnish his reputation."

"Who's been talking about him?"

"Some nutjob who got pulled out of a burning building last night. Name's Grange, I think. He's been talking crazy."

"Crazy how?"

"Says vampires made him kill a bunch of prostitutes from the district."

"And Nightingale?"

"Grange says he was there, too. Says he killed the vampire and nearly killed him."

"Is that true?"

"Beats me," Pearson said, shrugging. "Honestly, I don't think they even wasted their time asking."

The Madame nodded slowly. "I want to talk to Grange," she said.

Pearson choked on the smoke as he took a drag. The cough turned into a laugh. "He's a psycho. What would you want to talk to him about?"

"Business."

"That might be tough," Pearson said as he plucked the cigarette from his mouth. "It's a different precinct; I don't know the guys there so well."

"We'll pay," the Madame said.

Pearson shrugged and grabbed the phone from his desk. "Let me make a few calls."

After a fiver to the man at the front desk and a fifty to the detective working the case, the Madame sat in a drab, gray room in the basement of the Fifth District, where she could hear the muffled howl of prisoners and the police who yelled at them to quiet down. Pearson paced the room with her while they waited, smoking another cigarette, tossing it to the ground, and grinding it out under his shoe when the door finally opened.

Grange came in first, sallow, head drooped, and hands cuffed. Detective Larrabee—a mustachioed cop in a wrinkled shirt with a loose tie—came in after him, pushing the prisoner down into a chair, cuffing Grange to the table.

Pearson put his arm around the other detective and said, "Come show me where you boys keep the coffee in this place."

Larrabee looked over his shoulder at the Madame. "You just want to leave her alone with this creep?"

Pearson shrugged. "She's his lawyer, remember? We can't be eavesdropping." He looked back at the Madame. "Besides, she can handle herself."

The two policemen left, closing the door behind them, leaving the Madame alone with Grange sitting across from one another over a featureless metal table. The Madame sat straight, ankles crossed, turning slightly to rest one arm on the back of her chair. Grange sat with his head hung low, staring at the floor. Slowly, he lifted his head to meet the Madame's gaze, her eyes unwavering when he looked up.

"I didn't know I had a lawyer."

"I'm not her," she said.

Grange looked confused. "Then you aren't here to help me?"

"That depends," she said, "on whether or not you help me first."

"What kind of help?"

"Answers."

"I don't know nothing."

"I think you do," she said, pointing to the bandage on his neck. It was grimy and needed to be changed.

"I already fell for that," Grange said. "Cops been talking to me all morning, just for a laugh."

"I'm different."

"Yeah?" Grange asked spitefully. "Different how?"

Slowly, theatrically, the Madame pulled off the glove from her right hand and laid it on the table. She hiked up her sleeve past the elbow and leaned forward, holding out her tattooed arm for Grange to see clearly. Above the bloody dagger along her forearm was a set of disembodied teeth, the canines elongated and sharp—the teeth of a vampire. "Different enough to know what's out there."

Grange's eyes widened in surprise, and he leaned forward like a hungry dog. "You one of them?"

"No," the Madame said, bringing her sleeve back down into place. "But I work with them." She pulled her glove back over her hand. "Tell me what happened. Tell me about the man called Nightingale."

"That rat bastard," Grange said under his breath. He looked up and met the Madame's gaze. "He's the one who done this to me." Grange reached up to his neck with his shackled hands and pulled the grimy bandage down to reveal the fresh brand. The shape of the cross was ragged, but distinct. Grange's neck was a mess of puffy, angry flesh. "He's an ugly sonuvabitch with a big nasty scar down his neck. Only his isn't a cross."

"Tell me about the scar."

"Says he got it killing a vampire," Grange said. "That's what he does. He hunts them down and kills them."

"Why?"

"For money," Grange said. "Those girls hired him."

"What girls?"

"The whores. From the District. They're the ones who hired Nightingale."

"You're certain?"

"That's what he said to the one I got last night. The cops don't believe me that he was there; they think it was that whore who beat me up." Grange was speaking faster, more agitated, his voice rising with every word. "Like she could even try." He began coughing violently, hacking into his shackled hands. The Madame sat across from him, watching in disgust.

"You're sick," she said when Grange's fit was over.

"That's why I needed the vampire. He was going to cure me."

"I'm sure," the Madame said flatly. "Is that all you know about Nightingale?"

"You'd have to ask the whores to know anything else."

"I will," she said.

"Now what about me?"

"What about you?"

"You said you would help me. I answered your questions. Now what are you going to do for me?" Grange stared at her like a hungry animal from the other side of the table, his slack-jaw curling into a disgusting smile.

"Of course," she said, reaching into her purse and producing her tarot cards. "Have you ever had your fortune told?"

Grange shook his head. He was confused again. "I ain't ever had much fortune to tell, ain't got much future left either."

"It's not about the future," the Madame said. "And it has nothing to do with wealth. It's about insight. It's about helping you make choices." She placed the cards, face down, on the table. "Choices that make things easier for you."

Grange looked surprised for a moment, making the Madame pause. "Is everything all right?" she asked.

"Where'd you get them cards?"

The Madame narrowed her eyes. "Why do you ask?"

"I seen one before."

"A tarot card?"

"Yeah, but just like that, with the bats and all on the back."

"Where?"

Grange lowered his voice and leaned in. "Nightingale had it. Asked me what it meant right before he put this brand on my neck."

"And what did you tell him?"

"Nothing," Grange said, shaking his head. "It's all I knew."

"Good," she said.

"What are they for?" he asked.

"They're for our friends," she said, shuffling the cards and placing three of them face down on the table before turning them over. "The Wheel of Fortune, the Five of Pentacles, and the Three of Swords."

"What do they mean?" Grange asked eagerly.

"Bad fortune follows you," she said, her face turning grim. "Time and again, try as you might, you have always failed." She pointed to the Five of Pentacles. "Sometimes it was your own fault, sometimes it was the actions of others. Either way, you've been left alone, abandoned, shut out."

Grange's face folded into dismay. "Is there any hope for me?"

The Madame shook her head. "I see pain, drawn out longer than it should. Your lungs will tear themselves apart and you'll cough out the bits of yourself little by little until you die, in agony, gasping for breath and choking on your own bloody phlegm."

Grimacing, Grange brought his shackled hands up to his face, holding it. "I knew it," he said, beginning to sob. The sobs turned to coughs.

"There is only death for you." She pointed to the last card, the Three of Swords. This one had a heart suspended in a storm of gray clouds and pierced bloodlessly by three blades. "Either by their hands," she said, turning the card to face Grange and sliding it towards him, "or by yours."

Grange, raising his head from his hands, looked at her, confused. "My own?" he asked.

"Even a man whose life has been entirely out of his control still has a choice on how it ends," she said. "You need not know the agony that awaits you."

As Grange sat thinking across from her, the Madame gathered up the other two cards, leaving the Three of Swords in front of the dying man. She tucked them back into her purse and started to leave.

"Don't you need this one?" Grange said.

"No," the Madame said. "That one's for you.

"I thought these were just for your friends."

"They are," she said, feigning a smile.

Grange raised his shackled hands once more, grasping the card. As he raised it, he saw—hidden on the table beneath the card—a double-edge razor blade.

"Goodbye, Grange," the Madame said as she opened the door and exited to the hall.

Outside, Pearson and Larrabee were waiting for her, making small talk, holding paper cups of coffee, laughing about something. As the Madame sauntered away from the room, the two men looked up at her.

"I'm finished," she said, and Larrabee nodded.

"He give you what you needed?"

The Madame shook her head. "He's insane."

"I told you he was a nut job," he said to Pearson.

Pearson put out his hand. "There's just no saving some people."

Larrabee gave Pearson a handshake and gave a cordial nod to the Madame. "If you wait here, I can show you two out."

Pearson began to accept, but the Madame cut him off. "Thank you, Detective Larrabee, but we wouldn't want to trouble you further. We'll find our own way."

Larrabee shrugged and nodded. "Then I'll see you around," he said, mostly to Pearson, and then walked back into the interrogation room.

"How'd it go?" Pearson asked.

"He's filth," she said. "But he won't be a problem."

"What does that mean?"

"It means we need to leave."

Pearson put out his hand, gesturing dramatically for the Madame to lead the way. They were outside before they heard the alarm.

Somewhere deep in the precinct's lockup, Grange was bleeding out on the floor of his cell—a razor blade dangling from his limp fingers, and a tarot card, spattered with his blood, lay carelessly beneath the bed, unnoticed by all the officers.

CHAPTER 18

FRANKLIN BONAPARTE SAT AT the counter. He'd spent the morning making a few calls to collectors, the ones interested in Voodoo and tarot. None had seen a card like the one he described, but they were all eager to buy if he found a set. He thanked them all and told them he'd drop a line if he found something; they agreed to do the same.

He'd skimmed through a stack of books about tarot and fortune telling, searching for anything that might tell him more about the cards. But even in his own library, he came up empty. Frustrated, he pushed the books aside. He needed a break.

The bell above the door rang as it opened. The man who stepped inside was stocky, older, haggard. His face was creased with heavy wrinkles. His hands looked hard from years of labor.

"Hello," Bone said as the man approached.

The man, looking lost, pointed at the box beside Bone marked VAMPIRE WARDS.

"How much are those?"

Bone raised an eyebrow, leaned on the counter, and handed over a pouch. "You seem like a man with a specific problem."

The older man shrugged. "Just a rumor."

"Plenty of those in this city."

"Too many," said the man. He extended his hand. "Name's Willis," he said. "John Willis."

Bone took the man's hand. "I'm the one they call Dr. Bone."

"I know. Folks say you're the man to see about things like this," Willis said, lifting the bag. "These things really work?"

"Never had a customer say they didn't," Bone said, then added, with a smile, "Of course, if they didn't work, I don't suppose they'd come back either."

Willis chuckled uneasily. "I ain't ever bought something like this in my life."

"Not a superstitious man?"

"Oh, plenty superstitious, just never believed in monsters."

"What brings you round here, then?"

"Well," Willis said, looking around, embarrassed. "A guy I know got killed last night."

"By a vampire?"

"No, well, not exactly," Willis said. "He got shot."

Bone laughed this time. "Friend, I can tell you right now, as much as I'd like to sell you something, I don't think anything in my shop's gonna work against that, least of all what you got in your hand."

"Don't I know it," Willis said. "But the thing is, last night, before he got killed, my friend, Bull, was going on about vampires. Said he's seen them on the docks. Now, I don't know why he got shot, but I can't seem to shake what he was telling me. Almost like his dying made his story seem more real."

"Almost like someone's trying to keep him quiet?"

"Exactly," Willis said. "I'm taking his shift tonight, and I want to make sure I'm safe, just in case he wasn't telling tales."

"Well then," Bone said, leaning forward on the counter, putting on his salesman smile. "What you have there's got everything you'll need to vanquish any undead foe: holy water, a cross, garlic extract, a rosary, and a big ol' wooden stake that you gotta plunge right into the heart of whatever evil thing is chasing you."

"And that'll do it? A stake to the heart?"

"You act like that's an easy thing."

"Guess you're right," Willis chuckled. "I ain't ever done nothing like that."

"Me either, friend," said Bone. "I've got people who do that for me."

"Think your people might be able to help?"

"Maybe. He's very particular.

"What's his name?"

"Nightingale. Sebastian Nightingale," Bone said. "But before he helps, he's got to make sure what he's going after is the type of thing that needs killing."

"If Bull was telling the truth, then I guarantee these things need it bad."

"Next time I see my boy, I'll send him around, have him take a look. In the meantime," Bone pointed to the bag of vampire wards Willis had in his hands, "You gonna want to take that, keep yourself safe?"

"Absolutely," Willis said, putting it on the counter and reaching for his wallet.

"Excellent choice," Bone said, opening the cash register, which chimed cheerfully.

As Willis was digging for dollar bills, he looked at the stack of books about tarot. "You tell fortunes here, too?"

"No, sir," Bone said. "Just a recent interest. Are you in need of spiritual guidance as well?"

Willis shook his head. "I don't want to know whatever's coming," he said. "But you know about tarot cards?"

"A bit more than I did this morning."

"Can you tell me what this one means?"

Willis pulled the tarot card from his wallet, the one Lady Sabine had given him, and passed it to Bone.

"The Ten of Wands," Bone said. "It's about burdens and hard work, that sort of thing. A single card doesn't mean much, though. Tarot's all about context."

As he handed the card back, he turned it over. Bone stopped, shocked by the familiar Romani designs and two bats flapping across the night sky. His tone changed—joviality and salesmanship gone. His voice was tight and firm. "Where'd you get this?"

"They said I needed it for tonight." Willis put a few crumpled bills on the counter.

Bone lowered the card, placed his hands on Willis's money, and slid it back. "Friend," he said, "this one's on me."

CHAPTER 19

THE ST. LOUIS CATHEDRAL's pale facade looked ashen in the dreary light of the rainy afternoon. It was the tallest structure around Jackson Square, and its three spires pierced the mottled sky. The tallest, the bell tower, was crowned with an imposing, black cross that was almost lost in the fog that had settled over the city.

Toby stared up at it. He'd passed the alley where they'd found Bull that morning. He hadn't really meant to end up there, but he had. As he wandered the city at lunch, his mind circled what had happened and his part in it. He didn't feel guilty, exactly, but disliked that his last memory of Bull was him storming off, angry at something he and Cramer had done.

He'd been raised going to church; his mama always insisted on it. They'd get dressed in their best clothes for mass. He'd never really understood it, but it always eased his mind. He'd see familiar faces, all praying, acting kind towards his family, always pretending his father wasn't at home, sleeping off a bender.

That's what brought him back, from time to time, when he found himself thinking too much. He'd wander back to the familiar, welcoming feeling, and sometimes it would remind him of his younger days, when things were simpler, and he could go back to not thinking so much.

Toby climbed the stone steps and opened the heavy wooden doors. He took off his hat as he entered, twisting it in his grip. The pews held a scattering of parishioners, kneeling in prayer, heads bowed, hands desperately clutching their rosaries as they mouthed their devotions.

The tall, arched ceilings of the nave were intricate, and a gallery overlooked the pews. Toby moved quietly down the center aisle, headed for the altar. He paused near the confessional booths and scanned the schedule. Relief ran through him when he saw Father Renault's name.

In the last few years, Father Renault had been a presence around the docks. He'd worked bread and soup lines, offering food to the longshoremen during strikes, helping them make ends meet for their families, even the guys who never came to church. He offered prayers and even dipped into the church coffers when there wasn't enough work for the laborers. Toby had always liked him; the priest reminded him of growing up.

He stepped inside the dark confessional, sitting uncomfortably in the small, wooden space. The window between the two booths slid open, and Toby could just see the familiar face of Father Renault sitting on the other side.

"Afternoon, Father. Uh, bless me, for I have sinned. It's been—" Toby paused and whistled. "Well, it's been a good long while since my last confession." Toby caught his breath after speaking, and Father Renault remained silent. "I been drinking too much, and cussing, and I've felt lustful feelings towards some women." Toby continued. "But what's really bothering me today is, well, I've got this nasty feeling. A friend of mine, a man on the docks, he ended up dead this morning. They shot him right outside the cathedral, matter of fact. He was a good man, hard worker. But I was giving him a hard time right before he died."

"Who was your friend?" Father Renault asked.

"Bull. Bull Buford. Worked with me at the docks."

"And what did you say to him that's made you feel this way?"

"He was talking crazy talk," Toby said. "Saying things that didn't make sense. Talking about, well, talking about vampires and such."

"Vampires?"

"I know, Father, it's crazy, them's kids' stories and that. That's what I was razzing him about. But, Father, honest, I think that might be why he died."

"And what makes you think that?"

"Because other men have come around, asking things about them, too. Asking about Bull and the things he said. I ain't been too involved, but my friends have. Cramer, well, he's been talking to them all morning, telling them all the things Bull's said. And to be honest, I'm scared for him now, too. He's getting mixed up in things, and I don't think he should be—I don't think I should be either."

"That's a wise choice," Father Renault said. "But, tell me, who has been asking, and what did Cramer say?"

Chapter 20

Gino was quiet in the trunk, and Petey slept most of the drive back to the Green Manor—Charlie was grateful for both. He breathed a sigh of relief when he turned from the road to the long driveway. Petey blinked himself awake on the rutted road as they passed the overgrown trees. Charlie pulled around the fountain and parked, stretching as he stepped out of the car.

"Hoo boy." Petey stepped out and stared up at the house. "Your family owned this place?"

"Yeah," Charlie said.

"Why don't you fix it up, live here?"

"Look at it."

"I am, it's huge. You'd be like a king or something," Petey said. "It must have been quite the place back in the day—does it have a name? All these big places had names."

Charlie walked briskly to the back of the car. "It's the Mansion of Worms."

Petey frowned. "Not much of a name for a place like this."

"It's the name it deserves," Charlie said. "Now help me unload this guy."

Petey joined him at the trunk. Charlie pulled the gun from his trousers, popped the hatch, and eyed the lump bundled in the rug. He poked the shape with the barrel of his gun—no reaction. He jabbed again, harder; still nothing. Charlie tucked the gun away and grabbed one side of the rug as Petey took the other. They hoisted it out of the trunk and carried it through to the front door of the once-grand manor.

The house was quiet. Vermilion must have gone back outside to his brother's coffin, and Charlie had no idea where the girl might be—probably sleeping too. But even the frogs and snakes seemed to have disappeared.

"Where we taking this guy?" Petey asked, hefting his end of the rug.

"Out back," Charlie said. "I saw a cellar out there earlier. We can stash him in there."

They walked through the house, exiting out the back, where they could hear the faint buzz from a swarm of mosquitoes somewhere above the dense overgrowth of the lawn. Charlie glanced at the graveyard and the mausoleum where Vermilion slept. He turned, leading Petey to the side of the back porch, where the cellar door was hidden in the bramble. He tore the plants away and flung the wooden doors open. Stone steps led beneath the house, into the impenetrable black below.

With Gino between them, Charlie descended first. At the base, he snatched the lantern from a post, heard oil slosh, and flicked his lighter to spark the thick wick. The basement was as sprawling as a catacomb, broken up into a grid of rooms separated by dense rock walls and supported by wide stone columns. Cobwebs gathered in every corner, hanging down like drapes. It smelled like damp earth and decay, and the dirt floor was pockmarked with muddy puddles.

Holding the lantern, Charlie had the rug tucked under his other arm, and they went deeper into the cellar. They passed the coal shoot and large furnace, cold storage rooms—some of which had broken furniture piled inside of them—and a meat locker where bones had been discarded and the shriveled carcass of a pig lay on the floor. Whether it had been left behind or if the poor animal had wandered in and gotten lost, Charlie wasn't sure.

They stopped in the room beneath the kitchen, where a short flight of stone steps led up to the plantation house. They dropped Gino to the floor, and Charlie opened the door, allowing some light to enter. He hung the lantern on a rusty hook, giving them a bit more.

Unrolling the rug, they hoisted Gino up, tying his hands to one of the rafters with a discarded chain they'd found in the old meat locker. It groaned with the weight of the man suspended from it, dirt and dust falling to the ground. Gino hung with his feet dangling just above the ground.

"Where's the guy you want to show him to?" Petey said, dusting off his hands.

"He's resting, I think," Charlie said.

"Don't you want to go get him, show him what you've got for him?"

"Show me what?" Vermilion's voice came from the darkness behind them.

Charlie and Petey both jumped, turning towards the door as Vermilion stepped into the light.

"I didn't know you were there," Charlie said.

"I've been watching," said the vampire as he came closer, circling the men. He walked close to Gino's body, circling it. "Wondering what you've brought me."

"That's Gino Gentil," Charlie said. "He works for Anton Lazaretto."

"Those names are significant?"

"You ain't heard of Lazaretto?" Petey said. "You fresh around here?"

Vermilion looked at Petey. "And what is this?"

"He's a friend," Charlie said. "He helped me bag Gino."

"I'm sure you'll make yourself useful," Vermilion said, uninterested. He returned to Gino's body, holding the man's chin in his icy grip.

"I was thinking about what you said about needing cash," Charlie said. "I think this guy can get it for us."

"How?"

"Ransom," Charlie said. "Gino is one of Lazaretto's top guys, and Lazaretto is loaded. He'd pay anything to get him back."

"Lazaretto?"

"He's a gangster," Charlie said.

"He's ruthless," Petey added. "He runs the whole city."

"The club you were at last night," Charlie said. "That's Lazaretto's place—one of them, anyway."

"Ruthless, you say?" Vermilion said, still studying Gino's face.

"Yeah," Charlie said, "But don't worry about that. I figure that's where you come in. You've already offed a couple of his guys. With you around, they won't be trouble. Lazaretto is sure to pay."

"We should ask him," Vermilion said, letting Gino's head drop.

"If you can get him up," Charlie said, shrugging.

The vampire reached up and grabbed Gino's wrist, digging his sharp fingernail into it. Blood began to trickle down, and the big man stirred back to consciousness, crying out in pain.

Vermilion stepped away, back near the shadows as Gino's gaze landed on Charlie.

"You little rat bastard," Gino said, snarling. "I'm gonna kill you."

"You're Anton Lazaretto's man," Vermilion said, standing at the edge of the light. "Yes?"

"If you think you can get to him through me, you're wrong."

"Would he pay for you?" Vermilion asked.

Gino laughed. "Lazaretto wouldn't pay a single red cent. Especially not to this one." He nodded towards Charlie. "He'll cut every one of you down—and he'll make it slow."

"He's a killer, then," Vermilion said.

"A butcher," Gino replied, his lip curling up like a growling dog's.

"And you kill for him, too?"

"More men than you can count."

"How fortunate."

"Fortunate?" Charlie asked.

The vampire turned to him. "There's more than ransom in this."

"Then what are we supposed to do with him?" Charlie furrowed his brow.

"Fret not," Vermilion said, smiling as he licked Gino's blood from his hand. "He still has a use."

The vampire's eyes trailed back up to the hanging man as small, dainty hands wrapped around Gino's body from the back, climbing up his torso and latching onto his neck. Gino thrashed, trying to turn, trying to see who—or what—was behind him, but his hands were too tightly bound for him to move. He kicked his legs frantically, but to no avail. The hands tightened around his neck, and the small body pulled itself up until the face of the thing came up behind him, young and innocent. It was the face of Juliette—her long, blonde hair cascading down her shoulders as she clung to the man, her legs wrapped around his midsection. She dug her nails into Gino's flesh, grabbing his head and wrenching it back to expose his neck. She bared her fangs, happily, hungrily, giggling in glee.

As she plunged her teeth into Gino's neck, he let out a gurgling howl of pain while Vermilion gave a hearty basso laugh and Petey looked on in silent, petrified horror.

"What are you doing?" Charlie asked.

"I'll tell you," Vermilion said. "But first, we'll need a bag."

CHAPTER 21

AFTER SOME COAXING AND a few bills from Nightingale's wallet, the headmistress of the Sacred Heart Academy proved to be helpful. She handed over everything she had about the girls: their records of transition, admittance papers, and photos. Each of them had already been placed in affluent homes, working as maids or au pairs, earning a small wage along with room and board as they learned the skills believed to make them useful to society. "No drains on the system," the headmistress had said as she gave Nightingale and Magdalene the addresses each of the girls was staying at.

As they left the school and walked back to the car, Magdalene flipped through the files.

"Anne-Marie is in Lakewood, Louisa is in Audubon, and Antonia is in the Garden District," she said.

"Let's start with Antonia, then," Nightingale said. "She's the closest, and I've got a friend over in the Garden District we can see—I think you'll like him."

"What does your friend do?"

"He's in antiques."

"Not vampires?"

"A bit," Nightingale said, getting into the car. "But he's on the commission side of things."

"How does it work?" Magdalene asked as she climbed into the driver's seat and started the car. "Your business, I mean. How do you get clients?"

Nightingale answered as they started for Antonia's. "My friend I was telling you about sends a lot of it my way," he said. "He has a bit of a reputation for dealing with the occult. Whenever something suspicious comes his way, he lets me know."

"He's your fixer, then?"

"Exactly," Nightingale said, with a smile. "I get paid, and he takes a cut—a finder's fee."

"How benevolent," Magdalene said.

The detective chuckled. "Good deeds don't pay the bills."

"How did you even get started in this business?"

"Been in it a long time," Nightingale said. "Even when I was a cop. Knowing about vampires let me pick up on things the other cops missed. So, I'd take care of it."

"You'd kill them?"

"What else should I have done?"

Magdalene was silent for a moment as she considered. "I don't know," she said. "I suppose you had to kill them."

"Judges and juries aren't exactly equipped for this sort of thing," he said. "Death is the only way to deal with them."

"Do you ever feel guilty about it?"

"Should I?" Nightingale asked.

"They're living beings—or something close to that, right? Surely, they don't want to die."

"They're monsters," he said. "They drink blood and make other vampires. I don't feel any worse than I do swatting a mosquito."

Magdalene nodded pensively. "I don't know if I could do it," she said. "Even knowing what they are, I don't know if I could end a life."

"You don't end theirs, then they'll end someone else's. I'd rather have their blood on my hands than their victims'."

Silence fell between them as the radio warbled on and rain continued to fall, plinking atop the roof of the car, the windshield wiper squeaking across the windshield.

"How did you end up in New Orleans, detective?"

Nightingale chuckled. "Vampires, of course. I had a friend down here who needed some help with one. Turns out, there's a lot of them down here, so I stayed. I transferred onto the force, and when I was tired of that, I started my practice."

"How long ago was that?"

"Almost a decade now."

"And you like it?"

"I do," Nightingale said. "And what about you? How did you end up in this place?"

"That's a simple question with a long answer, detective," the sister said.

"I guess it'll have to wait, then," Nightingale said. "We're here."

The tall trees of the Garden District made the place seem darker beneath the gloomy sky than it should have been. Beautiful homes were set back from the street, hidden behind wrought-iron fences and tall brick walls covered in vibrant ivy. Magdalene made the final turn and parked in front of the home where Antonia had been sent.

It was an old-money mansion, three stories tall, white as alabaster. Dressed in Victorian details, the house was framed by slender columns, and plants overgrowing their hanging baskets filled the spaces between them. The sidewalk was bordered with neatly trimmed hedges that had grown a foot higher than the ornate fence in front. The yard was filled with willow trees, their drooping branches hanging down to the ground like the hair of a drowned woman. Shrouded in the foggy, dismal day, the house looked gloomy and lonesome.

The gate was open, and the two of them took the long path to the house together. Nightingale and Magdalene stepped onto the porch, which wrapped around the whole of the home, and stopped outside the double doors. Magdalene rang the doorbell; they could hear the chimes inside, but no one answered.

Nightingale peered through the window beside the door, which was covered in a curtain made of lace and sheer. Through it, he could make out the fuzzy shapes of the interior—but nothing moved.

"Try again," he said, still looking through the window, holding his hand up above his eye to block the glare. Magdalene rang the bell, but still no one came.

"Perhaps they're out," Magdalene said.

"The lights are on," he replied.

"Some people leave them on."

"Maybe," Nightingale said as he stepped away from the window and knocked briskly on the door. The door popped open and slowly creaked ajar. He looked at Magdalene doubtfully. "But I don't know many who leave their house unlocked."

Nightingale pushed the door open wider and put a foot across the threshold. Magdalene's hand shot out, grabbing his forearm.

"What are you doing?" she said in a quick whisper.

"Investigating."

"Investigating what?"

"We'll see," he said, shaking his arm loose and walking inside. "Hello?" he said, his voice echoing in the entry. "The door was open; is there anyone home?"

Silence. Just as before, there was no sound or movement—only the gentle, rhythmic ticking of the grandfather clock that stood against the wall near the stairs.

"Sebastian," Magdalene said, still standing outside. "I don't know about this."

The detective waved her in. "Come on," he said. "Close the door."

As Magdalene did, she turned to Nightingale. "I don't think we should be here."

"Me either," he said, stepping further into the house. "Something doesn't feel right." He left the entryway, stepping into the hall, the grand staircase ahead of them. To the left, he could see a library, and to the right, there was a sitting room. He turned to the left, peeking in at the shelves of leatherbound volumes. Magdalene went to the right. When she gasped, Nightingale spun around. Her hand covered her horrified expression; her eyes were wide with shock.

Antonia was there, on the floor beside a toppled chair, a puddle of blood beneath her. The young girl's face was expressionless, as still as the photo they had of her. Eyes open, she looked like a wax figure trapped in her final moment of distress. Dressed in a maid's uniform, her hair pulled back tightly, the only color she had was from the deep, red gash that ran from ear to ear below her jaw.

"My God," Magdalene whispered, her hand falling from her mouth. "Who would have done this?"

"I don't know," Nightingale said. "Let's take a look."

"Shouldn't we call the police?" she asked.

"We will," he said. "Once we're finished."

He crouched beside the girl, inspecting the slice across her neck. It was a fine, clean line right across the throat, severing the arteries. The blade was so sharp, she may not have even felt the fatal cut. Whether she felt it or not, the end of her life had not been pleasant. Her lip was split from a blow to the face, and beneath the cut, deep bruises marked her neck. Her arms were marked too, where someone had held her down. Her hands were scraped and bloody from fighting back. He shook his head, disgusted.

"Poor thing," Magdalene said, crouching beside the girl, taking her lifeless hand in her own.

Nightingale examined the room and the signs of struggle there—a shattered vase, an overturned plant pot, a corner of the rug scrunched up, and a red, crescent-shaped mark that could have been from the heel of a shoe. He touched it, and his fingers came away wet.

"What is that?" Magdalene asked.

"Blood," he said. "A footprint." He looked ahead and saw a second mark, and a third, and then a whole line of them beyond that, each one lighter than the one before it until they reached the stairs and disappeared. "And they go that way," he said, pointing.

The two of them followed the tracks, stopping at the wide base of the staircase, and looking up at the dark hallway above.

"The killer's?" Magdalene asked.

Nightingale nodded.

"Should we follow?"

He looked at her apologetically. "We have to."

She gave him a firm nod and linked her arm through his as they ascended.

The upstairs hall was dark; the doors were closed, and the lights were off. Nightingale and Magdalene paused on the landing. The sister opened her mouth to speak, but stopped when she heard the click of a door latch somewhere down the hall. She tightened her grip on Nightingale's arm and whispered.

"What was that?"

Nightingale pulled the heavy revolver slung beneath his arm. He looked back at the bloody footprints they'd followed up and his eyes flicked to Magdalene. "I don't think we're alone."

With his gun up, they started down the hall in the direction of the noise. When they turned the corner, they found another staircase that led up to the third floor. Magdalene pointed.

"I think it came from up there," she said.

"I think you're right."

They climbed the stairs. At the top, the hallway was short with only three doors—all of them closed, making it the darkest part of the house. They started down the hall and stopped outside the last door on the left. A bloody smudge was on the brass knob.

Nightingale and Magdalene looked at each other in silence. Nightingale nodded, his gun ready, and reached for the door-knob.

The door flew open before Nightingale could open it, knocking him off balance and sending him to the floor, his gun skittering down the hall. A masked figure sprang from the darkness inside the room, dressed all in black, a dark sack over his head.

Magdalene launched herself at the figure, throwing a wild punch at his head. The masked man turned, backhanding her across the face, then grabbing her throat. Their eyes met, and the killer hesitated. With another wild thrash, Magdalene swiped at the killer's neck and scratched him.

The masked man gave a muffled cry as blood streamed from the cuts. He let go of Magdalene and took off down the hall.

Nightingale clambered to his feet, grabbed his gun, and raced after the masked man. The detective took the stairs two at a time, jumping down the last three and running around the corner. As he did, he caught a glimpse of the masked man as he headed down the stairs, towards the front door.

Nightingale sprinted to the landing, where he leveled his revolver.

"Stop!" he shouted.

The masked man turned without slowing and, rather than running out the front, rounded the post at the foot of the stairs and took off down the hall, towards the back of the house.

Nightingale took a few bounding steps down the stairs, then vaulted over the railing, landing so hard that the chimes of the grandfather clock rang out in cacophony. The door down the hall was swinging on its hinges, where the masked man had just pushed through.

Scrambling, Nightingale ran towards it, bursting through the doorway into the kitchen. He had little time to look around. Just as he entered the room, a China cabinet came crashing down over him, raining fine pieces of porcelain that shattered around him on the floor and knocking him to the ground. Disoriented in the darkened kitchen, Nightingale only caught a glimpse of the back door opening and the black-clad figure rushing outside into the rain.

Pushing the off himself, Nightingale climbed back to his feet, fine China shattering beneath his feet. He ran to the door, but it was too late—the backyard was empty and there was no sign of the masked man, only willow trees swaying in the rainy wind. He holstered his gun and gave a heavy sigh. Blood trickled down his face from a gash above his eye. Nightingale touched it, then blinked the pain away and walked back inside.

Climbing over the broken cabinet, the detective pushed his way back out the door and into the hallway. He was startled when he came face to face with Magdalene, who stood on the other side, the poker from the fireplace in her hands, raised over her head. She began to swing it, but stopped when she recognized him.

"I heard the crash," she said. "I wasn't sure who would be coming back through the door."

"I should have stayed upstairs," he said.

"I did, for a moment," Magdalene said, bringing the poker back down to the ground and leaning on it like a cane. "And look what I found while I was up there."

She handed him a tarot card, identical to the one they'd found in Juliette's hiding place.

"I think the killer was looking for this," Magdalene said. "He was in Antonia's room, the drawers all open, but I found this in her coat."

Nightingale took the card. "Nice work," he said.

"That's not all," Magdalene said. "This is the killer's, too."

She handed over a small, silver cross, which Nightingale took too.

"I grabbed it when I scratched his neck."

It was tarnished with age, and along one edge was an inscription. The detective ran his fingers along it, then squinted.

"There's something written here."

"I know," Magdalene said. "*Praestare Aut Providere*. Any idea what that means?"

"No," he said. "But when we talk to the cops, leave this out of it."

Nightingale sat on the front steps under the eave, a bandage covering the gash in his forehead. Magdalene stood behind him on the porch, her arms folded across her chest. Another man, this one older with dark gray hair and deep worry lines across his forehead, had one foot on the first step, leaning out of the rain. He held a skinny top-fold notebook in one hand and a pen in the other. He tapped the pen on the pages as he read back his notes.

"Let me make sure I got this right: You're on a case, needed to talk to the girl. You heard a noise inside, found the body, and spotted the killer running out the back door."

"That's right," Nightingale said. He turned, glancing at Magdalene, who nodded.

The light outside had grown dim; the grey sky turned towards black, and the rain was beginning to pick up with fat, cold droplets as fog rose from the river. They had lost most of the afternoon waiting for the police to finish with them as the day began its shift to night.

"And you didn't get any look at his face," Westcott said, looking back up from his notebook.

"Nothing."

"You really aren't much help, are you, Night?"

"You're a smart guy, Westcott," Nightingale said. "I'm sure you'll find your man."

"No thanks to you," the other man said, folding his notebook closed. He looked up to Magdalene. "You're sure he's not leaving out anything important?" he asked. "He's done that to me before."

"The killer was wearing a mask," Magdalene said. "Neither of us saw his face."

"All right, then," Westcott said. "I definitely trust you more than him."

Inside the house, a dozen officers milled about. Some were collecting evidence, others were taking photos, and most were just standing around, not even trying to look useful.

"Just one more question," Westcott said. "What are you working on anyway that you needed to talk to the girl?"

Nightingale leaned against the banister beside Magdalene. "Missing girl," he said.

"We thought they might have known each other," the sister added.

"What about the killer? You think he might be related, too?"

"Be a hell of a coincidence otherwise," Nightingale said.

"Maybe we can help each other out," Westcott said.

"I've got all the help I need," Nightingale said, pointing his thumb back at Magdalene. "She's a better partner than you were."

"What about the other girls?" Magdalene said. "Maybe he can check on them."

"Other girls?"

"Yeah," Nightingale said. "They all came over together."

"We can look into them, if you don't mind," Westcott said. "Might give me something useful on this case."

Reaching inside his coat, Nightingale handed over the paper with the girls' names and addresses to Westcott. "Just stay out of our way," he said.

"You won't even know I'm working on the case."

"Sounds like old times."

Westcott smiled. "Anything you want me to ask them?"

"Maybe there is," Nightingale said. He took the tarot card from his pocket and showed it to Westcott. "Ask them if they have one of these."

The worry lines in Westcott's face crumpled in confusion. "What is this?" he said.

"It's a tarot," Nightingale said.

"I do live in this city, Night. I know what a tarot card is. I mean, why's it so important?"

"I don't know yet."

Taking the card, Westcott turned it over to see the back. "Wait a minute," he said, looking at the design. "I've seen this before."

"A card like that?"

"Just this morning."

"Where?" Nightingale asked.

"Hold on," Westcott said as he looked towards the house through the open doors. "Pearson," he shouted. "Come look at this."

Detective Pearson, dressed in a hip-length leather coat with an unlit cigarette dangling between his lips, stepped out. "What do you need, Westy?" he said as he leaned up against one of the columns. He glanced briefly at Magdalene.

"Look at this," Westcott said, holding the card out. "Isn't this the same as that card I found this morning?"

"I thought that was nothing."

"Maybe it's not."

"No," Pearson said. "I don't think that's the same, but I don't really remember."

"I swear it is," Westcott said, looking closer at the card.

"What body?" Nightingale asked.

"In the Quarter, just outside the square. A stevedore got a bullet between the eyes," Westcott said.

"Westy," Pearson said, interrupting. "You think we should be talking about that?"

Westcott looked up at his partner. "You don't know Detective Nightingale? He's a friend."

Pearson cocked his head to the side and took the cigarette from his mouth. He chuckled to himself. "You're Nightingale?"

"You've heard of me?"

"A bit," Pearson said. "Where'd you get this card anyway?"

"I found it."

"Yeah, where?"

"Got my fortune read."

Pearson's face broke with a smile, and he let out a cold, flat laugh. "Funny guy," he said. "We could use more guys like you on the force. Why was it you left again? Some sort of scandal?" He looked towards Magdalene. "Something to do with a woman who turned up dead."

"We don't talk about that," Westcott said, cutting his partner off.

"Of course," Pearson said.

"Maybe you should go see if they're wrapping things up in there."

Pearson gave Westcott a salute. "Sure thing, cap'n," he said before walking back into the house, putting the cigarette back in his mouth, and clapping his hands. "And good to meet you, Nightingale."

"Pleasure," the detective said under his breath.

Westcott hit Nightingale in the arm. "Don't mind him," he said. He handed the tarot card back. "But you might want to ask around the docks about that."

"Thanks," Nightingale said, returning the card to his pocket.

"I'll let you know what I find out about those other girls."

Nightingale shook the detective's hand. "You take care of yourself," he said, nodding towards the house where Pearson had just disappeared.

"You too," Westcott said. He climbed the stairs and shook Magdalene's hand too. "And I'm glad Night's finally got a good influence. See if you can't make him a decent detective again."

"I'll do my best," she said.

As Westcott walked into the house, Nightingale put his hands in his pockets and looked at Magdalene, motioning towards the front gate with his head.

"Let's get out of here," he said. He stepped off the steps and headed towards the street.

"What was that about?" Magdalene asked as she caught up with him.

"Just an old, sad story."

"There was a scandal?"

"It's not important," Nightingale said. "What's important is finding Juliette."

"Of course," Magdalene said.

They stopped at Magdalene's car parked on the street, standing beside it. Nightingale rested his hand on the car's roof near Magdalene and hunched over to talk to her quietly. He took the silver cross from his pocket and pressed it into Magdalene's palm.

"Take this," he said. "Bring it to my friend, the one I told you about here in the Garden District; he might be able to help us. Ask him what the inscription means, find out if it's important."

"He speaks Latin?"

"He speaks everything," Nightingale said.

"And what about you? Where are you going?"

Nightingale took the tarot card back out of his pocket. "To the docks."

CHAPTER 22

MADAME LOVEBITE PARKED ON Villere as the streetlamps turned on, some glowing red—the glass orbs changed out or painted. A woman, with curly black hair tucked under a cloche hat and wrapped in a navy blue reefer coat, approached the car and knocked on the window. Madame Lovebite rolled it down; the woman leaned in through the open window, her arms resting on the edge of the door.

"You looking for some company?" the woman asked.

"You could say that," the Madame said.

The woman scrutinized the Madame. "You might have better luck at Saloon La Frou's."

"That's not what I'm interested in," the Madame said. "I need to talk to someone."

"Talking costs too."

"What doesn't?" the Madame said. "I'll pay."

"Then you can talk to me."

"Get in."

The woman opened the door and climbed inside. "You can call me Ethel," she said. "What do you want to talk about, sweetie?"

"The woman who was taken last night," the Madame said. "Where is she?"

"Oh," Ethel said. "That kind of talking. That will cost you double."

The Madame remained unamused. She opened her clutch, which was resting on the dashboard. She took out a wad of bills and tossed it onto the other woman's lap. "That should cover it—and anything else I want to know."

Ethel snatched the money up greedily and tucked it away into her brassiere. "She's one of Florence's girls, at the Mahogany Box. I think they call her Lillie, but I don't know if she's seeing anyone right now."

"Show me," the Madame said, her hand on the gearshift.

"That'll cost too."

Staring at the prostitute, the Madame's brilliant, green eyes seemed sharp and unsettling in their luster. The world around them was dark and drab and grey. But the green eyes cut through that—like green flames, burning hot, searing through the other woman.

"Show me," the Madame repeated.

Ethel pointed forward. "Head up a block, turn left, then another block up. It's got a big, glitzy sign, you can't miss it."

"Good," the Madame said. "Get out."

She did, and the Madame left her on the curb, driving off around the corner.

The Mahogany Box was a burlesque draped in faux luxury, all velvet and black lace. It sat up against the street, so the patrons didn't have too far to stumble when they left. A small foyer had a coat check; beyond that was a room filled with tables, a stage covered by a flowing, red curtain, a long bar along one wall, and a staircase leading up to the second floor, marked by a velvet rope at the base. A sign hung from the rope that read PAYING CUSTOMERS ONLY. The windows were all covered with heavy drapes, and the light all came from the red-tinted wall sconces. The Mahogany Box wouldn't be busy until later, but there were already a few patrons there, one sitting at the bar, two sitting at the high cocktail tables in the middle of the room. All of them looked like they'd been there for a hundred years, like they'd melted into the place, hunched over and silent, unmoving.

Madame Lovebite took a seat at a table and lit a cigarette with the Ronson lighter. She took a napkin and placed it down as a young woman in a frilly black dress that stopped high above her knees approached.

"There are no shows for another hour, but can I get you anything to drink?"

"Just a tonic with lemon," the Madame said. "I'm here to see someone."

"You have an appointment?"

"No, just a name," the Madame said. She reached into her purse and took out another wad of bills, this one fatter than the one she'd tossed at Ethel. She slid it across the table. "I want to see Lillie."

The waitress's eyes widened. She palmed the bills and hid them discreetly behind her back. "I'll have your drink in just a moment," she said before retreating to the bar.

From her seat, the Madame could see the girl talking to the bartender, their eyes glancing towards her. She pretended not to notice, smoking her thin, black cigarette. The waitress left the bar, throwing one more glance towards the Madame, then disappeared behind a curtain to the back rooms.

Madame Lovebite watched the room. She looked at the barflies nursing their drinks. She noticed the sideways glances of the women working there; all of them wondering what she was doing. Some of them spoke to the bartender. The Madame continued to smoke, appearing disinterested. She saw more discreet looks. She saw the rumor start to spread: she was there to talk to Lillie. Lillie, who'd been attacked. What could she want with Lillie?

The front door opened, and Ethel walked in, taking a seat towards the back of the room, laying her coat and hat across the seat of a chair. When one of the waitresses approached, Ethel and the other woman bowed their heads, speaking in hushed tones, like vultures. Ethel pointed to the Madame, and the other woman shook her head. The Madame flicked the tip of her cigarette into the ashtray.

When her drink finally arrived, it was a different woman who carried it, this one with a bob of red hair. She set it down on the napkin that the Madame had laid out. Petite and muscular, the redhead took the seat across the table, laid down the wad of cash that the waitress had taken, then folded her arms across her chest.

"I'm told you wanted to talk to Lillie," she said.

The Madame took a final drag of her cigarette before snuffing it out in the tray, grinding the tip into the pile of ash. "That's right," she said. "And you are?"

"Ruby. Lillie's not taking customers right now," Ruby said. "She's under the weather."

"I heard," the Madame said. "That's exactly what I wanted to talk to her about."

"I don't think she'll ever want to talk about that."

The Madame reached out and pushed the wad of money towards Ruby. "Perhaps you can find someone who does."

"Nobody knows what happened but her."

"I'm not interested in what happened," the Madame said. "I only want to know about the man who saved her."

"I guess you haven't read the papers," Ruby said. "No one else was there, so I can't say I know who you're talking about."

The Madame's crimson lips curled into a half smile. "I'm talking about the man named Nightingale," she said, watching Ruby's face for recognition. "He's a detective, has a scar on his neck—and according to the police, he was here all night, with you, in fact."

For a fraction of a second, the Madame could see a falter in Ruby's composure. It was almost imperceptible, and quickly replaced with a harsher, harder mask of defiance. "I spend a lot of nights with a lot of men," Ruby said. "As for the man you're talking about—like you said, he was with me last night. Hard for him to be in two places at once."

"And do you know where I might find him now?"

"I don't," she said. "We don't talk about that sort of thing. We don't do much talking at all."

"He's the silent type, then?" the Madame said with a flat smile.

"A man of action, more like," Ruby said, coyly. "And he doesn't like questions."

"You two have that in common."

"That depends on the questions."

"What if I asked about the other girls, the ones who got killed?"

Ruby tossed the Madame a skeptical glance. "What do you know about them?"

"I know there were four others, that your friend, Lillie, would have been number five if she hadn't miraculously escaped. And I know what did it to them."

"You do?"

"I do," the Madame said. "Bloodless bodies, bite marks on their necks. There's only one thing that kills like that."

"Vampires," Ruby said.

"Vampires, the Madame repeated. "And I hear that's Mr. Nightingale's specialty."

Ruby leaned back in her seat, folding her arms across her chest again. "You'd have to ask him about that. Like I said, we don't talk about that sort of thing."

"Why do you think I want to see him?"

"When he comes around, then," Ruby said. "I'll let him know you were looking for him. I didn't catch your name, though."

"Lovebite," she said. "Madame Lenora Lovebite."

"Quite the name," Ruby said.

"It's my favorite."

"I'll let you finish your drink, Lenora."

"I think I'll leave it."

Ruby held up the wad of money. "And your change?"

"Keep it," the Madame said. "Just remember to keep an eye out for Mr. Nightingale."

"Detective, I think," Ruby said. "It's Detective Nightingale."

"Of course," the Madame said, and then stood from the table, walking to the doors. The women in the room watched her leave with inquisitive eyes, only breaking their gaze to look at one another questioningly. The men at the tables were still unaware she'd even been there.

As Lovebite stepped outside, she took shelter under the eave of the building and lit another cigarette. She took a long, hard drag and flicked the ash sharply from the end. Taking a deep breath, she looked up towards the stormy sky and clenched her jaw.

The doors to the Mahogany Box opened, and Ethel stepped out like a teenager sneaking from her room at night. She waved the Madame over, who took another pull from her cigarette and blew out the smoke before approaching.

"I got something you might want to know," Ethel said.

"How much is that going to cost me?"

"I'll be fair," she said. "But not here. Meet me around the corner."

The Madame took one more hit and then tossed her cigarette to the ground, grinding it with the tip of her shoe.

"Lead the way."

The two women kept to the edges, ducking into the shadowed alley beside the building. Garbage cans, crates, and broken pallets concealed them from view.

"Talk," the Madame said.

"I take payment up front," Ethel said, sounding brazen.

The Madame scowled and reached into her purse. Instead of money, she pulled out a thin stiletto blade. She brought it to Ethel's throat, the tip tracing a slow line along her neck. Ethel recoiled in sudden fear until her back hit the wall. Lovebite jabbed the tip of the blade under Ethel's jaw, forcing her to stand tall on her toes.

"You've earned enough today," the Madame said. "Now talk, before I silence you."

"Dr. Bone," Ethel said. Her neck was tight with tension.

"Who's that?"

"It's who Ruby called, right after you left. She told him you came around asking questions."

"Any idea who he is?"

"He knows your detective, I think."

"And where can I find him?"

"She called Bywater Fifteen Forty-one. That's all I know."

"Bywater's in the Garden District, isn't it?"

"I think so," Ethel said, "Yes, I'm sure it is."

Madame Lovebite pulled the knife away from Ethel's throat and slipped it back into its sheath inside her purse. "Then I'll pay Dr. Bone a visit."

CHAPTER 23

LAZARETTO LOOKED OUT HIS window, watching the rain. What little light there had been was disappearing, and the world was going dark. Streetlights, string lights, and other unnatural lights flickered on. The blinds cast shadows across Lazaretto's face. He was silent, thinking. He was entirely alone. Downstairs, he could hear the band playing, muffled as they practiced for the night's guests. The only other sound was the occasional clinking of ice in his glass as it melted.

He had come to power through brute force. As a young street tough with no one to count on, he fought and killed his way to the top of the pile. Before him, gangs ran everything in this city; there was no organization, no order. It had been a free-for-all. With so many gangs on the streets, they constantly clashed. The lines weren't even drawn along ethnic groups. The Irish fought with the Irish, the Cajuns fought with the Cajuns, the Haitians fought with the Haitians, and, of course, the Italians fought with the Italians. They were as busy fighting themselves as fighting each other.

And Lazaretto was in the middle of the fray. He was young and strong back then, full of vigor, vinegar, and violence. At sixteen, he cracked a man's head open with a lead pipe in the middle of the street. The man owed him money, a gambling debt. He was twice Anton's age and had lost badly to the kid at alley dice. When it came time to pay, he didn't respect the young kid enough to think he had to pay up. Lazaretto gave him plenty of chances. For weeks, Lazaretto reminded him, and the man kept blowing him off. A fire burned inside Lazaretto. It wasn't just that the man disrespected him; he didn't respect the rules of the street. He owed a debt, and he had to pay, one way or another.

It was a rainy day, much like this one, so many years ago. Lazaretto needed the money. His own debts were coming due. He talked to the man one last time to remind him about the money. The man told him to buzz off. Lazaretto made an example of him. He started with his fists; the man went down easily. When that wasn't enough, Lazaretto found something else. To be honest, he didn't even know where he got the pipe. Maybe years ago, he could have told the story with more clarity, but time had clouded his memory. Now, all he remembered was the pipe in his hands, the sound it made on the man's head, the crunch of a cracking skull, and the way blood was carried across the bricks in the rainwater, swirling away like smoke in the wind.

The man had a roll of cash in his pocket, which Lazaretto took. But he earned something greater that day—he gained a reputation. Suddenly, a boy who was once just another kid with nowhere to go—probably headed for the docks or jail or one of the city's many cemeteries—rose above the rabble. He was a killer now, a criminal, a brute who could take care of himself. The gangs all wanted him, and he soon rose to the top. Gaining control of the city took longer, but Prohibition helped. He had a foothold at the docks. When alcohol was banned, he saw an opportunity. By the time the ban started, he already had warehouses full of Caribbean rum, ready to sell.

After that, it had been easy. In ten years' time, Lazaretto had become a king, a legend of the streets. He controlled everything, built his clubs, managed his empire.

It was during those ten years that he first met the man called Monsieur Du Vide. He knew plenty of men who could bring him booze, but Du Vide brought him the best, and their relationship had grown strong as the money began to pile up.

Now, though, almost another decade had passed since Prohibition ended, and since then, things hadn't felt right to Lazaretto. He felt dulled, slowed down, like he'd lost some of that fire that had been burning in his belly since that rainy day as a youth, when a man wouldn't pay his debt. The game was changing, and Lazaretto, for the first time in his life, wasn't entirely sure how to change ahead of it.

His ice clinked in his glass.

How old would that man be now? The one he'd killed in the street—Maybury, he thought his name was.

"He'd probably be dead now anyway," Lazaretto said quietly, absently to himself. What difference did it make in the end?

Lazaretto brought a big hand up to his face and rubbed his eyes. He rolled his shoulder and rotated his neck. Everything popped and snapped; he'd been standing by the window, staring for too long. He turned, grabbed the glass from his desk, and walked to the bar on the other side of the room. He dumped the ice, ready to make another drink for himself, but then he stopped, putting his fists on the countertop, knuckles down, leaning against them. He looked at his reflection in the mirrored wall behind the bottles.

Things were slipping because he'd been slipping. And as he stared at himself, wishing he still had that fire in his belly, he wondered if maybe he'd already slipped.

There was a frantic knock at his door.

"Come," he shouted.

A man spilled into his room, tossed to the floor, Slits Nicotero behind him. "I found this piece of garbage skulking around outside," he said.

Frenchy came in after them. "I told him to bring him up to you."

Lazaretto looked back and forth between the two men's faces, shrugging and putting his hands up in confusion.

"It's Charlie the Cheat," Slits said, answering the question he knew his boss was asking.

Then Lazaretto understood. He grabbed the man on the floor by the hair and lifted his head up to face him. "Charlie 'The Cheat' Baptiste," Lazaretto said to him, grinning. "It's not often I get involved for a few lousy bucks, but you've made yourself a special case."

Charlie's face was smashed up, his lip and nose were bloody. He looked up at Lazaretto, an expression of unsettling calm on his face.

"What was he doing?" Lazaretto asked without looking away from Charlie's bloodied face.

"Not sure," Slits said. "We saw his buddy Petey out there, too. We've got him downstairs for now. He was carrying this, though." Slits passed Lazaretto a heavy, pearl-handled pistol, which Lazaretto took in his big hand, feeling the weight of it.

"Big piece for a little man," Lazaretto said. "You coming here to settle your debts for good?" He pointed the gun at Charlie, who had managed to get up onto his knees. "Pow," Lazaretto said, pretending to shoot the man on the ground.

"It's not just that, Boss," Frenchy said. "That's Gino's gun."

Lazaretto stopped and looked at the gun in his hand. Recognition sparked in his eyes. This time, Lazaretto spoke slowly, his words clear and precise. "Last night, Fat Phil and Knuckles take you away, and they end up gutted in a swamp. Next, I send Gino to your place. Now, you show up here with his gun."

Charlie's bloodied lips parted in a wet smile. "When you gonna learn to stop sending guys after me?"

Lazaretto whacked Charlie across the face with the automatic, blood and spit spraying across the rug.

"I'm not even gonna ask if you have the rest of my money. I'm just going to kill you."

"Wait," Charlie said. He started to stand up, but Slits kicked him in the back of the knee, sending Charlie back to the ground. "I don't have your dough, it's true, but I've got something better."

"What?"

"A proposition."

Lazaretto looked at Slits and Frenchy. His mouth was open in disbelief, and the other two had the same look, each of them turning to look at the other. They all started to laugh together.

"A proposition?" Lazaretto said. "A *business* proposition? You think I'd ever get into business with you?"

"Hear me out."

Lazaretto turned to Frenchy. "Close the door." He rubbed a big hand over his face, pinching the bridge of his nose. "The only reason you're not dead right this instant," he said, raising the gun again, leveling it to Charlie's forehead, "is because I haven't decided if I want to do it for what you done to Gino, or if I'm going to turn you back over to Slits for what you done to Fat Phil and Knuckles."

"If you listen to me, all that becomes worth it."

"What could you possibly say that's worth my time?"

"It's not just what I have to say," Charlie said, "I brought you a gift too."

"Yeah? And where is it?"

Charlie's eyes flicked over Lazaretto's shoulders; the crime boss turned to look. Framed in the window, standing outside, was a tall, lanky figure in a long, flowing overcoat, blacked out by shadow. In one hand, he held a cane, in the other a burlap sack. Uneasiness and dread washed over Lazaretto. Instinctively, he raised the big pistol and fired. The shot boomed, and the bullet passed through the glass, but the figure was already gone, vanished.

Following their boss's lead, Slits and Frenchy both drew their guns. Making sure they didn't lose him, Slits grabbed Charlie by the neck and forced him to the ground, putting his foot on the man's back to keep him in place.

The three men, their guns drawn, watched the windows. The shadowy figure appeared again, this time in another window on their right. No one hesitated this time; each of them fired, once again hitting nothing but glass. Rain and sounds of the city came pouring into the room through the shattered, empty frames.

For a third time, the figure appeared, and the three men spat out another barrage of bullets, shattering the glass. The wind whistled through, blowing the blinds and rain inside. And when the figure appeared again, the gangsters fired wildly, shredding the wood panels and sending the blinds clattering to the floor until their guns went dry. Once again, the window frame was empty.

"What is this?" Lazaretto said, his fear came out like anger.

The figure appeared a final time in the glassless window frame. With the blinds gone, the men could clearly see it as its long arms reached down, working its spindly fingers under the frame and forcing it up. With a jerk, the latch broke, and the window slid up easily.

A long leg came in first, followed by the rest of the dark figure, moving spider-like into the room. The three men watched impotently as the figure came into the light. It looked like a man, with its neatly trimmed Van Dyke and brushed-back hair, but there was something about him that was repulsive, unnatural. It was the way the light played off his skin. The man was pale, unnaturally pale. The memory of Maybury splashed through Lazaretto's mind—with his head cracked open, blood spilling out of him, the man he'd killed so long ago had the same sickly pallor as the one in front of him. This figure, this person, whoever or whatever he was, looked like a corpse.

"Who are you?" Lazaretto asked.

"Your gift," the pallid man said.

Searching for some sort of foothold in reality, Lazaretto looked over his shoulder at Slits and Frenchy. They, too, stared at the figure, as if entranced. Then Lazaretto's gaze trailed down to Charlie, who nodded at him slowly. The mob boss lowered his gun and turned back to the figure in front of him.

"You can dodge a few bullets, I'll give you that," Lazaretto said. "But what makes you so great?"

"I can do much more than that."

"Oh yeah, like what?"

"This."

The pallid man stretched out his long arm, holding the sack, and tossed it to the floor at Lazaretto's feet, the contents landing on the hardwood with a thump and a squish.

"What is this?" Lazaretto asked.

"Look and see."

Slowly, cautiously, Lazaretto knelt on the ground, opening the bag and peering in. When he could see the contents, his eyes widened.

"My God," he said. "You did this?"

"He's the one who did the same to Knuckles and Phil," Charlie said, still pinned to the floor beneath Slits' knee.

"What is it, Boss?" Frenchy asked.

"Look for yourself."

Frenchy stepped around his boss while Slits leaned forward, craning to see inside. Lazaretto opened the bag more so that they could get a good look. When Frenchy saw what was in the bag, he stepped back, horrified, then, covering his mouth, he ran to the adjacent bathroom to throw up.

Slits wasn't so queasy. He squinted to see. "That looks like Gino," he said. "What's left of him."

Lazaretto nodded. "It is." He looked to the pallid man. "You've killed three of my guys, you bring the remains of one, and for what?"

"The proposition," Charlie said from the floor. "Like I said."

"Which is?" Lazaretto asked, still with his eyes locked on the figure in front of him.

"No more of your men need to die," the pallid man said.

"But someone needs to?"

"Only if you say so."

"You'd do that for me?" Lazaretto said.

The lips of the pallid man peeled away, revealing his sharp fangs in a sinister smile. "For a price," he said.

Lazaretto set the pearl-handled gun on his desk. He grabbed his empty glass from the bar along with a fresh one and set them down on the desk. Unscrewing a bottle of booze, he put a splash of brown spirit into each. He opened the cigar box on his desk, brought it to his lips, and clipped off the end, which flew carelessly to the floor. He grabbed his lighter and ignited it, the flame illuminating his face from below.

"Then, let's talk."

CHAPTER 24

NIGHTINGALE WALKED ALONE THROUGH the fog; the sun hidden behind the grey gloom. River buoys clanged as they bobbed in the water, but the sounds were hushed, seeming distant in the eerie stillness. Somewhere far off, a seagull cawed.

Along the waterfront, the rain was more like mist. Nightingale's hat was pulled tight. His hands were in his pockets. Gusts of wind blew the tails of his long coat out behind him like a battered flag. There wasn't another soul in sight.

The harbor was a water-logged sprawl of storehouses—full of goods being brought in and shipped out—dotted with offices owned by cargo companies and flanked by the tall steamships they chartered. It stretched down the edge of the river as far as Nightingale could see, until it trailed off and disappeared into the mist. He stopped outside the gates to light a cigarette and check his pockets.

His money clip was running light after the headmistress and the man at immigration, and he hoped he wouldn't need too much to get the answers he was looking for. These stevedores were blue-collar guys, which might make them humble, but it could just as easily make them greedy.

He had Juliette's ticket and exit visa, along with the ones they'd taken from Antonia. He also had both of their tarot cards—that's what he would be asking about first. After taking a long drag, he lipped the cigarette and put his hands back in his pockets. He was as ready as he was going to be.

Passing through the gates to the harbor, he saw the first signs of life somewhere in the mist, movement of men carrying burlap sacks and wooden crates from ships to warehouses. They looked like apparitions in the ghostly fog. He walked past the workers, most of them ignoring him, while a handful took a moment's pause to look curiously at the stranger in their midst.

Nightingale headed to the break house, a dilapidated building next to the union bureau and beneath the foreman's office. The sour wooden planks in front were littered with cigarette butts and bottle caps. Before he entered, he added his cigarette to the heap. He took one final drag and tossed it to the warped wood, grinding it out with his toe.

The door creaked as he walked inside, the hinges rusty from the damp air. The place was full of lockers and ratty armchairs where the men would bum around between shifts. A dartboard hung on the wall, and a radio played tinny music softly. Two of the chairs were occupied; the man closer to the door was old and stout, with a red nose and rosy cheeks. The other was wiry and thin.

"If you're looking for work," said the red-nosed man, barely glancing at him, "it's all spoken for."

"I've already got work," Nightingale said. "That's why I'm here."

The red-nosed man sat up and eyed him carefully. "What's your work, friend?"

"Private detective," Nightingale said. "And I have a few questions."

"We ain't a fan of questions," the red-nosed man said.

"We ain't no friend of cops, either," said the skinny one, his voice thick with a Cajun accent. "We had enough of them earlier."

Nightingale raised his eyebrow. "You had some trouble?"

The two men looked skittish. "We didn't say that," said the red-nosed man.

"Cops don't show up for no reason," Nightingale said.

"A friend of ours got killed last night, is all," said the skinny one.

"Shut your mouth, Toby," the red-nosed one said. "We don't owe him nothing."

"Down in the Quarter? That's what I want to talk to you about."

"You and everybody else," Toby said.

"I told you to shut your mouth."

"Who else has come around asking besides cops?" Nightingale asked.

Neither of the two men spoke. They just sat there, button-lipped, looking at each other for some notion as to what they should say. Nightingale watched them both, deciding if he should pull out his money clip when the door behind him opened.

"What's going on here?"

When Nightingale turned, he saw an older man standing there, his wrinkled face weathered and dark.

"Just asking some questions, friend," Nightingale said.

"You a cop?"

"A private eye."

The weathered man cocked his head. "Nightingale?"

The detective looked at him, confused. Before Nightingale could speak, the man reached out his hand. "The name's Willis," he said. "And boy, am I glad to see you."

Nightingale took Willis's hand, still not sure how the man knew him. The longshoreman had a strong, firm handshake and a rough, calloused hand. "I didn't know I'd had the pleasure," he said.

"We haven't yet. But we got a mutual acquaintance." Willis reached into the bag he had slung over his shoulder, and he pulled out the sack of vampire wards. "Dr. Bone said you were the man to see."

"Any friend of Bone's," Nightingale said with a smile. "What brought you to the good doctor?"

"This," Bone said, taking the tarot card from his pocket and showing it to Nightingale. "That's why he told me to find you, said you'd want to see it. Told me you could answer some of my questions, too. Didn't expect to have you wandering into the docks, though."

"Where'd you get this?" Nightingale said as he took the card, turning it over to study it.

"Here," Willis said.

Toby, who had been watching the two men silently, spoke up. "That's just like the one Bull shown us."

"Quiet, you," the red-nosed man said.

"It's OK, Cramer, Nightingale's gonna help us out," Willis said. Then he looked toward the detective. "That's why you're here, right?"

"Not exactly," Nightingale said, shaking his head. "I need some help too."

Cramer jumped up from his chair. He shook a finger at Nightingale. "We don't need no trouble here," he said, his voice trembling.

"Cramer," Willis said, "We already got trouble."

"This one's just gonna bring more," Cramer said. "Lazaretto, he don't want none of us talking to nobody."

"Lazaretto's the reason we're in this mess," said Willis.

"It ain't him, it's something else, something more sinister."

"Like what?" Nightingale asked.

"I ain't saying nothing," Cramer said. "I ain't gonna get on the wrong side of this. I ain't gonna end up like Bull."

The old man leapt up from his chair. He pushed past Nightingale and Willis, yanked open the creaky door, and hurried outside.

"What's that about?" Nightingale asked.

"We all been a little jumpy since the news about Bull."

"And since Lazaretto's been sending his guys around," Toby added.

"Lazaretto still runs things around here?"

"We're not quite sure," Willis said. "That's the problem." He pointed to the tarot card that Nightingale was holding in his hand. "There's somebody new, somebody bringing something in that none of us can quite explain."

"Vampires," Nightingale said.

Willis nodded and lifted the bag of wards. "I wouldn't have really believed it, but the winds are changing around here."

"Listen," Nightingale said. "I'm looking for a little girl who was taken. She had a card too." The detective fished one of the tarot cards from his pocket and showed it to Willis and Toby. "This was in her things. She came through her earlier this week, from France by way of Morocco on a boat called the Myrkranna."

On the other side of the room, Toby's eyes went wide. "A Casket Girl," he said, not to anyone in particular.

"A what?"

"A Casket Girl," Willis said. "That's what they call these young girls who've been coming in lately."

"They arrive on the black boats," Toby said. "Late at night—carrying coffins."

"Coffins?"

"Coffins," Willis said. "They say they're travel trunks, but the rumors say it's not clothes inside."

"It's vampires, like you say," Toby said.

"Any idea where they take them?"

"Nobody knows," Toby said.

Willis pursed his lips and narrowed his eyes as he thought. "Tautopolis would."

"Who?" Nightingale asked.

"The foreman. He'd have the records in his office, I'm sure of it."

"Can you get me in there?"

"Follow me."

Nightingale followed Willis outside, and Toby trailed behind them both. As they passed beneath the old staircase that led to the foreman's office, the door opened quickly, like someone had been waiting for them, and Eugene stepped out onto the balcony, clutching the rail.

"Hey, Willis!" he shouted. "What's going on down there?"

Nightingale and Willis looked up at the balding man. As Toby noticed Eugene above, he scurried quietly back inside the break house, shutting the door behind him.

"Nothing, boss."

"I see a lot of new faces."

"You the foreman?" Nightingale shouted to him.

"Yeah. You a cop?"

"Close enough."

"If you ain't a cop, you got no right being here, harassing my guys."

Nightingale shot a look at Willis, trying to tell him to play along. "They're not being very helpful," he said.

"That's because they know what's good for them," Eugene shouted back. He scurried down the stairs to talk to Nightingale face-to-face. As he did, Cramer stepped out of the office too, watching everything from above. Once Eugene was at the bottom, he stalked toward Nightingale, wagging an accusing finger. "Now listen," he said. "You ain't got no right being down here, so you got exactly sixty seconds to make yourself scarce or I'm calling the authorities to do it for you."

Nightingale took a step forward so that he loomed over Eugene. "Go ahead and call, then."

Eugene shook his head. "You don't know who you're messing with." He took a step back and then retreated to the stairs, scurrying his way up.

"I've got an idea."

When he was about halfway up to his office, Eugene turned back and snarled. "You got no idea. You'll be sorry!" Then he ran the rest of the way up and slammed the door.

"He's serious," Willis said. "And it ain't the police he's gonna call."

"I'm sure," Nightingale said.

"Thanks for covering for me, by the way."

"It wasn't all for you," Nightingale said. "I need you in his good graces. Now, can you get him out of that office?"

Willis smiled. "You just make yourself scarce."

Taking the stairs two at a time, Willis ran up to the foreman's door and knocked feverishly. When it opened, Tautopolis stood in the doorway. "That hawkshaw still here?"

"He took off, ran towards the warehouses."

"Bastard," Tautopolis said. "I just called someone in, but it'll be a minute 'til they get here. Help me find him, will ya?"

"Sure thing, Gene," Willis said. He looked over the fore-man's shoulder, where Cramer leaned against the desk. "You too."

Tautopolis looked behind him. "Willis's right. Get out here, help us look for this detective. Lazaretto ain't gonna be too happy about any of this."

The three men came down the stairs, and Toby poked his head out of the break house. "What's going on?"

"Looking for that detective," Cramer said. "Come give us a hand."

Toby joined the pack as they ran out past the break house, towards the storerooms and warehouses, Willis leading the way. When their footsteps and voices were distant, Nightin-gale came out from around the corner. In the fog, everything was dim, and the lights glowed like paper lanterns. Everything was still again, and Nightingale was alone.

He made his way up to Tautopolis' office. When he tried the door, he found it locked. He cursed under his breath. There wasn't another way into the dilapidated building—none that he could see anyway. Running his hand against the doorframe, he found a gap at the top and the bottom where the whole thing slanted slightly to the left. He pulled a pocketknife and scraped away at it; the wood was soft, rotting in the wet air around the docks. After he'd carved a bit away, he took a step back, leaning against the railing, then raised his foot. With a flat thud, he kicked, and the frame gave without resistance. Nightingale rushed forward, grabbing the knob before the door hit against the wall, and then closed it behind him.

The office was stuffy and dim, the only light coming from a desk lamp partially hidden behind a stack of unfiled papers. Nightingale hoped that Willis had been right, that Tautopolis was organized enough that he'd have a record of where those coffins were going.

He walked past the desk to the row of filing cabinets behind it, and found the drawer marked SHIPPING AND RECEIVING. Pulling it open, he found that the files were marked by date. He took Juliette's ticket from his pocket, reading it again in the low light. She had arrived on Monday night, so he found the file and brought it to Tautopolis' desk, where he began to flip through it, glancing at the names of the ships until he found the Myrkranna.

When he heard a creak outside, Nightingale paused, standing motionless, watching the door, holding his breath, and listening for another noise. A moment passed, and everything remained silent. Must have been the wind, he thought, as he cautiously looked back down at the file in front of him.

The cargo was listed as machine parts and porcelain pieces, with four passengers riding steerage. The names of the girls weren't listed, but the company that chartered the ship was. Nightingale tapped it with his finger.

APOPHRADES, INC.

There was no address listed, but Nightingale returned to the filing cabinet, where he opened another drawer labeled IMPORTER REGISTRY. These files were alphabetical, and the names and information of companies were typed out on index cards. He flipped through the A's until he found what he needed. He pulled out the card for Apophrades, Inc. and slipped it into his pocket.

Nightingale closed the drawer and retrieved the file from the desk, then returned it to the other cabinet. He passed the desk, walking back to the door, when he heard another creak outside. He froze again, but this time, it wasn't just the wind; the door opened, and the red-nosed man named Cramer stepped inside.

The old man's eyes went wide when he saw Nightingale, who was shadowed and backlit by the light on the desk. He opened his mouth to call out, but Nightingale grabbed him by the lapels, clasping a hand over his mouth and dragging him inside the office. Nightingale kicked the door closed.

Pulling his gun, Nightingale stuck the barrel into the man's gut, making sure he knew what it was, then he slowly took his hand away from Cramer's mouth. "There are two ways out of this," Nightingale said. "You keep your mouth shut and you get a pocket full of cash, or you open it and you get a belly full of lead." He shook the old man by the lapel. "What's it gonna be?"

"The cash, the cash," the old man wheezed.

"Good," Nightingale said, taking his money clip from inside his coat and stuffing the remaining wad of bills into the pocket of Cramer's coveralls. "Now, where are the others?"

"I don't know," Cramer said, frightened. "I snuck off, came in here to sit."

"Then, sit," Nightingale said. "And forget I was here."

"I don't want any more trouble."

"You seemed to want it the first time you came running in here to rat me out."

"I was scared," Cramer said. "We all are."

"Then be scared," Nightingale said. "Either you're in this mess, or you're out. You don't want trouble, then don't go looking for it."

"I won't, I won't, I swear."

"Then take that cash and go drink it away," Nightingale said. He put his gun back in the holster and peeked out the door. When he didn't hear or see anybody else, he opened it all the way. "But don't let me see you again."

Nightingale went down the stairs, listening for Tautopolis and the others, hearing nothing but the distant sounds of the river and the men working it. He headed for the corner of the building, ready to duck into the shadows and escape, when he heard a soft whisper and stopped.

"Over here," came a voice from the darkness, and he knew it was Willis.

He followed the sound until he saw the broad frame of the longshoreman hiding behind a stack of crates that leaned against a warehouse. Nightingale hustled to him and ducked around out of sight.

"You get what you needed?" Willis asked

"I did."

"Good. Now you've got to get out of here," Willis said. "Whoever Gene called is going to be on their way."

"Thanks," Nightingale said. "Take care of yourself."

"You too, detective," Willis said. "But I got one more question for you, first."

"Hit me."

"Do any of these knick-knacks Bone sold me actually work against vampires?" Willis held up the bag of vampire wards.

"They'll give you a fighting chance. Why, you expecting to find some?"

"Tonight," Willis said. "The Casket Girls are coming in."

Nightingale took the bag, opened it, and pulled out the stake. "You put this in the heart," he said. "Fire works too, but otherwise you've got to get the heart."

"That's it?" Willis asked.

"It's harder than it sounds."

"For sure."

Nightingale put out his hand. "Stay safe," he said. "Don't do anything stupid."

"Too late," Willis said.

Willis stayed in the shadows as Nightingale took off into the evening. He was walking fast through the fog. He was headed for Bone's, where he'd meet Magdalene. He checked his watch as he headed for the gate. It was getting late, with any luck, though they could take a look at Apophrades, Inc., and maybe follow them back to the docks when the boat came in.

As he walked through the gate, two broad-chested men, with guts that hung over their belts, stood in front of him, next to their car.

"You a detective?" one of them asked.

Nightingale stopped. He knew trouble when he saw it. He reached into his coat, feeling the cross brand in his pocket, but grabbed a cigarette instead. Playing it cool, he lit it, flicking his lighter shut and dropping it back into his pocket.

"Why?" he asked, taking a drag. "You lose something?"

"It's him," the other one said, "Look at the scar, just like Tautopolis said."

Nightingale smiled, blowing smoke out into the mist. "So, you're the ones the foreman called." Nightingale took another hit from his cigarette. "You got here faster than I thought you would."

"We been hanging around close today," the first one said with a grin.

They moved together, lunging toward Nightingale, who dodged backward. He flicked his cigarette into the first one's eyes, the hot ashes flying into his face. The big man howled and put his hands up, grabbing his own forehead. Nightingale feinted again, then threw a punch that landed across the other man's jaw, which must have left his ears ringing.

Nightingale was feeling confident until he felt a big hand clamp down on his shoulder and spin him around. It was the man he'd flicked the cigarette at; his eyes were red and full of rage. Nightingale was off balance from being turned unexpectedly, and the big man brought a heavy fist right across Nightingale's face. Stars burst in front of Nightingale's eyes, and a high-pitched buzz in his ears drowned out all other sound.

The man that Nightingale had clocked was in front of him now, with an evil grin on his face. He brought another fist down across Nightingale's face. He heard something pop as he collapsed to the ground.

Then the two men really went to work. Each of them held Nightingale down with one hand and pounded their fists into him with the other. After the first few dozen hits, it almost didn't matter. Nightingale was numb; the blows seemed distant, far away, like they were in a dream. Then the man who'd had the cigarette in his face kicked Nightingale, planting his loafered foot right into Nightingale's stomach, forcing the air out of his lungs and bringing all that pain right back into sharp reality.

Nightingale felt like pulp; his body pulsated with it as he gasped for breath. His face was slick with blood. His sides flared with a fiery ache. He felt like he was going to throw up.

Mercifully, the two men stopped beating him. In his frazzled, disconnected mind, he figured they only stopped because there wasn't much left of him to hit. The ringing in his ears was fading, slightly, and he could hear the two men talking, sounding distant and underwater. He couldn't follow anything they said, only managing a few words that dotted their conversation, like "boss," "club," and "questions."

Darkness crept in around the edges of his vision like a vignette. He felt weightless for a moment and realized the two men had picked him up off the ground, dragging him to the trunk of their car. They tossed him inside, and before they closed it on him, Nightingale saw Willis running up to the gate, a few other stevedores trailing behind him. Then the lid came down, and everything went black.

CHAPTER 25

WHEN THE DOOR TO the Emporium Historia opened, it chimed. Madame Lovebite walked inside. The shop, filled with curios from distant times and places, was empty of people. She looked around, peering beyond the shelves in search of anyone present. Her eye caught the box of vampire wards on the counter, and she stepped over, smiling amusedly at the idea. A door towards the back clicked open. Out stepped a man—older and handsome, distinguished by the lines on his face and the gray in his hair. He was just as the Madame had imagined him. "You must be Dr. Bone," she said.

She could see the man searching her face, trying to figure her out, wondering where she came from and how she might know his name. Calmly, the look faded, and the man came back to himself, casually walking up to the counter to greet her.

"And you must be the most beautiful woman I've seen all day," he said, offering his hand. "I am the good doctor. What can I do for you?"

The Madame took his hand and smiled courteously. She pointed to the box of vampire wards.

"Go right ahead," Bone said, walking behind the counter.

The Madame picked up a pouch and untied the twine that closed the bag, emptying the contents onto the counter in front of her. She sifted through them, touching the cross, the garlic, and the holy water, spreading everything out evenly.

"Interesting business you have here," she said.

"I deal in all manners of the occult."

"Like the tarot?" she said, pointing to the stack of books that were still laid out on his counter.

"I'm trying to learn," he said.

"I could teach you."

"You're a fortune teller?"

"I dabble," the Madame said.

"Enough to be dangerous."

The Madame smiled. "You might say that."

"Show me what you've got," Bone said. He reached beneath the counter, pulled out a tarot deck, brushed away the vampire wards, and set the cards down in front of the Madame.

The Madame slipped off her silk gloves, placed them carefully on the counter, and positioned her hands on either side of the tarot deck.

"Interesting tattoos," Bone said, studying her hands, looking at the moons, the birds, the thorny vine of roses, and the bloody knife up her wrist. "Beautiful, in fact."

"Thank you."

"You know, in Egypt, they've found mummies covered in tattoos, most of them women."

"Do you have any of those hiding in here?"

Bone chuckled. "I should be so lucky," he said. "The archeologists who found them noticed the markings were significant and unique. They thought the tattoos were used to tell the women's stories."

"Were they happy ones?"

"Some of them," Bone said. "Some say the Egyptians were the ones who spread the custom around the world. Of course, yours don't look Egyptian. If I didn't know better, I'd say some of these designs look European, maybe even Romani."

"You have a very good eye, Dr. Bone."

"I like to learn."

"Then let's learn," she said, pointing to the deck of cards. "Touch the deck."

Bone reached out and rested his fingers on the deck as instructed. The Madame placed her hand over his, holding it in place. "Touching the deck creates a bond between you and the cards. You only need to touch it briefly. And when it's your deck, you shouldn't let others handle it too much."

"Why is that?"

"Because it's the reader who needs the strongest connection. The interpretation of the cards is more important than the cards themselves."

"Where did you learn all this?"

"My grandmother," the Madame said. "Now take your hand back, and I'll do a simple reading—three cards." She cut the deck and took three cards, laying them face-up on the counter. The first was THE HERMIT, an old man in a long robe holding a staff and a lantern on top of an icy mountain at night. "You're a seeker," she said. "But your search often leaves you solitary."

She pointed to the next card, TEMPERANCE, where a winged angel hung above a flowing stream, pouring water between two goblets held in her hands. "You're patient," the Madame said. "And balanced. You have a serenity about you, one that's regarded and trusted." Touching the final card, she said: "The Queen of Pentacles. You've been trapped deep in thought, as you often are."

"It looks like she loves gold," Bone said, pointing to the picture of a woman dressed in a fine gown, sitting on a throne, hugging a gold coin to her chest.

"Pentacles can signify wealth," the Madame said. She looked around the shop. "But you find wealth in knowledge, not gold."

Bone chuckled again. "True enough," he said. "Is that it?"

"That's what the cards tell me," the Madame said. "The cards are clearer the more direct your questions are."

"And the more complicated the reading, is that right?"

"It is. More cards give you more insight."

"Let me try that on you, then," Bone said. He collected the cards, shuffled them, and then cut the deck three times before stacking them neatly again. He looked up at the Madame. "I saw this one in a book," he said. "Tell me if I'm doing it right." Then he peeled off six cards from the top of the deck, placing them face-up on the counter in the shape of a triangle—three cards on the bottom, two in the middle, and one at the very top.

The cards were a hodgepodge of the major and minor arcana, with the Fool, the Two of Wands, and Justice along the bottom; the World and the Queen of Swords in the middle; and finally, the Sun at the very top. Bone put his hand up to his chin, stroking his goatee, making throaty sounds to make it obvious that he was studying them.

The Madame watched amused. It wasn't very often she sat on this side of a reading. Bone looked up from the cards, meeting the Madame's emerald-green gaze.

"You're conflicted," he said. "You find yourself trying to change, but you keep ending up in the same place where you started."

The Madame was taken aback. "That's not what the cards say."

"I know," he said. "It's what you're telling me." He pointed at her hands. "The raven and the dove, light and darkness. The cycles of the moon, always changing, always remaining the same."

"You're supposed to read the cards," the Madame said.

"You said it was the reader who was the most important," Bone said. "I'm just reading you."

"Maybe these aren't about conflict," she said, raising her hands. "Maybe they're about acceptance—all of us have light and darkness, and sometimes nothing changes, even when it seems to."

"Even when we want it to?"

"That's not what I said."

"Then what are you looking for?" Bone asked.

"Who said I was looking for anything?"

"Everybody who comes into my store is looking for something." He pointed to the bag of vampire wards. "And not everything is a trinket for sale."

The Madame fixed a sharper gaze on the man across from her. Slowly, she reached for her gloves, slid them back onto her tattooed hands, and then clasped them together on the counter.

"I'm looking for someone," she finally said.

"Did you think you'd find that someone here?"

"No," the Madame said. "But I think you know him."

"Does he have a name?"

Just as the Madame opened her mouth to answer, the door chimed loudly and swung open. Startled, she spun around and reached down toward her thigh holster, ready to draw her pistol. Seeing the man rush up to the counter with his eyes fixed on Dr. Bone—and realizing he wasn't there for her—she relaxed and left her weapon untouched.

"Bone, we gotta talk," he said quickly.

"Willis," Bone said, "what happened?"

"Nightingale, they got Nightingale."

Bone shot a glance at the Madame, who remained calm as she reached into her purse to pull out a lighter and a cigarette. He turned back to Willis. "What are you saying?"

"He came down to the docks asking questions. The foreman didn't like it, so he sicced Lazaretto's men on him."

"Is he alive?"

"For now, but they beat him bloody and tossed him in the trunk," Willis said. "I heard they were taking him to the club."

"The Rag & Bone?"

"Sure enough."

"Damn that fool," Bone said under his breath. He looked to the Madame. "I'm sorry, I have to take care of something."

"It's all right," the Madame said, taking a pull from her cigarette. "So do I."

CHAPTER 26

CHARLIE STOOD ON THE balcony, gazing over the club's crowded floor and watching the revelry below. With the windows shot out, Lazaretto's office wasn't suitable for conversation, so they'd relocated to one of his private rooms instead. Now, through tall windows, the casino sparkled beneath them, and the stage hosted the big band playing as usual. A pretty waitress arrived, delivering a drink and a cigar. When he asked her to keep his tab open, she responded politely—there was no tab for friends of Mr. Lazaretto. He didn't need to worry about it.

A friend of Mr. Lazaretto. Her words echoed in his mind—bolstering him, puffing up his chest, and reigniting his dreams. Power. Success. Respect. He looked at the waitress, smiling. She met his gaze and smiled back. To Charlie, it wasn't just friendly—it was a lingering smile, the kind reserved for powerful men. The kind that lingered. He was a friend of Mr. Lazaretto's, now, dangerous and mysterious. An object of attraction.

The waitress would have to wait. Drink in hand, Charlie stepped back to the table where Lazaretto sat, Frenchy at his side and Vermilion across. In the corner, Slits Nicotero chewed on a toothpick and looked sullen.

"Let me get this straight," Lazaretto said. "You want me to let Charlie's debt go and forgive you on the killings of Gino, Knuckles, and Phil. In return, you'll work for me, going after the heads of the other bosses in this city."

"That's what Charles and I had discussed."

Lazaretto frowned. "I've got a few problems with it. Nothing we can't work out, though."

"What kind of problems?" Charlie asked, taking a seat. "You come out on top; I just don't want to be hunted by your goons no more."

"I'm sure that's not all you want," Lazaretto said. "That's not all anybody wants. Living is one thing, lifestyle is another; that's what you all really want."

"What do you mean?"

"Riches," Lazaretto said. "That's what you're after, am I right?"

"I thought that's what we were discussing," Charlie said.

"Far from it." Lazaretto turned to the vampire. "Vermilion, according to your plan, you wouldn't be much more than a contract killer. A useful one, an efficient one, for certain, but nothing more."

"What do you have in mind?" Charlie said, taking a sip from his drink.

"Bigger," Lazaretto said.

"Bigger what?"

"Your whole plan needs to be bigger."

"What do you mean?"

"Look around, you two. You think I got here by taking the small route, eking by? Charlie, that's why you're a two-bit hood. You never had vision. And Vermilion, I get that you lost everything from those goddamned krauts, but come on, you come here thinking you're going to start fresh, and this is the best you can do? It's pretty obvious you were born rich. You've never had to fight for anything you had. No offense."

The vampire waved his hand.

"You got a better plan?" Charlie asked.

"I like to think that I do," Lazaretto said. He stood from the table, cocktail in one hand, cigar in the other. As he began to pace, he sloshed his drink while he talked. "This is an opportunity like no one's ever been given in this city—maybe anywhere in the world. But we don't care about that; we're not greedy." Lazaretto paused, waiting for Frenchy and Slits to chuckle. Charlie looked confused. Vermilion remained expressionless. "Sure, we could go with your plan: bump off the heads of our opposition, take control of their organizations. But that's messy. Hostile takeovers? They're always ugly. Loyalists vie for control and try to keep you out. And once you *do* gain control, you gotta send more manpower to keep things in order. Half the time, it's more work than it's worth."

"Then what are we even doing here?" Charlie asked.

"I'll get to that when I want," Lazaretto said, taking a drink. "First, let me tell you about my mother. When I was a kid, she told me stories from the Old Country. To hear her tell it, you'd think the hills were crawling with monsters. I never thought much of them, but tonight, well, maybe Mama wasn't wrong about certain things. One story in particular stands out in my mind. She told me about the Striga—a witch, long dead, who would crawl out of her grave to suck the blood of men and young boys alike, luring them in and turning them into her slaves. By the end of it, she had a whole army of them."

Lazaretto looked at Vermilion, raising his glass to him. "Now, my bloodsucking friend, maybe you can enlighten us, but is there any truth to my dear dead mother's bedtime stories?"

"I know no striga."

"But is what she said true? Can you make men into slaves?"

Vermilion's grey lips parted in a sneering smile. "I can make men into vampires," Vermilion said.

"How many?" Lazaretto asked.

Vermilion looked at the men sitting across from him, his eyes slowly passing from face to face before he answered. "An army's worth," he said after leaving them in silence.

Lazaretto gave a triumphant laugh and finished his drink, slamming the glass back onto the table. "There you have it," he said, opening his arms to the table. "Our answer."

"What answer?" Charlie said.

"We're going to raise an army. We're going to control this whole city—hell, this whole region—with an army of vampire soldiers. That's how you earn your keep. You build me this army, and you help me keep control. What do you say?"

Charlie looked at Vermilion, who continued to look at Lazaretto. The vampire reached for the glass in front of him. He'd ordered absinthe when Lazaretto insisted on everybody having a drink, but hadn't touched it until this moment. He raised the glass in his hand, nodding towards Lazaretto. "I think we have an agreement," he said before taking a sip.

"Perfect," Lazaretto said. "We'll give you a quarter of the profit for your work."

"A quarter each?" Charlie asked.

"No," Lazaretto said, scoffing. "For the two of you to split."

"For what we're going to give you, we deserve at least half."

Lazaretto laughed boisterously, his belly shaking. "Half?" he said. "I offer you a quarter and you want half? You're lucky to be above ground still, and you want half?" Lazaretto turned towards Vermilion; his fat finger pointed at Charlie. "Is this guy serious? Half?"

The vampire shook his head, raising the glass to his lips once more. "A quarter is more than generous," he said.

"See?" Lazaretto said. "I knew one of you could be reasonable. And while we're all being reasonable, there's one more thing we need to talk about."

"What is that?" Charlie asked angrily.

Lazaretto turned his head slowly to Charlie. "It's something we need to discuss over drinks," he said, raising his empty glass. "Hop on over to the bar and let that pretty young thing know we're running dry."

"I'm not your waiter."

"I know. She is. Now go tell her."

Vermilion nodded at Charlie and waved him away. After shaking his head at the group of them, he stormed off towards the bar.

When he was out of earshot, Lazaretto took the opportunity to lean across the table and whisper to the vampire. "I'll be honest, I'm not sure why you're running around with that joker."

"He's family," Vermilion said.

"I had family, too." Lazaretto looked around at the private room and the men sitting around him. "I traded up."

"You've done very well for yourself."

"You can too," Lazaretto said. "You do what you want, but you ditch the baggage, we can go thirty percent instead of twenty-five. And that would be all yours, no need to split it." Lazaretto sat back down and raised his eyebrows. "Think about it."

Charlie returned, annoyed. "She's got the order—now what is it you want from us?"

"I normally don't do this without the drinks, but I can see you're an anxious man, Charlie, so I'll go ahead and get started," Lazaretto said. "Before we jump into bed together, there's one bit of business I'd like you to take care of—call it a trial run. You do this, and the debt you owe is forgotten, Charlie, the bounty is off your head and Vermilion—my dead men will be bygones."

"What is it?" Charlie asked.

"Since we're getting into the business of vampires, I think it's important that we take care of the competition." Lazaretto pointed to Vermilion. "And I think you might know them."

"Who is it?" Charlie asked.

"They call him Monsieur Du Vide."

"Who is that?"

"Do you know, Vermilion?"

The vampire nodded cordially and turned to Charlie. "He's the man who arranged for my passage—his organization, at least."

"Perfect," Lazaretto said.

The waitress brought the drinks to the table, setting them down in front of each of the men. She asked if there would be anything else they needed, but Lazaretto said no and sent her on her way with a slap on her rear.

"I want Du Vide dead," Lazaretto said. "And his lady friend, the one called Madame Lovebite, I want her dead too. We kill them both and anybody else from their organization that gets in our way, and we take control. We do that, then we get a pipeline of vampires coming into this country."

The door to the room opened, and a potbellied thug in a fedora poked his head inside, looking around the smoky room. When he saw Slits sitting in the corner, he stepped inside and quickly walked to him and whispered in his ear. Slits nodded and buttoned his jacket.

"I'll be back, boss," he said. "Something's come up."

"Don't be long," Lazaretto said. "You're going to want to be here for this."

Slits headed off with the thug, closing the door behind them.

"So, what do you say?" Lazaretto said. "We have a deal?"

Vermilion hunched forward over the table to talk to Lazaretto. "How exactly do you expect us to take care of Monsieur Du Vide?"

"That's your business," Lazaretto said. "Anyway you want. If you want to bring me back a souvenir, I'd be happy to have it."

"Where do we find him?"

"He's around," Lazaretto said. "In fact, he's got a shipment coming in tonight, ain't that right, Frenchy?"

"That's what the Madame said." Frenchy leaned forward in his seat. "That will lead us right to Du Vide. It still leaves the Madame, but we can figure that one out after tonight."

Lazaretto looked across the table to the vampire. "What do you think?"

Vermilion held his cane, looking at the features of the bird skull like an artist studying a painting, tapping his finger on it as he thought. "Tonight, then," the vampire said. He turned to look at Charlie, then nodded. "We are ready."

"What about Petey?" Charlie said. "We could use the extra help."

"Your friend stays with us," Frenchy said before Lazaretto could answer. "Until the job is done—as an assurance."

Lazaretto nodded in agreement. "Tonight then," he said. "Frenchy, you take these two to the docks, wait for the shipment, see that they get where they need to go."

"Of course," Frenchy said. "We can leave now."

Charlie raised his glass, having missed the last toast, but nobody moved to meet him. "Now we can celebrate," Charlie said, holding his glass in the air, alone. "Maybe we could head upstairs first, enjoy ourselves a little."

"The third floor?" Lazaretto said.

"Yes," Charlie said, suddenly feeling sheepish. "That's where the real action is, right?"

"Let's not get ahead of ourselves. You two take care of my Du Vide problem, and then we'll head up." He pointed to Frenchy. "Let's get moving," he said.

Charlie settled back in his seat, looking disappointed. He sipped from his glass quietly. The door opened again when Slits returned, walking briskly to the table.

"You just missed it," Lazaretto said. "This partnership might just work out."

"Great, Boss," Slits said. "About that—I think you're going to want to come see this?"

"See what?"

"The problem," Slits said.

"What is it?"

"My guys, they picked up somebody from the docks. Eugene said he was asking questions."

"What kind of questions?"

Slits looked over at Vermilion. "About vampires."

Lazaretto looked grim. "Let's not keep him waiting, then," he said, standing from his seat. Frenchy and Charlie did the same, but Vermilion finished his absinthe before joining them.

The group of them headed for the door, the waitress telling them all to have a good night as they left. Slits hung in the back, pulling Frenchy aside as Vermilion and Charlie walked ahead with Lazaretto.

"You sure about this?" Slits asked.

"Lazaretto is," Frenchy said.

"Yeah, but vampires? Raising an army, taking control of it. Don't it all seem a little dangerous?" Slits said. "And sudden?"

"He's gotten us here, hasn't he?"

"Sure," Slits said. "But never like this."

"It will be fine," Frenchy said. "We'll take care of Du Vide tonight, get us out of this whole business, and then we can talk some sense into him."

"And the vampire?" Slits asked.

"We can take care of that too, when the time comes."

"You sure?"

"Let's just get through tonight," Frenchy said. "One problem at a time."

CHAPTER 27

NIGHTINGALE WASN'T SURE HOW long he'd been out.

When he finally came to, his head throbbed, ears rang, and ribs ached. They had left him on the floor of a cold, dark room, which helped his head. They hadn't bothered to tie him up but had taken everything: his gun, wallet, and coat. He lay in his suit, checking if anything was broken. As far as he could tell, nothing was—it just hurt like hell.

In the windowless room, time lost meaning. Nightingale focused on his breathing and replayed the events of the day. He wondered about Magdalene. He was glad she hadn't come to the docks, though maybe things would've gone smoother. Or maybe she'd be in the next room. He doubted these types would spare a woman, even a nun. She'd saved him enough trouble already.

As he put the pieces of his mind back together, he tried to focus on what he'd seen today, what he'd learned. He tried to remember Juliette, to think about her, to remind himself why he was doing this.

At some point, he heard music start. It was distant and muffled and mixed with the sounds of people. Lots of people. It sounded like they were having a good time. It didn't help his headache.

The door unlatched, spilling harsh light into the dark. Dagger-like pain stabbed his eyes; he closed them tightly. Footsteps echoed around him as he was hoisted up by the arms. Nightingale kept his eyes closed and his head down as they dragged him down the hall.

They him into another room, and tossed him in a chair. They stripped his suit coat off him, took out his cufflinks, and pushed up his sleeves. They made sure to go hard on him as they pushed him around; more than once, he got a punch to the gut when he wasn't moving the way they wanted him to. They men backed off eventually, and when he heard the door close, Nightingale took three deep breaths before slowly opening his eyes.

The room was stark; a single, naked bulb hung overhead. The walls were bare brick curving overhead. There was a table in front of him and a chair on the other side of it. Faintly, he could still hear the muffled rhythm of music and movement above him.

He took another deep breath. Something inside him stung sharply. He hoped it wasn't serious. His hands were bound behind the chair; ankles secured to the legs. Nightingale stretched his neck and heard his spine crackle. He was in rough shape.

The door opened again, and this time the light wasn't so searing. The two thugs—the same ones who had jumped him outside the docks—stepped back inside, this time accompanied by a third man. He was long and skinny, with short hair beginning to thin at the widow's peak. He had a glass in his hand, which he set down on the table before taking the seat across from Nightingale.

One of the thugs brought a bundle to the table, laying it out in front of the other man—Nightingale's coat, his cufflinks resting on top, his gun, the bullets, the tarot cards and papers, his brand, everything Nightingale had carried in his pockets. Hiding the aches and pains that flared over his body, Nightingale raised his head, trying to look defiant.

"Got a smoke?"

The two thugs were expressionless, but the other man sneered. He reached into his coat and grabbed a packet of cigarettes. He tossed it down on the table in front of Nightingale.

"I don't think we need all that," the man said, pointing to the ropes. One of the thugs walked to Nightingale, flicking open his switchblade as he loomed over the detective, then cut the ropes with a quick swipe of his knife. The ropes fell to the floor, and the thug pulled them away as Nightingale rubbed his wrists. He reached for the pack of smokes and fished out a cigarette, lipping it.

"So, this is Lazaretto's place," Nightingale said. "And if I remember my mugshots, you're Slits Nicotero." He pointed a shaky finger at the man across the table.

"My boys here say they picked you up at the docks, but you don't look like a dock worker to me," Slits said.

"I'm a detective."

"Then what were you doing on the waterfront?"

"My job."

Slits turned his head, talking to the two thugs. "Loosen him up a little more," he said.

The two thugs grinned at Slits' order, each pressing a fist into their opposite palm as they approached Nightingale. One thug grabbed Nightingale's arms from behind and hoisted him out of the chair while the other, a big man, faced him. The thug holding him back restrained Nightingale by his arms; the other began to land heavy punches into Nightingale's torso. The first blow knocked the wind out of him and sent the unlit cigarette flying. Each punch left him gasping, pain radiating through his body until his vision darkened at the edges. Just when he thought he'd pass out, they finished and dropped him back into the chair.

Keeping his head down, Nightingale braced himself against the table's edge. He felt like vomiting. His breaths were slow, deep, ragged. The two thugs hovered above, just waiting for the next order.

"This can be easy, or it can be hard, detective," the man on the other side of the table said. "And I'll be the one to decide. If you're helpful, I'll make this easy for you. If you continue being your difficult self, I'll make sure whatever's left of you in the end will still tell us what we want to know."

Nightingale didn't answer. He was still trying to gather himself.

Slits reached across the table to Nightingale's coat, grabbed the detective's wallet, and flipped it open. Inside the flap was a gold badge: shield-shaped, with an eagle on top and an eye in the center. The words 'PRIVATE INVESTIGATOR' circled around it. Slits tossed the wallet back onto the table and began sorting through the rest of Nightingale's belongings.

He picked up the revolver, hefting it in his hand. "Good weight," he said, genuinely seeming impressed. Using the gun's barrel, he pushed aside the lighter and a rosary. When he found the brand, he put the gun down and picked it up, slipping it on over his fingers, clenching his fist around it, like they were brass knuckles. He held up his hand, examining it, looking down at the metal cross.

"Interesting tools for a detective," he said.

"I take," Nightingale wheezed, "interesting jobs."

"And which of your interesting jobs brought you down to our docks?" Still going through Nightingale's things, he had moved onto the rosary, holding it up, rubbing the cross with his thumb.

Nightingale paused. He didn't think he could take another beating, but he didn't want to crack. He'd give Lazaretto's people just enough.

"I'm looking for a girl."

"That ain't what Tautopolis told us," one of the thugs said. "He said this guy was asking about some of the shipments—Du Vide's shipments."

Slits raised an eyebrow. "What do you know about Du Vide, detective?"

"Never heard of him."

"You must not be a very good detective, then," Slits said. He picked up the card that Nightingale had taken from Tautopolis' office and lifted it up so that the detective could see the name Apophrades, Inc. on it. "What were you looking for at the docks? It wasn't a little girl, not many of those around those parts."

"The one that took her."

"A man?"

"Sure."

"A vampire," Slits said, almost making it a question. Nightingale raised his head to look at the man across from him. The two thugs looked at each other, confused. "Keep him awake," Slits continued. "Lazaretto's going to want to talk to him."

The two thugs just nodded as Slits left, shrugging their shoulders after the door closed. Nightingale let himself collapse on the table. When one of the thugs put his hands on him, Nightingale waved him away.

"I'm awake, you loaf, but you touch me again, I might not be," he said. "See how your boss likes that."

The two thugs backed off. Nightingale breathed heavily, his forehead resting on the table, his elbows on his knees. It hurt to swallow. It hurt to talk. Every inch of him seemed to ache and burn with bruises. Slowly, he started to get a handle on it. The pain wasn't going away, but he was getting used to it, at least. He felt like he could sit up, just as he heard the door open.

Raising his head, he was able to watch as Slits came back in, followed by a broad, behemoth, who walked in, draped in fine clothing, his bald head reflecting the light of the bare bulb. He knew the face; he'd seen it in newspapers and case files alike.

"Anton Lazaretto," Nightingale said, trying not to slur his speech.

The large figure loomed over the detective, resting his fists on the table, knuckles down, blocking out the light.

"You're the detective," Lazaretto said. "The one poking his nose around my business."

"To be fair," Nightingale said, wincing. "I didn't know it was yours until now."

"What do you know about vampires?" Lazaretto said. Noticing the confused expressions on the two thugs, he looked up at them. "You might as well know. There are vampires around. You'll be meeting one soon enough."

"You serious, boss?" one of the thugs asked.

"You ever know me not to be?"

The thug stayed silent and took a step back.

"You're working with them?" Nightingale asked.

"With one," Lazaretto said. "Call it an experiment."

"It ends poorly," Nightingale said.

The mob boss looked at the items on the table, pushing aside the rosary and the tarot cards, grabbing the cross brand and slipping it over his fingers, flexing his hand into a heavy fist.

"That a threat or something?"

"It's just the truth."

"You're calling me a liar?"

"No. Just telling you what I know."

"I'm stupid then? In over my head? Some kind of idiot doesn't know what he's getting himself into?"

"Yeah," Nightingale said. "That's the one."

Lazaretto looked up at the two thugs, raising his hand. The two thugs knew what it meant. Before Nightingale could even react, the big men were on him, hoisting him out of the chair once more by the arms. Still shaky from his beating before, Nightingale took a moment to get his legs underneath him. The two men pinned him up against the wall, and Lazaretto came around the table to face him.

At first, it looked like Lazaretto was going to ask him another question, but instead, he hit Nightingale with a left hook. He still wore the brand around his fingers, and the metal cut into Nightingale's side. Lazaretto pulled back, hitting him again and again. The last time Lazaretto hit him, Nightingale felt something give, followed by the warm trickle of blood down his side. Lazaretto stepped back, sitting against the edge of the table, and the two thugs dropped Nightingale to the floor. On his shirt, where Lazaretto had been hitting him, was the bloody mark of a cross, the red spreading out across the fabric.

"You act like a hard man, but you ain't nothing," Lazaretto said. "You ever killed a vampire?"

Nightingale couldn't talk; his arms were wrapped around his stomach as he lay on the floor, but he managed to nod.

"If you can do it," Lazaretto said. "So can I. Just like I done to a thousand other men. Just like I'm gonna do to you." The mobster flexed his shoulders, making his back crack. "Take this hunk of garbage out of here, leave him where nobody's gonna find him."

As the two thugs moved in to grab Nightingale, there was a knock at the door. Slits answered it, putting his head out into the hallway. There were muffled voices, and when Slits stepped back in, he talked to Lazaretto.

"It's Madame Lovebite," he said.

"What does she want?"

"To talk to him," Slits said, pointing to Nightingale.

Lazaretto frowned and shrugged his shoulders. "What do I care?" he said. "Let her in."

Slits opened the door, and Madame Lovebite stepped into the room, her heels clicking on the cold, hard stone floor.

"You want this lump of meat?" Lazaretto said to her, pointing down to where Nightingale lay.

"If you're finished with him," she said.

"I was about to be," Lazaretto said. "But you can have a moment with him first, if you like."

"I would," the Madame said.

"He seems to know something about your business."

"That's exactly what I want to talk to him about."

Lazaretto nodded and snapped his fingers. "Get him in the chair," he said to the two thugs. As they grabbed him and dragged him back to the seat, Lazaretto crossed to the door. "You've got a few minutes," he said.

"I appreciate that," the Madame said. She pointed to the two thugs. "But I want to talk to him alone."

"However you like," Lazaretto said, snapping his fingers again; the two thugs filed out. Before he left, Lazaretto tapped the card from the docks on the table, his fat fingers falling over Apophrades, Inc. "And this prick knows more than he says he does."

The heavy metal door shut behind them, leaving the Madame and Nightingale alone. She took the seat across the table, sitting down to look at the man sitting opposite her. He was bloody and bruised, wheezing as he breathed. One hand was held to his side, the other rested on the table, clenched into a fist.

"Detective Nightingale," she said. "I've been looking for you."

He stared at her with bloodshot eyes, taking heavy breaths through his nose that puffed up his chest. He opened his mouth to speak, closed it quickly to swallow, then opened it again. "Madame Lovebite," he said. "You're not part of Lazaretto's entourage. That must mean you're with Apophrades, Inc."

"You've been working hard, I see."

"I get that way when I'm trying to find a little girl."

"A little girl?" the Madame asked, masking her confusion.

"The ones you use to bring the vampires over," Nightingale said. "She was taken."

The Madame took a breath, making sure she was composed before speaking. "I imagine it's confusing, ending up in a place like this for something like that."

"Why are you here?"

"I told you; I've been looking for you," she said.

"Why?"

"I was going to try and stop you."

"From finding a child?"

"From finding things you weren't supposed to know about."

"Of course," Nightingale said. "The business."

"I have interests to protect."

"I've seen how you protect them."

"What do you mean?"

Nightingale nodded towards the tarot cards on the table. The Madame reached out, turning them over so that they faced up, sliding them side by side so she could see both. "Where did you get these?" she asked.

"One belonged to the missing girl, Juliette," he said.

"And the other?"

"That was Antonia's. She traveled with Juliette."

"She gave it to you?"

"No," Nightingale said. "She was dead."

The Madame choked back her surprise once more, only giving the slightest tilt of her head.

"Huh," Nightingale said. "I guess somebody at the office didn't tell you."

"We don't kill young women."

"Somebody did," Nightingale said.

The Madame picked up the tarot card, looking at it, studying the sullen figure on the boat. Only seeing the woman's back, she'd never noticed how frightened she appeared, covered by an old blanket, crossing to a new land—one that promised a fresh start, but was likely just as cruel as the one she'd left. She set the card back down on the table.

"Have you ever had your fortune read, detective?"

Nightingale scoffed. "I don't think I have much of one left."

"Would you let me read yours?"

"Why?"

"I want to know what kind of man I'm talking to."

"Fine," he said.

The Madame reached into her purse, taking out her deck of cards. Nightingale noticed they looked identical to the ones he'd been finding all over the city, but he wasn't surprised, and it wasn't worth the effort to ask about them.

"Touch the deck," she said.

Nightingale did, reaching out his hand and tapping the deck, leaving bloody fingerprints behind. With her delicate hand, she shuffled the cards, the bloody one disappearing somewhere into the deck. When she finished, she set it down, cutting the cards in half, tucking the top half beneath the bottom, and peeling off the first card. It showed a young man, hair blowing in the wind, standing on a hillside, wielding a sword.

"The Page of Swords," the Madame said. "You're a passionate man," Detective. A man of action. Look how the page leans to one direction, holding his blade, but he looks off in the opposite direction, eyes open to the world around him. The Page of Swords is curious, and with his questions, he brings change."

She took the next card from the top of the deck, setting it down beside the other. This one depicted a man and a woman standing naked together, gazing up at the heavens where a radiant angel looked down upon them. A wry, half-smile crossed the Madame's face. "The Lovers," she said. "In reverse."

"What does that mean?"

"Discord, detective. Disharmony."

"That sounds about right."

"Sometimes the Lovers mean you have inner conflict. But it can also mean that you will soon face a tough decision. See the angel, here," she said, pointing to the figure at the top of the card. "It's Raphael, whose name means 'God has healed.' He's supposed to remind us that, when making a decision, no matter how tough, you must trust your values—no matter how much we may want to take an easier path."

A pained smile crossed Nightingale's face as the Madame reached for another card. She stopped her hand when she realized it was the card with Nightingale's bloody fingerprints. She took it, softly, and laid it down with the others.

"The Hanged Man," she said, pointing to the figure on the card. He hung from a tree, upside down, one foot tied to it, the other crossed behind it at the knee. His hands were bound, but his face was stoic and calm.

"The Hanged Man," Nightingale repeated. "One sympathizes."

"Sometimes," the Madame said, "The Hanged Man represents surrender—but I don't think that's what he means for you." She pushed the card forward, just a bit closer, so that Nightingale could see it. He's a man alone, apart from the world, viewing it in a way no one else does. One foot is bound, the other is free—he has a foot in both worlds, where he's free to make his own decisions, but still held prisoner by some other force. Although seeing how calm he is, one has to wonder if it's a punishment of his own making."

Nightingale surveyed the cards, then looked up to face the Madame. She was staring at him—or through him, more like, with those piercing green eyes.

"Everyone I've met who's been connected to Apophrades, Inc. had a tarot card. Like the ones from the girls, the ones with the design just like the deck here," he said.

"Do you have a question, detective?"

"I do," he said. "What card do you have?"

The Madame was surprised, leaning back in her seat. Then, reaching into her purse, she took a lone tarot card out, placing it face down on the table and sliding it across to Nightingale. He reached forward, taking the card and flipping it over.

Sitting in front of a veil was a beautiful woman dressed all in white; she wore a cross around her neck and had a crescent moon at her feet. On either side of the woman was a pillar, one white and one black. The left one was marked with a B, and the other with a J. At the bottom of the card was the woman's name.

THE HIGH PRIESTESS

"What does this one mean?" Nightingale asked.

She pointed to the black pillar "B," she said, "for Boaz—'*in his strength*'." She pointed to the other column with the J. "Jachin, '*he will establish*'." She leaned back in her chair. "Duality, Detective Nightingale. The acceptance of such is the only way to get through the veil."

Nightingale smiled. He watched the woman across from him, beautiful and dangerous. He knew the type. "You see duality," the detective said. "I see conflict."

"That's because we all see what we want to see."

"And what do you want to see? Do you want me dead or alive?"

"I'm afraid, detective, that's no longer my decision."

"If only you'd found me first," he said.

"If only you'd been easier to catch."

The door opened behind the Madame, and Lazaretto walked back in, flanked by the two thugs, Slits filing in behind all of them.

"Time's up, Madame Lovebite," Lazaretto said. "I hope you said your goodbyes to this piece of garbage."

"You sure you don't want me to take care of him?" she said.

Lazaretto laughed. "We'll save you the trouble."

"Good riddance, then," she said, looking to the detective.

"All good things," Nightingale said, looking back at her.

"But I think we need to have a serious discussion," Lazaretto said. "You, me, and Monsieur Du Vide. We've got one private dick snooping around; there are going to be others."

"You're absolutely right," she said.

"How about it, then? Let's go see the Monsieur right now."

"He doesn't like visitors."

"I don't like prison," Lazaretto said. "Take us to him."

"Fine," Madame Lovebite said. "But whatever happens, it's all on you."

"Oh, trust me, sweetheart," Lazaretto said through his cigar. "I know." He turned to the two thugs. "Make sure nobody finds this guy."

The Madame gathered her cards from the table, putting them back in her purse, giving Nightingale one last look before Lazaretto escorted her out of the room, his fat hand on her slender back. Slits took a moment inside. "Make it ugly," he said to his men before bringing a cigarette to his lips. and lighting it.

As the door closed, the two thugs nodded and smiled, their eyes fixed hungrily on Nightingale. The detective put up as much of a fight as he could, which didn't amount to much beyond sporadic struggles. They dragged him out of the room and down the hall, through a back door, and into the alley where they had parked their car. They slugged him once more in the stomach before tossing him back into the trunk. One of the thugs had grabbed his belongings, bundled them up in his coat, and held them all under his arm. He tossed it all into the back seat and they drove off, out of the city.

In the darkness, Nightingale wasn't sure how long they had driven. He wasn't even sure he'd been awake for the whole thing. His stomach was sticky with blood, his head and body pulsed with pain. He could feel the gash across his ribs from where Lazaretto had been hitting him with the brand. He felt every bump and pit in the road as they jostled away, each time a jolt of pain travelled down his body like a lightning bolt.

He heard the back tires on gravel, and the car gradually slowed down, finally coming to a rolling stop. They didn't kill the engine, but Nightingale heard their two doors open and their footsteps as they came around to the back of the car.

The trunk popped open, and they hefted Nightingale out, tossing him to the ground. They slammed the trunk closed and then dragged him a few feet in front of the car.

They were in an open pit, full of rocks. The city lights were a way off in the distance, and the only light out here came from the headlights. The two thugs stood in silhouette in front of him. One of them opened his coat and drew a pistol.

Nightingale got up on his knees, facing towards the men, the bright lights shining in his face. He sighed. "Let's get this over with."

"No last words?" the one with the gun asked.

"I'll see you in hell," Nightingale said.

The two thugs turned towards each other and, surrounded by the blinding light, he could see them shrug.

"If that's all," the thug said, raising the gun.

Nightingale took in a final, deep breath, waiting for the shot.

But the shot didn't come; instead, there was a roar and a flash of light behind them. Nightingale realized what it was a split second before the two thugs did, but it was enough. He tossed himself to the ground, rolling out of the way, just in time to see a flash of powder blue in the dark and hear the bone-crunching collision of metal on metal.

CHAPTER 28

SISTER MAGDALENE SAT IN her car outside the Emporium Historia. Nightingale had left her at the house where they'd found Antonia, leaving in a cab for the docks. She'd felt fine while she was with him; now, alone in her car, the full weight of the violent death they had discovered pressed down on her. She tried to push it from her mind, but she continued drifting back to the memory of the body, the young girl, how frightened she must have been, how confused. Her eyes blurred with tears, and her hands shook, overcome by the horror she'd witnessed. She wished she'd never seen it. Magdalene forced herself to dry her tears and step from the car into the rain, seeking comfort in being near someone—anyone—other than the haunting ghost of the young girl.

She had removed her veil at the house and kept it off. She wanted to feel the rain in her hair and on her face. She hoped it would wash away her tears. She held the silver cross in her hand, clutching it tightly, and stepped into the store.

"Good evening," said the man behind the counter without looking up from the book he was reading. He was sitting on a stool, leaning forward. He licked his index finger as he turned the page. When he finally looked up, he straightened his posture. "Oh," he said, surprised. "Hello, Sister."

Before even introducing herself, Magdalene crossed the room, almost running to the counter, so grateful to not be alone any longer with the memory of the murdered girl. "I know Nightingale," she said. "And I need your help." Then the tears came rushing out.

Dr. Bone fixed a pot of tea and poured it into a steaming mug for her. He took Magdalene to the back room as she sobbed. She told him about the missing girl, hiring Nightingale, and helping with the investigation. She ended with the discovery of Antonia's body. By the time she finished that part of the story, her tears had dried up, and her unease had lessened in the company of Franklin Bonaparte.

"Night always had a knack for picking the tough ones," Bone said, stroking his goatee. "And you say he's gone to the docks now?"

"That's right," Magdalene said.

"Good," Bone said, nodding. "I've made a friend down there today. He can help our intrepid detective—he had a tarot card too."

Magdalene sipped her tea. "What are they, the cards?"

"Identification, we think," Bone said. "Helps them keep track of people and who they are, what they mean to the organization."

"Crooks and killers," she said.

"It seems to be, yes."

"I hope he's safe out there," the sister said.

"He will be," Bone said, taking Magdalene's hand. "He's too stubborn to do otherwise. You just sit tight here until he gets back."

"There's something I'm meant to ask you," Magdalene said, reaching into her pocket, pulling out the silver cross. "This is why Sebastian sent me here, he said you might be able to help."

Dr. Bone took the bifocals from his pocket, clipped to a gold chain. He set them on the tip of his nose as he took the cross and held it up to examine it.

"From the killer?" he said.

"That's right, I took it—" Magdalene paused, remembering the attack, "—when I scratched him."

Rubbing his thumb along the inscription, he read it out loud. "*Praestare Aut Providere.*"

"We weren't sure what it meant. Neither of us speaks Latin."

"To perform or provide," Bone said, looking over his glasses and smiling at Magdalene. "That's why Nightingale keeps me around."

"What do you suppose that means?"

Looking towards the ceiling, Bone lowered the cross, setting his hands in his lap. "I've heard that before somewhere," he said. He snapped his fingers and held one of them up. "Just a moment," he said, standing from his seat and stepping out into the store. She could hear him, humming to himself, and after a moment, he returned, this time with a book in his hand. He took his seat again as he flipped through the pages.

"Here it is," he said as he tapped his finger on the open book, a triumphant smile crossing his face. He turned the book around, laying it open on the coffee table in front of Magdalene. "That's the motto of military chaplains."

"He was a soldier."

"Seems like it, or one gave him the cross." Bone brought the cross back up to his face, studying the rest of the markings.

"We weren't sure about the rest of it," Magdalene said. "We thought they were Roman numerals."

"You're correct," Bone said.

"You know what they mean?"

"Three hundred and twenty-nine," Bone said. "And then eighty-three."

"Not a date, then."

"No," Bone said, leaning forward and showing the cross to Magdalene, pointing to the numbers. "The 329th Infantry Regiment of the 83rd Infantry Division. Army."

Magdalene took the cross back, reexamining the inscription. "No wonder this man knew how to kill."

"Nasty thing we put our boys through out there. We're all afraid we might do it again if Europe keeps going the way it is."

The bell above the front door chimed, and they looked up at the noise. "We don't usually get customers this late in the day," Bone said. "Or in this weather. You don't think you could have been followed, do you?"

She shook her head. "I don't think so."

"Probably nothing, then," Bone said. He put up his hand, motioning for Magdalene to stay put. He stepped back into the store, where Magdalene could hear him greet someone with a muffled woman's voice responding.

Easing toward the door, Magdalene peeked through; she wanted to see who was there. Her skin prickled with goosebumps; after the day she'd had, her nerves were feeling frayed at the ends.

Inside the shop, Bone sat behind the counter next to the cash register. His voice was low, but Magdalene could tell he was talking about tarot, reading the cards. He spoke with a woman seated across from him. Her black hair shimmered in the overhead lights. She held herself with elegant poise and wore a beautiful black dress. Her coat was lined with fur, and her hands, surprisingly, were covered in tattoos. The woman turned her head slightly. Magdalene retreated a step backwards.

The woman turned back to Bone and watched him read the tarot for her. Bone smiled as he spoke. He was quite charming, Magdalene thought, especially when he was trying, which he was with this woman. She saw him touch her hands, motioning towards the tattoos on her wrists. Magdalene wished she could hear more of what they were saying.

As she thought that, the front door flew open, the bell chiming again. Magdalene could see that it had startled Bone and the woman as much as it had startled her. She could see that the woman's hand had slipped under the fold of her dress, and it slowly came out as the man talked, which she found curious.

The man at the door seemed to know Bone, and in his quick speech, Magdalene couldn't hear what he said at first. And then she understood—it was Nightingale, something had happened at the docks, he'd been taken to a place called the Rag & Bone.

Magdalene wanted to rush to her car to help him, but she didn't want to leave with the woman still there. That problem was solved quickly. The woman in black gathered her things, and as Bone excused himself, so did she, saying that there was something she needed to take care of.

As the bell chimed and the door closed, leaving Bone and the other man alone in the shop, Magdalene emerged from the back room.

"What happened to Sebastian?" she asked.

"They got him."

"I'm going to get him."

"He's at the Rag & Bone," Bone said. "It's not the kind of place for a sister to be, that's for sure."

"I wasn't always a sister," she said. She checked her purse for her car keys and moved towards the door.

"These are Lazaretto's people. Might even be the ones who killed that girl you found. You don't want to get mixed up with them."

"It's my fault Nightingale's mixed up in this," she said as she started to walk outside.

"Wait," Bone said, and Magdalene halted. Bone reached under the counter and pulled out a small, rectangular box. He handed it to Magdalene. "These are silver bullets. When you get to Night, he might need these." She took the box, and Bone grabbed her hands, wrapping his around hers. "And none of this is your fault. Night gets mixed up in a lot of things, whether he has help or not."

Magdalene tried to smile. "I'll make sure he gets these," she said, and then left.

"Be careful," Bone shouted after her.

It was raining hard again as she drove her powder blue Studebaker through the streets. Water washed up against the tires. The heavy car moved sluggishly through the puddles. Finding the Rag & Bone wasn't hard; she'd passed it plenty of times. The bright lights in the dark night acted as a beacon. She drove past and turned the corner, parking where she could see the back entrance. She stopped and thought a moment. If they had Nightingale, he'd be in the back somewhere. It was nowhere she could get. Magdalene felt overwhelmingly helpless. Gangsters. Vampires. She was lost in a world of killers and thieves. What could she possibly do?

She clutched at the cross that hung around her neck.

Something, she thought. *She had to do something.*

Quickly, Sister Magdalene removed the white wimple from her shoulders and the scapular hanging beneath. She laid them both on the seat beside her. She was left in her black tunic and tucked the cross into her collar. She stepped out of the car and into the rain, leaving her religious garb behind. From the front of the building, jazz music played. She heard the buzz of conversations and drunken revelry. For a moment, she felt strange without the religious pieces of her outfit, but they would draw too much attention. She closed the door and crossed the street quickly.

There was no traffic, and she saw no pedestrians. Even with the noise in front of the place, the back of the club felt still and empty. When she reached the alley, she walked in the shadows. A gutter ran down the middle of the path, water streaming down it. Rats scurried along the foundations of buildings, and the rain pattered against rooftops and trash cans. Maybe, she thought, there would be a way in, a kitchen or something. Some way to get inside. Maybe she was foolhardy, but she didn't know what else she could do.

Magdalene turned a corner beside the building, down a narrow passage that ran between the club and the building beside it. She stopped as soon as she turned, as she interrupted a man and a woman in the narrow space, the woman's dress hiked up above her thigh, the man's hand firmly placed on her buttock, their lips locked in a lustful kiss. They pulled apart suddenly as the sister came into view, retreating to other corners.

"I apologize," Magdalene said, flustered, averting her eyes. The man cleared his throat, adjusting his tie, and the woman smoothed out her dress. Magdalene pointed behind her. "I was just—" she paused. "Is there a door to the kitchen. I'm a waitress."

The man coughed and pointed to the other side of the building. "Cooks smoke over there," he said.

"Perfect. Thank you," Magdalene said. "I'll be on my way."

She turned and left; her cheeks red as she hurried to the other side of the club. The building was large, the biggest on the block, by far. There were no windows on this side of it, either, only a storm cellar door that she assumed led to a storeroom built beneath the club.

When she reached the other side, she turned the corner. There was a door there, a red one with a small glass window at eye level. She knocked, and when the door opened, a baby-faced man answered it. He looked Magdalene up and down and smiled.

"What's a pretty little dish doing knocking on the back door?" he asked. "You lost or something?"

Magdalene put a hand on the man's chest. "I found you, didn't I?"

The man smiled. "This must be my lucky night."

"Not yours," Magdalene said. "Lazaretto said he had someone here, a detective. I was told I needed to see him."

"The detective they dragged in here earlier?"

"That's the one."

"I don't think he's exactly taking guests," the doorman said. "Not sure they'd need something like you."

"Well," Magdalene said. "You can take that up with Mr. Lazaretto if it's so important to you."

"OK, OK, I don't think we need to do that." The man looked behind him. "Come on in," he said. "Let's go find out if your man's even here still."

"Oh?" Magdalene said. "I'm too late?"

"Maybe," the doorman said. "I heard they were taking him out of here."

Magdalene straightened her back, pushing out her chest. Her hands were shaking, but she clasped them over her stomach to hold them still. She felt flushed, her stomach was a tight ball, and her heart pounded. "Then we'd better hurry," she said.

"Follow me," the doorman said, not seeming to notice the tension.

He led her to a dark hallway and opened a door marked PRIVATE. It opened onto a short flight of stairs that took them beneath the club. The air grew colder, and the sounds of the club became muffled. Down here, the walls were brick, and the lights were dim, and the few doors there were plain and heavy. The hallway was empty, except for a single man sitting alone in a chair, flipping through a magazine; a drink sat on the floor beside him.

"Hey, Mikey," the doorman said to the man in the chair. "I got a special guest here who wanted to see the detective they brought in. He still around?"

Mikey looked surprised. "You just missed him," he said. "Paul just brought him out back."

The doorman turned to Magdalene. "Sorry, Sweetie," he said. "Guess you don't get to pay him a visit."

Mikey in the chair said, "I didn't hear nothing about no girl."

"I guess you're not important enough," Magdalene said.

The man in the chair looked hurt. "Well, don't you worry, sweet thing," he said. "Paul will show him a helluva time before putting him on ice."

Magdalene's head swam. "They're going to kill him?"

"That's the rumor."

"Oh well," she said. "Guess I came out for nothing."

"I wouldn't say nothing, honey," the doorman said.

"How long ago did they take him?" Magdalene asked, ignoring the man's advances.

"Not even a minute," Mikey said. "I guess if it means that much to you, you could try and catch them."

"Which way?"

Mikey pointed down the hall to the storm cellar doors. "Through the back."

"Thank you," Magdalene said. She took off running down the hall, pushing the doors open as she went. Rain splashed on her face, and just as she crested the top of the stairs, she heard a car engine come to life only a few feet away. As it rumbled off down the alleyway, she turned and ran in the other direction, towards her powder blue Studebaker. As she tore open the driver's side door, she saw the taillights of the other car disappear. She jabbed the starter and her car rumbled to life. Cranking the wheel, she turned her big boat of a car, heading in the direction she'd seen the taillights go.

Pressing the pedal down to the floor, she sped through the rainy streets, lights whizzing past her windows as she gunned the car quickly down the road. The taillights were ahead; she recognized the car as the same one she had seen in the alleyway. And when she saw it, she finally slowed down, keeping her distance.

There was traffic in the city, and she kept an eye on the other car, letting three or four other vehicles get between her and them. As they got away from the Quarter and downtown, the traffic cleared, and the rain got heavier. The other cars disappeared, and she allowed the distance between them to grow wider and wider. They were headed out of town.

Anxiously, she tapped the steering wheel with the palm of her hand, hoping she wasn't too late, hoping it wasn't Nightingale's body they'd pull out of the car and toss. She drove slowly, matching their speed, which only made her more anxious. She focused on their taillights; two small red dots ahead of her, like beady little bat eyes staring back at her.

When the taillights disappeared, she panicked, speeding up to see where they went. They had turned off the road. There was a gate that had been left open; a sign hung crookedly on it, reading "GENTILLY QUARRY." She killed her headlights and drove through the darkness, slowly, hearing the tires crunch over the wet, crushed limestone. She rolled down her window, despite the heavy rain, listening for the other car. She could hear them up ahead, driving slowly, too.

They were northeast of the city, the lights of New Orleans bright in the stormy night. She could smell the lake, rancid and swampy. As she crested over a hill, she could see down into the basin. Surrounded by high piles of gravel, the other car sat, headlights shining brightly in the darkness. Two men were leaving the car, heading toward the trunk. Magdalene parked at the edge of the bowl, watching them.

They opened the trunk, and in the red of the taillights, she could see them struggling to pull something out, but in the dim light, she couldn't quite make it out—until they dragged Nightingale to the front of the car and tossed him to the ground under the bright headlights. He was badly beaten, but he pulled himself up to his knees, facing the two men in front of him, resting against the hood of their car.

When the two men pulled guns, Magdalene knew she had to act. She wanted Nightingale to see her, so before she gunned the engine, she flipped on her headlights. Jamming the pedal to the floorboard, the heavy Studebaker lurched to life, roaring loudly in the rain, spitting gravel behind her in a high rooster tail. She could hear it and feel it blasting against the undercarriage. Then the car shot forward.

The heavy car raced down the hill, and right before she smashed into the back of the parked car, she honked the horn, giving Nightingale one last chance to know what was happening, hoping he'd be able to get out of the way, and that the two armed thugs wouldn't be as quick.

The two cars connected with a calamitous crunch of metal on metal. The back window of the parked car busted out, and the open trunk crumpled as the heavy Studebaker rammed into it. The momentum of the sister's car propelled the other one forward, and both of them moved through the limestone pit until the other car crashed into a pile of gravel, spilling it over the hood and burying it up to the windshield.

Quickly, Magdalene threw the car into reverse and backed up. Her smashed bumper was caught on the crushed backend of the other car, and her wheels spun on the wet ground. She looked behind her, the night colored by the bright red of her taillights. She saw a figure stand up, dazed. She thought maybe it was Nightingale, until the figure raised a gun towards her. She jammed the gas pedal once more, and with a wrenching scrape, the cars separated. She turned the steering wheel hard, and the front end swung around, clipping the man who'd pointed a pistol at her, sending him flying backward to the ground.

She put the car into park and quickly got out to look at him. As she ran through the rain, she surveyed the damage all around her—the wrecked front end of her own car, with one headlight shattered and useless, and the bumper hanging loosely from one side, the other end touching the ground, ripped away from the chassis. She could see the other car behind it, buried and wrecked, smoke sneaking out from under the hood. Then there was the man lying still on the ground. She put a hand to her mouth as she ran towards him.

The body was motionless, and as Magdalene looked at him, she thought for certain he was dead. Then a shadow fell across his body, and the sister turned to look. Another figure was between her and the Studebaker in the beam of the one remaining headlight. She knew this figure wasn't Nightingale either. This man was bigger, stockier, his shoulders coming up where his neck should have been. This man, she knew, was dangerous, and when he too raised a gun towards her, her body tensed, ready to jump away, to try and escape. But she didn't need to.

Out of the darkness, Nightingale dove at the man, his arm wrapping around the man's middle section, tackling him to the ground, his gun skittering away across the gravel. Magdalene moved to grab it, and as the two men wrestled on the wet stone beneath them, she held the gun, ready to shoot if she needed to.

The bigger man punched Nightingale in the face, sending him tumbling backwards. Magdalene almost shot then, but Nightingale was on him quick enough, throwing a right hook and then a left, spinning the man around and sending him to his knees beside the sister's car. Before the man could recover, Nightingale rushed up behind him, grabbing the man's head by his wet hair, pulling it back, and then smacking his face hard against the fender of the blue Studebaker. The man wheezed and collapsed to the ground, and Nightingale, unsteady at first, took a wide-legged stance, his shoulders hunched, his breathing heavy.

Magdalene lowered the gun and tossed it away, embracing Nightingale in the rain.

"I thought you were dead," she said breathlessly in his ear.

"So did I," he said, "until you came around."

Magdalene felt his warm body against hers. It was strong; his damp clothes clung tightly to his skin, and she could feel his muscles working beneath them. In the same second that she felt them, though, she tore away from him, embarrassed and bashful. She felt suddenly uncomfortable, and her eyes wandered to everything save Nightingale. When she saw the man she had clipped with her car lying on the ground, she gasped again and ran to his body.

"He isn't dead, is he?" Nightingale asked.

Magdalene placed a hand on his neck to check his pulse. Nightingale helped pull him over onto his back, and they could hear his ragged breathing, and in the last remaining headlight, they could see his chest rising and lowering, slowly and unevenly.

Together, they hefted both of the men to their car, forcing the front doors open against the weight of the gravel that buried them. Once both men were in the front seat, Nightingale gathered his things they'd taken from him and used his pair of handcuffs on the men, threading the chain through the loop of the steering wheel.

"That will keep them there until morning," Magdalene said when he had finished.

Nightingale put his other belongings away, slinging his arms through his shoulder holster, tucking his heavy revolver under his arm, and then covering it with his long black coat. He walked to Magdalene's car and looked at the bumper that hung crookedly off the front of the car. With a swift stomp, he kicked the bumper off with his heel and then tossed it to the side.

"We've got to get out of here," he said to Magdalene.

"You're right," she agreed. "We need to get you to a doctor or someone."

"No," Nightingale said. "Take me to the docks."

"The docks again? Are you crazy? Why do you need to go there?"

Nightingale checked the chamber of his revolver, snapping it closed. He looked at her, washed red in the taillights. "To find the dead."

CHAPTER 29

AFTER THE NUN LEFT, Bone told Willis there was nothing more for them to do. Nightingale had been in worse, he'd said, but he didn't sound too confident. Either way, Bone said, Willis was more useful at the docks. He'd left Bone's shop after lingering as long as he could. He didn't want to go back yet. He still had the vampire wards, the bag discarded, the different pieces of the kit tucked into his pockets. As the night became darker, he became more nervous.

After leaving Bone's, he stopped by the Port of Call, where he got himself some dinner—a tough chicken-fried steak with roasted potatoes and a tall glass of beer. He sat alone, eating, drinking, and thinking about what Nightingale had told him. Get the stake into the heart, no matter what.

Willis jumped when someone slapped his back and sat down beside him. He turned to see that it was Cramer. Toby was there too, taking a seat behind the red-nosed man.

"Quite the excitement today," Cramer said.

"Too much to want to talk about it," Willis said, sullenly.

"Can you believe that detective?"

"Those Lazaretto boys sure did work him over," Toby said.

"It's a good thing I gave Gene the heads up," Cramer said.

"Yeah," Toby agreed. "Good thing."

"What are you talking about?" Cramer said. "You was spilling your guts to him, telling him everything we wasn't supposed to."

"Yeah? Well, I was running all over, looking for him while you was in Tautopolis' office taking a break."

"My heart ain't good for running," Cramer said. He reached into his pocket and took out a wad of bills. "Now who's drinking with me? Toby, I know you want one. What you say, Willis?"

Willis didn't say anything.

"Come on, boy, speak up, you want a drink or not?"

"Not with you," Willis said. He pushed his half-finished plate of food away from him and took his coat from the back of the chair.

"Now, come on, what's that about?"

"I ain't drinking no more," Willis said. "I got work."

"Oh," Cramer said. "The boat, that's right. You enjoy that extra money. Maybe you can buy me a drink when you're done."

"Looks like you done alright yourself. You get that for ratting out that detective?"

"What do you care about it?"

"You probably got that man killed," Willis said. "And you're flashing your wad around like you're proud of that."

"Life's rough. It's the name of the game, out here."

"I ain't playing it no more, not tonight, not ever."

"Yeah, well, you think about that when you're spending Lazaretto's money."

Willis, looming over Cramer, grabbed the old man by the collar, lifting him out of his seat.

"What's all this about?" the red-nosed man said frantically.

"Stand," Willis said.

"Why?"

Willis cocked his fist back and landed a right hook across Cramer's jaw. There was a heavy thud, and the old man's head snapped to the side. He fell backward onto his chair, which broke beneath his weight, the splintered wood flying out from beneath him.

The bar went silent as everyone turned to see what had happened. Toby jumped to the ground, cradling Cramer's head, the old man's eyes rolling.

"What was that for?" Toby asked.

Willis ignored him, picking up the wad of cash from the table and tossing it so that the bills fluttered to the floor. "Drinks for the house," Willis said. "But no more for him, he's had enough."

There were chuckles as Willis left the bar, the men unsure what to make of it. When one of them shouted to the barkeep, "You heard the man!" the bar erupted into laughter, and Willis walked into the fog.

The solitude was pleasant as he walked to the docks. He hadn't worked a shift this late since he was a kid, just getting started. He had his hands in his pockets, walking past the closed storefronts—the storefronts turning to warehouses as he got closer to the harbor. He'd never thought much of his work until tonight. He'd never asked what was being brought in or taken out. He'd never cared. But he was left tonight wondering if maybe he should have. Either way, he was done after tonight. He'd been saving all his life, living comfortably, but wisely, not spending all his money like some of those fools—the types like

Cramer and Toby. He'd planned to work a few more years, then retire somewhere quiet, somewhere along the river where he could buy a little place and spend his days fishing and his nights dancing. He'd always planned to do it with his wife, but she'd passed some years before. Now he'd do it for her.

He was just about to the front gate of the docks when he saw a flash of light. He turned, and he saw a blue Studebaker parked down an alley facing him. Its headlights flashed on again before the passenger's door opened, and a figure stepped out.

"Heading to work?" the voice said—it was Nightingale, Willis could tell, though he sounded pained.

"You're alive," Willis said, leaving the street and heading down the alley to the car. As he got closer, he could see the rough shape Nightingale was in, the bloody shirt, the bruised face. He was holding his side, his teeth clenched in pain when he wasn't talking. No wonder his voice had sounded that way.

"Just barely," Nightingale said. "Can you get me inside?"

"The docks? You're crazy, you need to go to a hospital."

"That's what she says, too," Nightingale said, nodding toward the car where Willis could see Sister Magdalene sitting behind the steering wheel. "Now, can you get me in or not?"

Knowing there was no convincing the detective of anything else, Willis thought for a moment. "There's an old entrance on the north side. It's boarded off and locked from the inside. I think if I met you over there, I could open it.

"Good," Nightingale said. "Then I'll meet you there."

CHAPTER 30

MAGDALENE WASN'T WRONG, AND neither was Willis—Nightingale knew it. Going in now was a bad idea, but there wasn't time. The trail was red hot; if he waited, it would go cold fast. Something bigger than just a missing girl was happening. Everything was on the edge, and he had to see it through; if he didn't keep moving, everything could disappear in an instant.

While the sister waited with the car, he moved in the direction Willis had pointed, slipping through a narrow alley bordered by the dockyard's tall fence and the backs of waterlogged warehouses. The door was exactly where Willis promised, boarded up just as he'd said. Quickly, Nightingale pried the boards loose, the rotted wood coming off easily. The gate was latched on the other side, though, and the gap was too narrow for him to get his hand through. When he heard someone approach, he ducked into the shadows, but the figure that came to the door was familiar.

"You there, Nightingale?"

"Right here, Willis," he said, stepping back into view.

"Let's get you inside." Willis unlatched the heavy bolt, and together they wrenched the rusty gate open. "The boat's already here. I'll show you where it is, but you wait for me to make a move."

"You don't need to get any more involved."

"I am involved," Willis said. "Now this is my turf, so you do things my way, or I'll kick your ass right back out of that gate."

"Fair enough," Nightingale said, "Lead the way."

Moving behind the warehouses, they passed the break house and moved up the river. Then they finally saw it: a tall, black boat, like a shadow on the water. If not for the lights on the opposite bank, which gave it a ghostly outline in the fog, the ship would have been totally lost in the night. The gangplank was out, and a group of men huddled beside it, loafing around the outside of a warehouse.

The ship's captain—a gray-bearded man in a black turtleneck and captain's hat—was conferring with another: a tall, pale man with angular features and greasy hair. His thin mustache chased the curve of his narrow lips, and his double-breasted suit was cut to fit his wiry frame.

"Wait here for me, I'll see what's going on. When I've got a lay of things, I'll come back for you."

"Sure thing," Nightingale said, silently grateful that he'd have a chance to sit in the cool river air while he waited. After he planted himself on a crate, Willis disappeared around the back of the warehouse, coming out on the other side, heading for the ship. The pale man held out his hand to stop Willis from getting any closer. From where he sat, Nightingale could just barely make out their conversation.

"Can I help you?" the pale man said.

Pulling the tarot card from his pocket, Willis showed him the image of the workman on the front, then turned it over to show the bat on the back. The pale man nodded, then pointed to where a group of other longshoremen was gathered. "Wait over there with the others," he said. "We'll be ready soon."

Willis nodded and walked past the two men and posted up against the leg of a crane near the other stevedores. Just a few minutes passed before headlights appeared from the direction of the front gate. From the height of the lights, Nightingale could tell they belonged to a truck. He could hear the rickety chassis as it came to a stop. The pale man and the captain, casting long shadows down the dock, approached the front of the vehicle, where another figure, who had climbed out of the cab, met them.

As if they'd been waiting for their cue, Nightingale saw movement on the deck of the ship, shadows coming down the gangplank. In front was a sailor, who reached the bottom first, stepping aside as the figures behind him filed off and headed towards the truck.

They were girls, seven of them. Each looked frightened and cold in the foggy light. They stared at the ground as they walked, clutching small cases, no bigger than overnight bags, and nothing else. When they reached the truck, they stopped. The pale man inspected their papers, then handed them to the driver. Their voices were hushed. Nightingale could tell they were talking, but couldn't make out what they said.

One by one, the girls passed to the back of the truck and climbed in. When they were all inside, the driver walked to the back, closed the doors, and returned to the front, where he shook hands with the pale man and the captain, and then climbed back into the driver's seat. The truck backed up before it turned around and drove off into the night, the taillights disappearing down the docks.

There was a grumble as the huddle of silent longshoremen broke and they walked, single file, onto the boat. Nightingale could see them silhouetted against the lights as they headed down the hatch and disappeared below deck, to the rusty underbelly of the old steamer.

He waited, watching the pale man and the ship's captain. Once the longshoremen were aboard, the captain called his men from the ship, and they left, heading down the docks, toward the city. The pale man remained, standing motionless, the river breeze kicking up the tails of his long coat.

It felt like ages before Nightingale saw any of the long-shoremen reappear. Silently, they emerged from the ship, two by two, lugging long, narrow, black boxes. Like coffins, they were narrow at one end, wider at the other, closed with strong leather straps. There were seven of them, one for each of the girls who had left the boat. Willis was the last man out, holding the back end of one of the trunks. He looked toward the darkness where Nightingale was hidden, trying to see if he was still there, then snapped his head back forward to focus on his work.

Nightingale couldn't see where the longshoremen went, but after another few minutes, the group of them returned to the ship, heading up the gangplank, but Willis was nowhere to be seen. Behind him, Nightingale heard the scuff of workmen's boots, and he turned to see Willis poking around the corner of the warehouse, waving him to come.

Sitting for so long had let the ache in his muscles set in, and Nightingale's joints throbbed dully when he began to move.

"Come with me, detective," Willis said in a whisper when the detective was close. "Have I got something to show you?"

Together, they moved quickly and quietly down the dock. Willis took the lead, staying close to the warehouse walls and pausing at corners to check for movement before proceeding. They kept to the shadows, which was easy as there was hardly any light in this part of the harbor. Willis signaled for Nightingale to follow as he turned a corner. Heading for a small, broken-down storeroom, Willis pointed toward the building.

The door was chained and locked, so Willis led them around to the side of the building, where a stack of pallets sat below a high window. He climbed atop the pallets and jumped, grabbing the ledge and pulling himself up. The glass was broken, and Willis was able to slip his arm in to unlatch it. With little sound, the tired longshoreman, ready to retire, slipped inside the old building, then he reached down, taking Nightingale's hand in his firm grip, and hoisted him up after.

Inside, water dripped from the ceiling. Misty rain collected along the beams and fell to the wooden floor. Crates and boxes were stacked along the walls of the creaky building. A beam of hazy light came in through the windows, revealing the line of seven coffins in the middle of the floor. Willis approached them, clearly still awestruck by what he was witnessing. To Nightingale, Willis didn't strike him as a man of superstition. Certainly, he was struggling to wrap his mind around the idea of these black boxes holding the bodies of the reanimated dead—the bloodthirsty stalkers of the night.

"These are the ones?" Nightingale said.

"I can hardly believe it, but yes."

"How does it work, then? The smuggling, I mean."

"I was talking to the others, and as far as I can tell, these things are all coming from Europe, along with the girls."

"And the coffins stay here?"

"Not for long," said Willis. "Someone's coming to pick them up right now. They call them the *undertakers*."

"Then we'd better get to work."

"What kind of work?"

"You got that wooden stake from Bone?"

"It hasn't left my side."

"Give it to me," Nightingale said. He knelt beside the black box, unfastened the buckles quickly, and opened the lid, which squealed in want of oil. Inside the box, washed in the pale light, was the body of a woman. She looked young, her skin pale, her lips plump and red as roses. She wore a black, high-collared dress with a lacey fringe. Her hands, which were covered in golden rings, were clasped over her stomach, clutching a tarot card.

While Willis held the lid, Nightingale reached in, gently pulling the card from her hands. He knew the design on the back too well at this point; he wanted to know what image was on the front. It was just as he suspected: the card was marked with DEATH.

The vampire stirred. Her eyes snapped open. She clearly caught the sharp scent of blood that soaked Nightingale's shirt. In the darkness, he saw the red ember burn in her eyes. Her mouth split, revealing her vicious teeth. Her lips peeled back in a wicked grin. She hissed and lunged, fingers splayed, nails curved like talons.

Nightingale was quick, though. He raised the wooden stake over his head and thrust it down into the vampire's chest. The vampire fell back, her eyes opening wide in shock and pain, blood gurgling from her mouth. Her arms fell to the sides of the coffin as her body began to quiver and shake, her dark eyes rolling over white as she gasped for breath.

The detective brought his hand down over the stake, driving it further, deeper. The vampire lurched forward, her eyes locking onto his. He could still see the fire in them, that red glare burning in the back of her black pupils; it had grown dimmer, though, more distant. Her pale skin looked soft in the light. With one hand, she grasped Nightingale's wrist and held it, not aggressively, though. She looked at him with her fading eyes, and with one final, gasping breath, she asked him a simple question.

"Why?"

The vampire fell back into the coffin, dead, returned to the grave from which she'd risen.

"Jesus, Mary, and Joseph," Willis whispered.

Nightingale wrapped his hand around the stake and pulled it from the vampire's chest, with a wet sound of suction. His hands were covered in the thick, dark blood of the vampire. "It gets easier," Nightingale said.

Willis let the coffin lid down slowly, and the detective fastened the straps around it. He started for the next coffin when he saw that Willis was kneeling on the ground, his hands clasped in prayer. "Lord," he said, "take her back—I beg you."

"You a religious man, Willis?"

Shaking his head, Willis said, "My wife was. I've found myself praying more now that she's gone, though. Sometimes it gives me comfort." Then he added, "It seemed like the right thing to do."

"Well, put in a good word for me," Nightingale said. "We've got six more of these to go."

Bowing his head, Willis returned to his prayer. "Just give me the strength to finish Nightingale's work, Lord, and forgive me for it—and please forgive him too."

"Amen."

Chapter 31

The car was parked outside the docks in the shadows between two streetlamps; the headlights off, the engine dead. Charlie sat in the driver's seat, Frenchy beside him, and Vermilion in the back seat. The vampire had insisted on taking their car—the one they'd stolen from Fat Phil and Knuckles. Charlie figured it was Vermilion playing mind games, using the car of Frenchy's dead compatriots to assert dominance in some small way. But if Frenchy had recognized it, he hadn't shown any sign of it.

They'd been waiting at the docks for the better part of the night, sitting mostly in silence. Charlie had grown a bit stir crazy—he tapped his foot, checked his watch, then settled again. Frenchy and Vermilion, unbothered, seemed content to wait quietly. A conversation rose and fell here and there, but neither Frenchy nor the vampire would answer questions. The rain's steady patter filled the car. It was endless.

Charlie was relieved at the first sign of movement. Stevedores arrived one by one. A truck came and went. After hours of waiting, their prize finally arrived. Four hearses drove up, entered the docks, and disappeared behind buildings. Even Frenchy stirred from solitude. He adjusted in his seat, sat up straight, and cracked his neck.

"When they leave," he said, "we'll follow—but not too close."

"I've followed people before."

"I'm sure," Frenchy said. "I just want to make sure this is done right. Are you ready, Vermilion?"

"I am."

"And you're certain you can convince these vampires to help us out?"

"I am," the vampire said again.

"Good. This is a big play we're making. I want it all to go smoothly."

The three of them went silent as they saw headlights approach. Out of the gates came the first hearse, long and black with narrow, menacing windows. Three more followed behind it, leaving the docks and heading back to Du Vide's.

"Let's go," Frenchy said.

Charlie started the car, and they crept forward, keeping the headlights off. They drove around the corner, where they could see the taillights of the hearses driving away. They followed after them, finally turning their headlights on when they were farther from the docks, and they entered the city itself.

They swung onto Canal Street, heading toward the park before taking another turn on Brad Street, passing the fairgrounds and heading up through Gentilly. They turned before the new lakeshore developments and the Industrial Canal. The street was dark, all but one of the streetlights was off, and the only other life around seemed to be in an all-night diner a block away.

They drove past the street, seeing where the hearses pulled in, and headed around the block, killing the lights as they approached. Charlie parked the car again, not needing to worry about being seen in the utter darkness.

The car was parked outside a wrought-iron fence. A long, gravel drive led to an old, white mansion—three stories high. Its central tower rose above the eaves. The house was silhouetted against the gunmetal sky. A few lights glowed inside. By their soft light, Charlie could see a wide porch with columns rising from the foundation to the roof. The mansion sat at the peak of a low hill. The grounds were scattered with sycamore and oak trees, resurrection ferns coiling around the trunks. At the base of the slope, near the gate, stood a long, white, wooden sign.

GOLGOTHA HILL MORTUARY

"Here we are," Frenchy said. "Du Vide should be inside."

"Good," Vermilion said. "And just to be certain, we remove him, and we get what was promised to us."

"That's what Mr. Lazaretto said."

"And you, Mr. DeAngelis, what do you say?"

"It don't matter what I say."

"It seems to matter," Vermilion said. "Or so it seemed when you were speaking with Mr. Nicotero."

"I don't know what you're getting at."

"You told him you'd deal with the problems one at a time, isn't that right?"

Frenchy started to look nervous. "I was just putting him at ease, is all," he said. "Lazaretto always makes good on his promises."

"That will be one of us, then," Vermilion said, his lips curling up at the corner into a devious grin.

From the backseat, two tiny hands reached up, grabbing Frenchy around the neck.

"The hell?" he shouted.

As he did, Juliette appeared from behind him. She grabbed his neck and pulled herself up from her hiding place along the baseboard. Frenchy fumbled for his gun. Too slow. Before he could yell, the little girl's teeth sliced into his neck. Frenchy screamed. He fell back against the window. Juliette climbed over the seat and bit him again. Her fangs dug in deeper.

Charlie sat horrified beside the two of them, unable to look away. "What are you doing?" he asked, still watching the carnage.

Vermilion, still smiling, leaned forward, patting the young child on the head. "Now, my dear, not too much. We need him alive."

Stirred from his alarm, Charlie looked at Vermilion. "Alive? What do you mean? What is happening?"

"Our plan," the vampire said.

"Our plan? This isn't our plan."

"It is now," Vermilion said.

"But Lazaretto, we need him."

"No," Vermilion said. "Not anymore." He stroked the girl's hair as she lapped blood from Frenchy's neck. The man was pale and unconscious, but breathing. His arms hung limp at his side, and he sat crumpled up against the door. "We're through with Lazaretto tonight. He dies in there," he said, pointing at the mortuary.

"Then why are we even here?"

"Because Du Vide dies too," Vermilion said. "They all do. Tonight, we claim our empire. We take Lazaretto's power, we wield it, with the help of our delicious friend here, and we rule this city. With Du Vide's operation, we can bring in help.

We'll control the city, from the shadows, of course, and reap the benefits."

"And the other gangs?"

"Leave them," Vermilion said with a wave of his hand. "Let them have their meager scraps, who will they be to stand up to us?"

"So, Frenchy will be our slave; he'll still talk to the men. They think he's loyal to us, so they go along with it?"

"Precisely," the vampire said.

"And Du Vide?"

"The woman, this Madame Lovebite, she'll do the same for us here."

"You're certain?"

"Do you still doubt me, Charles?" the vampire asked.

Charlie looked over at Juliette, who gave a final slurp at Frenchy's neck and drew her mouth away with a smack of her lips. She turned towards Charlie, smiling, her mouth and jaw covered with blood. "No," Charlie said. "I don't"

"Good," Vermilion said. "Then let us finish our work."

The three of them exited the car; Vermilion paused to gently wipe the girl's mouth before kissing her on the forehead. Taking Juliette's hand, Vermilion led her towards the mortuary gate, and Charlie followed a few steps behind.

Near the base of the hill, the driveway forked. The wider lane continued up towards the mortuary, circling the front of the building. A smaller drive branched off, running around to the back and sloping down so it was hidden from the street.

Vermilion chose neither path. He stepped off the gravel into the trees and ferns. The dense foliage stopped most of the rain. It plinked the treetops overhead, making the wet leaves rustle.

Light wisps of fog lurked over the grass. Stacked against the tree trunks, partly overgrown with ferns and vines, were slabs of marble, which Charlie realized were tombstones yet to be engraved.

They made their way through the overgrowth, towards the back of the mortuary, where the gravel driveway turned into an open lot. The four hearses were parked there, backed up to the mortuary. Two bay doors were open in the back of the building, light flooding out onto the wet gravel. Six men in black suits huddled near the cars. One of them opened the back of the first hearse and, with the help of another, pulled a coffin from the back, setting it down inside the morgue. The others followed suit, opening the remaining hearses. One long box after another came out into the light.

"Distract them," the vampire said to Charlie.

"How?"

The vampire reached into his coat and pulled a tarot card from his pocket. He handed it to Charlie, who turned it over. In the low light, he could see it was the Death card. "With this," the vampire said

"What is it?"

"Their sign," Vermilion said. "They'll think you're one of them." He took the little girl's hand and continued through the shadowy trees around to the other side of the mortuary.

Charlie shook his head, taking the pearl-handled pistol from his belt and making sure the safety was off. He tucked it back in and hid it beneath his suit coat. He chewed on his lip and huffed, then walked out of the brush towards the hearses.

"Excuse me," he said, walking into the light beaming out from the mortuary doors. He held the tarot card out in front of him. "Can I ask a favor?"

The men stopped their work, turning to look at him. They squinted in the light, looking at the card in Charlie's hand.

"You're not supposed to be here," one of them said. He was a middle-aged man with a thick mustache.

"You're the undertakers, right?" Charlie asked.

The men looked at each other, and the mustachioed man spoke again. "I'll get you where you need to go, but we can't be talking here."

"That's fine, that's fine," Charlie said. "Whatever you need to do."

A man on the far side of the hearses coughed, his hands reaching up to his throat as blood streamed through his fingers. The other undertakers turned to look at him. On the edge of the light, Vermilion appeared, walking slowly, his coat blowing in the wind, his cane in hand. He drew his arm back, bludgeoning a man across the face with the heavy bird skull handle. The man spun and fell to the ground, his jaw hanging out of place.

One of the undertakers reached for a knife but cried out in pain as Juliette appeared beside him, grabbing his arm and sinking her sharp teeth into his wrist. She clawed her way up his chest, biting into his neck in a bloody spray.

The last two undertakers ran back towards the mortuary. Charlie stopped one, clocking him over the back of the head with the pearl-handled grip of Gino's pistol, and the last one fell to the ground, tripping over Vermilion's cane. The vampire loomed over him. He pinned the man down to the ground as Juliette crawled over, giggling. She lunged viciously at the man's neck and dug her teeth in, leaving him gurgling his last gasping breath.

Vermilion surveyed the carnage before him, his mouth curling up into a cruel smile once more. Juliette sidled up beside him, and he patted her head. Charlie walked towards them.

"Now what?" he asked.

"Now we find our help," the vampire said. He walked to the nearest coffin and unfastened the latches. Turning his cane around, he raised the lid open with his handle. Inside was a vampire—a plump man in a powdered wig, his face ashen with makeup, a black beauty mark drawn on his top lip. His mouth hung open, slack, though, and his eyes stared out into the void. His chest was bloody, and in the middle of it, right where his heart would be, was a gaping hole.

Vermilion's jaw clenched in fury. He turned to another coffin, opening it as quickly as he could. There was a woman in that one, dressed in a crimson gown. Like the first, she too was dead, a hole in her chest where her heart had been pierced.

Together, Charlie and Vermilion removed the other coffins from the hearses, laying them on the ground, opening them as the rain began to fall harder. Of the seven coffins, there were three women and four men, all of them vampires, all of them dead, staked through the heart—one of them with the stake still planted in his chest.

Vermilion's top lip quivered as rain streamed down his face. Charlie approached him as Juliette sat on a casket just inside the mortuary doors.

"What do we do now?" Charlie asked.

Vermilion turned, wiping a bloody hand through his hair, sending streaks of red down his pale face. "The same as before," the vampire said. "We kill them all."

CHAPTER 32

"SNAZZY PLACE HERE," LAZARETTO said as he stepped onto the porch of the Golgotha Hill Mortuary and through the red, wooden double doors. Inside, dark hardwood floors stretched beneath a wide Oriental rug. The wainscotting on the grey walls ran from floor to ceiling. Candle sconces fixed to the walls cast flickering light, concealing the corners in deep shadow. Dozens more candles perched in tall candelabras around the room, their hot wax dripping down the sides, adding to the shifting gloom.

A black-suited man with a solemn face and long features waited just inside the doorway. The Madame pulled her tarot card from her purse and flashed the image of the High Priestess to him as she passed.

"These are my guests," she said, motioning back towards Lazaretto and Slits. "We're here to see the Monsieur."

"Of course," the solemn man said, bowing his head slightly, then turning on his heels and heading through the double doors on the right side of the entry hall.

Opposite the doors, on the other side of the entry, was a showroom filled with ornate caskets, richly stained to deep browns and so polished they reflected the flickering light.

Ahead of them, across from the front doors, was the chapel. Rows of pews faced a podium at the far end of the room.

"We can wait in here," the Madame said, motioning towards the chapel. "Or you can take a seat in the hall." She motioned towards a few padded benches that were arranged beneath the front windows.

"I think I'll stand," Lazaretto said. "I don't imagine your boss will take long."

"No," the Madame said. "I'm sure he'll make time for you quickly."

Lazaretto tried to smile but failed. He looked up at the staircase, his eyes following it. They continued to the next floor and then to the next, all the way up to the top of the tower. Slits busied himself looking at some of the art; tall portraits hung on the high walls, depicting figures dressed in garb from the French Regency.

Pointing around to the grandeur that surrounded him, Lazaretto said, "You must be doing all right."

"You know our business," the Madame said. "You're doing fine yourself."

"I've noticed the bottom lines getting fatter, too," he said. "Must be nice having a fortune teller around, predict the future, to know when trouble is coming."

"It doesn't work like that."

"Oh yeah? How does it work?"

"It's all about interpretation and perception."

"Interpretation and perception," Lazaretto said, nodding. "That's good. I was getting a little nervous looking at this tower, thinking about the card you gave me earlier. That sort of thing might give a person the wrong idea."

The Madame gave a crooked courtesy smile. "The Tower isn't all about doom," she said.

"Wish you'd told me that earlier," he said. "I've been fretting about it all day." He took the card from inside his coat. "Been carrying it around too."

She took the card from him. "You're thinking too much about the man," she said. "There's more to it than just him. See the tower here, how it's white against a dark sky? That can mean a reveal is coming, that the truth will be brought out from the darkness."

"Interesting," Lazaretto said. "What else can it mean?"

"Betrayal," she said. "From the hands of someone close."

"Very interesting."

The doors to the right of the entry opened, and the solemn man stepped out. "Madame Lovebite," the solemn man said. "The Monsieur would like to see you first—privately."

"Of course," the Madame said. "You'll excuse me, Anton."

"We'll wait," Lazaretto said, twirling his finger in the air.

The door closed, and Lazaretto walked to Slits, talking to him in a whisper.

"What do you make of this place?" he said.

"It's big," Slits said. "Who knows what he's hiding in here?"

"Any sign of our new friend?"

"Nothing," Slits said. "We'll have to wait and see."

"He better be here soon," Lazaretto said. "I don't know how long this conversation's going to be."

"If we need to, we can always take care of business ourselves," Slits said. "Your new friend ain't the only killer you know."

Lazaretto patted Slits on the back. "Don't worry," he said. "You're not being replaced. I'm only making things easier for us all."

"I just don't trust him," Slits said. "Any friend of Charlie the Cheat and all that."

"I know, I know," Lazaretto said. "And we'll take care of that business when we need to. Let's worry about tonight and get done what needs to get done."

"Sure thing, boss."

"Just be ready, I'm not so sure what's waiting for us."

Slits nodded. The door opened again, and the solemn man entered the entryway. "Monsieur Du Vide will see you now," he said.

"Let's not keep him waiting then," Lazaretto said.

With the solemn man leading the way, they followed him down a narrow hall. Like the entryway, it was lit by candles, the walls covered in paintings. At the end of the hallway, there was an alcove with a door. The solemn man opened it and motioned for them to enter.

The room beyond was richly appointed. Bookcases, stained a deep brown, lined the walls. A stone fireplace dominated one side, a fire crackling within as the room's only light, so that shifting shadows moved over books and furniture. The Madame sat in an overstuffed chair facing an oak desk. Behind it, tall windows looked out towards the lake. They were streaked with rain, and Lazaretto could see the flashes of lightning out over the water. A man leaned against the desk. His figure was dark, cast only in the dim light of the dying fire. He was dressed in grey pinstripes, his neck covered in a black cravat. His mustache was thick, well-groomed, his face covered in graying stubble. His wavy hair was black as the night behind him, only just peppered with gray. Shadows moved over him as the fire quivered.

"Monsieur Du Vide," Lazaretto said. "It's been too long."

The Monsieur nodded, opening his hands towards the over-stuffed leather chairs in front of him.

"Come," he said. "Sit. You're here to talk."

Lazaretto stalked forward to the chairs, passing the rows of books and the fireplace, and taking a seat in the middle. Slits took the seat next to him as the Madame stood from her own. Du Vide walked to the bar cart in the corner. He took a glass, fixing himself a drink of something brown.

"Can I get you anything?" he asked without turning to look at the other men.

"No," Lazaretto said. "I've had enough tonight already."

"Where I'm from," Du Vide said, "there's a saying that business without drinks must be a serious business." He left the bar cart and took a seat behind his desk, leaning back in the chair, lightning flashing out in the distance behind him. "So, what serious business have you brought me so late this evening?"

"There's been a detective asking questions around the docks."

"I know about him," Du Vide said. "Nightingale. Should I be more concerned about him than I am?"

"No," Lazaretto said. "We've taken care of him already."

"Then why are we having this conversation?"

"I'm worried about the future."

"Of course, Mr. Lazaretto. So am I," Du Vide said. He took a sip from his glass. "Why don't we wait for our other partner to arrive?"

"Other partner?" Lazaretto said. "What other partner?"

"You haven't met him. You haven't needed to."

"And when does he get here?"

"Soon. Once he's finished his work."

Lazaretto shifted in his seat uncomfortably. "And what kind of work, exactly, does this other partner do?"

"He makes arrangements," Du Vide said. "And he also cleans up messes."

"Well, good," Lazaretto said. "Because I've got to tell you, I've been noticing a lot of messes with this operation, and I ain't too happy about it. Seems like I might need to do some cleaning up, too."

Du Vide smirked, reaching into his drawer and pulling a pistol from his desk. "There's another saying I know about serious business," he said. "Serious business happens at the other end of a gun."

Lazaretto put up his hands. "Hold on there, Du Vide, I thought we were at least going to wait for your other man to show up."

A muffled scream came from the hall. Slits and the Madame turned to look, but neither Lazaretto nor Du Vide moved, keeping their eyes locked on one another.

"He's going to have his work cut out for him," Lazaretto said, smiling.

The door opened slowly, creaking on its old hinges. A draft swept in from the open door, stirring the fire briefly, causing it to swell. A figure entered, tall and pale, his gold-handled cane tapping on the floor, a bolero hat covering his face. Vermilion smiled, his fangs protruding from his sinister mouth.

"Glad my man showed up first," Lazaretto said.

A gunshot rang out through the room as lightning flashed in the distance and bedlam broke loose in Golgotha Hill.

CHAPTER 33

"Now, CAN WE GET you to a hospital?" Sister Magdalene said, driving through the rainy streets.

Nightingale winced in the seat beside her. "No," he said. "I'll be fine. I'm not even bleeding anymore."

The sister shook her head in disagreement. "You're pushing too far."

"Finding the girl is far enough. Now slow down, don't let them see you."

After finishing their bloody work at the docks, Nightingale and Willis exited through the back gate. They shook hands, and Willis left, heading far away, he said. Nightingale thought that was the right idea. He'd gone back to Magdalene, who'd been watching the street. She'd seen the truck come and go, but couldn't make out the driver. He told her about the undertakers. Almost immediately, four hearses arrived at the docks. When they left, Magdalene began to follow. That's when they noticed another car easing out of the shadows to trail the hearses as well. They kept their distance, watching where everybody was going.

Nightingale could tell the sister was tense, so he wanted to get her mind off the situation. "You never told me, by the way, what did Bone say about that cross?"

"The Latin was a motto for chaplains during the war," she said, sounding relieved to have something to talk about. "The numbers were for a unit."

"It belonged to a vet?"

"I guess so. It doesn't really narrow it down, though."

"The numbers might," Nightingale said. He pointed ahead of them. "I think you'll turn up here."

Magdalene followed as they left the main roads, heading up toward the lake and turning off before the Industrial Canal. Now separated from the more populated areas, the streets around them were empty, dark, and quiet, save for their makeshift procession.

"Father Renault was in the war," Nightingale said.

"You're not suggesting he killed the girl, are you?"

"I'm not saying anything, but I'm not going to discredit it either," he said. "At the very least, he might know the other chaplains around here, might be able to help."

"When I see him, I'll be sure to ask."

Nightingale tried to laugh, but it hurt. Instead, he pointed again. "Here," he said. "That's where they turned."

As they reached the corner, they could tell there was no sign of the cars they'd been following. "Did we lose them?" said Magdalene.

"I don't think so," Nightingale said, looking out past a wrought iron fence and grassy knoll that led to the Golgotha Hill Mortuary. Pulling out the card he'd gotten from the foreman's office at the docks, he checked the address. "This is it," he said. "Apophrades, Inc."

"It's a funeral home," Magdalene asked.

"I think it's more than that," Nightingale said. "Sure is quiet, though."

"I think I see a car up there," Magdalene said, pointing through the windshield where a black sedan sat parked against the curb.

"You're right," he said. "And I think there's somebody in it." Nightingale shifted towards the door, opening it, looking back at Magdalene as he got out. "Wait here. I'll be right back."

Pulling his revolver, Nightingale walked gingerly towards the other car. He moved cautiously through the dark. He stopped by a lightless lamp post and watched the vehicle. There was definitely somebody in there, but they weren't moving. Crossing the street, he walked behind the car, looking in through the back windshield. The person inside sat perfectly still. He walked to the passenger door, staying low as he moved, and opened it.

The man fell out. Nightingale caught the body in his arms before it hit the sidewalk. There was blood on the door and covering the man's front. Dragging the man from the passenger seat, he pulled him in front of the car. He rested him against the bumper. In the streetlight, Nightingale had a better view. He could see the bite marks on the man's neck. He was still warm. His chest moved with shallow breaths.

Magdalene walked from her Studebaker, wrapping her coat around her to protect against the wind and rain. "Is he dead?" she asked.

"Not yet," Nightingale said.

"Do you know who he is?"

"He's Frenchy De Angelis," Nightingale said. "One of Lazaretto's guys. His red right hand, in fact."

"Lazaretto must be here, then."

"That's what he and the Madame talked about. Or whatever's left of him in here—these are vampire bites. And if they got Frenchy, who knows what's going to happen to Lazaretto."

"What's going on?"

"I don't know," Nightingale said, stroking his rough chin as he thought. "But I think they're all in danger."

"What sort?"

"I'm not sure yet." He looked over his shoulder at the mortuary. "But they must be inside."

"Nightingale," she said. "Sebastian. This is a bad idea. I don't think you should go."

"Someone has to," he said. "And nobody else is around." He walked back to the powder blue car, opening the door. He grabbed one of the guns they'd taken from the thugs that had tried to kill him at the quarry. He handed it to Magdalene.

"You know your way around one of these, right?"

Magdalene didn't reach for it. "Yes," she said. "But I don't want it."

"Take it," he said. "Take it and wait out here. I'm going to go have a chat."

Shaking her head, Magdalene stepped to her door, reaching inside and grabbing the box of bullets that Dr. Bone had given her as she left. "Then take these, at least," she said, handing the box to Nightingale. "Bone sent them. He said they were silver." She nodded towards Frenchy. "And I think you might need them."

Nightingale smiled as he took them, opening the box and setting it on the hood of the car. He cracked open the chamber of his revolver, removing the other bullets and loading it with the ones from Bone. He dropped the other rounds into his coat pocket.

"How are you going to get in?" Magdalene asked.

Nightingale paused, a curious look crossing his face as he felt something in his pocket. He reached in and pulled out a tarot card. "With this," he said, showing it to Magdalene.

The sister stepped forward, touching the card as she looked at it. "The Hanged Man?" she asked. "Who's that?"

"He's me," Nightingale said, tucking it back into his coat. He took the thug's gun and forced it into Magdalene's hand. "I'll be right back."

The detective crossed the street as Magdalene watched, reluctantly stepping into her car and closing the door as he vanished into the foggy, rainy night—a thunderstorm raging somewhere across the lake.

He hustled up the driveway, his side hurting where he'd been punched. He wanted to stop and take a breath, but he didn't want the sister to see him in pain. So, he continued to run all the way to the door, where he paused to catch his breath, holding himself steady against one of the columns. His head was feeling fuzzy, and he could feel a headache gathering somewhere in the back of his skull. He shook it off. It would have to wait.

Walking to the double doors, he knocked, pulling the tarot card from his pocket. When the door opened, a solemn-looking man answered.

"Can I help you?" he asked.

Nightingale held the card up. "No," he said. "I'm here to help you."

"Who are you?" the man asked.

"Madame Lovebite gave this to me. Is she here?"

"If you'd tell me who you are—"

"Is she here?" Nightingale asked again, more forcefully. "Is Anton Lazaretto with her?"

"Yes," the man said.

"Bring me to them," Nightingale said. "I think they're in danger."

"From what?"

Fed up, Nightingale pushed his way past the man at the door. "From vampires."

The solemn man walked down the narrow hall, Nightingale following close on his heels. They stopped at a book-covered alcove with a thick wooden door. "They're inside," the man said. "Let me see if they'll talk to you."

"Be quick," Nightingale said.

The man nodded. As he turned toward the door, a pale hand reached out from the shadow of the intersecting hallway, grabbing the man by the neck and pulling him back towards the darkness. The man yelped and then screamed as fangs bit viciously into his throat.

Nightingale rushed forward, throwing his weight against the vampire, who dropped the other man to the floor. The vampire dug his nails into Nightingale's bloody side, and the detective gritted his teeth in pain. When the vampire released him, he dropped to the floor beside the doorman, who sputtered blood from his mouth, opening and closing it like a fish on the deck of a ship. The vampire raised his cane, swinging it like a bat and smacking the detective in the ribs. Nightingale curled up in a ball.

The vampire stepped over him, opening the door and stepping inside. Nightingale, still wincing in pain, rolled over, pulled his revolver, and drew a bead on the vampire. His vision was blurry, but he took the shot, which bellowed out loudly in the small space. Through the gun smoke, he could see the vampire stumble. Nightingale rose to his feet and ran through the door, throwing his weight into the vampire and knocking the monster to the ground.

On the opposite side of the room, Monsieur Du Vide had his own gun raised, pointed at Lazaretto. When the commotion came, he took his eyes off the mafioso just long enough for the fat man to scramble behind his chair. Slits did the same. Du Vide fired into the cushions, but the padding was enough to stop the bullets.

Slits and Lazaretto pulled their own guns, raising them above the overstuffed chairs, and fired blindly. Windows shattered, and the sound of rain rushed in. The cold air whooshed in, and the fire dimmed.

The Madame dove behind the desk, and with Du Vide, they pushed the heavy piece over, giving them cover. She hiked up her dress, pulling her pistol from its holster. She ejected the clip, checked it, then jammed it back in, pulling the slide back and chambering a round. She popped up from behind the desk, firing towards Slits and Lazaretto, her bullets punching into the tanned leather of the chair.

Across the room, Nightingale and Vermilion rose to their feet. Nightingale pulled his revolver, but the vampire clawed it away, knocking Nightingale back to the ground.

Scrambling back up, Nightingale reached into his pocket. Grabbing the brand, he wrapped his fingers around it. He lunged towards the vampire, taking a wild swing that landed across the monster's jaw, making the thing howl in pain. As the vampire stumbled backward, Nightingale lunged again, throwing himself into its stomach and tackling it to the ground.

Two of Du Vide's men, dressed in black suits, ran into the office, pistols raised, searching through the commotion of the dark room, trying to see what was happening. Before they could act, Lazaretto and Slits opened fire, dropping both of them to the ground.

"Vermilion!" Lazaretto shouted. "Get over here! End this!"

The vampire pulled the detective up. Nightingale took another swing but missed, and the vampire knocked him against the bookcase, sending heavy volumes toppling to the ground from the highest shelf. Winded, Nightingale tried to stand, but the vampire took another swing at him with his cane. He raised his arm, taking most of the blow that certainly would have broken his jaw if it had landed, and fell to the ground.

Du Vide rose from behind the desk and fired at the vampire. Vermilion ducked, the bullets pounding into the books above him. Slits rolled out from behind his armchair and fired towards Du Vide, the bullets splintering the wood. As Du Vide ducked back down, Vermilion ran forward towards Lazaretto, crouching.

The vampire huddled close to Lazaretto, and for the first time, he noticed the nauseating scent of death coming from Vermilion. He was perfumed, and the smell of burnt gunpowder hung heavy in the room, but the smell was still pronounced this close to the monster.

"Get on with it!" Lazaretto said, still shouting.

Vermilion's lips curled up in a smile, and his blood-covered lips parted, his fangs protruding from his mouth. Lazaretto moved back, suddenly frightened, seeing the hungry look in the vampire's eyes. It seemed as though the vampire was about to lunge forward at him, but Nightingale came rushing from the other end of the room, throwing himself against the vampire once more, sending the two of them sprawling to the floor.

Stunned, Lazaretto crawled backwards towards Slits.

"Let's get out of here," he said, shaking away the shock. "Go!"

Slits looked at the tall windows and shot out the glass. He turned towards the desk, firing at it recklessly as he helped Lazaretto up with his free hand. He pushed his boss towards the windows, covering him as Lazaretto climbed over the window frame and threw himself out onto the hedges outside. Slits took one last look at the room, still firing, the desk splintering, Vermilion and a Nightingale wrestling on the ground. As Slits jumped through the window after Lazaretto, they could all hear sirens in the distance.

CHAPTER 34

CHARLIE WAS WAITING IN the morgue. Vermilion had said he wouldn't be long, and when Charlie had objected, Vermilion had looked at him fiercely. "Stay with the girl," the vampire said.

"What if something goes wrong?" Charlie had asked.

"Go to the cemetery, the Saintes-Maries. Take the girl and wait for me there if you have to."

"But—" Charlie began, but Vermilion glared, eyes blazing.

"Stay," the vampire said. "Care for her. I want nothing to happen to the little one."

Charlie scowled, but obeyed. He slumped onto a stack of coffins by the bay doors.

Juliette continued feeding on one of the men, her teeth buried into his neck, suckling the blood. Charlie tried not to watch, though he found himself staring in morbid fascination. He thought again about the girl asking him about being a vampire, and he wondered what that would be like. How could anything find that desirable, he wondered.

He eyed the line of open coffins recently unloaded from the docks, all holding dead vampires. He approached the one still impaled, tugged the stake free, and inspected its bloody, pointed end. Returning to his seat, he marveled at how such a simple weapon could end something that seemed so strong.

Gunshots rang out—a boom, then a volley. Charlie jumped down from the coffins, shoved the stake in his pocket, and drew Gino's gun. Juliette looked up, blood on her face.

"War?" she said.

"Close, kid," Charlie said. "Don't worry about it."

"Where's Papa?"

"Somewhere up there. Don't worry about it, I said. He'll be back and we'll be gone."

"He said we'd be powerful, like before."

"Yeah," Charlie agreed. "Like before." Then he paused. "You were with him before?"

"In France, our home. Before the war came and we fled."

"No kidding," Charlie said. "I had no idea."

"You're his son, yes?"

Charlie laughed. "No."

"Maybe you can be."

Charlie looked at the little girl, wondering what she meant, when he heard the door that led upstairs open. He ducked behind the coffins, grabbing the little girl and pulling her close to him. He brought a finger to his lips, telling her to be quiet, and she nodded in understanding.

"What's going on up there?" he heard someone ask.

"No idea," said another.

"We should go up."

"Lemme see if there's anyone down here."

Footsteps neared, two sets. Charlie gripped his pistol tighter. The footsteps stopped.

"My God," he heard the second voice say. "They're all dead."

Charlie surveyed the bodies strewn across the gravel, some inside the morgue, some left outside in the rain, all of them covered in blood.

"You got your gun?" the first voice asked. "Let's go have a look."

The footsteps resumed, moving faster this time. Charlie looked at the girl and the hearses outside. Too far to make a run for it, he knew, especially with the girl in tow, and he didn't want to think about what Vermilion would do if anything happened to her. As the footsteps neared, he took a deep breath and exhaled, puffing out his cheeks. He popped up from behind the coffins and fired.

The two men were on the stairs, almost to the bottom, dressed like the others had been, in dark suits. Wood splintered around them as the bullets tore through the railing. One of the men fell backward, clutching his leg, screaming. The other one grabbed the man's arm and pulled him back up the stairs, firing towards Charlie with his other hand.

The top of the coffins splintered as bullets tore into them, and Charlie dropped behind them. The gunshots echoed through the morgue, booming loudly. Charlie's heart pounded, and as he listened to the gunshots and the bursting wood above him, he heard another sound, a wailing sob—the frightened cry of a child.

He looked beside him at Juliette. She was curled up, kneeling on the ground, hands covering her ears, rocking back and forth, giant tears rolling down her cheeks and her blood-stained chin. Her eyes were shut tightly, and her whole body quivered in fear.

Charlie put a hand on her back, crouching down low to her ear. "Juliette," he said, "Juliette, what's going on?"

She didn't answer, just continued rocking and crying.

The booming gunshots stopped, and Charlie looked over the top of the coffins, firing his own gun again before the volley from the stairs continued.

He looked back down at the little girl.

"Juliette, snap out of it," he said. "We've gotta take care of these guys."

"The war," Juliette said, finally breaking her silence. "The war."

She repeated the phrase again and again, not speaking to Charlie or to anyone, just saying the words, half mumbling them to herself.

Charlie growled in frustration. The girl was no use right now; he had to do something. He looked at the hearses outside in the rain and back to the girl. He whispered into her ear. "Juliette," he said. We're leaving. We need to run when I tell you."

The girl stopped speaking but continued rocking on the ground. He didn't know if she heard him or understood, but he was right; they needed to leave. He rose once more, firing back towards the stairs. He grabbed the girl, pulling her up, dragging her across the floor. At first, she hung limp, then she found an unsteady footing, stumbling along with Charlie.

"Walk! Walk!" Charlie shouted as he moved backward, firing into the stairs, the two men huddling around the corner. The booming stopped when his pistol clicked empty, and for a moment, Charlie looked at it in shock. The two men on the stairs didn't hesitate. They turned the corner, guns out and raised, ready to fire.

Charlie scooped up Juliette and ran. The gunshots rang out behind him, the bullets hitting the walls and doors as he rushed out into the rain.

He tossed Juliette into the hearse, sprinted to the driver's door. Keys were in the ignition. He jumped in, slammed the door, and hit the gas. As one gunman stepped out, the tires gripped the wet gravel, and the car lurched forward.

Charlie turned the wheel sharply, the back of the hearse spinning wide. He gunned the engine and sped up the drive. The gunmen fired at them, but it was too late; he and the girl were gone.

CHAPTER 35

MAGDALENE TURNED THE GUN over in her hands as she waited, the rain hitting against the roof of the car. It was a small .32 caliber revolver, nothing notable, but still capable of killing someone. She looked up towards the mortuary and wondered what Nightingale was doing, wondering if he was safe.

She thought back to the day before, when Juliette was in the convent. Just a little girl who wanted to draw. How, the sister wondered, did that lead her here, sitting in a car with a gun in her hands, hoping she wouldn't need to use it.

Through the rain-washed windshield, she saw the man by the other car's bumper suddenly slump into the road. She gripped the gun and bolted from the car, sprinting across the street to him. Reaching his side, she shoved the revolver into her habit's pocket and pressed her hand to his cheek, afraid he might be dead.

The man murmured when she touched him, but she didn't understand what he said.

"We should have never left you out here in the rain," Magdalene said. "Frenchy, can you hear me?" She looked around, frustrated, thinking of what to do. She tried to pick the man up, struggling to sling his arm over her shoulders. She could at least move him out of the rain. Headlights appeared at the far end of the street, and in the darkness, Magdalene froze, watching them approach.

A rumbling truck drove down the street towards them, slowing as it came closer. Just as it reached the gates, the headlights revealed Magdalene and Frenchy, and the truck stopped abruptly, the brakes squealing as it came to rest. It sat there for a moment, the windows looking black in the night. Then the driver's door opened, and someone stepped out around the front.

"Sister Magdalene?" the figure asked. The voice was familiar.

"Father Renault?" she said.

Stepping into the headlights, Magdalene could see she was right. The priest's features came into clear view.

"What are you doing here?" he asked, glancing at the mortuary.

"I'm—" the sister paused. "I'm helping this man."

Father Renault seemed to relax, if only just slightly. "Always the good Samaritan," he said. "Let me help, it's raining."

"No," Magdalene said, gently lowering Frenchy back to the ground. "It's OK—what are you doing here, Father?"

"I—" this time it was the priest who paused. She could see the struggle in his face as he wrestled between a lie and the truth. When his face resolved, he spoke again, this time clearly, confidently, even condescendingly. "I'm going to the mortuary," he said. "To see Monsieur Du Vide."

"And what reason could you possibly have to do that?" she asked.

"Magdalene, dear Sister Magdalene, I'm going to let you in on a secret." Renault stepped forward. "I work for the Monsieur—with him, rather."

"Doing what?"

"His is a peculiar business, and it requires the help of young girls. They travel from overseas. I arrange the travel, and I arrange for them to find lodging and work."

Magdalene's wet hair was plastered to her face. "Why does he need young girls?"

"Sister, there are things you don't need the answer to."

"This thing, I do," she said. "I care for some of those girls. What do you do to them?"

"Nothing, I don't do anything to them. They bring cargo for the Monsieur, and I make sure they're taken care of."

"Vampires, you mean," Magdalene said.

"You know quite a bit about this, don't you?" Father Renault smiled. "Should I regret disagreeing with the Mother Superior and letting you have your detective?"

"I just want to know why, Father, why are you working for a man like that?"

"You don't understand," Renault said. "I care for those girls. I'm protecting them, saving them."

"Then why did we find one dead this afternoon?"

Renault looked at her blankly. "I suppose accidents happen. Come inside, meet the Monsieur, we can ask him about it together and make sure it never happens again."

Sister Magdalene squared off against him in the street. He stepped forward, hand out. She resisted stepping back and slid her hand to the pocket where the revolver hid.

"All right," she said. "I'll meet him."

The father looked relieved and pleased, a smile crossing his face as his features relaxed. "Good," he said. "Perfect. Come with me and we'll sort this out. You'll see why I do what I do."

"Thank you, Father," she said, "for showing me how I was wrong."

"It's all right, child, these are strange times we live in. We all have to make compromises for the greater good."

"Yes," she said. She stepped toward Renault. "Before we go, though, I do have one more question."

Renault raised an eyebrow. "Yes? What is it?"

"You served in the war, didn't you?"

Renault seemed confused. "I did, yes."

"I thought so."

"Is that all?"

"Yes," she said, continuing toward the truck.

"Perfect," he said. "Let's get out of the rain." He turned toward the mortuary, expecting the sister to follow behind him.

She stopped walking, and from behind him she called out. "*Praestare aut providere.*"

Renault froze, turning slowly to face her. What did you say?" he asked, and when the sister didn't answer, he asked, "Where did you hear that?"

"Which company did you serve in?" she said, blurting it out.

"Regiment," he said, smiling, no joy behind it. "The 329th, 83rd division. Why? What's going on, Sister? Why all these questions?"

"Did you kill all the girls, or just Antonia?"

Behind him, from the mortuary, Magdalene heard the pops of gunfire. She forced herself not to look, not wanting to take her eyes from the priest in front of her. Father Renault pursed his lips, his face went cold, and the façade of friendliness was completely removed.

"I told you, Magdalene, we all have to make compromises."

"We do," she said. She reached into her pocket, pulling the revolver out and pointing it at Renault.

He raised his hands. "You don't really want to do that, do you?" He took a step towards her.

"Stay back," she said.

"Let's be reasonable. Put it down."

"Why would I trust you?"

"Because," he said, "I know what's best. And trust me, you don't want to pull that trigger; you don't want that on your conscience. Take it from someone who knows."

"A killer," she said.

"Yes," Renault said, nodding. "A killer."

Renault made a sudden move, reaching behind him, his priest's cloak flying out around him. Before he could finish the movement, though, a shot from Magdalene's gun rang out in the night, and thunder rumbled distantly.

The priest fell to the ground, his body sprawled out, a pistol lay beside him.

Magdalene moved forward, gun outstretched, aimed at Renault. His face was fixed upward, a dark hole beneath his left eye, the glassy stare unblinking.

She stepped backward, confused, horrified, disgusted. She dropped the gun into the street, not wanting to touch it, not wanting to look at it.

From the city, sirens wailed. Panic seized her; they must be for her, she thought. She dashed to her powder blue Studebaker, started it, and sped away, leaving Renault's body behind, lying in the middle of the street.

CHAPTER 36

"I THINK THAT GODDAM vampire was going to kill me," Lazaretto said, panting as he ran after Slits across the grass toward the street.

"Why do you think that?"

"Hold on, hold on, I gotta stop."

Slits turned. "We better get out of here, boss, those sirens are getting closer, and Du Vide could come tearing out of that place any minute."

"I know. Damn. This night," Lazaretto said. "That son of a bitch vampire—you should have seen his eyes. If it wasn't for that detective busting in..."

"Just your luck, our boys weren't too good at their jobs."

"We'll handle that later. I still want him dead—Du Vide, the missus, and that goddamned vampire." Lazaretto gulped air. "First, we gotta get out of here."

Slits nodded and grabbed his boss by the arm. He pulled him along. They started running again. Then a roar of an engine came from behind the mortuary. Both men looked back. A hearse pulled onto the driveway and sped toward the road, the driver gunning the engine.

Then the engine quieted, and the hearse slowed. Like a predator stalking the savanna, it seemed to Slits like they were being watched through the windshield. Suddenly, the car jerked toward them and barreled ahead, tearing across the lawn.

"Go!" Slits shouted, yanking his boss's arm. He pulled his gun, firing backward at the hearse as they ran.

Slits fired until his pistol was empty. The engine behind them growled. Sirens whined closer. The car gained, matching them turn for turn. Lazaretto struggled for air, dragging his heavy frame across the field.

The headlights reached them, cresting the low-rising hill, catching them in their beams. The driver of the hearse gunned the engine, running Slits and Lazaretto down.

At the last moment, as the car hurtled toward them, Slits darted sideways and slammed into Lazaretto, shoving him clear of the hearse's path. Slits tried to jump away, but the hearse's hood clipped him. He tumbled over the windshield, rolled across the roof, and flew off the back, finally crashing down the hill in the grass. Lazaretto, pushed just in time, was only grazed on the side by the car and spun to the ground from the impact.

The hearse screeched to a halt, tearing up turf. Slits stayed prone, rolling onto his stomach, head spinning and body throbbing. He watched as someone jumped out, ran to Lazaretto, and dragged him to the hearse. In the glow of brake lights, Slits recognized Charlie Baptiste.

Slits tried to shout, fumbling with his gun as he attempted to reload, but the effort was lost in his haze. All he could do was lie there, barely moving, and watch as Charlie opened the hearse's back door, pulled Lazaretto to the car, then hefted the big man's weight up and shoved him inside by the feet.

Charlie never looked at Slits. He slammed the door, ran to the front, and sped off, crashing through the gate and onto the street.

Drawing a heavy breath, Slits staggered up, wincing. Pain shot through his bruised side, and his head was still foggy as he limped toward the street. The sirens grew, shrill and relentless. He made it to the street, one hand holding his side, the other hand holding his gun. In the road in front of him, still running, was a truck, the lights shining out onto the slick road, the body of a man sprawled out beneath them. Slits looked at the body cautiously. It didn't move as he approached, and he could see the white priest's collar.

"They're killing priests now in the street," he said to himself. "This night. This whole damn night."

Slits bent down, grabbed the pistol by the body, and found another nearby. He stuffed them away with his own. Squinting, he saw another man slumped by the other car. "Frenchy? That you?"

He limped toward the car. Frenchy De Angelis lay in the gutter, neck bloody.

"That rat bastard," Slits said. "The vampire got him."

He checked Frenchy's pulse. "You lucky son of a bitch," he muttered, relieved. "They didn't finish the job." Grunting, he lifted Frenchy and eyed the car. "Ain't this Fat Phil's car?"

Frenchy didn't answer.

"We gotta get out of here," Slits said.

He opened the back door, set Frenchy on the seat, then hustled to the driver's side. Popping the dash panel, he yanked the wires. Sparks flew, the engine caught. Slits threw it in gear and sped off, sirens blaring, the mortuary fading in the mirror.

"This night," he said, shaking his head. "This goddamned night."

Frenchy didn't say anything.

CHAPTER 37

As NIGHTINGALE FELL TO the floor, he heard the gunshots and saw Lazaretto take a run for the window. The vampire scrambled up and followed, stepping to the window frame and pausing there, hunching like a gargoyle before jumping down. Nightingale leaped forward, catching the vampire's coat, sending them both tumbling to the ground. Nightingale landed hard, and he felt something snap beneath him.

There was no sign of Lazaretto or Slits, only the vampire who rose to his feet, holding the broken handle of his cane—the thing that had broken Nightingale's fall. The vampire bared its fangs as it lurched forward.

The detective picked up the broken shard of cane from beneath him, wielding it like a knife, the sharp end pointed toward the vampire.

"I want Lazaretto," the vampire said. "But I'll kill you if I have to."

"Take a shot, you bloodsucking bastard," Nightingale said. "I don't like vampires."

The two of them rushed together, the vampire bearing its fangs, its claws outstretched, Nightingale with the broken cane in hand. As they collided, the vampire's claws dug into

Nightingale's side. He shouted in pain, then brought the cane down, slashing across the vampire's face.

Blood sprayed against the wall. The vampire howled, tearing its claws from Nightingale's side, sending more blood splattering to the ground. The vampire fell backward, clutching its face, as Nightingale tumbled down the hill towards the back of the mortuary. Behind him, the vampire writhed on the ground, and Nightingale crawled down to the gravel lot behind the building.

Hearses were parked there, their doors open, coffins stacked outside. Their lids were open, revealing the twice-dead occupants inside. There were other men there too, dead, on the ground, their throats torn out. Nightingale crawled to the coffins, sitting up against them.

Every inch of his body ached. The fresh slashes along his left side stung with burning pain; the laceration from Lazaretto had opened again, and blood was running from the wound. The other bruises and cuts from the two thugs seemed like faded memories compared to what else he'd endured since leaving the docks. He fought for the will to stand back up, to finish his business here, but he was struggling to find it.

The vampire appeared around the corner of the house, stalking towards Nightingale. The bloody, ragged cut on its face went from its forehead to its cheek, through its right eye. Nightingale fumbled for his revolver, taking it from his holster. As he raised it weakly, he heard shouting behind him.

Gunshots rang out in the commotion, sending the vampire fleeing for cover around the building, disappearing in the shadows. Nightingale peeked over the lid of the coffin and saw two men, Du Vide's, he guessed by the way they were dressed.

They each had their guns raised, walking out through the open bay doors, one of them limping, a bloody bandage tied around his leg.

When they saw Nightingale, they turned their guns on him, chewing up the top of the coffin. He ducked as bullets and splintered wood flew overhead. He crawled along the ground to one of the hearses, ducking behind it. He had to get away from here.

He raised his revolver, firing towards the men—one, two, three, four times—as he ran for the other side of the house, the loud shots booming in the night. Dodging between cover, he reached the far side of the mortuary, then he struggled up the hill, the Golgotha Hill, he assumed from the name, and made it around to the front.

Ignoring the pain, Nightingale ran, sprinting for the street. He didn't look behind him, but his body was tense, waiting for the gunshots, or worse, waiting to feel the vampire behind him, bearing down on him with sharpened fangs. But neither came. He reached the gate, clutching it for stability, taking just a moment to breathe. The sirens were louder; the police were getting close.

He looked for Magdalene, but she was gone, no sign of her or the Studebaker. The other car was gone too, the one they'd found Frenchy in. There was only a truck, still running, a man lying on his back in the street in front of it.

Nightingale stumbled towards the body, recognizing Father Renault even with the extra hole in his face. He made the sign of the cross, then climbed into the truck, shifted it into gear, and pulled away towards the city.

Taking the long way around to avoid any cops, Nightingale breathed through the pain, driving with one hand, clutching his side with the other to try and stop the bleeding. He checked his revolver; he had one shot left. That had been lucky, he supposed. After tonight, he'd take any luck he could get.

The detective headed towards his office, but first, he would stop at a parking lot a few blocks away to ditch the truck. He'd wipe his blood from the seat and leave it. In a few days, somebody would call it in, and nobody would ever know where it came from.

Even in his condition, he felt like he could walk a few blocks. He'd sleep in the office, and in the morning, he'd find someone to patch him up. Then he could start to piece the night together, figure out what he'd stumbled into, and how Juliette was involved. Before any of that, though, he'd need to find Magdalene.

The streets were empty and dark as he pulled the truck around to the parking lot. He killed the engine, and after sitting for a minute, he climbed out. He took a handkerchief, wiping blood from the leather seat, and closed the door. He walked around to the back to see what was in there, and when he reached it, he found the doors were open.

Hairs tingled on the back of his neck, and instinctively, he grabbed his revolver. Just as he broke leather, he felt cold hands grab him from behind, pulling him backward, and then he felt the icy breath on his neck.

Nightingale fired. The hands released him as another familiar howl of pain filled the air. He spun around, falling to the ground. Writhing before him, clutching its bleeding leg, was the vampire.

Reaching into his pocket, Nightingale searched for the rest of the silver bullets Bone had sent, but they were gone, lost somewhere in the scuffle. His office, he thought, he had rounds there—he only hoped he could make it. Without wasting another moment to think about it, he climbed to his feet and ran as fast as he could, leaving the vampire clutching its leg, black blood seeping from its wound.

Nightingale cut behind buildings, his body on fire with pain. He held his side as he stumbled down an alleyway washed in the harsh light of a streetlamp. He made a tight-lipped grimace with each painful step—a dark red stain growing across his white shirt, and warm blood trickling through his fingers.

As he tripped over a trash can, rats scurried for the shadows. Leaning against the grimy wall for support, he hurried on as fast as he could, leaving a smeared trail of fresh blood that shimmered in the streetlight.

He rested his head against the wall and clenched his jaw as he pulled his hand away from the raw, ragged wound. The whole thing stung, sending waves of pain radiating out across his body. He pulled the bloody handkerchief from his pocket, wadding it up. He took another deep breath, and he shoved it into the wound. Pain swelled up inside him, and his mouth tasted like pennies as the corners of his visions throbbed red. It was enough for now to slow the bleeding.

Once he made it to the street, he hurried towards his building. When he reached it, he stopped, fishing for a heavy ring of keys that jangled with the weight. When he finally fumbled the keys into the lock, he put his weight against the doors and pushed his way into the lobby.

The place was full of shadows. The lobby was wide, tiled in white marble, and furnished with black leather armchairs. It was cold inside, and his footsteps echoed against the walls like he was stepping into a mausoleum.

He headed for the stairs and started up them, a few crimson drops falling to the pearly white floor. Each step was an effort, and he pulled himself along on the banister. When he reached the top, he stopped, holding on and breathing heavily. He lifted his head in determination as he headed for the office door across the way, the one marked NIGHTINGALE INVESTIGATIONS.

He unlocked the door and pushed it open, leaving a bloody handprint just below his name.

Nightingale dropped his keys to the floor and collapsed beside them, kicking the door closed with his foot. He sat on the floor, propped up against the empty secretary's desk, catching his breath.

Pulling the handkerchief, he examined the wound. His shirt clung to his body from all the blood. As he peeled it away, fresh jolts of pain coursed outward, reaching his toes so that they tingled, almost in ecstasy. The claw marks were distinct, but they would heal, like all the others.

He checked his other side, where the cross had been cut into him. It had already bruised, but he checked his ribs and none of them seemed to be broken. He breathed a sigh of relief and let his body relax, lying there on the floor.

Nightingale's head shot up when he heard the noise three floors down of the front door opening and shutting. The vampire—he'd followed the blood—and Nightingale hadn't locked the door.

In the otherwise silent building, he could hear the footsteps—deliberate and distinct—as they came up the staircase, echoing in the empty, soundless building. The vampire made it to the second floor and started for the third before Nightingale could stir himself back into action.

He scrambled to his knees and moved for the door. He managed to bolt it shut and put up the chain before collapsing back against the wall of the vestibule.

As the footsteps came closer, Nightingale pulled his gun from its holster. With a flick of the wrist, he opened the cylinder and dumped the empty shells. Slowly, quietly, he snapped the cylinder shut. His box of bullets was in the top drawer of his desk, one room away, but as he prepared to make a move for them, the vampire stopped right outside his door.

Nightingale held his breath. Light came through his office window, marking the room with long bars of shadow. Low enough to be hidden in the darkness, he stared up at the frosted window, watching and waiting. There was no light in the hallway, so there was nothing more but an empty void beyond it. The vampire hadn't made a sound since he'd reached the door. It was listening, waiting—just like he was.

Movement caught his eye, something ghostly pale in the lower corner of the glass, close enough that Nightingale could tell that it was a face. A long tongue pressed against the glass and licked at the bloody handprint. The blood streaked up, and the pale face pulled away. Then the doorknob moved slowly, and the door rattled gently as it was pulled against the frame, stopped by the heavy bolt. Nightingale wished he had a round in his gun as the doorknob stopped turning. He expected the glass to break and to see the wretched face of the monster peeking through.

But it never came.

Instead, the vampire moved away, its footsteps leading away from the door and down the hall. It didn't go downstairs; instead, it opened a far door around the corner.

When Nightingale heard it close, he jumped to his feet, shaking off the fog and stars that clouded his head. He limped to his desk and tore open the drawer. Grabbing the box of bullets from inside. Loading the gun quickly, he spun the chamber closed.

Above him, Nightingale heard movement. He looked out his window at the fire escape. The vampire had climbed to the roof and was heading down to his window.

Nightingale moved to the front of the desk, where he'd be concealed. The clambering came closer, until it stopped, and the vampire's shadow appeared in the window, falling across the floor in a hideous form.

The figure was tall and lean, with long limbs; he could tell it was staring into the room, gazing into the dark.

It raised a hand to the window, its sharp fingernail tapping against the glass quietly. It began to tap louder and louder, scraping against it.

Nightingale cocked the hammer of his gun back quietly. He closed his eyes and took a deep breath, letting it out slowly before he sprang from his hiding place.

But the vampire was gone.

No one stood on the fire escape, and the shadow that had washed across the floor had vanished. All that remained was a long, jagged scratch down the glass.

Nightingale rushed to the window and looked out into the street. It was just as empty as it was before, washed out in the bright glow of the streetlight—except now there was a car out front. Long and black and menacing.

There was a click of heels on the tile floor outside, and then a knock at the door behind him. Nightingale hobbled toward it, unlocking it, gun still raised.

Madame Lovebite was waiting in the hallway.

"Rough night?" she said as she breezed past him, wearing a smirk across her crimson lips. She shrugged out of her black, fur-lined coat, hanging it on the rack as she took a seat on the couch.

"No small thanks to you," he said, closing the door and leaning against the wall for support.

"My hands were tied," she said, taking her gold case from her purse and plucking out one of her long, black cigarettes, bringing it to her lips. "I'm glad you're not dead, though. We need to talk."

"What about?"

She lit her cigarette, taking a drag and blowing out the smoke.

"I have a job for you."

PART III
Two Needles in the Neck

PART IV

CHAPTER 38

"Why would I ever want to work for you?" Nightingale asked.

"Because, detective," Madame Lovebite said, "We're on the same side now."

"Are we?"

"We are," she said. "The vampire in Du Vide's office—you've been after him all day."

"You might have told me."

"I didn't get the chance," she said, drawing on her cigarette. "You dove out the window before I could speak. Besides, you looked like you had things under control."

"Does it still look that way?" he said, limping to his desk. He tossed his revolver down and snatched his crumpled pack of cigarettes, lighting one. "He about killed me, and there would've been another round if you hadn't shown up."

"He was here?"

"You scared him off," Nightingale said. "What does that say about you?"

"Maybe he knows what I came here to talk to you about."

"And what is that?"

"I want you to kill him, detective."

Nightingale laughed through his cigarette. "You see what he did to me. What makes you think I'd want to go after him?"

"For the girl, of course," the Madame said.

"And what makes you think I'd still want to find her?"

The Madame looked surprised. "Are you not?"

"Look at me," he said. "Do I look like a guy ready for another fight? I got out of this by the skin of my teeth. If I had one ounce of sense, I'd never look for another vampire in my life. If I saw you on the street, I'd cross to the other side. If I saw a nun—" Nightingale paused and let out a weary breath. "Well, I'd make my excuses and be done with it. It's a rotten business I've gotten into, as rotten as yours, and a man can only take so many beatings before he gets wise to that."

Madame Lovebite took another long drag from her cigarette before speaking. "I have to say, I'm shocked," she said. "I think I had you figured all wrong, detective. You seemed like a man who would never quit."

Nightingale pulled out the tarot card from his pocket and flashed it to the Madame, then tossed it onto his desk. "Why? Do you think you can look at me and some cards and know everything about me? Well, you don't. It takes a lot more than that to know a man."

"I know plenty, detective."

"Yeah? Like what?"

She watched him over her cigarette, its tip glowing. "You're not a man who does something because he enjoys it; he does it because no one else will."

"Your cards tell you that, too?"

"No," the Madame said. "It's a gift."

"Don't give me any of this hocus pocus mumbo jumbo, Madame Lovebite."

She smirked. "All right, then," she said. She closed her eyes. "There's a woman crying in a graveyard. The wind is blowing her long, red hair back, and leaves are rustling past her feet. She's dressed all in black, and she's clutching a handkerchief to dry away the tears." The Madame paused, adjusting her shoulders, keeping her eyes closed. "Someone approaches, a shadow—it's you, detective. You're there with her. You put your hand on the small of her back. And she turns, folding herself into your arms. You say her name, whispering it—*Marianne*."

"That's enough," Nightingale said sharply, his voice suddenly tight with emotion.

"You don't want me to go on?"

"We both know how it ends."

"Then we both know you're a man who sees things through to the end."

"Maybe I've changed," he said, voice heavy. "Or maybe it's this God forsaken city—and that's on you."

"How so?"

"I kill one of those things, and you bring in a dozen more. What's the point?

"You think you make things better."

"I used to," he said. "But maybe that's changed, too. Maybe I'm only making it worse. You ask your boss about that dead girl I found yet?"

"No," she said, tightening her jaw. "I haven't had the opportunity."

"Find one," he said. "Or are you afraid you might be wrong about your boss, too?"

Dropping into his chair, Nightingale turned from her to the rain streaking his window. The Madame rose, smoothed her dress, and stamped out her cigarette in the ashtray.

"Detective," she said. "You and I both know what's inside you. We both know how far you're willing to go. And we both know that's what frightens you."

When Nightingale didn't answer, the Madame walked around the desk to face him. Nightingale's eyes were closed, his chest slowly rising and falling, the cigarette still burning in his hand.

She shook her head and chuckled. Leaning over, she took his cigarette and crushed it in the tray with hers. Spotting the tarot card—the Hanged Man—she took out a pack of matches and placed it beside the card. Then she shrugged on her coat and left, locking the door behind her.

CHAPTER 39

"WHERE ARE WE GOING?" Lazaretto asked from the back of the hearse.

"We're going to have a chat," Charlie said, knuckles tight on the wheel. Juliette knelt beside him, facing backwards, eyes wide as she watched Lazaretto in silence.

"What about?"

"About you wanting to kill me," Charlie said.

"You got it all wrong, Charlie."

"Shut up," he snapped, his jaw clenching. "Vermilion told me all about your little deal you offered him."

"It was business, Charlie, you should understand that. I've got to keep that overhead low."

"I'm sure that's all it was."

"It was. That's why I'm willing to make you a deal, too."

"I don't need a deal," Charlie said. "Vermilion and I have it worked out."

"Your vampire buddy's dead," Lazaretto said.

Charlie slammed on the brakes, his hands shaking as the engine stalled out. The hearse slid for a moment on the wet asphalt, coming to a jarring stop in the middle of the road.

"He's lying," Juliette said frantically, her chest heaving as panic flashed in her eyes. Her mouth hung open in distress, her small, sharp teeth just barely visible.

"What do you mean he's dead?"

"What do you think I mean?"

"Did you kill him?"

"No, it was this detective, a man named Nightingale. He busted in after your vampire friend disrupted my meeting with Du Vide."

Juliette shouted, "He's lying!"

"Then how am I here and Vermilion isn't, huh?"

Charlie turned around, facing forward in his seat. He stared blankly at the rain-slicked road ahead, jaw set tightly, and his breath fogged the window as the rain came down.

"You're sure he's dead?"

"Pretty sure," Lazaretto said. "This Nightingale guy doesn't seem to know how to stop."

"We have to go to the graveyard," Juliette said. "We have to wait."

Charlie ignored her; he looked at Lazaretto through the mirror. "What kind of deal do you want to make?"

"Same deal as before," Lazaretto said. "Du Vide's still alive, I think. I need him gone. You take care of him, all your problems go away."

"Vermilion's alive!" Juliette shouted, her voice cracking as tears welled up in her eyes. "We have to find him!" She was growing more frantic, gripping the seat until her knuckles turned white.

"Let's go back to my club," Lazaretto said. "We'll talk about it—third floor this time. And we'll let your friend Petey join us, too."

Without a word, Charlie started the car.

"Where are we headed, Charlie?"

"Let's get a drink," he said.

"Good choice."

Juliette screamed, her face contorted with anguish, and tried to grab the wheel from Charlie. He shoved her away. "Crazy little brat," he said, his voice rough. "Stay in your seat."

"But Vermilion—"

"He's dead," Charlie said. "You heard the man."

"He's not!" she shouted, her voice ragged with emotion. She reached for the wheel again, clutching it so tightly her arms trembled. Charlie struggled to pry her hands off, but her grip was fierce. He wrenched one away, and she dragged it across his chest, her sharp nails raking his skin. Charlie yelled out in pain and, almost reflexively, slapped her in the face, knocking her back into her seat.

Juliette hissed, getting ready to lunge at Charlie. He pulled the stake from his pocket—the one he'd pulled from the vampire's chest back at the mortuary, and he swiped at her. Juliette dodged out of the way, and the stake plunged into the seat. The little girl pushed herself up against the door.

Pulling the stake from the seat, his hand trembling, he raised it, face twisted with rage and hurt. Juliette's eyes widened in fear. She opened the door and dove into the street, landing hard. Charlie slammed on the brakes again as Juliette rose, drenched and wild-eyed, before running off into the dark.

"Good riddance!" Charlie shouted after her.

She looked back once, stopping for a moment and shouting back at him. "You'll be sorry!" Then she disappeared into the dark.

Charlie closed the door harder than necessary and slumped back into the driver's seat, his shoulders sagging as he let out a shaky breath.

"Dames," Lazaretto said from behind him. "Even the young ones."

Charlie grunted. "How about that drink, then?" he said, as he pulled away, headed for the club.

CHAPTER 40

VERMILION LIMPED THROUGH THE street, his leg and face bleeding; his gouged-out eye was swollen and dark. Consumed by a burning rage and an unquenchable thirst, he moved unsteadily, using a stone wall for support. He shuffled along until reaching the gate of the Cemetery Saintes-Maries, where he stopped and collected himself.

He rattled the gate. A heavy chain and padlock held it shut. He shook it again, louder this time, but it didn't budge. A light appeared among the tombs and came closer. Vermilion watched with his remaining eye as the man he'd dealt with before—long coat, bolero hat—stepped into view and raised his lantern, peering at him from behind the gate.

"You're in bad shape, friend," the man said.

"Let me in."

"You were here before, right. You checked out?"

Vermilion nodded.

"Alright," the man said. "Remember, we charge five dollars a night. Any victims you got, we don't want them here, and if anybody's looking for you—we don't want none of your trouble."

"Let me in," Vermilion said again.

"I said we charge five dollars."

The vampire fished out his cane's golden raven skull. "That's pure gold. That more than covers it."

"I should say you're right," the man said, nodding. He pocketed the piece and unlocked the gate. As he closed it, Vermilion stepped behind him, knocking off his hat. He grabbed the man's hair, yanked his head back, and bit into his neck, muffling any scream.

Vermilion drank deeply, feeling the man's life fade away. He let the man drop, then crawled to lap up the last of the blood.

He retrieved his cane top from the man's pocket and dragged the body between two mausoleums. He tossed the keys in after it, doused the lantern, left the gate open, and entered the cemetery.

He wiped blood from his mouth as he passed open tombs. Most vampires were out hunting, but some lingered in the cemetery, whispering by the desecrated chapel. Vermilion ignored them, passing silently to avoid the groundskeeper's notice.

He found an empty mausoleum and stepped inside. A coffin lay on the floor, lined in red velvet. He lay down and closed his eyes, satisfied by the gatekeeper's blood. His thirst eased, and he rested, knowing his leg would heal, but his eye would take time.

As he rested, his mind turned to the detective. He longed for the man's blood, but Madame Lovebite and Monsieur Du Vide had intervened. He intended to destroy them, and Lazaretto, whose escape still burned in his memory. He would have another chance—all would feel his wrath.

Vermilion opened his eyes as his name echoed among the mausoleums. He rose from the coffin, pausing to listen—the call came again. He immediately recognized the tiny voice as Juliette's, the little girl's.

He limped to the door and stepped into the rain. Other vampires emerged, curious. Vermilion followed Juliette's voice. When she rounded a corner, he moved as quickly as possible. She ran to him and hugged him, and he touched her golden hair.

Crouching down to Juliette's level, he took her arm and met her gaze directly.

"Be quiet, child," he said. "We don't want to draw attention to ourselves."

"I'm sorry. I had to find you," she said, whimpering. "I knew you had to be alive."

"Of course, I am." He looked around. "Where's Charles?"

"He tried to kill me," she said.

"Explain," Vermilion said, voice cold as ice.

"The fat man said you were dead, and then Charlie tried to kill me."

"You're certain?"

The little girl nodded. "The fat man said he'd make him a deal. They're going to talk at his club."

"Charles," Vermilion said to himself. "I had such high hopes."

"What are we going to do?" Juliette asked.

"We deal with them. Then we finish this."

"But you're hurt?"

"Rest first. They're not running," Vermilion said. "If they think I'm dead, all the better."

"You'll kill them?"

"Of course, I will," Vermilion said. "It's what we do best."

CHAPTER 41

IT WAS THE KNOCK on the door that woke Nightingale up. His body was stiff and sore as he sat up in his chair behind the desk. Outside, the rain had stopped, but the sky was still gloomy and dark, and the streetlights shone through the window. He turned around in his chair, clicking the banker's lamp on over his desk. The clock there said it was just after nine in the morning.

He blinked away sleep. On the desk, beside the tarot card he'd tossed down, lay something else: a matchbook. He picked it up and examined it.

THE HOUSE OF THE RISING SUN

TAROT - PALMISTRY - TEA LEAVES

He flipped open the cover, and inside was written an address and a phone number.

The knock came to his door again, snapping him fully awake. Nightingale opened his eyes wide, pocketed the matchbook, and forced himself to rise from the chair. He staggered to the door, finding Sister Agnès standing there, her posture tense with urgency.

"It was bad news for me the last time one of you stepped into this office."

"That's exactly what I need to talk to you about, Sebastian," Agnès said. "Magdalene needs you."

Nightingale sighed. "Take me to my place," he said. "Then we'll go see her."

When they reached his apartment, Nightingale showered and changed. He tossed his torn clothes onto the floor to be burned later. He put his coat back on and headed out the door. He got in the car with Agnès, who drove them back to the convent.

"What happened to her?" he asked.

"I thought you might know."

"She disappeared on me last night."

"She's been in the chapel, praying and crying ever since she got back."

"She didn't sleep?"

"She told me she couldn't," Agnès said. "You need to talk to her, Sebastian."

"I don't know if I can help."

"I think you can," she said. "She's hurting. You understand that."

"This whole case has been a mess."

"Are you any closer to finding the girl?"

"I don't know if I can, sister," he said. "You told me there was something strange going on. What did you mean?"

"The girls that they've brought in, from France, not just to our convent but to orphanages and boarding schools all over the city, there's been talk about vampires. It was never enough to act on it, but I've been worried something like this might happen."

"The nails in the shutters, the ones at the convent—that was you, wasn't it?"

"I thought it would protect the girls."

"Maybe it did," Nightingale said. "This one just had help."

"Had I known what this would do to Magdalene, I never would have sent her. I would have come myself."

"I'll talk to her," he said. "I'll see what I can do."

The fog lifted as they neared the convent, revealing the alabaster building. They stopped outside the gate. Agnès parked, and the two of them walked through the grounds to the chapel doors, Agnès leading the way. She stopped on the steps.

"Sebastian," she said. "Be kind to her."

"Who do you think I am?" he said, as he opened the door and stepped inside.

The chapel was dim. It took a moment for Nightingale's eyes to adjust. At first, it seemed silent. Then he heard the quiet sob of a young woman. As the darkness cleared, he could see her figure on one of the pews, her head bowed, her hands clasped, her body quivering.

He approached her, his footsteps loud and intrusive in the silent chapel. He turned down the row and slid next to Magdalene, resting his hands on the pew in front of them.

"I lost you last night," he said. Magdalene didn't look up. She kept her head bowed, and she continued to cry softly to herself. "Had me worried," he continued. "But I figured you knew how to take care of yourself." Nightingale frowned, wanting to reach out his hand to her, but not knowing if it was right. "I saw the father out there," he said. "I think I know what happened."

Finally, Magdalene looked at him. She had dressed herself again in her full habit, the veil back over her head, her blonde hair once more hidden away. Her eyes were red and puffy, the wet trail of tears streaking down her face.

"I killed him," she said, whispering hoarsely as if the words didn't want to escape.

"I know," he said. He touched her face to wipe away a large tear that rolled down. "I know."

She backed away from his hand, wiping her own tears away, drying them on her sleeve. "I can't—" she started, before pausing to find the words. She took a deep breath before speaking again. "How do you do it, detective? How do you kill without it destroying you?"

"I don't think about it," he said, sounding colder than he wanted.

"It's *all* I can think about," Magdalene said before breaking down into tears once more. She buried her face in her hands for a moment, hiding away. He touched her back, but she recoiled. She looked up at him through wet eyes. "I've tried to wash it away, but I can't seem to forget. All I want to do is change it, but I can't. I took a life. I made that choice, and it's final."

"If it wasn't him," Nightingale said. "It would have been you lying out in the street. And he wouldn't have been crying in a church about it."

"How can you know?"

"You think he shed a single tear for Antonia?"

Magdalene shook her head, tears still falling. As she collapsed against Nightingale, he wrapped his arms around her, sensing the depth of her grief. He closed his eyes, feeling both her pain and his own wash over him. For a moment, they sat together, alone in the chapel, the angels and saints carved into the walls watching in silent witness.

"Her name was Marianne," he said. "The one Pearson was talking about."

Magdalene's sobs slowed, her breathing rough but becoming steadier as she listened to Nightingale.

"He was wrong, though. I didn't leave the force because of her; I was leaving *for* her." Nightingale sighed. "I was on a case; her husband had been killed. It was vampires. I knew it, of course, and I was able to tell her about it. She believed me; she'd seen things. She knew what I had to do, and she wanted me to do it; she wanted her husband to be at peace. So, I did it. I put him down. She was there when I put him back in his grave for the last time.

"With everything that had happened, though, she wanted to leave. She couldn't be here anymore. She wanted me to go with her; she wanted to feel safe. I agreed. We were going to leave. She had a family home up north, in Maine, along the coast. We would go there for a while, find a way to start again, leave all this death and misery behind us. So, I quit the force. I thought maybe I'd be a carpenter or something, maybe a fisherman. I didn't quite know, and I didn't care. I just wanted to leave with her.

"It didn't happen that way, though. I had taken care of her husband, and the vampire who bit him—a woman. But it wasn't enough. Another vampire came looking, and he found Marianne. He turned her into one.

"I killed him, but not before I had to put a stake through Marianne's heart too. In her eyes, as she died, I saw something in them, something I recognized—something that recognized me."

Magdalene had stopped crying, and as Nightingale spoke, she had slowly raised her head, watching him as he talked. He was staring off into one of the dark corners of the chapel, where the flicker of the votive candles didn't quite reach.

"Do you worry about it?" she asked.

"I did what I had to do," he said.

"Not that," Magdalene said. "Do you worry about your soul?"

"I don't know if I have one anymore," he said. He pulled his collar down, showing more of the ragged scar that ran down his neck. "Sometimes I think the vampire that bit me got enough of its poison into my veins that I lost it."

"I don't think that's true," Magdalene said. "You're a good man, Sebastian Nightingale."

"I hope you're right," he said. "I hope whatever it's taken from me, there's something left to salvage."

"Is that why you do what you do?"

"It is," he said. "If I kill enough of these monsters, maybe I can save myself from being one too."

"Then you need to find Juliette," Magdalene said. "Bring her back. Let all this count for something."

He nodded. "And you?"

"I'm making my peace," she said. "How did you make peace after Marianne?"

"I drank," he said. "But then I stopped. I failed her; I had to own that. And then I did what I had to—I owned that too."

"Then that's what I'll do, too," she said. "Now go, find that little girl, for both our sakes."

Agnès was still waiting outside on the steps as Nightingale stepped out of the convent.

"How is she?" she asked.

"Stay with her," Nightingale said. "She needs someone with her."

"Where are you going?"

"To finish this," he said. He nodded back towards the chapel. "For her, if nothing else."

"And for you, Sebastian," Agnès said. "Don't forget about yourself."

He pulled his collar up around his neck and brought the brim of his hat down low over his eyes. He stalked down the street to the payphone on the corner. He stepped into the booth, dropping in a nickel. He pulled Madame Lovebite's matchbook from his pocket. When the operator connected, he gave her the number from inside the cover.

"Crescent-1013," he said.

The operator connected him with a click, and when someone answered the other end, he recognized Madame Lovebite's voice.

"Hello?" she said.

"It's Nightingale."

"I thought you'd be calling."

"Of course, you did," he said. "You just hired me."

CHAPTER 42

TWO SHADOWY FIGURES WAITED in the dark alley across from the Rag & Bone. One was tall and lean. The other was short, coming up just to the taller one's waist. Rats crawled past their feet, unbothered by the intruders. The taller of the two bent down. The motion was fluid, but stiff. His leg still badly hurt.

"Juliette," he said. "Are you ready?"

The little girl looked up into the last good eye of Vermilion Donatien du Baptiste, the Marquis du Sang, and nodded.

"Good," he said. "Then let us begin."

They left the shelter of the alley and crossed the street. Passing the club, they made their way to the rear of the building. There, the hearse Charlie had stolen waited, parked beside a cluster of garbage cans. No one was inside.

"He's here," Vermilion said. "They both are."

The little girl nodded again.

The vampire looked up at the building, to the fire escape that ran along the side. From one of the platforms, a narrow ledge led to a small balcony in the corner, where Lazaretto had his office. The windows had been hastily boarded up after being shot out the night before.

"You go and wait," he said to Juliette, pointing to the window. "When the building goes dark, you do what you have to do, but remember to send them to me."

"I will," she said.

He kissed her forehead. "I know you will."

"When will we go home?"

"Soon," he said. "As soon as we finish here. Everything will be better. Everything will be set right."

The little girl kissed the vampire's ring. He lifted her to the fire escape ladder. She grabbed the rung and climbed. Vermilion watched as she peeked through the window. When she saw there was no one inside, Vermilion nodded to her, and the little girl crawled through.

Vermilion walked past the hearse to the side of the building, where the junction box hummed quietly with the current. For a moment, he studied it, considering the metal pipes that ran from the box to the building. He walked back into the alley and found a discarded scrap of wood, sturdy enough to work. When he returned to the junction box, he forced the piece of lumber behind the conduits and pulled them away from the building.

The tubing bent, coming loose from the box and revealing the wires inside. Vermilion kept pulling. The wires grew taut, then snapped. They crackled at first, then went dead. The junction box ceased to hum.

In the silence, he waited. Inside, confused shouts echoed as men called out, unsure what happened. He nodded. That part was done. As the men shouted inside, Vermilion went to the fire escape, climbed past Lazaretto's window, and continued higher.

When he reached the roof, the screams inside began. Confusion had turned to fear, and he knew Juliette was playing her part, just as he'd trusted her to do. For the first time since the previous night, a cruel smile curled his mouth. Yes, he thought, everything will be set right.

Chapter 43

"How did you sleep, Mr. Baptiste?"

It was the same leggy blonde from the night before who'd helped with the drinks during their meeting, before the mess. He had spent the night in one of the Rag & Bone's private third-floor bedrooms. He'd finally made it to the top, but he'd be lying if he said he wasn't a little disappointed. It was just like the rest of the club, done up in the same Rococo style. The third floor had a bar and gambling tables, just like downstairs. Only the private rooms set it apart, but he'd seen plenty of brothels before. Perhaps it was the people who made it something special, the rich and the powerful who came up here to drink and gamble so they didn't have to mix with the rabble below. He hadn't experienced that level of luxury yet, but after talking with Lazaretto last night, he was sure he'd have plenty of opportunities.

He smiled at the blonde as he adjusted his tie. He'd slept and washed, and for the first time in days, he felt good. Even with Vermilion, he'd had to stay at that filthy house—the Green Manor, the Mansion of Worms. Now, though, he was where he belonged. He just had one more thing to do for Mr. Lazaretto, and then everything would be set right.

The blonde brought in a mug of coffee on a tray and set it down on the dresser. She returned Charlie's smile.

"Mr. Lazaretto is waiting for you at the bar," she said.

"Tell him I'll be there in a minute."

She nodded and backed out of the room, and he listened to her heels clicking down the hallway.

The club was mostly empty this early, but faint sounds came from downstairs as cleaners readied for another night. Charlie shot his cuffs, puffed out his chest, and smoothed his outfit as he admired his reflection. Yes, this was how things should be.

He glanced at Gino's pearl-handled pistol next to the coffee. Considering it, he decided to leave it—why ruin his suit's line? He took the coffee and headed for the bar.

The chairs were all turned up on the tables, ready for the cleaning crew. The place was dim—the windows up here were all still shuttered. A few of the lights were on around the place, and Charlie could see Lazaretto sitting at the counter, a smoky ring, like some infernal halo, hanging over his head from the fat cigar he was smoking.

"Look at you," Lazaretto said as Charlie took the seat next to him. "Looking like a million bucks. Not bad for the night we had."

"I clean up all right," Charlie said. "How about you?"

"Leg's still stiff, but I guess that should be expected when someone slams into you with a car."

Charlie laughed, but Lazaretto didn't. He looked at the boss, confused, not sure if it had been a joke or not. Embarrassed, he took a drink from his mug of coffee. "When do we get started on our business?" Charlie asked, trying to distance the conversation from his laugh.

"First things first," Lazaretto said. "I thought you might want to see your buddy."

"My buddy?"

Lazaretto looked behind him, snapping his fingers at a wiry man beside the door, his hat pulled low across his eyes. He nodded and left through the door. Lazaretto turned back to Charlie. "Petey Beech," he said.

"Petey, of course," Charlie said. "I'd totally forgotten."

"I thought you might have, but don't worry, I didn't." Lazaretto chuckled. "I never forget."

The wiry goon came back in, Petey following behind. When he caught sight of Charlie, he shouted his name in excitement.

"Buddy, am I glad to see you," he said, coming up to Charlie and giving him a slap on the back.

"You too," Charlie said. He looked at Petey's bruised face and the blood on his rumpled shirt. "They treat you all right?"

"Eh," Petey said. "Nothing I couldn't take. I'd like to get my gun back, though. Little baby cost me a fortune." He looked at Lazaretto.

"We should talk about that," Lazaretto said, rising from his stool. "Get us three drinks, honey," he said to the blonde, then turned back to the two men. "I figure it's not too early, with how busy we've all been."

Charlie and Petey both shrugged, following Lazaretto to a table. The wiry man was already ahead of them, pulling chairs down and setting them on the floor for the three of them to sit.

Lazaretto sat at the table. Petey and Charlie sat across from him. The waitress delivered their drinks—all gin—setting them on napkins. Petey grabbed his. Charlie kept his on the table, watching Lazaretto, who puffed his cigar, something cruel curling his mouth.

"Should we get down to business?" Charlie said.

Taking the cigar from his mouth and tapping the ash off into a tray, Lazaretto nodded. "I think we should," he said. "I want to make sure we're all on the same page."

"Me too," said Charlie. "Because going after Du Vide isn't going to be easy."

"Ain't that the truth?" Lazaretto said.

"Especially now that he knows we're coming after him."

Lazaretto nodded, slowly bringing the cigar back to his mouth.

Charlie continued. "And he's going to stop shipments, right? He knows he can't bring anything through you now. We don't know where to find him, or where he'll be. He's going to hide. But we have to act fast. It has to be us who makes the first move, right?"

Lazaretto leaned back in his chair. The grin that had been hovering around the corners of his mouth came to life. "I don't want you to have to worry about any of that, Charlie."

"Why's that?"

"Because you're not going to be going after Du Vide."

"That's what we talked about last night."

"I know," Lazaretto said. "I say a lot of things when somebody has a gun on me, but that don't mean I mean them."

Charlie stared at Lazaretto from across the table, dumbfounded, as Lazaretto reached inside his coat and slowly brought out a gun. Lazaretto rested his forearm on the table, pointing the gun directly at Charlie. Seeing the weapon, Petey quickly put up his hands and slid his chair back away from the table. The waitress, eyes widening at the sight of the gun, turned and quietly left the room.

"At least I gave you one night up here. That's what you wanted, right?"

"You lying son of a bitch," Charlie said through gritted teeth.

"You really want to go there?" Lazaretto said. "The guy who cuts out on a debt he owes, kills every goon I send his way, then comes crawling in here with promises only to stab me in the back?"

"Listen, Lazaretto—"

"Mr. Lazaretto," the wiry man said, cutting Charlie off.

"Mr. Lazaretto, look, that wasn't my idea, that was Vermilion's. He's the one who betrayed you. I was happy to work for you—you told him to kill me, for Chrissakes."

"Because I don't trust you, Charlie. I never did, and I never will. So, say goodbye to all this."

"I'm more than happy to work for you, too," Petey said, sweat starting to bead up on his forehead.

"Shut up," Lazaretto said, not even looking at Petey. "You die too. You whole rotten lot."

"Lazaretto—Mr. Lazaretto—let's talk here. Let's be reasonable."

Lazaretto shook his head, raising his arm from the table, pointing the gun at Charlie.

Just as he was about to take the shot, the power cut out and the room went dark. Morning light came in around the shutters, giving them just enough light to see each other's dark silhouettes.

"See what's going on," Lazaretto said in the darkness. The wiry man ran to the door. Lazaretto stepped away from the table, his gun still levelled at the figure he thought was Charlie. "Don't either of you move," he said. "I can still see enough to blow both of you away."

"Get it over with," Charlie said.

They heard confused shouting downstairs as Lazaretto's men checked the breakers, desperately trying to find the problem. Then they heard someone scream—a man. He cried out, but the agony and fear were cut off abruptly. Charlie and Petey looked at the doorway. Lazaretto still watched them, the gun pointed directly at them.

There was another cry, and another, the sounds of confusion growing louder as more people cried out, trying to understand what was going on and why the lights were out.

The next scream they heard was closer than any of the others, and the double doors flew open. Grey light came bursting in along with the wiry man, who ran towards Lazaretto.

"We gotta get you out of here, boss," he yelled.

"Why? What's going on?"

"It's—" Just as the wiry man opened his mouth to speak, he fell to the ground, pushed from behind. In the light, Lazaretto, Charlie, and Petey could all see the dark figure of Juliette on top of him as she bent down and bit into his neck with a gristly, wet chomp. The wiry man howled in pain, and she bit down again, harder. The wet noise gave way to a crunch as the wiry man fell silent.

"The little brat!" Lazaretto shouted, bringing his gun around and firing at her shape.

She scurried away across the floor, the bullets tearing into the floorboards as Lazaretto fired at her. Charlie and Petey both dove out of their chairs, scrambling to escape while Lazaretto kept firing at the little girl. Noticing them fleeing, Lazaretto turned and fired blindly towards their moving shapes, the bullets striking tables and some smashing through the blinds, letting in more grey morning light.

Lazaretto tried to chase after them and, turning quickly, tripped over the chair where Charlie was crouched. He fell, tumbling directly onto Charlie and Petey. All three tumbled to the floor, then scrambled upright in the darkness, bumping into one another as they regained their footing. They heard the little girl hiss somewhere behind them.

She climbed onto the table in front of them, knocking over their drinks. She crawled toward them, spider-like. Lazaretto fired, but his gun clicked empty. Stunned, he froze, unsure what to do, fear gripping him.

Charlie made the first move; he turned and ran towards the hall, headed for the private room he'd spent the night in, where he'd left Gino's pistol. As he moved, Juliette jumped for him, reaching out her tiny hands to try and grasp him.

Petey jumped between them, knocking the little girl away and sending Charlie back to the floor. As Charlie rose to his feet, he saw the little girl skitter to her feet. She grabbed Petey by the lapels of his suit and pulled him forward, meeting his neck with her fanged teeth. There was a cry in the dark, and a sound like raw meat being sliced into strips, then the slurping noise of the little girl lapping up the blood.

Without looking back, Charlie ran down the hall. Lazaretto, no fool either, ran too, headed for the wall behind the bar. Pushing a padded section of the wall, he opened a hidden door that led to the roof.

Huffing and puffing as he ran, Lazaretto still clutched his gun as he forced his massive frame to make it up the stairs. He hoped that the little brat would be too busy to come after him. He'd head to the roof, make for the fire escape, and go down into the alley. From there, he'd be free and clear to get away.

This whole damn thing had turned into a mess—Charlie the Cheat, he should have known it would lead to more trouble than it was worth. He should have shot him the moment he saw him last night.

He heard more screams and gunfire from inside. His men could take care of the girl, he thought. Even as a vampire, she was so small and frail that she wouldn't make it out of there. Then he could focus on Du Vide, finish what that damnable vampire had started. That traitor, Lazaretto thought as he pushed his way through the door to the roof, a gust of cool, wet air hitting him as the mist blew in over the river. At least he didn't have to worry about him.

As Lazaretto headed for the fire escape, he heard the clanging metal as someone came up the other side. The heavy-set mafioso came to a sliding halt on the rooftop as Vermilion appeared in front of him, climbing up the ladder. He had lost an eye, and he moved slowly, stiffly, as he came up over the ledge. In the morning light, his one good eye glowed red.

"How good to see you again," the vampire said.

"You're dead," Lazaretto said. "You're dead."

Vermilion nodded. "I know," he said. "As are you."

Lazaretto raised his gun but remembered it was empty. Instead, he threw it as hard as he could at the vampire and turned to run the other way. He crossed the roof, headed for the front of the building, stopping when he reached the ledge. Below him was the patio, where the band played on clear nights. There was a balcony, though. He could make it; he could jump. It was farther than he'd like, and he'd have to be sure not to overshoot it, but he could do it. He readied when he felt the vampire directly behind him—close enough that his breath was on Lazaretto's neck, the tiny hairs standing on their end.

Vermilion's hand came down on his shoulder, the icy grip forcing him to turn around. Lazaretto was a large man, both wide and tall, but the vampire measured up to him—something he hadn't noticed until this moment. The lank frame was the same height as he was, perhaps even taller. Lazaretto felt deflated in the vampire's presence.

There was hunger in Vermilion's good eye, a cruelty with a touch of pleasure on his face. Lazaretto could think of nothing to say, nothing to do. He just stared at the vampire for what seemed to be ages in a single moment. They stood together on the windy rooftop, another storm blowing in. It would be here soon. Lazaretto chuckled.

The vampire pulled Lazaretto forward, snapping the big man to him. His mouth open, his fangs bared, he plunged them into the big man's neck. Lazaretto let out a cry, cut quickly short as the razor-sharp teeth dug in deeper, slicing into his throat, and then tearing it away. Blood sprayed across the rooftop and onto Vermilion as he licked his greedy lips. Lazaretto looked at him almost in amazement, then Vermilion let go of his shoulder. As the vampire's hand came away, Lazaretto felt free; he felt light.

He tumbled over the edge of the building, blood still squirting from his neck.

CHAPTER 44

ACROSS THE STREET FROM the Rag & Bone, Slits Nicotero sat in the driver's seat of Fat Phil's car; Frenchy sat next to him. His neck was bandaged; they'd had a chance to find a doctor in the night who agreed to patch him up without asking any questions. They'd gotten at least a little bit of rest in the car before driving towards the Quarter, where they'd ended up outside the Rag & Bone.

Frenchy had wanted to go in, see Lazaretto, and start working on what they would do next. But Slits had said they would wait. Something hadn't felt right to him. Maybe it was nerves from the night before; he was still sore from being mowed down by the hearse, but something in his criminal brain told him they should stay put.

It wasn't too much longer until they saw the lights go out, and then they heard the gunshots.

"We've got to go in now," Frenchy said, his voice weak and wavering.

"And what? Go in guns blazing?" Slits said. "No, thank you. For all we know, it's cops in there, or Du Vide's people—or worse."

"Anton needs us."

"Anton's got other guys. I'm not risking my neck, and you shouldn't risk what's left of yours."

"We should have never made that deal with Charlie the Cheat."

"I knew it, you knew it, it was Lazaretto who got greedy."

"He's still our boss," Frenchy said.

"For now," Slits said, eyeing the club. The gunshots stopped, but the lights stayed off. He pointed at the roof. "Look—someone's up there."

Frenchy leaned forward, wincing as he craned his neck to see. Slits was right. He could see someone on the roof, silhouetted against the grey sky. He squinted, trying to see if he was right about what he saw. "I think that's Lazaretto," he said.

"I think you're right."

"What's he doing up there?"

As Frenchy asked the question, another shape appeared. A tall, thin figure approached Lazaretto from behind and turned him around. The two figures stood close together. The tall one leaned in, as if whispering into Lazaretto's ear.

"What's going on?" Slits said. "Are they talking?"

The two figures came apart. Lazaretto fell backwards over the ledge of the roof, clipping the railing along the third-floor balcony. This sent him spinning out toward the patio. His heavy frame plummeted, rotating twice—heels over head—before landing on the ground with a heavy, pulpy thud.

Slits and Frenchy both jumped in their seats, startled and silent. They looked out at the club, neither one knowing what to say. The tall figure disappeared, walking away from the ledge. Both men sat perfectly still in the car.

Slits moved first. He leaned forward under the dash, connecting the wires he'd pulled from the column and touching them together. There was the sound of sparks. Then the engine roared to life.

"What are you doing?" Frenchy asked.

"Leaving," Slits said.

"Shouldn't we do something?"

"No," Slits said. "We don't have a boss anymore."

He pulled out of the alley and turned onto Bourbon Street. Frenchy looked like he wanted to say something else, but he never thought of it. Instead, he sat back in his seat and touched his aching neck as the two of them drove away.

CHAPTER 45

CHARLIE SEARCHED IN THE darkness for the gun, patting the top of the dresser in his room. When he felt the cold steel, he smiled, and relief surged through his body. He wrapped his fingers around the pearl-handled grip and went dashing back out into the hallway, headed towards the bar. He was going to kill that little girl, send her back to Hell, and be done with the whole thing.

He'd find Lazaretto, and he'd finish him too, send him packing with that little brat. Then, maybe, he'd find whatever money they had stashed around here, and he'd take off. The hearse was outside; the keys were still in it. He'd head for Atlantic City, like he should have done two nights ago. He'd ditch the hearse for something better along the way, but first he had to take care of business here.

As he walked among the tables, he listened. The room was silent. Downstairs, he still heard commotion, but it had died down. No doubt a lot of people had left after the gunshots. Outside, he heard the first distant wail of sirens, and he cursed. He'd have to be a lot faster than he'd thought. He had to find the girl and Lazaretto quickly—he just hoped he'd have time to grab some cash.

Charlie picked up his pace, weaving through the tables, trying to see anything in the dark room. The sirens were making him anxious, and he was having trouble concentrating. He wondered if he should just make for the cash now and get out of there. The girl wouldn't be able to make it out of the city, anyway. Right?

He stumbled over something on the ground, making him fall to the floor. He scurried onto his back, sitting up, and looking to see what he'd tripped over. His first thought had been that it was the girl, that she'd tried to ambush him, but in the dim light, he could see he was wrong. Laid out in front of him, on his back, was Petey Beech. His eyes were open, his neck torn apart with a huge, bleeding gash running along the side.

This was his fault, he realized. And the pang of regret hit him like a hammer. Poor Petey, he'd never thought he'd say that, but for as much of a runt as he was, he didn't deserve something like this.

"You sonuvabitch," Charlie said, turning to search the room. "Stop hiding!"

"Charles."

Charlie turned in the direction of the voice. He didn't need to see to know who it was. Vermilion's tall frame was outlined in grim light, and the little girl stood beside him, her face covered in blood—some of it Petey's.

"They said you were dead," Charlie said.

"They lied."

"I didn't know."

"You should have," Vermilion said. "The girl told me what you did. Said you attacked her."

"She attacked me!"

"You've betrayed me, Charles." The vampire moved forward, slowly, walking among the tables. Juliette walked with him.

"Betrayed you? What are you talking about? I was trying to survive, trying to get what was mine, what I was owed. I thought you were dead."

"No more excuses, Charles. That's all you've ever had." The vampire moved closer.

"Vermilion, look, you've got it all wrong. I didn't know you were still alive." Charlie began to back away as the vampire approached. "We're family, you and me."

"And I should have known," Vermilion said. "My family betrayed me before, left me, forgot me. They stole everything from me—I had to find a new family. I had to make one of my own. One that understood me. Then the war came and took that from me, too. This little one is all that I have left."

"Vermilion, I—" Charlie fell backwards as he tripped over a chair. As he fell, the two vampires moved forward so that they leered over him. Two dark shadows loomed in the dark room. "I didn't know," Charlie said to them, his voice small.

"You never know, Charles. That has been your failing. The answer has always eluded you." Vermilion knelt in front of Charlie, his clawed hand reached out, touching Charlie's chin. The touch was icy and repulsive; Charlie's skin began to crawl.

With a sharp fingernail beneath Charlie's chin, Vermilion led him forward, bringing their faces close together, almost like lovers. The sirens outside were getting closer.

"Know this," Vermilion said. "When I first arrived, and I searched for what remained of my family, I planned to kill them all, take what they had, and rebuild. But all I found was you, penniless, broken down, worthless. I would have killed you, too, but I saw purpose in you. I saw a use. Nothing great, of course, nothing remarkable. I saw an idiot, a tool to be wielded, something to be cast aside when it no longer served my needs." The vampire leaned in close to whisper in Charlie's ear. "And even in that, you've been a disappointment."

The vampire bit down on Charlie's neck. The pain was immense as the two needle-like teeth pierced into the soft flesh. Charlie could feel blood trickle down his neck, and he could feel tears roll down his cheeks. He was filled with sadness, anger, and regret. His life had been worthless, but he didn't want it to end. His hand tightened around the pearl handle of Gino's pistol, and he brought it up against Vermilion's chest.

Charlie pulled the trigger three times. Blood splattered against the floor, and the vampire gasped as he fell back, collapsing onto a table.

Juliette growled and lunged for Charlie. He swung the pistol toward her and fired. The report of the gunfire was deafening. In the darkness, he could see Juliette fall into a slump on the floor.

Clutching his neck, Charlie dragged himself to his feet and ran for the private rooms. He headed into the one he'd slept in, kicking the door closed behind him. He threw the bolt, and he crawled under the bed, where he lay there, gun pointed toward the door until his heavy eyelids fell closed.

CHAPTER 46

LOVEBITE HUNG UP AND walked downstairs. At home, she'd waited in her bedroom for Nightingale's call. Her pistol pieces were laid out on her vanity, where she'd been cleaning and oiling them. Du Vide sat by her birds, the raven out again as he gently petted its head.

"Nightingale will do it," she said. "I'm going to meet him."

Du Vide nodded. "I thought he would. You can always count on his type to come through."

"And which type is that?"

"The valiant ones," Du Vide said. "No matter what it costs them, they always do what they think is right."

"I think he's more complicated than that."

"Whatever he is, he'll do the job. Just remember what we talked about. He knows too much."

"You're sure?"

"He knows everything."

"He won't go to the police."

"I'm not worried about the police," Du Vide said. "I'm worried about him—as I said, his type will do anything if they think it's the right thing to do."

"All right," the Madame said.

"You sound reluctant."

"It's a waste," she said. "He was only in it because of a little girl."

"Yes, well, these things can't be helped sometimes."

The Madame crossed the room to the chair facing Du Vide and sat down. "Speaking of little girls," she said. "Did you tell Renault to kill the other ones?"

"You asked me not to."

"I know," she said, watching him closely. Du Vide didn't flinch.

"Whatever Renault did, died with him."

"What does that mean?"

"It means that all of this has cost us enough already, and we need to finish it—this vampire, Lazaretto, and your dear detective Nightingale. Then we can get business back to normal."

The phone rang. The Madame picked up the receiver on the table beside her. It was black with ornate, gold trim.

"Hello?" she said.

It was Pearson, he sounded shocked.

"Get over to the Rag & Bone."

"What happened?"

"A massacre," he said. There was a pause, then a whisper. "Lazaretto's dead."

The Madame raised an eyebrow, surprise flickering across her features, before she hung up the phone.

"What was that about?"

"Business," the Madame said. "Urgent business."

"You'll take care of it?"

The Madame headed for the stairs, she needed to put her gun back together; she wanted it before she picked up Nightingale.

"I always do," she said.

CHAPTER 47

NIGHTINGALE WAITED ON THE corner by the pay phone, smoking, grateful that it wasn't raining anymore. Three cigarette stubs lay on the ground by his feet. His body was sore, but the pain had gone—now it only hurt when he moved, so he didn't. He leaned against the side of a building, thinking things over, judging the score.

When he saw the mean-looking, black Mercury sedan round the corner, Nightingale pushed himself off the wall and tried to loosen up his sore muscles. The Mercury pulled up alongside the curb. The window rolled down, the Madame was inside, her fur-lined coat buttoned up to her neck.

"Get in," she said.

He lowered himself gingerly into the seat, wincing as he moved, and then looked over at her. "You got any leads for me?"

"One," she said. "A big one. Lazaretto's dead—I think it was our vampire."

"That doesn't sound like a lead," he said. "Sounds more like a dead end."

"We'll see," she said. "We'll see if you're as good as you seem to be."

She put the car into gear, and the engine growled as she drove off towards the Rag & Bone.

"Let's be clear about something first," Nightingale said.

"You have conditions?"

"Who doesn't?" he said. "Nothing happens to the nun."

"Which nun?"

"The one who was with me," he said. "If you don't know her name, I'm not going to give it to you. But nothing happens to any of them. It's not their fault you and your people got them involved in this dirty business. She doesn't know anything that can hurt you, and she doesn't want any part of it. You leave her alone."

"You have my word."

"Your word, huh? I guess that's the best I'm going to get."

"The word of a Romani is a bond," she said. "You can trust it."

"Yeah?" he said. "You ask your boss yet about the other girls he killed?"

"I did," she said.

"And? What did he say?"

"Nothing," she said. "A lot is going on."

"Interesting," Nightingale said.

"What's interesting, detective, is that you asked me to spare a nun and not you." She glanced at him briefly. He didn't look at her, just watched the road as they passed over it.

"Let's get this thing done, and we'll see where we're at," he said. It seemed like they would travel the rest of the way in an uncomfortable silence until Nightingale broke it. "I do have one question, though."

"Only one?"

"Why the girls?" he asked.

"It was easier that way," she said.

"Nothing about it sounds easy."

"We needed someone with the vampires to keep an eye on them. With Europe the way it is right now, the only exit visas we could secure were through the church, and even they could only get them for young girls, with sponsors out here."

"Renault."

"That's right."

"That didn't work out too well for him," Nightingale said. He shifted in his seat. "So, the girls would get the visas, pretend the coffins were their trunks, come over here, and start fresh."

"We have people on the other side arranging things on their end."

"Do they have tarot cards too?"

"We all do, detective—even you."

"I'll be sure to keep it handy," he said. "We're almost there."

The street in front of the Rag & Bone was full of cop cars, some of which still had their lights flashing. Madame Lovebite parked down the block, so she and Nightingale could walk. When they reached the police line, a uniformed officer stepped in front of them, raising his hand.

"I'm sorry, you'll have to take your stroll somewhere else," he said.

"It's all right, officer," Pearson said behind him, running up from the club's patio. "They're with me."

The officer looked confused. "Who are they?"

"You don't recognize this guy?" Pearson said with a smirk. "That's Sebastian Nightingale, the greatest detective in New

Orleans." He pushed aside the police barrier so Nightingale and the Madame could pass. "And his lovely assistant, of course."

Once they were past the officer and the cars that had parked up onto the curb, the Madame grabbed Pearson's arm.

"What happened?" she said.

"We don't know yet," he said, shrugging. "Maybe you can figure it out. It's some nasty business, though. Somebody hit this place hard."

"You said Lazaretto was dead."

"He is," Pearson said. He turned, pointing to the club. "You can see them scrape him off the pavement if you like."

The Madame walked forward, Nightingale and Pearson trailing behind. A white cloth, stained red, covered the body. Blood leaked out of it, pooling around the cobblestones.

"He's all busted up," Pearson said. "Probably hit the rail on the way down, got his neck shredded too."

The Madame looked over at Nightingale, giving him a knowing glance.

"Were there any survivors?" Nightingale asked.

Pearson shrugged. "There were gunshots, and everybody scattered after that. We're trying to round them up, but Lazaretto didn't keep great books, so we can't be sure who was around. Right now, it looks like all we've got are corpses.

"Witnesses?"

"Not many. Got a few shopkeepers who say they saw a car driving away down the back alley after the shots. They said it was black, might have even been a hearse."

"A hearse?" the Madame asked.

"That's what they're saying."

"No one saw the driver?" Nightingale said.

"Not a great look, no. Like I said, we don't have a lot right now. Your old buddy Westcott is upstairs if you want to go see him; he might have something more to tell you."

Nightingale nodded and headed for the doors, an officer opening one of them for Nightingale as he passed through. As Madame Lovebite moved to follow him, Pearson grabbed her arm.

"Hey, I wanted you to know, your new buddy there knows quite a bit."

"I know," she said.

"Good. Because yesterday he asked me and my partner to go check on a couple girls. They both had one of these," he said, handing her two of the tarot cards. "I'm guessing that ain't a coincidence."

The Madame looked at the cards, each one with the identical image on the front, a woman and a young girl crossing a river in a boat. She looked at Pearson. "The girls were dead?"

"Somebody slit their throats," he said. "There was another one too, that's where I met your friend. I searched the place, but I didn't find a card. I'm guessing he's got it already."

"Thank you," she said.

"Don't worry about it, that's why you and Du Vide pay me, right?"

The Madame nodded.

"You want to go in now?" he asked.

"No," the Madame said. "I need to take care of some business."

"Bigger than this?"

"Yes," she said. "Tell the detective I had to leave." She paused. "And tell him to come see me when all of this is over. He can find me at home. Tell him he doesn't need to worry."

Pearson furrowed his brow. "Whatever you say. I'll keep you updated on all this."

The Madame left, pushing past the barriers and hurrying to her car down the block. Pearson watched until she was out of sight, then turned back toward the club and went inside. He climbed up to the third floor, where Westcott was standing by the bar with Nightingale beside him.

Open windows and floodlights brightened the third floor. Two more bodies lay under sheets. Westcott pointed at one as Pearson approached.

"As far as we can tell, there was a lot of gunplay, but neither of these two got hit. Their necks were torn up, but that was it," Westcott said. "And Lazaretto fell from the roof, but that's all we got. Whoever hit this place knocked out the power, but we're not sure what happened exactly."

"Gang war is the best guess," Pearson said.

"We can't think of anybody who would have the guts to pull this off."

Nightingale nodded, taking it all in. "So, who are these guys?"

"This sorry lump over here," Westcott said, pointing at the body nearest the stairs, "is Bobby Boucher, 'The Butcher'. He was one of Lazaretto's, not a top guy, but on the rise. The other one's Petey Beech, a local gambler. Had a bit of a sheet—drunken disorderly, nothing heavy. Not sure why he was doing up here. His kind didn't usually make it this high up in Lazaretto's club. The third floor was pretty exclusive, and this guy was small-time."

"And that's all of them?"

"Up here, yeah," Westcott said. "There are a few more downstairs, all Lazaretto's, all of them lower down on the rungs, all with the same torn-up necks."

"Mind if I take a look around?"

"Be my guest," Westcott said. "Just let me know if you find anything we can use."

"Of course."

Nightingale walked past Petey's body, pausing to study it. There had to be a reason someone like him was up here. He crouched to better examine the blood on the floor. He saw where Petey had been bleeding, but nearby was another puddle that didn't look like it came from him. Nightingale knelt beside it for a closer look.

There was a pile of bullet casings not far off and another trickle of blood a little further away. Nightingale pulled his pen light from his pocket and shone it over the blood. He looked ahead, and there was another splatter. They seemed to be leading towards a hallway marked PRIVATE.

Nightingale looked back. Pearson and Westcott were busy on the other side of the room, talking to another officer. He returned to the blood, following the trickle down the hall, walking past the private rooms that the police had busted open, their doorframes splintered and torn off their hinges.

He made it about halfway down the hall before the blood disappeared. Then he turned back. The last drop of blood was right outside one of the doors. Nightingale slipped inside.

Shining his pen light around the dark room, he spotted another splash of blood on the carpet near the bed. He got onto his knees and looked under it. The first thing he saw was the business end of a gun barrel, which made him jump back. He grabbed the gun, pulling it out from under the bed—a hefty .45 with a pearl handle. When he pulled the gun, a hand came with it. Nightingale looked under the bed again, shining his light. This time, he saw the rest of the man. The hand that had been on the gun was outstretched; his other hand was clutching his bleeding neck. As Nightingale shone the light in the man's face, he winced and let out a groan.

Quickly, Nightingale shut the door to the room and grabbed the man's hand, pulling him out from beneath the bed. He sat him up, and with the pen light in his mouth, he pulled that man's hand away from his neck to look at the wound. It was still bleeding, but slowly, and Nightingale could see the bite marks. He took the penlight from his mouth and held it up, shining it into the man's face. Then, as quietly as he could, he slapped the man's cheeks, telling him to wake up.

Slowly, the man's eyes opened. His skin was pale from the loss of blood.

"You're alive," Nightingale said.

"Who are you?" the man on the floor asked.

"A detective. Detective Nightingale."

The man looked surprised in his daze. "Nightingale?" he said. "Lazaretto's going to kill you."

"Who isn't?" Nightingale said. "Who are you? What are you doing here?"

"Charlie," the other man said. "Charlie Baptiste."

"Charlie," Nightingale said. "Look, you've lost a lot of blood, and we need to get you some help, but you need to tell me what happened first."

"Vermilion," Charlie said, sounding more coherent, acknowledgment returning to his eyes. "The vampire."

"Vampire?" Nightingale said. "You're sure?"

Charlie nodded. "I'm sure," he said. "I brought him here."

Nightingale leaned back, looking at the man with suspicion. "You brought him here?"

"I did," Charlie said. "To Lazaretto. Then to the mortuary. Then he tried to kill me."

"Vermilion," Nightingale said. "He was at the mortuary last night."

"That's right."

"And he attacked you here."

"Yes."

"Charlie, I need you to tell me, do you know where he went?"

"I shot him," Charlie said.

"He got away."

"I don't know, then."

Taking Charlie by the shoulders, he shook the man, trying to jostle him to consciousness. "Listen to me, Charlie, think. You said you brought him here, you brought him to see Lazaretto. Where did you bring him from? Where was he before?"

"My house," Charlie said. "The old family homestead."

"Where is that?"

"The swamp," Charlie said. "That god-forsaken swamp."

"You have an address?"

"It's the Mansion of Worms," Charlie said. "That old rotten place, full of ghosts."

"The Mansion of Worms?" Nightingale said to himself.

"That's what they call it."

Nightingale heard footsteps towards the end of the hall. "Hey, Night," came Westcott's voice. "You doing okay?"

"Dammit," Nightingale said under his breath. He let go of Charlie, who fell over to the floor, and walked to the door, sticking his head out.

"I got a live one here," he shouted down the hall. "But he's hurt, we need a medic."

"You serious?" Westcott said, starting to head down the hall.

"Of course I am, but he needs help, fast, go get someone. I've got him for now."

"Sure, sure," Westcott said, turning around and running towards the stairs. "Get me a medic," he shouted to Pearson and another officer. "We got a witness."

As Westcott disappeared down the stairs with Pearson and the cop, Nightingale went back to Charlie, pulling him back up, this time slapping him across the face hard. Charlie's eyes shot open, and Nightingale pulled him up by his lapels. "Listen, Charlie, we don't have much time. I need you to tell me exactly what happened."

"Vermilion, he's a vampire. He's family, family from way back," Charlie said. "We took a girl."

"Juliette?"

"Yes. We brought her to the house."

"The Mansion of Worms?"

Charlie nodded.

"You were helping the vampire?"

"He said he'd give me what I wanted. He said he would solve all my problems. That's why we came here, to see Lazaretto. That's why we went to the mortuary."

"You idiot," Nightingale said, dropping Charlie back against the bed.

"I know," Charlie said. "I know. It all went bad."

"You lived, though."

"I lived."

"You were lucky." Nightingale reached into his coat, wrapping the cross brand around his fingers. "You're bleeding, though, Charlie. I've got to take care of that so that you keep on living." Nightingale took a wooden stake from inside his coat and put it in Charlie's mouth. "Bite down on that," he said. "For the pain."

Then, Nightingale took out his lighter, flicking it open and striking a light. He held it up to the cross until he could feel the metal getting hot. He snapped his lighter shut and pulled Charlie's head to the side.

"This is for your own good," Nightingale said, as he brought the cross up to Charlie's neck and placed the hot metal on his skin over the bite.

The metal seared Charlie's flesh, and he bit down hard on the wooden stake, a scream of pain burbling out of him. Nightingale pulled the cross away and took the wooden stake from Charlie's mouth. Charlie collapsed on the floor, panting for breath.

"You won't make the same mistake twice," Nightingale said. He could hear the commotion coming up the stairs as he walked out of the room.

When Nightingale got to the end of the hall, Westcott was running with two men dressed in white smocks. "He's in the room, down the hall, on the floor," Nightingale said. "He's delirious, lost a lot of blood. And he's got a bad burn on his neck."

"He tell you anything?" Westcott asked.

"Just nonsense," Nightingale said. "I wouldn't believe anything he says until he gets some more blood in him."

"Lucky for him you found him."

"Yeah," Nightingale said. "Lucky him."

"You want to stick around, see if you find anybody else?"

"No," Nightingale said. "I've got something else to look into."

"Still on your case, right?"

"That's right."

"Where are you headed then?"

"To find a mansion of worms."

CHAPTER 48

HEADLIGHTS APPEARED IN THE swirls of misty fog that rose up from the ground, under the thick trees that covered the long drive that led to the Green Mansion. The hearse crept towards the house, pulling around the old, broken fountain out front, until it came to a squeaking halt.

The driver's door opened, and Vermilion spilled out of the car, clutching his chest. Charlie had missed his heart, but there were three large holes blasted into his chest. He coughed as he picked himself up off the ground, holding onto the car for balance; blood splattered from his mouth.

He walked to the other side of the car, opening the door and pulling Juliette from her seat. Her eyes were closed, and her body was limp, but her chest slowly rose and fell with breath. Charlie's shots had mostly missed her, but one had caught her in the neck, grazing her, covering her clothes in her blood. The wound had been dressed with white gauze. He carried her to the doors, kicking them open. Another flurry of bats was startled out of their rest and went flapping into the swamps.

Vermilion brought the girl to a moldering sofa in the parlor, tearing the dirty sheet off and laying her down on the bare cushions. He brushed her hair back off her face, smearing blood across her forehead.

"Juliette," he said in a whisper. "My poor, sweet girl. Wake up."

Slowly, her eyes opened. When she tried to speak, she winced from the pain. Vermilion brought a finger to her lips.

"Don't talk," he said. "It's all right. We're home now."

"Not home," she said softly, her voice hoarse and pained.

"I know," he said. "But it's the only home we have." He continued brushing her hair with his hand. "There's something I need you to do for me. Do you think you can?"

The little girl nodded.

"You're hurt," he said. "I need you to rest, out of sight. And I need you to stay hidden, no matter what you hear."

"Why?" she managed to ask.

"They may come for us," Vermilion said.

"We killed them."

"There will always be more, little one," Vermilion said. "And I fear they may be on their way. The police may not be fools. I will wait, I will watch, and see who comes. But you must stay hidden, you must stay safe. You're weak, and you may have a chance to survive if you let them think you're just a little girl, let them think you're my victim."

"I'm not."

"Let them believe it, though. It's better that way."

Tears began to well up in the little girl's eyes. "But you—"

"I will do what needs to be done—just as you will," he said. "Now, rest."

The little girl closed her eyes, squeezing out more tears. Vermilion wiped them away and picked her up. By the time he reached the door to the cellar, she was asleep again. He brought her down beneath the house, into the cool underground, where he knew she liked it best. Gino's body, headless and bloody, still hung from the rafters. He laid the girl down on a soft nest of old sheets and went back upstairs, giving her a long, lingering look before closing the door.

Vermilion walked back to the hearse, pulling open the back doors, where a man dressed in white was tied and gagged. When he saw Vermilion, he gave a muffled scream and tried to squirm away, but Vermilion grabbed him by the ankles and pulled him out of the hearse. The man fell to the ground with a thud.

The vampire crawled over the man, pinning him down, staring into his eyes.

"I thank you, doctor," Vermilion said, "for your care of the little girl, but you have one last service to render."

Vermilion pulled the white collar of the man's shirt down, revealing his plump neck. It was already bloody where Vermilion had drunk before. Now, he would finish the job. He sank his fangs into the man and greedily slurped until the doctor stopped squirming and his blood had run dry.

Leaving the body in the mud, Vermilion walked to the house, wiping his mouth and chin clean. He still limped from where the detective had shot him the night before, and his chest erupted in sharp pain with every breath. He felt the blood in his belly, and he felt life returning to his joints. He was in no shape to fight, but he would if he needed to—for his own survival, and especially for the girl's

He walked to the back door, toward the cemetery, and walked among the mausoleums and tombstones. Reaching out his hands, he touched them gently. The graves of his brother and his brother's offspring. Some of the names he knew, others he didn't. Some had been names from the old family, passed down to the new generations, just for them to be laid to rest here in this muddy, swampy earth.

When he reached Bernardin's tomb, he sat down on the stone steps that led up to the entrance, lowering himself slowly to the ground. The pile of bones that had been his brother sat beside him. He reached down, picking up the skull, holding it out in front of him, staring into the empty eyes.

"At least I saw you one last time, brother," Vermilion said. "It gives me great joy to have seen you like this." He looked out over the graves. "And whatever hell you wretches find yourself in, I'll be sure to find you as I pass to my own."

Smashing the skull against the steps, Vermilion sent pieces of shattered bone scattering across the dirt.

"But we shall see when that will be," he said, as he leaned against the doorway to the mausoleum to rest.

CHAPTER 49

NIGHTINGALE TOOK A CAB to the Emporium Historia. The shop was empty, except for Bone, who was resting behind the counter. He was stirred when the bell chimed above the door, and Nightingale walked inside. A wide grin grew across Bone's face.

"You're not dead," Bone said, grinning. He hugged Nightingale, slapping his back and making the detective wince.

"I came close, though," he said.

"I can see that," said Bone. "You look like you've been dragged through hell."

"Magdalene got to me in time."

"And where is our fair friend of the cloth?"

"At the convent. Resting." Nightingale paused. "She had a rough night, too."

"You can do that to people," Bone said. "But is the job done?"

"Not yet," Nightingale said. "It will be soon, though."

"You'd better hope so," Bone said. "It doesn't look like you'll last much longer."

"All I need to do is last long enough. But I need to find a place first."

"And you need my help?"

"When don't I? I'm looking for a plantation house outside the city."

"You know who owned it?"

"A family named Baptiste, I think."

"Let's see what we can find."

Bone walked to the wall of books as Nightingale sagged against the counter, still in too much pain to hold himself upright for long. When Bone came back, he had a stack of heavy tomes, and he set them down on the counter.

"You know when it was built?" he asked.

"I didn't have time to ask."

"We'll start at the beginning, then, see what we find." He opened the leather-bound cover of the first book, the pages yellowed and musty. "Anything else you know about the place?"

"They called it the Mansion of Worms. Pretty lousy name for a home, though."

Dr. Bone stopped, looking up over his glasses. "It was a lousy family who lived there," he said, and closed the book.

"You know it?"

"Heard stories about it all my life. Rich family, came to America full of hope and dreams built on the backs of slaves, of course. They found nothing but the worst ways to fulfill those dreams. They all died in squalor, I think."

"Good riddance," said Nightingale. "But I know at least one of them is still alive—and another one who's already died once."

"People say they were cursed because of something they did, back in Europe, in the old country. I never heard what it was; people said all kinds of things, like witchcraft or plague-spreading. But one story I heard was that they were haunted by a terrible secret, and that drove them all mad."

"Maybe that secret has come home."

"Maybe that secret needs to leave."

Nightingale nodded. "You have any more silver bullets?"

"What happened to the ones I sent last night?"

"I told you it was a rough one."

"Lucky for you," Bone said, "I got one box left." He pulled a box of ammunition from below the counter and slid it toward Nightingale. "Is this all you need?"

"There is something else," Nightingale said. "I need you to get word to Magdalene. Not right away, but sometime, if I don't make it back."

"What are you planning, Night?"

"I'm doing what has to be done," he said. "That's what I need you to tell her. Tell her that whatever happens, it wasn't in vain. She doesn't need to carry it with her."

"Just come back, Night, you won't have to tell her that at all. She'll know."

"Just tell her for me, in case."

"Of course," Bone said solemnly. He rounded the counter as Nightingale emptied the bullets into his pocket. The old man reached for Nightingale's hand, shaking it, clutching it tightly. "When you get back, if you need a patch, Sadie'll be happy to do it."

"The seamstress?"

"She's good with a needle and thread."

"Thanks for everything, Bone." Nightingale took his hand away. "Now there's one more thing."

"What is it?"

"I need to borrow your car."

CHAPTER 50

NIGHTINGALE HAD THE MAP laid open on the passenger seat as he drove through the swamp. The sun was setting. The dusk sky turned purple above the thick tree branches overhead. He worked his way to the X Bone that had marked. He said it was tucked behind a grove of trees, but it was the only building for miles, and it would be hard to miss.

The detective had taken it slow, not wanting to stick Bone's heavy old truck in the mud as he crossed pitted roads that hadn't been cared for in decades. As the sun was setting, though, Nightingale was getting nervous. He needed to get there soon.

His heavy revolver hung beneath his arm, loaded with some of the silver-tipped bullets Bone had given him. The cross brand was in his pocket, along with wooden stakes, his pen light, and a pair of pliers he'd found in Bone's truck. His pack of cigarettes was on top of the map, and the number of cigarettes inside was dwindling. His chest still hurt, and his legs felt weak, and he couldn't take a deep breath without the pain in his side growing sharp, but he was as ready as he was going to be.

Nightingale felt strangely alone after the past two days. He thought about Magdalene, how she'd cried in his office, how she'd cried in the church, but in between those two times, she had been vibrant and curious. She had been better at the detective work than a nun should have been—and if it weren't for her, he'd have been buried face down in a rubble pit.

When Magdalene hadn't been there, he'd been with Madame Lovebite. She couldn't have been any different than Magdalene, but he recognized something in her. His business was dirty, just as dirty as hers. Better men found jobs that weren't tied so closely to death, but better men were getting harder to find. Madame Lovebite hadn't let him forget that.

He watched the road before him as the headlights revealed mile after mile of scraggly trees and rutted dirt. He stopped the truck when they revealed something else: an old sign, with an arrow, grown into the bark of the tree.

GREEN MANOR

1 MILE

Nightingale kept going, slowing the truck when he saw where the trees had been cut away and the road turned off into a long driveway. He pulled just inside to get off the road, and then he killed the engine.

The sound of crickets chirping in the overgrowth surrounded him. He started down the long driveway, pulling his revolver from his holster. He held it down by his side and moved slow through the fog. An owl called out in the distance. Bats squeaked, their leathery wings flapping as they hunted bugs as the sun set. He thought, perhaps, he'd chosen the wrong road. It seemed to go on and on. Then, with another step, he saw the dark facade of a building rise from the mist.

As he drew closer, the structure came into clearer view—the tall columns, the wide porch, the many broken windows on every level of the home. This was the Mansion of Worms.

He walked around the moss-covered fountain and faced the door. A hearse was there—same as the ones he'd seen last night outside the Golgotha Hill Mortuary. No one was inside. As he moved around the back, he found the body of an old man in a doctor's uniform. The man was slumped on the ground, dead. His neck torn open where the vampire had bitten him. Nightingale looked up at the house. The vampire would be inside—inside, with the girl.

The doors had been left open, swung wide. He stepped into the entry hall, looking up at the grand staircase before him. He thought of the story Bone had told him, and he wondered what spirits haunted these empty halls. But then he focused. He wasn't here for spirits; he was here for something worse.

Reaching into his coat, he pulled out his wooden stake, grasping it in his hand, ready to strike. He moved through the house as quietly as he could, searching the shadowy corners as he passed them.

He moved from room to room. Stepping cautiously through doorways, he brushed aside the stained and faded curtains. He checked beneath the old, dirty sheets that covered the furniture, searching every corner. Still, he found nothing. He was alone—or seemed to be.

Nightingale made his way to the back of the house, passing through the open French doors into the backyard. He peered into the overgrowth, seeing only fog in the dying light. He stepped onto the grass and crossed toward the graveyard, where he searched among the tombstones for a sign of the vampire. All he found was the dead, resting, as they should be. Outside a mausoleum, he found a pile of bones—freshly dumped. The skull was shattered into pieces. Nightingale picked one up, examined it, then tossed it aside with the rest.

When he turned around to face the house, he saw a light flickering in the window. A curtain that had been pulled aside dropped. He couldn't see the figure inside among the shadows, but someone was there watching him.

Checking his revolver, he walked back to the house, faster this time, but even more cautious. When he stepped back through the back doors, he saw the house had transformed. Candles in every sconce flickered with flame, hidden behind their frosted glass, and the candelabras on tables danced with light.

"Vermilion," Nightingale said, raising his voice to be heard through the house.

"Detective," the vampire's voice hissed back.

Nightingale took a wary step into the house. The vampire was somewhere inside, but his slithering voice seemed to fill the whole space, and Nightingale couldn't tell where he was. He moved towards the front of the house, his hand steady on the grip of his revolver.

"I found Charlie," Nightingale said, his voice still raised. "He told me where to find you."

"He's weak," the vampire's voice came again.

"You sure did a number on him." The detective passed into the drawing room. The plaster had cracked and fallen from one of the walls, revealing the boards behind it. The chandelier hung crookedly from the ceiling. The sofas, still covered with their sheets, sat askew, one of them overturned. "I suppose that's what loyalty gets you from a vampire."

"He betrayed me first." Vermilion's voice sounded close. Nightingale spun around, towards the open doorway behind him. When he thought he saw a shadow move, he fired his revolver, and the loud boom echoed in the high rafters. More bats fluttered down from the attic, squeaking frantically as they raced outside through the open doors, out into the burgeoning night.

When the ringing in his ears faded, Nightingale stood still, listening, trying to hear any movement from the other rooms. It was only Vermilion's voice, carried through the empty, desolate manor, that he could hear.

"Missed me, detective," the vampire said.

"Come out and meet me," Nightingale said. "I won't miss twice."

"You're so eager to kill," the vampire said, hiding somewhere in the house.

"Only you," Nightingale said, stepping slowly into the next room, the floor covered in dead, dried leaves that had blown in over the years.

"You're wrong," the vampire said. "You're a killer."

"You don't know anything about me."

"I know monsters."

Nightingale stopped, listening again for the vampire's voice. A cold chill climbed up his spine.

"We're not so different," the vampire continued. "We're both hunters. We're both spillers of blood."

"I'm only here for the girl," Nightingale said.

"So am I, detective."

The vampire's voice seemed to come from right behind him. Nightingale turned quickly, aiming from the hip; he fired twice, blowing huge holes into the old plaster walls, sending dust and debris in every direction.

"Why can't you just let us live?" the vampire asked, now sounding distant.

"Because," Nightingale said, "you're evil."

"You truly believe that, detective? You truly think we're on different sides of this?"

"I'd ask the doctor outside what he thought, but it's hard to talk when your throat's ripped out."

"That was survival, necessity."

"That's how you live," Nightingale said. "You kill because you have to."

"So do you, detective."

"I don't have to kill."

"Then don't," the vampire said. "Walk away, leave me be. Let me live out my days in this rotting old mansion, let me commune with the ghosts that haunt these halls. What is it to you if I remain here?"

"Because you won't stay here. You'll go out, you'll feed. You'll take someone's life to keep yours going." Nightingale left the room he was in, passing back to the entry hall, walking beneath the stairs, listening to the vampire, trying to follow his voice that rang out all around him.

"Would you notice, detective? People die every second of every day. War rages across Europe, and what do you do to stop it? Plague ravages an African village, and do you even know about it? A homeless man freezes to death on a bench; did you ever offer him refuge? I am a natural force, part of this world, and fighting against me only draws you into the fray."

"Come on out, then," Nightingale said. "Let's start a fray of our own."

A scratch above him made Nightingale look up. Clinging to the wall like a spider was the one-eyed vampire, Vermilion. With a hiss, he launched at Nightingale. The detective raised his revolver, but Vermilion slammed into him, knocking them to the floor. The stake slipped from Nightingale's grip, and his revolver discharged, blowing a hole in the wooden stairs.

The vampire clawed at Nightingale as the detective kicked him away. Tossing the vampire aside, Nightingale struggled to his feet, his body flaring with pain. Opposite him, the vampire moved stiffly, weakly. Nightingale could see the ragged wounds in Vermilion's chest. He smiled and brought up his fists.

The vampire bore its fangs, stretching out its long fingers, revealing its sharp nails. The two of them rushed towards each other, Nightingale throwing a punch that landed across the vampire's jaw, Vermilion, raking his claws over Nightingale's chest, tearing at his shirt.

The two of them came apart, and Nightingale moved for his revolver that lay on the ground. He was able to grab it, lift it, and just as he was about to fire, the vampire swiped at his arm. There was another deafening boom as the gun went off, firing into the ceiling. Plaster blasted off the walls, and the grand chandelier that hung overhead spun, the old chain nicked with a ricochet. A candelabra fell from a table against the wall, hitting the floor, and the flames from it licked at the tattered wallpaper and began to climb.

Vermilion grabbed Nightingale's hand, forcing the gun upward. Bats flurried overhead, the last of them disturbed from their sleep in the attic and empty rooms, filling the space above them, circling the chandelier. The vampire lunged for Nightingale's neck, but the detective grabbed Vermilion by the throat, forcing him away. Then, with his free hand, the vampire reached out, grabbing Nightingale by the neck too, his sharp claws digging into him.

Nightingale could feel the blood trickling down his throat. At only an arm's length, the vampire gnashed his teeth angrily, his one eye burning with fury, the flickering light from the candles and the fire climbing up the wall burning within it. The vampire's thumb moved over his throat, pressing hard, and Nightingale gasped for breath.

With his gun still forced up over them, Nightingale fired. The shot blasted a hole in the ceiling. The rotted old beams gave way, and the heavy chandelier came loose, the chain tearing its way from the attic above. Nightingale and Vermilion fell away from each other as the chandelier crashed down between them, breaking through the floor and sending shards of glass raining over them.

Nightingale was first to his feet, rushing past the broken chandelier to where the vampire was collecting himself. Clutching his chest, Vermilion got up too, slowly, his back curled as Nightingale descended on him.

With a heavy blow, Nightingale brought his empty revolver down across the vampire's face. Blood splattered from his mouth. The vampire swiped back at him, clawing at his coat. There was a stinging pain in Nightingale's side, a fresh wound added to the raging pain from the abuse he'd already suffered. The detective swung again, catching the vampire with a blow to the body. Nightingale huffed as his body cried out for rest.

He and the vampire both stumbled, catching their balance and standing once again to face each other.

Reaching into his pocket, Nightingale pulled out the cross brand, wrapping his fingers around it, wearing it over his fist. Vermilion snarled. Both stared at the other, their chests heaving with ragged breath. They were both hurting, both wounded, both tired.

It was the vampire who moved first, taking two wild swings, one with each hand, clawing for the detective. Nightingale stepped backward, dodging both attacks, and then lunged ahead, fist cocked back, bringing it across the bridge of Vermilion's nose. The metal of the cross cut into Vermilion's face, and Nightingale felt the old bones in the vampire's face give as the punch connected. They both fell; the vampire knocked backward, Nightingale carried to the ground by his own momentum.

The fire burned hot and bright as it continued up the wall of the entryway, peeling plaster from the ceiling and climbing into the attic. Flaming debris began to fall around them, setting more fires throughout the old, ruined house. The rotted wood burned with a dirty flame; thick clouds of smoke rose from it.

Nightingale picked himself up off the floor, stumbling toward the vampire. He pulled Vermilion onto his back, his face bloodied, his nose broken, his last good eye half open.

"Killer," the vampire said, spitting blood at the detective.

Picking up his wooden stake from the ground, Nightingale steadied it on Vermilion's chest. He raised his revolver high overhead and brought the butt down onto the stake with a sickening crunch. Vermilion howled in pain as the stake pierced him, his eye opening, full of fear. Nightingale brought the revolver down again, and again, driving the stake in further and further, tearing through the vampire's heart. Vermilion continued to screech in pain until, with one final hit, the stake was driven deep into the vampire's chest. He let out a gurgling cry and then went still.

The crackling fire burned all around Nightingale. He tucked the revolver back into its holster and pulled the pliers from his pocket. He opened the vampire's mouth and pulled the unholy fangs from his skull. Hands covered in blood, he dropped the fangs and the pliers into his pocket.

He heard coughing behind him, and Nightingale turned. In the hallway, beneath the stairs, was a little girl dressed in a blue nightgown. There was a bloody bandage on her neck, and she looked at Nightingale, seeming lost.

"Juliette," he said.

The little girl coughed again. "Help?" she said and then collapsed.

Nightingale scooped her up in his arms and carried her through the burning rubble. Night had fully descended on them, and as they walked down the long driveway, back to Bone's truck, the Mansion of Worms burned orange in the mist, thick clouds of black smoke rising from it as the flames consumed what was left of the old Baptiste family.

CHAPTER 51

MADAME LOVEBITE WENT HOME first, but Du Vide had gone. She knew where he would be; there were few places he went. She got in her car and made the long drive to the edge of town, towards the lake, until the Golgotha Hill Mortuary came into view.

She drove through the gate and parked by the building's steps. The door was unlocked; no one was there to greet her. Without seeing another soul, she went straight to Du Vide's office and pushed inside without knocking.

Embers smoldered in the fire. Du Vide sat at the far end of the room, behind his desk in his tall chair, gazing out the window. A breeze blew in through the shattered pane where Lazaretto and Slits had crashed through. His desk, righted, still carried scars from the previous night. The former chairs in front of his desk were now heaped beside it, splintered by the fight.

At the sound of the door, Du Vide turned to see who had entered. He smiled at the Madame before turning back towards the windows. "You're not finished, I assume," he said. "That would be fast. Lazaretto was dead, though?"

"You had them killed," the Madame said.

"Whom?"

"The girls. The girls from the boat—the ones I asked you to spare," she said.

"Renault and I agreed it was the best choice for us to make," he said with a resigned sigh. "We had to protect ourselves."

"Protect yourselves?" the Madame said. She pointed to the window, to the broken furniture, to the bullet holes in the top of his desk. "Is that what happened?"

"Lenora—" he began, but the Madame cut him off.

"No," she said. "I told you I would handle it. There was no need to kill them."

"And this was you handling it?" Du Vide said, raising his voice. "Anton Lazaretto, a private detective, and a vampire all found their way into my office—this office—and look what they did. Was that you handling it? Imagine what would have happened if I hadn't had Renault do what he did."

"They would be alive," the Madame said.

"Yes, and what about us? What about our business?"

"It's over," the Madame said. "Can't you see that?"

The Monsieur slammed his fist down on his desk. "I have fought too hard for this," he said. "I have taken our people out of impoverished slavery, and I have built an empire. Do you know how many centuries our people languished under the rule of the strigoi? I did what none of them could: I made us the masters, and the vampires travel with our blessing."

"But at what cost, Du Vide?"

"Everything, anything," he said. "That is how we survive. That is how we live."

"And what about them? Those girls, why don't they get to live?"

"Because of bad luck," Du Vide said.

"I don't believe in luck," the Madame said.

"You've been reading too many cards," he said. "Not everything is left up to fate."

"Only half is fate."

"And the other half?"

"Choice," the Madame said. She raised her pistol, aiming it at Du Vide.

"Choice," he said, his cavalier grin raising the corners of his mouth. "You've made yours then."

"You lied to me," she said. "And you wanted me to kill for it."

"Killing has always come easy to you."

"No, it hasn't," the Madame said. "Not one death has been easy, least of all yours."

Monsieur Du Vide nodded, meeting the Madame's eyes. Suddenly, he shifted to his right, quickly reaching toward the drawer in his desk where he kept his gun. Before he could grip the handle, however, the Madame fired her pistol. Three shots echoed in the large room. Du Vide collapsed into his chair, slumping over sideways, blood seeping from three wounds in his chest.

The Madame took a deep breath, then walked around the desk to Du Vide's body. She reached into the inside pocket of his coat and pulled out a tarot card. Like hers, like those given to the girls, the vampires, and the dock workers, it had the familiar design on the back—bats with fluttering wings on a field of ancient Romani design. Yet the front was different. A man in a red silken robe stood behind a table. Each suit of the minor arcana—the sword, cup, coin, and wands—was laid before him, under his control. One arm was raised over his head, the symbol of infinity floating above. The other arm pointed to the ground, where his name and title were written at his feet.

THE MAGICIAN

The Madame took her lighter from her purse and lit the card on fire. She watched it burn away, dropping it into an ashtray as the flames blazed higher and hotter. She made sure the whole card burned—no sign left for anyone. As the flames died, she took one of her long, black cigarettes—the last one in her case—brought it to her lips, and lit it, taking a drag. She left the room and the mortuary. Madame Lovebite climbed into her black Mercury sedan and drove down the long driveway to the street, turned towards home, and left.

PART IV

A Stake Through the Heart

CHAPTER 52

MAGDALENE HAD BEEN KNEELING beside Sister Agnès in prayer when the heavy knock came to the door of the chapel. The two women opened their eyes, looking at each other questioningly.

"Who could that be at this hour?" Agnès asked.

Both women rose from the pews and walked to the doors, opening one of them slightly.

Wind was gusting outside, and the sky was dark. Another storm was approaching, and it would arrive soon. A man stood on the threshold, his dark coat billowing in the wind, his hat pulled down tight, covering his eyes. A little girl was carried in his arms.

"Sebastian," Magdalene said, pulling the door open wide. "You're back."

The detective shuffled in through the door, the little girl asleep in his arms.

"You found her?" Magdalene said.

Nightingale nodded. Sister Agnès brought a quivering hand up to her mouth. "The poor thing," she said. Moved into action, she took the little girl, cradling her over her shoulder. She rushed back into the chapel. Magdalene took Nightingale's arm, steadying him as they followed the other sister. Nightingale's shirt was covered in dry blood, and he limped across the stone floor.

"And the vampire?"

"Dead," Nightingale said.

"I was so frightened," Magdalene said. "I thought, when you left, that might be the last time I saw you."

Nightingale forced a smile. "You can't get rid of me that easy."

Agnès laid Juliette down gently on one of the pews. "Watch her," the sister said. "We need to tell the Mother Superior."

"Are you sure?" Magdalene asked.

The older woman nodded. "This girl needs caring; we need to tell her what's happened."

"All right," Magdalene said. "We'll stay with her."

Agnès nodded and hurried through the other doors into the convent, leaving Nightingale and Magdalene alone in the chapel.

"I've been thinking about what you talked about earlier," he said. "About worrying for my soul."

"You have?"

"I think maybe it's time I start worrying about it, while there's some part of it left worth saving."

"I've been thinking too," Magdalene said. "And I don't know if the convent is the right place for me."

"Why not?"

"I don't feel at home here anymore," Magdalene said. "Bad memories."

"Plenty of those to go around," Nightingale said with a sad smile.

"Maybe we all need a change," Magdalene said. She grabbed Nightingale's injured, bloodied hand—bruised from his fight with the vampire—and held it in hers.

The doors from the convent opened as the Mother Superior entered, Agnès following behind.

"Where is she?" the Mother Superior said. "You found her? Is she well?"

"She's hurt, but she's safe," Nightingale said.

The Mother Superior touched Juliette's head, and the little girl stirred but didn't open her eyes. "She's bleeding," she said.

"There's a fresh wound on her neck," Nightingale said, glancing at Agnès. "She'll need rest and care."

"I can look after the little thing," Agnès said.

"Good," the Mother Superior said, standing from the pew and stepping towards Nightingale. She pursed her lips as she looked over the man. "You don't seem like a man who talks out of turn."

"If you're worried about what I might say, don't worry. I don't want to ever think about this again."

"That's exactly what I wanted to hear," the Mother Superior said. "Now, if you would leave, we'll take it from here."

Nightingale nodded, turning away. Magdalene went with him.

"You don't have to go," she said.

"I should. I'm tired, I need some rest."

"Then come to me tomorrow, find me here. I'll need a ride anyway."

"Where are you going to go?"

"I don't know yet," Magdalene said. "Anywhere but here."

She kissed her fingers and then touched Nightingale's cheek. He smiled at her, and her eyes glistened. "Now, go," she said. "Rest."

Nightingale nodded, putting his hat back on, and stepped out into the night.

Magdalene closed the heavy door, and when she turned back around, the Mother Superior was standing behind her.

"You're leaving us," the old woman said.

"It's for the best," said Magdalene.

"I agree."

"I'll pack my bags tonight."

"And I trust you won't mention any of this once you leave?"

"Mother Superior," Magdalene said. "I don't want to bring any of this with me."

From the pew, Agnès gasped.

"What is it, sister?" the Mother Superior said.

"Get help, get Nightingale," she said frantically. "The girl—she's a vampire!"

Before the Mother Superior or Magdalene could do anything, Juliette's eyes opened, the candlelight overhead flickering in them like embers. She rose from the pew, biting her fangs into Agnès' neck. She cried out in pain as blood spurted from her.

Magdalene ran for the door, the Mother Superior following close behind her. Juliette tore herself away from Agnès' neck, blood dripping down her chin, and Agnès collapsed onto the pew. When Juliette saw the two women fleeing, she scrambled after them, moving on all fours like an animal.

When they reached the door, Magdalene pulled on the heavy knob, but the door had been latched closed. As she reached up to undo it, the Mother Superior screamed, pushing her out of the way.

"Run," the Mother Superior said. "Hide."

Juliette was there, running up to them, her mouth open and her fangs bared. Both women turned and ran, heading deeper into the chapel, passing by the pews. As they passed Agnès' body, Magdalene could see the old woman's eyes still open, the look of terror etched onto her face. She blinked away tears as she ran.

The little girl wasn't behind them. As they neared the doors to the convent, she appeared ahead of them, cutting them off from the other side of the pews. The Mother Superior and Magdalene backed away, crossing in front of the altar.

When Juliette jumped towards them, the Mother Superior pushed Magdalene away. "Go," she said. "Outside."

Magdalene hesitated for only a moment, but the Mother Superior pushed her again, towards the front doors of the chapel. As Magdalene ran back down the aisle, the Mother Superior grabbed a cross from the altar, holding it out in front of her.

"Unholy spawn of the devil," she cried. "You will not take us here."

Juliette lunged again, knocking the cross away, biting down onto the Mother Superior's neck. She gave a gurgling cry of pain and fell to the ground; Juliette was latched onto her like a parasite.

Magdalene slid into the heavy doors, throwing open the latch and pulling them wide. Before she could leave, though, Nightingale burst inside, revolver raised in his hand, as the rain began to pour.

CHAPTER 53

NIGHTINGALE LEFT THE CONVENT, reached into his pocket for a cigarette, and brought it to his lips. He lit it, standing by Bone's truck. He took a long drag and coughed, pain stinging his chest. As he smoked, rain began to fall. He felt his body relax as he exhaled. The rain felt refreshing as it washed over him, taking some of the blood with it. He'd have to shower. He'd be throwing away another suit. Maybe it was time for a change after all.

A scream came from inside the convent. Tossing his cigarette to the ground, he pulled his revolver and a fistful of silver-tipped bullets. Flicking open the drum, he emptied out the spent shells as he ran back to the convent; they tinkled on the sidewalk behind him. He loaded six shots into the empty chambers and then snapped the drum back into place. He reached the door and pushed, but the heavy doors stayed shut. He heard another scream, backed away, and then the latch clicked—the door flew open.

Magdalene was there, just inside, her face streaked with tears. He saw Agnès' body slumped on the pew, blood pouring from her neck, and he saw the Mother Superior on the ground, the little girl on top of her, lapping blood from the old woman.

Nightingale pushed past Magdalene, gun raised. The little girl howled at him, sprang up, and charged down the aisle.

"You said you would protect me!" Juliette shouted. Her eyes fixed on Magdalene, fiery in the candlelight and full of rage.

He aimed at the girl—small, frail, blonde hair flying, blue gown drenched in blood, fangs bared.

He fired. She flinched. He shot again; she fell with a yelp, rose, and he fired once more. This time, she stayed down, crawling slowly toward him and Magdalene. Blood trailed behind as she slid forward. Nightingale approached, cautious. Magdalene stared, hands over her mouth in shock.

He knelt by the girl. She growled, slashing at him. He caught her skinny wrist; she scratched his cheek but barely broke skin. He pulled her close. She cried, tears mixing with blood.

"You killed him," she said through her heavy sobs.

"I had to," Nightingale said.

"Why?" she asked.

"I don't know."

Nightingale drew back the hammer on his revolver and fired. The shot echoed in the high rafters overhead.

Magdalene cried. She rushed to Nightingale, pulling his arm, tears rolling down her face as she sobbed. "Please, Sebastian," she said. "Let's leave. Right now. Find a new life somewhere. Get away from all of this."

Nightingale shook his head, still cradling the little girl's body.

"I can't," he said. "This is where the monsters are."

CHAPTER 54

LENORA LOVEBITE WOKE TO the pounding on her door. It was late—too late for customers, too late for anything good. She put on her robe and tucked a knife into her sleeve, heading down the stairs.

With a flick, her neon sign came on outside. She opened the door just wide enough to see his face, half-washed in the red and blue light. Rain poured into the street behind him. He was soaked, his clothes dripping, still covered in blood.

"Detective," she said. "It's a little late."

"She's dead," he said, his voice gruff. "The little girl, Juliette."

'The Madame looked concerned. "What happened?"

"I killed her," Nightingale said. "I thought you should know."

"Why?"

"She went bad." Nightingale's lip curled in a snarl. "I had to put her down."

Lenora hesitated, hand half-raised to comfort him. Her mouth opened, but words failed as he turned away. She called after him, but by the time she did, he had reached the edge of the neon glow. "You didn't kill her," she said. "She was already dead." He stopped at the sound of her voice. Lenora gripped her robe tightly, searching his back for a response. "It's not your fault, Sebastian. That vampire—he's the one who killed her. You didn't have a choice. They're monsters."

Nightingale didn't face her when he answered.

"Maybe we're all monsters."

He walked out into the rainy street, leaving her in the doorway. She watched him walk out into the night. When he finally faded into the fog, she slowly closed her door.

ABOUT THE AUTHOR

Alec Sousa is an award-winning journalist, writer, editor, and presenter. An avid traveler, he has ventured to twenty-five countries. He's backpacked through Europe, India, and Nepal; lived in Mexico; studied in the Middle East; and, once spent a week stranded in Eastern Europe. He currently resides in Utah with his wife, two sons, and their cats.

Visit *twofistedsousa.com* and subscribe to his newsletter.